THE COLLECTOR'S APPRENTICE

THE
COLLECTOR'S
APPRENTICE

A NOVEL

B. A. SHAPIRO

ALGONQUIN BOOKS
OF CHAPEL HILL
2018

Published by
Algonquin Books of Chapel Hill
Post Office Box 2225
Chapel Hill, North Carolina 27515-2225

a division of
Workman Publishing
225 Varick Street
New York, New York 10014

LIBRARY OF CONGRESS CATALOGING-IN-PUBLICATION DATA

Names: Shapiro, Barbara A., [date]– author.
Title: The collector's apprentice / B. A. Shapiro.
Description: First edition. | Chapel Hill, North Carolina :
Algonquin Books of Chapel Hill, 2018.
Identifiers: LCCN 2018010860 | ISBN 9781616203580 (hardcover : alk. paper)
Subjects: LCSH: Art—Collectors and collecting—Fiction. | Art thefts—Investigation—
Fiction. | Murder—Investigation—Fiction. | Paris (France)—Art—20th century—Fiction.
Classification: LCC PS3569.H3385 C65 2018 | DDC 813/.54—dc23
LC record available at https://lccn.loc.gov/2018010860

10 9 8 7 6 5 4 3 2 1
First Edition

For Albert and Violette

The question is not what you look at, but what you see.

—HENRY DAVID THOREAU

PART ONE

THE TRIAL, 1928

This isn't how it was supposed to be, Edwin. Instead of you and the collection, fear is my companion. It's settled itself somewhere between my stomach and lungs, often reaching its tentacles through to my fingertips, other times lurking in place, robbing me of the ability to take a full breath or swallow even the smallest morsel of food.

As I sit here on this unforgiving bench in the Montgomery County Courthouse waiting for the lunch recess to end, I close my eyes and imagine that after today's session I'll head back to my little house and you'll be there to pour us a glass of wine, that we'll share a cigarette and a laugh at the prosecution's allegations. Then I snap back and remember that you aren't waiting for me, that you're no longer able to listen or laugh. It's been seven months, and still I do this.

I'd hoped this morning would go better, that my lawyer, Ronald Jesper, who looks to be all of fifteen years old, would stand up to that pompous district attorney, Mr. G. W. Pratt. Initially the firm assigned me a senior partner as counsel, but after the partner persuaded the judge to release me on bail, he vanished, and I was turned over to this newly minted lawyer, the smell of the classroom still clinging to his suit. Ronald is so green he felt the need to tell me that Pennsylvania executes more convicted murderers than almost any other state in the country. Yet, I trusted he would repudiate the court's notion that I was the one responsible for your death.

Their lead witness was the policeman who had been the first on the scene. He described what Mr. Pratt prosecution kept referring to as "the fatal event" rather than "the accident," although any thinking person can clearly see that's exactly what it was. What else do you call a truck colliding with a car?

Painstakingly, the policeman answered each of Mr. Pratt's questions. Yes, it was a calm night, dark, no ice or snow on the ground or in the air. Yes, there was little traffic on the road. Yes, he had taken the truck driver's statement, but the fellow was not forthcoming, an unfortunate circumstance. For although the driver's only injury was a cut to the forehead from hitting the windshield, the wound became infected, and the man was dead within two days.

Next up were the photographs, over a dozen of them, taken from every angle, labeled Exhibits 1–17. Ronald objected, stating they were prejudicial, but the judge overruled him. The policeman identified each one: the position of the vehicles; the position of the body; even poor little Fidèle, growling and baring his teeth, refusing to allow the medics to tend to you. Then the district attorney passed them on to the jury. Two of the men looked away, and one of the women grew so pale I thought she might faint.

Mr. Pratt, looking so wise and gentlemanly with his thick gray hair and expensive pinstriped suit, collected the photographs. He walked over to the defense table and had the audacity to smile at me. "Perhaps you'd like to see these photographs of Dr. Bradley, Miss Gregsby?" He bowed slightly and held out the pack as if he were presenting a gift.

I didn't move. I couldn't look. It was bad enough imagining you like that. Imagining the effect of that big rig on your Packard. On you. Imagining your terror when you finally realized the truck wasn't going to stop.

"Don't take them, Vivienne," Ronald hissed, then stood. "Objection!"

This time the judge sustained, and the proceedings turned to motive. I'm the primary beneficiary, the heir, the inheritor, and therefore I have the most to gain from your death. Pratt implied that because I'm not your wife, this was particularly suspicious, although I have no idea why that would be the case. Two art experts testified to my portion of the estate. One figured the twenty-five hundred paintings and sculptures you left me are worth about $20 million, and the other estimated at least $25 million. Isn't it remarkable *that the art they all derided just a decade ago is now worth so much? As I always said, you were a true visionary.*

Edwin, why did you have to die now? Just when you finally proved to everyone that you were right all along. You, a man of such brilliance and creativity, who faced so many challenges and beat back every one. You didn't deserve this fate.

But then, so few of us receive the fate we deserve.

1

PAULIEN/VIVIENNE, 1922

Paulien is aware that being banished to Paris with 200 francs in her pocket isn't the worst of circumstances. But the city is vast and crowded and lonely despite all the noise and hubbub, not at all the way she remembers it. She wishes she were back in Brussels, filled with hope for the future, standing with her arms held wide as the seamstress made the final adjustments to her wedding gown. She looks down at the diamond on her ring finger. There is still hope. It's a crazy mistake, which George will straighten out.

His telegram read: NOT AS IT SEEMS. STOP. GOING AFTER SWISS BANKER WHO STOLE ALL THE MONEY. STOP. WILL COME FOR YOU WHEN SUCCEED. STOP. LOVE ALWAYS.

It pours the day she takes a bateau along the Seine, and she's unaffected by either the Eiffel Tower or her walk down the Champs-Élysées. Even a visit to the Louvre, a place of worship to her, leaves her as cold as the classical sculptures there. She worries about her parents and her brothers, wonders how they're holding up, what they're doing. She's edgy and skittish, startles at every sound, searches every face for a sign of George or her father.

Clearly she needs something more absorbing than sightseeing. She decides she'll look for a position in a gallery like the one she had in London after she graduated from college, gain a little more experience before she goes out on her own. George spoke about starting a new company. Why not here? It doesn't matter to her if she opens her gallery in London or in Paris or in Brussels for that matter. She smiles as she imagines asking her father's advice on which artists she should choose for her first show.

True, Papa and Maman were the ones who cast her out. *He has destroyed everything we have been building for generations—and you brought him here, allowed him to do this to us, helped him!* She can still hear her mother's words. *It is all gone. What we had, what you and your brothers and your children would have had. Everything that we are. Our name. Our proud name . . .*

The memory almost doubles Paulien over. But Maman will soon discover that she's worrying herself for no good reason. George will find the corrupt banker who cheated him and stole everyone's money. Then her parents will see they were mistaken to believe that there never was a banker or that George is a crook and a con man of the worst sort. George would never swindle them, never swindle her, of this she is certain. Paulien dons the one stylish suit she managed to shove into her valise before she left, tilts her hat at a rakish angle, and sets out to find herself a gallery.

It's a breezy late summer day in the most enchanting city in the world, and her spirits rise. She steps onto the teeming streets. Fashionable women with strappy shoes and short dresses drink coffee and smoke cigarettes, heads pressed together inside the red-fronted Le Pure Café. Tiny tables and wicker chairs pack the sidewalks, shops dazzle with the latest button-up boots and brimmed hats. The *boulangeries*, the marble facades, the cascading flowers, the promenades.

From under the bright green awning of Les Deux Magots in Saint-Germain-des-Prés, a handsome young man with a thin mustache calls out for her to join him. She flashes him a smile and walks on. Between the carriages and carts, Paulien catches sight of a Studebaker Roadster dexterously dodging the bicyclists and pedestrians. It's the same model as George's, although in bright yellow rather than navy blue, and her eyes follow the car's path until it turns at the corner. Perhaps he will come today.

She strolls into a gallery called Arnold et Tripp at 8, rue Saint-Georges. The street name is a good sign. The proprietor is at least fifty, with a heavy beard and what sounds like a Polish accent. She introduces herself and tells him about her experience at the Whitechapel Gallery, her studies at the Académie Royale des Beaux-Arts in Brussels and the Slade School of Fine Art in London, her childhood in a house with an extensive art collection.

He's happy to listen to her, but in the end he says, "I am so sorry, mademoiselle. As much as I would enjoy the company of a young woman as knowledgeable and beautiful as you, I have neither the resources nor the need." French men are such flirts. Even the old ones.

She moves on to Brame et Lorenceau, a gallery with connections to the Manet family. But there's no job there either. She speaks with Marcel Bernheim at Bernheim-Jeune and Henry Bing at Galerie Nunes et Fiquet with the same outcome. She stops by a gallery specializing in old masters—painters she appreciates but isn't drawn to—and then moves on to Boussod, Valadon et Cie, which sells only prints of the popular Salon artists. No luck.

The shadows lengthen, and Paulien starts back to her hotel. She passes the Durand-Ruel Gallery and almost doesn't go in, but then she recognizes a Cézanne on the far wall: the luscious brushstrokes; the turbulent, uncontrollable energy; the bevy of rare juxtapositions and color combinations. Home.

She steps into the hushed, musty-smelling gallery and approaches *Léda au cygne.* Cézanne. Her father's collection includes Cézanne's *Five Bathers*, which she fell in love with as a child: the vivid blues, greens, and yellows; the roughness of the tree bark; the soft, fleshy women frolicking in the sifting sunlight. There was something magical about the diminutive painting, just over two feet square, which soothed and touched her in a way she was too young to understand.

Paulien appraises the canvas in front of her, guessing Cézanne painted it sometime in the early 1880s. She isn't familiar with this particular picture, and although she prefers his more mature work, her heart slips. Those succulent blues against the yellow-orange of both the swan's beak and Leda's ringlets, the sexuality in every twist of their bodies, in every swirl of the fabric, the desire in the swan's grasp of Leda's wrist. She catches her breath. She misses George, wants him.

"I see you are admiring our *Léda*, mademoiselle." A deep voice interrupts her musings.

She turns to the stocky man with wide shoulders standing next to her. Although he's broadly balding, his unwrinkled skin hints that he can't be much more than ten years her senior. "I am."

"You are a devotee of Monsieur Cézanne?"

"Yes, but I prefer the work he did in the last decade of his life." She figures she might as well be honest, as there surely are no jobs to be had in this tiny gallery. "When he began to construct objects with color instead of line."

He bows slightly and then extends his hand. "Alexandre Busler," he says. "And I most heartily agree with you."

"I'm Paulien Mertens, and I suppose I'm a little surprised to hear you say that."

"Not every art dealer is so entrenched in the past that he cannot see what is the future."

She returns his bow. "I'm sorry if I mistook you for one of those."

"Apology accepted." M. Busler turns toward the Cézanne. "But this painting is not without merit, no?"

"No. Not at all. It's moving, provocative. All these curves—her hip, her arm, the swan's neck, even her hair and the back of her chair—flow so, so . . ." She wants to say erotically but substitutes, "Beautifully."

His eyes crinkle with amusement. "Yes, they do. As you say, so *beautifully.*"

Heat rises along her neck, and Paulien curses her pale skin, which constantly undermines her. "What I really like is how you can see his ideas evolving. Like here." She points to the face. "Her skin isn't classically smooth and pearly—it's blotchy. Made with thick brushstrokes. And with colors you wouldn't think of as skin tones: greens, purples, oranges."

M. Busler leans back and crosses his arms over his chest. "Would you like a cup of tea? Or perhaps something stronger?"

"Tea would be delightful, thank you." Paulien unpins her hat. Perhaps there is a job here.

He ushers her into a small alcove at the side of the gallery and prepares tea while they talk about Cézanne, Van Gogh, Seurat, Picasso, and her favorite, Henri Matisse. About when post-Impressionism began and who began it. After half an hour, they're Paulien and Alexandre.

"Listening to you," Alexandre says, "I would guess you are an artist. But your fingernails are too clean."

She smiles fleetingly. "Right now I'm looking for a position."

He appears confused.

"As an assistant. In an art gallery."

"But you are only a visitor to Paris, no? I hear from your accent that you are not French."

"Belgian. From Brussels. But then I was in London for school and stayed after I completed my studies. And . . . and now I'm living in Paris. Or will be soon."

"You would like to work here? At my gallery?"

"I would. Very much." Then she plunges into a recitation of her qualifications.

"Why did you leave London?" he asks.

She can't tell him the truth, so she says, "I didn't like it there. All that rain. And the English . . ." Her mother once told her that no specifics were necessary to convince a Frenchman of anyone's antipathy toward the British. "Well, you know how they are."

"Indeed I do." Alexandre stands and retrieves a pen and notebook from his desk. He gives them to her. "Please write down all your particulars, how I can reach you, the exact years you were at the Slade, worked at Whitechapel, anything else you think I should know."

When Paulien finishes, she hands the notebook back and asks, "So you have a position?"

"I would not have said so before you walked in, but perhaps there is something we can do. Although it will not be full time and will pay next to nothing. At least not at the start."

"That's fine," Paulien tells him. "It will be fine."

Alexandre squints at what she's written. "You are staying at Le Meurice?" he asks. "Why would you want a small position here if you can afford to stay there?"

"I, ah, I . . ." She's unprepared for the question, looks down at her ring. "Well, you see, it's that I'm going to be married. Soon. And my fiancé is, well, he's quite well off. So . . ."

Alexandre glances at her quizzically and then down at the notebook in his hand. "Mertens, Mertens . . . ," he mutters. "Belgium." Then he straightens up. "Aldric Mertens? Are you related to Aldric Mertens?"

Paulien is silenced by his harsh tone, by the cold glint of his eyes.

"You are the daughter," Alexandre declares, disgust creeping into his voice. "The one who was involved with that maggot Everard." He glowers at her. "It is no surprise then that you are so knowledgeable about art."

"Please, Alexandre, please let me explain. It's not what you—"

"My brother is dead because of . . . because of . . ." He chokes on the words, and his face reddens. "Your father, a supposed friend, persuaded him to invest, and he lost everything. Joseph could not bear the embarrassment, the failure. He . . . he left his wife a widow and three little boys . . . without a centime."

Paulien jumps from her chair and takes a step toward him. "Oh no. No. I'm so sorry. So very sorry. That's—"

Alexandre holds up his hands, and she stops. "You need to leave." His voice is raspy; he's close to tears. "And if you are smart, you will also get out of that hotel. Out of Paris. This city is smaller than it seems."

"But you don't understand. It's all a mistake. My father didn't know anything. And . . . and there wasn't anything to know. It will all be cleared up as soon as George finds—"

"Do not tell me your father just wanted to help Joseph make a few francs. No, your father was getting a cut of the profits, of this there can be no doubt. And you, engaged to marry that . . . that bandit!" Alexandre barks a laugh containing no humor, and his eyes are black with derision. "Obviously your fiancé is *well off.*"

"But he didn't. Papa didn't. And George didn't either. A Swiss banker stole all the money and George is going—"

"Get out of my sight!"

Paulien rushes for the door. She moves quickly away from the gallery, turns at the first corner, slithers into an alley, and pushes herself into a small notch between two buildings. *Merde.* No one has ever looked at her like that. With such disdain and contempt. Such scorn. She closes her eyes against the shame, but it doesn't go away.

When she composes herself, she hurries to the telegraph office. I MUST COME HOME, PAPA. STOP. PLEASE COME GET ME. STOP. NOW. Then she returns to Le Meurice to wait for him.

SHE HOLES UP in her hotel room, afraid of being seen, eating little, sleeping as much as she can. As the days pass and neither her father nor George appears, it begins to dawn on her that they might not. That she may be on her own. Surely it's just that it's taking George a long time to find the banker, but she's troubled that she's the only one who believes there's one to be found. And where is Papa? She writes a letter every day, sometimes more than one, but there is no response. She burrows deeper into the covers and sobs like a child.

But she isn't a child. She's an adult, almost twenty years old. When her tears run dry, Paulien drags herself from the bed. Although she wishes she were dead, she also wishes to live. She counts her money. Once she pays the hotel bill, she will have almost nothing left. What will she do?

How she will survive? She has no answers, but there is no doubt that she must pawn her ring and move to cheaper lodgings.

For the first time in days, she leaves the hotel and heads into districts she's never seen before. Her family spent many holidays in Paris, but none in these quarters of serpentine lanes and wooden buildings pressed tight to their neighbors. The women on the streets are pale and thin and look exhausted. They wear dresses of rough cotton, often covered by aprons; the dresses and aprons look as if they haven't been washed any more often than their owners. The men look even more downtrodden in their frayed pants and hats stained with sweat.

What must it be like to live in such poverty? To have so little and perhaps even less hope for the future? It occurs to her that this might be her own state, but despite the silence from home and George, she can't believe this is true. Still, she must proceed as if it is.

After visits to three pawnbrokers, she returns to the one who offered the most money. The shop is cramped and smells like the inside of an old suitcase. The proprietor leers at her as she pulls the ring over her knuckle. She's not going to cry in front of him, she's not, she won't. But it feels as if she's drowning. She imagines George returning to the shop to retrieve the ring, putting it back on her finger where it belongs. This calms her enough to take the money the man proffers, a fraction of what the ring is worth, one hundred francs. Which won't last long.

She has to locate a room she can afford, somewhere safe where she can stay until things work themselves out. She can't go home without an invitation, not after how quickly they assumed the worst of her, of George. How could they possibly believe she would swindle them? Her own family? Nor does she have enough money to leave Paris for another destination. She wanders the streets, wonders if she is walking in circles, finds nothing.

Finally she comes upon a sign for a women's rooming house on rue du Cardinal Lemoine. The arrow points to a door covered with chipped blue paint that's squeezed between a butcher and a dank shop that appears to sell gear for horses. She climbs a flight of stairs to another door in no better shape than the first.

Standing on the rickety landing, she tells herself that this, too, is a momentary obstacle. A tale she and George will laughingly tell their children someday: how Papa fooled Maman with one of his silly pranks and how well she survived on her own. George is such a jokester. Like the way he proposed marriage, allowing her to think one thing while he was busy planning another. She knocks.

A slender girl, stringy hair held tight to her forehead by sweat, answers and eyes her uneasily. "You lost?"

"I'm looking for a room."

The girl laughs, revealing a broken front tooth. "Not here."

"There's nothing available?"

"Not for you."

"But you do have a vacancy?"

"Va-can-cy," she mimics, looking Paulien up and down, taking quite an interest in her shoes. "What we got is a room in the attic. Not near swanky enough for you."

"Can I see it, please?"

"Hot in summer," the girl continues. "Freezing in winter. Cold water down one floor and a WC more like a closet with a slop bucket than anything else."

"How much?"

The girl narrows her eyes. "One franc a week." She tries to keep a sly smile from her lips and almost succeeds.

Paulien considers bargaining, as this is surely higher than the usual rate, but she says, "I'll take it."

"You got a name?"

A name. Paulien hesitates. She needs a new name. One that will hide who she is, a nationality that isn't hers. An English surname. A French given name. "Vivienne," she says, appropriating this from her favorite nanny. "Gregsby," she adds, appropriating this from a professor she admired at the Slade. "I'm Vivienne Gregsby."

"Well then, Vivienne Gregsby, give me enough to cover two weeks and it is yours."

Paulien guesses she's being taken again, that few of the women seeking shelter here have the means to pay so much in advance. She's aware she can't afford to be generous any longer, that the girl probably has more money than she does, but she hands her a franc. "I'll give you the other half tomorrow," she says, deciding against seeing the room, fearful she'll lose her nerve. "I'll be back in the morning."

Before she returns to Le Meurice for her last evening as Paulien Mertens, she sends her parents a telegram with her new name and address. Then she stops at a hairdresser and has a coiffeur bob her long blond hair and dye it dark brown. A completely different person gazes back at her from the mirror. She supposes it's Vivienne Gregsby.

2

VIVIENNE, 1922

Vivienne's room is tiny, just enough space for a narrow cot and two wooden boxes to hold her meager belongings. The sounds of squabbling between the two sisters who run the place and the screeching of chickens in the coops just below her window never seem to let up, and neither do the odors of raw meat and horses and leather. She can't return to her more familiar haunts, fearful of seeing Alexandre's loathing and pain on another face, so she spends her days roaming the streets of her new neighborhood, chain-smoking and trying to remain invisible.

She eats little, her stomach now shrunk to the size of a clenched fist, knotted like an old woman's fingers, and she's dropped at least ten pounds since coming to Paris. She's always been on the plump side, so this alters her appearance more than she would have thought. It also saves money. But not enough. She has eighty-six francs and must find a job.

Not an unpaid position, as she had in London, but one with a salary large enough to support her and allow her to save money to leave France. She's never thought much about a salaried position, or making money, for that matter. Her father's lessons in how to curate the Mertens collection never included the financial aspects, as she was raised to believe it was vulgar for a girl to consider such things. But now she finds herself without income or connections, disowned and disavowed, on her own in a world she doesn't understand, her lessons in piano, art, and elocution having prepared her for nothing.

Dark clouds shadow her wanderings. Papa, Maman, Léon, Franck, do they miss her? They know where she is, her new name, how to find her, but still no one has come. Do they think about her? Do they still love her? She would never have believed the answer to these questions could be no. She aches for them all. For George.

She yearns almost as much for the world of art. Her father is the fourth-generation owner of Mertens Mills and Textiles, the largest producer of cotton in Belgium, and he's also an art collector. She's dreamed of becoming a skilled collector since she was a girl, preparing to take over the family collection, which was started by Arrière-grand-père Mertens, ignored by her grandfather, and enhanced by her father. But her aspirations go far beyond simple stewardship. She's going to convert a large barn on the eastern end of their estate and create the Mertens Museum of Post-Impressionism, the greatest post-Impressionist art center in the world.

The majority of the Mertens collection, the seventeenth- and eighteenth-century European paintings purchased by her great-grandfather, is located in the formal north wing of their manor house and is open to the public five days a week. But the pieces she and Papa like best—the paintings he acquired over the past few decades against the advice of his friends, all of whom believed the works to be inferior and the artists mad—hang together in a room in the east wing, which they refer to as the colonnade because it opens into a hallway framed by two sets of Corinthian columns. Three by Henri Matisse, *The Music Lesson*, *Dishes and Melon*, and *Still Life with Gourds*; two by Pablo Picasso, *Head of a Woman and Young Woman Holding a Cigarette*; Seurat's *A Sunday on La Grande Jatte;* and Cézanne's *Five Bathers*.

Originally, these seven paintings were in the north wing with the more traditional works, but closed-minded patrons complained that they weren't art, only smudges by untalented pretenders, and Papa removed them to the colonnade. Growing up, she spent as much time there as she could, sneaking away from her nannies and tutors to be with the pictures.

The room was furnished with a few comfortable couches and chairs, and her preferred spot was directly across from Matisse's *The Music Lesson*, her favorite of the seven. She would curl up on the silver-blue sofa with her sketchbook and pencils, sometimes drawing and sometimes just looking, drifting, dreaming, allowing the paintings to transport her into a distant world.

Aside from the staff, she didn't have much company as a young girl. The family property expanded for miles in every direction, and her mother insisted she be educated at home by the same tiresome teachers who had taught her and her sisters eons before. Paulien's older brother, Léon, was too straitlaced to be any fun, and although she was crazy for her younger brother, Franck, he was too little to be much of a playmate.

Her mother, whose interests lay in gossip, parties, expensive jewelry, and being a beauty, was unhappy that her only daughter wasn't concerned with any of these things. Maman often predicted that, despite her pretty face, if Paulien didn't start acting more like a proper girl, she would be forced to "marry down," the worst fate imaginable. The paintings, on the other hand, were always there, welcoming her, opening up to her so she could crawl into their swirling emotions and bring them to life with her imaginings. Bring herself to life.

One day when she was about eleven, her father came upon her softly weeping in front of *The Music Lesson*. Embarrassed and afraid he'd think poorly of her, she jumped up and wiped her tears with the sleeve of her dress. "Hello, Papa."

"Why are you crying, my dear?" he asked.

She didn't know how to explain what she was feeling, but he hardly ever asked her a personal question, and she wanted to answer him. For him to take notice of her. She pointed to the picture. "I, ah, I always feel sad that the people are so alone. They are a family just like us—a sister and two brothers, but there is no father in the picture, and the mother is so far away. As if she does not care what her children are doing. And maybe the father does not either."

He gave her an intense look she couldn't read. "What makes you think they are alone? They are home together enjoying their amusements."

"I . . . I do not know," she stuttered. When he glanced at his watch, she blurted out, "Maybe it is because they are not looking at one another. The older brother is reading his book, the mother is knitting behind the house, and even though the small boy and the sister sit together at the piano, there's . . . there's something that seems to keep them apart. I do not ever want our family to be like that."

"Very good." Papa pointed to a wide band of gold—ostensibly the edge of a gilded frame—that cut between the heads of the two piano players, separating them. "Very good, Paulie." He glanced at her, at the painting, back at her. "You are an insightful girl. Not like your brothers, who cannot be bothered to sit still long enough to look at anything."

This comment astounded her. The times her father was at home instead of at his offices, he gave most of his attention to her brothers, once in a while glancing at her indulgently but dismissively. Just the night before, at dinner, he'd grilled Léon about his lessons in physics, threw out mathematics problems to Franck, but told her she needed to smile more if she was ever going to find a man to marry her. Her mother heartily agreed.

Delighted that for once she'd bested her brothers, Paulien cried, "This room is my favorite place in the whole wide world, Papa!"

He leaned over and kissed the top of her head. "I am glad it is here for you whenever you wish."

After that, he began to discuss the paintings with her, as well as his thoughts on how creativity was shaped and changed, on the future of art. Paulien reveled in his attention, the best hours of her days. One afternoon he pulled a chair close to where she was seated on the couch. "How would you like it if someday this was yours—the whole collection?"

"Mine?" She was the daughter, and although she knew she would always be taken care of, would want for nothing, she'd always assumed the properties would go to her brothers. "Léon and Franck—"

"Léon and Franck will have nothing to complain about. They have no feeling for art. And the collection deserves to be grown and nurtured by someone who does."

"I can do that," she told him. "I'll take good care of them. All of them. Even Arrière-grand-père's dark ones. And I'll find more to keep our special seven company—to keep me company."

For the next five years he trained her, changing the tenor of their relationship, sharing his devotion to art, deepening her own and their respect for each other. A businessman with an obsession for order, he claimed that this school of art, which was being called post-Impressionism, provided a respite for him, a means to step outside his restrained world. Paulien, on the other hand, a girl who flaunted rules and had a passion for the uneven and irregular, was drawn by the playful defying of traditional perspective and the artists' use of raw, expressive color.

Papa taught her not only about art but also about the art of collecting. About choosing always what she loved, but only those pieces that fit into her vision, works that would make the whole greater than its parts. He took her to museums and galleries and auctions. He explained that a true collector was unconcerned with what he acquired for himself or his family in the present; he was concerned only with what he acquired for posterity. A collector was a curator, a custodian, for art could not be owned in the sense a piece of furniture could be owned; it was timeless and meant to be shared.

Now all those teachings might be for naught, the Mertens family a reflection of the Matisse family in *The Music Lesson*: separated, disconnected, shattered. Just as she had told her father she never wanted them to be.

Vivienne craves a walk through the galleries and museums she once took for granted, visits to artists' studios, to discuss what's new, what's good and what isn't, to think about what would best fit her vision. She sees the barn transformed into an open and airy museum, white walls covered with bold hues and stylized abstractions. The tears fall.

She wallows in self-pity for a few weeks, spending money she can't afford on cigarettes and telegrams to Brussels that go unanswered. One afternoon she's so disheartened that she splurges on a half-dozen éclairs. She sits at a table outside the *boulangerie* and gobbles down three in quick succession. Then she throws it all up in a trash can. The stench of vomit combined with rancid rubbish is overwhelming, and she rushes to the street, gasping for fresh air.

She watches a woman with two little girls, each clutching one of her hands, as they come around the corner. Their clothes are well worn and the children's dresses are smudged with coal, but they're all singing "Frère Jacques," the girls' high voices appealingly off-key. When the verse ends, the woman stoops to drop a kiss onto the top of each child's head. The girls laugh and look up at her adoringly.

As the three of them reach the front of the *épicerie*, a rough-looking man with a scraggily beard whips off his hat, bows, and chivalrously opens the door for them. The woman smiles, curtsies, and enters the shop. The girls' giggles tinkle along with the bell on the door.

WITHIN A WEEK, Vivienne finds work at a tiny millinery shop, helping women who save their centimes for months, maybe years, to buy a hat. Except for the staff at the estate, Vivienne never knew women like this, and she's staggered by the life of privilege she grew up within, by what she had presumed was normal. She likes the customers, their quiet pride and shy pleasure when she places a hat on their heads.

Shoppers are scarce in this humble district, and the milliner can afford to have her only two days a week, which isn't enough to pay for her room and one meal a day. But it's dangerous to search for a job with a wealthier clientele in a fancier area; even with her name change, weight loss, and new hairstyle, she might be recognized. So Vivienne stays within these streets where she knows no one—and where no one she knows would ever be.

She discovers a café just off rue du Cardinal Lemoine that's in need of a waitress a few nights a week, and then she meets a painter who asks her to model for him, something she did at the Slade School as a favor for her friends rather than for money. He finds a few other artists who hire her also. Between the three jobs, she manages.

She's surprised to find she doesn't mind working. In truth, she enjoys it, especially the modeling, because she's back in the world of art and artists. She's perversely amused that the modeling would horrify her parents. Her mother would be even more horrified to learn that her daughter has made friends with some of the girls at the rooming house.

Adélaïde, who has been on her own since she was twelve and can turn a tattered piece of fabric into a dress that looks as if it came from an elegant store. Exquisite little Rachelle, who ran away from a Catholic orphanage and lives with a terror Paulien can now appreciate: that she'll be recognized, beaten, and sent back for more punishment. And Odette, who is fearless and takes Vivienne to dance halls on Saturday nights. They all recognize she's different but ask no questions, and for this Vivienne is grateful.

When one of her artists mentions that an American art collector, a Dr. Edwin Bradley, has lost his translator and needs someone to help him navigate the French art world, Vivienne asks for the details. She speaks fluent English, Flemish, and French. Also German and Spanish, although not nearly as fluently.

But can she? Should she? A job like that will put her in the middle of Parisian society. Her stomach cramps at the thought of it, but she hasn't been able to save any money, and this will surely pay more than she's making. Two months have passed since she arrived, and the fact that she no longer looks or even feels like Paulien Mertens has to count for something.

An interview is set up for the following day. She's to meet Dr. Bradley in the lobby of his hotel at noon. On her way, Vivienne fixes her eyes on the ground, her wide-brimmed hat pulled low over her face. She stays close to the buildings, steals around corners, amazed to realize that she's now more comfortable in the rooming house she shares with a dozen shop girls and three coops of chickens than in the rarified venues she's always patronized. She thinks about running back there but continues forward. She needs this job, and although she has no experience with job interviews, her mother has schooled her well in the art of charming a man.

The hotel turns out to be small and elegant, hushed and tasteful, the kind of place one would expect a wealthy European tourist to choose. Exactly the sort of person Vivienne doesn't want to encounter.

Fortunately, Dr. Bradley is waiting at the entrance when she arrives. "Miss Gregsby?" he asks in English as soon as she walks through the door.

"Yes," she responds, also in English. It still feels odd to acknowledge that she isn't who she's always been. She doesn't remove her hat until he leads her to a quiet spot toward the back of the lobby and she's had a chance to scan the room for familiar faces. Faces she fears. Faces she longs for.

Vivienne guesses Dr. Bradley is in his late fifties or early sixties and probably was a handsome man in his day. Some might say he still is: tall and powerfully built, with a patrician nose and a full head of hair, if liberally sprinkled with gray.

"Please sit," he says, and for the first time he looks directly at her. The force of his icy-blue eyes, deep with intelligence, is so intense that for a moment it seems as if he's looking directly into her mind, seeing all. Given her circumstances, this is more than a little disquieting.

She takes a cigarette from her pocketbook, and he lights it for her before lighting one of his own. She asks how he's enjoying Paris.

"I like it very much, but I don't think it likes me."

"And why is that?"

"I'm American and feel no need to hide it. If I decide I want something, I buy it."

This is an apt description of what the French most despise about Americans, and she says, "You're a man who reads his audience well."

"Why, thank you, Miss Gregsby." They're sitting kitty-corner in a pair of armchairs, and he rests his right foot on his left knee. "The very best art in the world is being created here—brilliant and bold and free spirited—and I'll put up with just about anything to get my hands on as much as I can."

She flashes him a broad smile. "If you don't mind my asking, how did you come to be a collector?"

"I once tried to be a painter," Dr. Bradley says, "but I wasn't a very good one. So now I collect. The next best thing."

"It is," she agrees. "Have you been doing it long?"

"About ten years. My good friend Bill Glackens—are you familiar with his work?"

Vivienne admits she isn't.

"You probably wouldn't be. He's from the United States. Extremely talented. A post-Impressionist, I'd say, but an American one. I own a number of his pieces. Bill took me all around Europe and showed me how to look at art, how to distinguish between what's good and what isn't, how to find what's extraordinary. And I was hooked."

"It must be wonderful."

"Do you know anything about art?"

"I studied painting at the Académie Royale des Beaux-Arts and the Slade School of Fine Art in London. Then I worked for almost a year at the Whitechapel Gallery outside the city. It's my dream to be a collector someday."

As soon as she tells him this, she realizes she shouldn't have. This is a job interview, and he's well within his rights to check on anything she says. If he does, he'll discover that Vivienne Gregsby never attended either school or worked at Whitechapel. He would have no reason to ask about Paulien Mertens, who had.

"Which artists do you most admire?" he asks.

Vivienne hesitates, knowing her answer could determine whether she does, or doesn't, get the job. *Brilliant and bold and free spirited*. She's heard that people in the States are even more critical of the new painters than Europeans are, but she takes a chance. "Matisse and Cézanne are two of my favorites, Matisse in particular—he's the one who taught me that I could never be happy unless I'm surrounded by great art."

"Anyone else?"

"Oh, there are many. But I believe Picasso and Braque are the future. That their work will propel the next wave of innovation."

"What is it about this type of painting that attracts you?"

"The new uses of color. Color as a power in and of itself, not just something you put on top of a drawing. Color as an encounter."

"An encounter?"

"Colors are more than just visual to me." She leans toward him. "They're experiences, emotions, tastes, smells. Blue calls to me, calms me, brings me to the beach, and tastes like salt water. Red is pizzazz, happy and sexy and full of life, a swirl of exotic dancers. And yellow, the morning, hope, the sweet smell of a newborn baby . . ." She trails off, looks down at her lap, embarrassed.

When she dares to raise her eyes, she sees that Dr. Bradley's demeanor has changed, that the harsh set of his mouth has softened, as have his eyes. "Is your French as fluent as your English?"

"Je parle très bien," she says, and the job is hers.

"Now that that's settled, let me tell you about my plans," Dr. Bradley says. "I own works by traditional masters such as El Greco, Rembrandt, and Michelangelo. As well as many pieces of African and Chinese art. But my collection—as my passion—is primarily post-Impressionist."

Vivienne sits up in her chair. This man appreciates the same artists she does. He's collecting their work, as she hopes someday to do. And he has just hired her to assist him in these efforts. For the first time in what feels like forever, she experiences a whisper of hope.

Dr. Bradley goes on to explain that his collection has grown so large that he's in the process of constructing a building where it can be properly seen. He lives in Philadelphia, Pennsylvania, which is somewhere south of New York City. Her knowledge of American geography is fuzzy at best.

"There's a lot of resistance to the post-Impressionists and more modern artists in Philadelphia," Dr. Bradley says. "I want people to have access to them, to my collection. To be able to learn more about the style, the artists—where they came from and where they're going—and come to value them as much as I do."

"There's a lot of resistance here also, although it's been ebbing since the 1918 *Painters of Paris and Nice* show. At least no one's saying the post-Impressionists are part of a plot to destroy European painting anymore. But everywhere people are afraid of new ideas, and we need men of vision like you to open their eyes."

He tilts his head as if this kind of compliment is simply his due. "I have to agree with you there, Miss Gregsby."

"Please tell me more about your ideas."

"A museum. Open to the public, but one without guided tours by so-called experts, and absolutely no little white cards with the name of the piece and the artist to distract the viewer. I detest those stodgy old places. I want warm, comfortable rooms where people will be encouraged to look, really look, and come to their own conclusions about what's in front of them."

"That sounds grand," she says, thrilled that he, too, views his collection as something to be shared.

Again, Dr. Bradley accepts her compliment as a given. "The new building is substantial," he continues. "It needs more art to adequately fill the spaces. And that's why I'm in Paris. For the next three weeks I plan to buy, buy, and then to buy more." He mentions a number of places he's already been to, including Gertrude Stein's, and a number he expects to visit before he leaves the city. "Then I go on to Italy to do more of the same."

Vivienne tries to hide her disappointment. Even if the pay is more than she's making, three weeks won't add much to her paltry savings.

And she'll have to give up the jobs at the millinery shop and the café, both of which will surely hire replacements. But maybe he'll stay longer than he expects. Or, if she does a good job, perhaps he'll take her to Italy to translate for him. Italian isn't all that different from Spanish. She could manage.

He explains that she'll be accompanying him on his purchasing rounds, starting at seven in the morning and possibly going well into the evening, seven days a week. Translating is her primary charge, but she's also to act as his secretary, helping him set up meetings and taking detailed notes on the transactions. "Can you handle all of this?" he asks.

"Of course," Vivienne says with less enthusiasm than she intends. It will be a very public three weeks. She'll be out and about in the city, easily seen by anyone passing by. The job carries significant risk.

But the places Dr. Bradley plans to visit aren't ones her family's conservative set is likely to frequent. Avant-garde galleries. Modern artists' studios. Gertrude Stein's salon. It's impossible to imagine any of the Mertenses' circle mingling with bohemian Parisian writers, painters, and collectors. Her father is the only one who might, but she's sure he's neither traveling nor purchasing art at the moment.

"I don't have time to waste." Dr. Bradley narrows his eyes. "If you aren't able to do this, I need to know now so I can move on."

"No, no," she assures him. "This sounds like a perfect job for me." She has no secretarial skills, isn't sure what that entails, but she can take notes and make appointments.

He gives her another of his penetrating stares, and she meets it. She must have convinced him of her sincerity, because he quotes an hourly rate three times what she makes as a waitress and salesgirl, four times what she makes as a model.

3

VIVIENNE, 1922

Combing a city for art is in her blood, and doing it in Paris with Dr. Bradley is a dizzying experience reminiscent of her days with her father, but almost better because of the expansiveness of Dr. Bradley's search and the limitless amount of money he seems to have to spend. Her pleasure is dampened only by the need to be on the alert for familiar faces.

They often visit six or seven venues—museums, private collections, galleries, antique shops, artists' studios—in a single day. And then after a late dinner, they go to the gallery owned by Dr. Bradley's Parisian dealer, Paul Guillaume, where Dr. Bradley holds court as painters and sculptors are called in to discuss their work with him. He says this is very different from the way he's treated in Philadelphia, where the art he's buying is at best ignored and at worst ridiculed.

One day she accompanies him to the mansion of the famous collector Christian Tetzen-Lund. For reasons she can't fathom, the wealthy merchant wants to sell Matisse's *Le Bonheur de vivre*, a masterwork her father believes changed the course of painting. It's enormous, formidable, revolutionary, and she immediately understands what Papa meant. She's swallowed up by it: the reds, the greens, colors inverted, planes flattened, forms slightly abstracted, high spirits everywhere. It may only be paint on canvas, but it's alive, and she wants to live inside Matisse's enchanting creation.

"I don't understand how anyone could not be moved by this," Vivienne says to Dr. Bradley. "How anyone could even think of ridiculing it."

He doesn't take his eyes from the picture. "They claim that Matisse is a fool. That everyone knows the sky isn't purple and trees aren't pink."

"Then they're the fools. Denying themselves the pleasure of feeling a great piece of art and instead just looking at the surface of it."

He nods at her in appreciation and starts bargaining with the broker on the price. Soon *The Joy of Life* is his.

The next day he buys a painting of a Tahitian woman crafted in brilliant triangles of blue and salmon by Paul Gauguin. The following day it's Van Gogh's *The Smoker*, a depiction of a man so close to the picture plane that he's almost in the room with you, created with paint squeezed directly from the tube, thick ridges of pink, olive, and yellow, juxtaposed with unpainted canvas. Vivienne is in awe.

Although she's been dropping a prodigious number of hints, Dr. Bradley hasn't asked her to accompany him to Italy yet. While she takes great pleasure in viewing art and speaking with artists, the vigilance necessary in Paris is wearing her down. She has to be somewhere else. Anywhere else. She does everything she can to impress him: working hard, taking detailed notes, making careful suggestions, using all her languages. Although this last skill is probably unnecessary when it comes to French, as Dr. Bradley apparently knows far more of the language than he lets on.

He waits for her to translate what he says and then waits for her to translate the response, but he always keeps his eye on the speaker instead of on her. Although he attempts to control his facial expressions, she can see that often he doesn't need her translation. He also listens intently to conversations between French speakers, who are more forthcoming than they might be if they believed he understood what they were saying, giving him an edge in negotiations. He's willing to pay a fair price, but never more than he needs to. The man is shrewd.

By midafternoon of her last day, Vivienne, Dr. Bradley, and Guillaume have been to three museums, an antique shop, and a show at the Galerie Au sacre du printemps. Guillaume, at least twenty years Dr. Bradley's junior, is starting to flag, as is she. But Dr. Bradley, who's already purchased two Modiglianis and a Soutine, is still raring to go. He declares that he must see the work of the Lithuanian sculptor Jacques Lipchitz before leaving for Rome. So it has to be that very day. There's no arguing with him. When Dr. Bradley gets it into his head that something must happen, it does.

"Lipchitz is a most disagreeable man," Guillaume grouses. The dealer is startlingly attractive, with a mustache, high cheekbones, and a generous smile. He also speaks English well, so there's no need for Vivienne to translate.

"If I bought only the work of artists I personally liked," Dr. Bradley tells him, "I'd have a very small collection."

"He may refuse to see us," Guillaume says. "He is angry with me at the moment."

"Does he need money?" This type of inquiry contributes to Dr. Bradley's reputation as a man without breeding or culture, but Vivienne doesn't agree. What many consider his uncouth American directness about money—particularly the willingness to talk about it in polite company—she finds refreshing.

"Lipchitz's name has been bandied about recently," Guillaume says, "but his commercial success has been limited. So yes, I suppose he does need money. Much of our current quarrel stems from a sale that fell through."

"Then," Dr. Bradley says, "lead on."

And indeed, when Lipchitz opens the door and sees who is standing on his stoop, he crosses his arms and demands, "What do you want, Guillaume?"

Guillaume nods at Dr. Bradley. "I have a collector who is interested in your work."

Lipchitz is a large man with longish brown hair and dark eyes that are almost black. "He can contact my dealer," he snaps. "I work through him, not you."

"This is Dr. Edwin Bradley from the—" Guillaume begins.

A plump woman with rosy cheeks comes into the doorframe. She holds out her hand. "So nice of you to stop by, Monsieur Guillaume. Please, do come in. All of you, please." She gives her husband a look that's easy enough to read: Do not turn away potential buyers.

Lipchitz stands aside and allows them to enter. The apartment is dark and tiny, filled with too much furniture that is too large for the rooms. All worn and tattered, inherited from someone's grandmother, Vivienne guesses. Yes, he's not selling many pieces.

Dr. Bradley smiles at Mme Lipchitz. "And you must be Berthe, the model for Amedeo Modigliani's *Jacques and Berthe Lipchitz*. A truly great painting."

Berthe is delighted, as Dr. Bradley undoubtedly intended. "Amedeo is a good friend. And a wonderful artist."

"He says the same about your husband, I'm sure."

Berthe turns to Jacques, who shrugs but looks at her fondly.

"I've heard many accolades about your sculptures, Mr. Lipchitz," Dr. Bradley continues. "And I was hoping you'd be willing to show some to me despite"—he motions toward his dealer—"whatever argument you might have with Guillaume, here."

Berthe gives her husband a little push, and he reluctantly leads them to a small room at the back of the apartment.

Vivienne is unimpressed with what she sees, mostly bas-reliefs, which aren't to her liking. Dr. Bradley looks at her, waiting for her opinion, something he's been doing more often as the weeks pass. She shakes her head.

Dr. Bradley turns to the artist. "Do you have any more besides these?"

Lipchitz looks as if he's going to say no, then apparently thinks better of it and concedes, "There are more in my studio. But it is a long distance from here."

Guillaume's mouth hardens slightly, which Vivienne takes to mean that the studio isn't far at all. "Do we need to hire a carriage?" she asks.

Lipchitz seems to notice her for the first time. "I suppose not, mademoiselle."

"And we can go there now?" she presses.

Lipchitz doesn't look happy, but he escorts them the four blocks to the studio, which is filled with so many sculptures that Vivienne doesn't know where to look first. Harlequins, guitarists, acrobats, Cubist variations of men and women whose body parts are realigned and fused at odd angles. Made mostly of bronze and stone, the figures are all dynamic yet graceful, their motion conveyed as the light catches their many planes.

The easiest way to describe the work would be to say Lipchitz is a three-dimensional Picasso, working in stone and bronze. Although this isn't fair and takes away from the sculptor's unique eye and style, both men are Cubists taken with the human form, both partial to musicians and musical instruments, so the comparison is impossible to avoid.

Dr. Bradley's face is impassive, but there's a small vein pulsing on his forehead that Vivienne has learned indicates he likes what he's seeing. She catches his eye and nods to a limestone sculpture of a woman whose elongated arms give the impression of wings. Vivienne has grown up with great art, taught by her father and her teachers to appreciate it. And this is great art.

Dr. Bradley points to the limestone figure. "How much for this one?" he asks Lipchitz.

The artist is clearly nonplussed by Dr. Bradley's abruptness, although neither Guillaume nor Vivienne are. "Ah, that one." He hesitates. "That . . . that one is ten francs." A ridiculously low price.

She writes the figure down as Dr. Bradley approaches a bas-relief of guitars juxtaposed with a basket of fruit. "And this?"

"Ten francs, also."

He points to a large alabaster statue of a woman lying on her side, her limbs as supple as if she were made of flesh. "This?"

"Twenty."

Dr. Bradley points the back of his pen at a tiny figure that appears to be a postman dancing.

"Thirty."

Vivienne walks over to a sculpture of a bather, fascinated with how it plays with the eye. A woman? A man? Coming or going? From the side or the front? She tilts her head toward the piece. Dr. Bradley contemplates the sculpture for a moment, then looks at Lipchitz.

"Forty."

This happens another five times, each time with a ten-franc price increase. Guillaume stands in the corner watching the proceedings, amused by the spectacle. Lipchitz seems to have decided that this is some kind of a game, that Dr. Bradley can't possibly be a serious buyer.

Dr. Bradley takes Vivienne's notebook and adds up the numbers, hands it back to her. She checks his arithmetic and writes: "This is a steal. Give the man a little more?" He glances at Lipchitz and proposes a figure 10 percent higher than the total. It's still a steal.

The artist couldn't have been more surprised. "You want all ten?"

"All ten."

Lipchitz looks over at Guillaume, who shrugs.

"Yes, yes, it is a fine offer," Lipchitz says. "But it is not, it is—"

Dr. Bradley hands the sculptor his card. Lipchitz reads it carefully, but the unfamiliar name does nothing to quell his reservations. Lipchitz is a relative newcomer to the Paris art scene.

"Do not be a fool, Lipchitz," Guillaume tells him. "No one else is buying your work."

Lipchitz glares at Guillaume, then holds out his hand to Dr. Bradley. "Yes," he says. "Thank you."

"As soon as you can, send all the pieces to the address on the card," Dr. Bradley instructs, as if he's purchased a load of lumber instead of some of the finest sculptures Vivienne has ever seen. "I'll pay the freight."

She finds it inspiring to work with a man who makes momentous decisions with such speed and certitude. Papa schooled her to take her time, to choose nothing randomly or arbitrarily, to select only the best pieces in an artist's oeuvre that fill a hole in the collection. But now she wonders if incorporating some of Dr. Bradley's spontaneity might have its place.

THEY STOP BACK at Lipchitz's apartment to gather up Berthe and head over to celebrate at the Café de la Rotonde, a haunt of writers and artists, both famous and not. While Picasso and Modigliani are frequent customers, the owner, Victor Libion, is known for allowing struggling artists to sit for hours sipping ten-centime coffees; he pretends not to notice when they eat the bread reserved for diners. If a man can't pay his bill, Libion takes a painting or drawing in exchange for what's owed and keeps it until the man can buy it back. The walls of the café are a veritable pawnshop of art.

As soon as Libion spies Dr. Bradley, he conjures a table and five chairs out of nowhere and places them at the center of the small room. Vivienne huddles in the middle of their group, the collar of her coat pulled high, hoping to hide her presence from the other customers, all of whom appear keenly interested in their arrival.

When they're seated, Libion brings over a bottle of wine, bows, and says, "On the house for one of my favorite customers. Welcome back, Monsieur Bradley."

"It is my pleasure, Monsieur Libion."

The restaurateur fills the glasses. "À votre santé."

Vivienne tips her glass to Lipchitz and Berthe. "Pour la gloire et la fortune."

After they order dinner, the procession begins. One by one, and in small groups, artists and dealers approach, either introducing themselves or greeting Dr. Bradley, exclaiming over his recent purchases, inviting him to view their work. Lipchitz and Berthe watch the parade with bemused fascination.

At one point, a tall, ungainly man in paint-splattered overalls slaps

Lipchitz on the back. "How'd you manage a seat at this table, Jacques?" he demands, a cigarette hanging from his lips.

"Monsieur Bradley was kind enough to purchase a number of my sculptures this afternoon."

The man glances from Lipchitz to Dr. Bradley to Lipchitz again. "No," he says, crushing his cigarette butt under his boot.

"Yes," Berthe informs him.

The man steadies himself on the table and mutters, "Congratulations." Then he slinks away.

Berthe, who's sitting next to Vivienne, asks softly, "There is something here we do not completely understand, yes?"

"You have no idea who Dr. Bradley is, do you?"

Berthe dips her head. "I am sorry."

Vivienne places her hand over the other woman's, pleased to be the one to give her the good news. "He's in the middle of amassing a large, possibly important, art collection."

"In America?"

"In Philadelphia, Pennsylvania. He's already acquired many works by Picasso, Gauguin, Toulouse-Lautrec, Matisse, and Cézanne. He's planning a grand museum."

Berthe grabs for her husband's hand and turns to Dr. Bradley. "Thank you so much for what you have done for us today, Monsieur Bradley. I cannot tell you what it means to us that you have understood Jacques's work and seen the merit in it. We have been waiting a long time for this moment." Tears glisten in her eyes, and she whispers, "May God bless."

When the dinner dishes are cleared, Vivienne asks M. Libion to call her a carriage.

"No dessert for you tonight, mademoiselle?" he asks in French. "This is a grave mistake. Chef has made a lovely plum tart for us this evening."

"It's okay, Libion," Dr. Bradley tells him, before Vivienne can translate. "She's had a long day, and I will eat two tarts." He turns to Vivienne.

"Will you join me for breakfast at my hotel tomorrow? We have much to discuss."

She's more than happy to oblige. *Much to discuss.* This is promising. M. Libion helps her into her coat, promises the carriage will arrive momentarily, and she steps into the cool October night. It feels good to be outside, by herself, after the noise and stuffiness of the café. She takes a deep breath, wonders what the morning will hold.

Behind her, the door to La Rotonde opens and closes, and she steps to the side so the patrons can pass, her eyes on the street.

"Paulien," a voice says softly.

Vivienne freezes. No. Yes. She whirls around, and he's there. She throws her arms around him. "George," she sobs. "Thank God. Oh, thank God."

He wraps her in his arms, holds her tight. "It's all right, doll," he soothes. "It's all right. No need to cry. No need at all." Then he kisses her. It's as it has always been, and she loses herself in the dense, rich deliciousness of him, the deliciousness of the life she can now reclaim.

"But . . . but what happened?" She presses a hand to his chest, not at all certain that he's real. "Did you find the Swiss banker? Did you get the money?"

"Hush, my Paulien. Everything is going to be just fine."

"I love you so much, and I was so afraid." She covers his face with kisses. "So you have the money? Everyone will get paid back? Oh, Papa and Maman will be so happy." She thinks of Alexandre's brother and realizes that not everyone will be happy, but she pushes the thought away. "Thank God," she says again.

He pulls her gently into the shadows of the next building. "I want you to come with me."

"Come with you where?"

"Anywhere you want. Let's leave right now."

She steps out of his embrace, wipes her tears with her handkerchief. "But we have to go back to Belgium first. Set everything right. We can get married there, as we planned. Move to London until you close down Everard Sureties, and then . . . then we can go wherever we like."

"There's nothing to close down. I was thinking New Zealand or Australia or maybe even America. Which one would you like best?"

"Nothing to close down?"

"It's complicated. But the only thing that matters is that now we can start our life together. Without any entanglements."

"Entanglements," she repeats. "I . . . I don't understand." But she fears that she does.

He raises an eyebrow. "Don't you?"

"Is there a banker?" she demands.

"There are many bankers."

"My father, his friends, everyone . . . you didn't do this, did you?" Her voice rises an octave. "Did you?"

"Oh, Paulien," he says, laughing. "I gave you enough hints. You knew exactly what was going on."

The world disappears. No wind, no cold, no noise, no cooking smells. All she sees is an opaque mist of white. It occurs to her that this must be what it's like to die, that she has died, and she goes calm. But when her vision clears and George's smirking face wobbles above her, she knows she's all too alive. "I knew nothing!" she says, and slaps him hard across the face. "You're a horrid, horrid man."

He presses his hand to his cheek, clearly surprised. "Does that mean no?" he asks with a slight smile.

"Are you out of your mind?" she cries. "I'm not going anywhere with you. Ever. Never."

George pulls her into a tight hug, then just as quickly releases her. "I wouldn't be so sure of that. As you know, I can be very persistent." He touches his finger to the brim of his hat, dimples, and walks into the shadows.

Her carriage pulls up in front of the café, and she dives for it, her body gouged out by the pain. A piece of her knew from the moment George disappeared, and more so with each passing day, but if she already knew, why does it hurt so much?

"Do you think you'll be back here soon?" Vivienne asks Dr. Bradley when they settle into the booth.

It had been a trying night, but now that she's been forced to confront the reality of her situation, it's even more imperative that she leave Paris, that she persuade Dr. Bradley to take her to Italy. George did destroy all those lives, including hers, there's no denying it. On purpose. Out of greed. And however unwittingly, she was a part of it. She's responsible for her own obtuseness, for her inability to see what even George claimed was right in front of her. She now understands why people believe she shares the blame. Because she does.

"I come to the city at least twice a year," Dr. Bradley is saying. "But it will be a bit more often in the next year or two. I have my eye on many works."

She pushes down her shame and heartbreak, forces herself back into the moment. "You've done so well in the short time you've been here. I can't tell you how much I've enjoyed the whole experience, but I suppose you know that."

"Good. Because I have a proposition for you."

Vivienne tries to appear blasé. "Oh?"

"I want to extend your employment for another month."

He does want her to come with him. "What do you mean, 'extend'?"

"As you know, I'm leaving for Rome tomorrow, but I'd like you to follow up on some of the works here that I'm still interested in."

"In Paris?"

"You have a good eye for quality art, and you can do some scouting for me. When I come back from Italy, you can show me what else I might want to buy."

She doesn't think she has the stamina for four more weeks. Especially now that her last fantasy has been stripped away, her culpability revealed.

"I'll double your salary."

She bites her lip. There really is no choice. Her jobs at the millinery shop and the restaurant have been filled. But even more important, this opportunity will give her the chance to impress Dr. Bradley with her skills and work ethic and maybe persuade him to offer her a position at his new museum.

Vivienne visualizes herself on a mighty ship. She's standing at the railing of the highest deck, watching France, all of Europe, slip into the mist. She turns from stern to bow, facing into the future, away from her mistakes and regrets, away from those she's hurt, away from those who might want to hurt her. She's remained invisible for the past three weeks; she can remain invisible for another four.

Dr. Bradley crosses his arms over his chest. "Well?" he asks.

"I'd be happy to."

He pulls a pack of papers from inside his jacket and lays them down on the table. "These are the artists and galleries I want you to visit. Guillaume will help you."

4

PAULIEN, 1920

Paulien was so engrossed in her work that she never heard him approach and only slowly became aware that someone was standing behind her. It was late spring, one of the first days without rain, and she'd set up her easel at the edge of a wood not far from campus. When she turned, he was staring at the painting, seemingly oblivious to her.

"I like what happens with the yellow here." He pointed to the top left of the canvas. "How it leads the eye to the yellow below without actually telling it to go there."

She was put off by the fine cut of his jacket, the gold glittering on his watch, and the confidence of his pose, not to mention the inappropriateness of his approaching her. A dandy pretending to be interested in art when he was only interested in flirting with her. She returned to her painting and tried to pretend he wasn't there. Although she had to admit she appreciated his comment on the yellow brushstrokes—and that he was very handsome. Exceptionally handsome.

But he didn't leave, just stayed behind her left shoulder, watching her paint.

Because she wasn't very good, she didn't like to be observed. Especially this closely. "Don't you have someplace else to be?" She knew it was rude, and that her mother would admonish her for speaking like that to such an attractive and apparently wealthy young man, but he unnerved her.

"Not when I can stand here and watch you work such wonders."

She didn't respond.

"I don't mean to bother you, but I'm drawn by the process of creating something out of nothing."

Paulien gave an exaggerated sigh, put down her brush, and twisted around. "Are you an artist?" she asked, although she doubted he was. No artist walked around in clothes like that.

He removed his hat and bowed slightly. His eyes, like warm pools of chocolate, were playful; matching dimples cut his cheeks. "George Everard," he said in a resonant baritone. "Man of no talent."

Despite the arrogance that allowed him to presume he could interrupt her, she felt the tug of him. She stood and dropped into a mock curtsy. "Paulien Mertens, girl of not all that much."

"I heartily disagree with your opinion, but I'm charmed to make your acquaintance, Paulien Mertens." Then he put his hat back on his head and walked away.

She watched him go, surprisingly disappointed by his leave-taking. She shook off the feeling and returned to her work. She didn't think about him again until about two weeks later when he strolled into the Princess Louise on High Holborn, where she was having a glass of sherry with two classmates from the Slade.

The girls often met there because it was in central London, close to the British Museum and Paulien's flat. It was also a beautiful place, with deep wood paneling and a ring of booths—where either single women or couples could be comfortable—circling a bar at which only men were allowed. And the food wasn't half-bad.

She recognized him immediately; he was difficult to forget, with his strong cleft chin and the clump of dark hair that lazily fell to his forehead. Not to mention those dimples. His suit was just as fine as it had been that day in the woods, but it was less formal and lent him an air of the urbane rather than the overly proper. She quickly ducked her head so that her long hair covered her face.

She waited for him to come over, but there was no tap on her shoulder, no friendly cry of recognition in that sultry voice she remembered.

She raised her head and surreptitiously watched him. He was sitting at the bar talking animatedly with another man, unaware of her. And she didn't want him to be unaware of her. She flushed at the thought and lit a cigarette.

"Why are you all red?" her friend Lannie asked. She followed Paulien's eyes to the bar. "Oh là là!" she cried. "Who is that dashing fellow?"

"I have no idea," Paulien said primly, coloring even more deeply.

Lannie elbowed their friend Bernice and shrieked at Paulien, "You're a damn liar, you are!"

"Shush," Paulien hissed at her. "He'll hear you."

"I thought you didn't know him," Lannie teased.

Bernice rested her chin on her fists. "Wish I knew someone as dreamy as that. Think he has a friend for me?"

"I've no idea who his friends are—or who he is," Paulien said, then corrected herself. "Well, I did meet him once, very briefly. I don't even remember his name," she lied. "And I'm sure he doesn't remember mine."

"Let's go find out." Lannie stood and grabbed Paulien's hand.

But Paulien pulled her down instead. "No," she said, more sharply than she intended.

Lannie held Paulien's gaze, and when Paulien dropped her eyes, Lannie laughed softly, but with affection. "Have it your way, Paulie. Although I'm guessing what you really want is to go straight to that bar."

Paulien acknowledged the truth of her friend's remark with a twisted smile, but when she looked back at the bar, George was gone.

SHE BEGAN DROPPING into the Princess Louise more frequently, becoming almost a regular despite the fact that she wasn't all that fond of sherry. But George didn't return. At night, she dreamed about him; sometimes he chased her and sometimes it was the other way around, but either way, no one was ever caught.

When she woke from one of these dreams, a deep longing consumed her, frightening her, and she had a hard time falling back asleep. It was ridiculous, she knew, there were other boys who sought her attentions, but they all seemed terribly young and unmannered.

And then one day he was there. She was by herself, waiting for Lannie and two other classmates to join her for dinner, filling the time by sketching the bar, which was as ornate as the nave of a grand church.

"Still creating something out of nothing, I see."

She sat completely still, savoring the inevitability of the moment. Then she lowered her sketchbook and pencil to the table and raised her eyes. "Hello, George Everard."

"I've been looking for you, Paulien Mertens."

Suddenly confident in the rightness of the world, she said, "And now you've found me."

5

GEORGE/BENJAMIN, 1922

Lisbon is a very agreeable city, and he wonders why he never thought to come here before. Not as dirty as Paris or London, much less frenetic. Safer. He's sitting on the terrace of an elegant hotel, overlooking the harbor, enjoying the breezes and the pretty women. Granted, the skirts here aren't as short as they are in Paris, but they're short enough. He thinks of the suitcases full of cash in his room upstairs and smiles.

He'll be boarding his ship in the morning. Heading back to the good old US of A. New York City this time. Another financial scam, but with a different tenor. He has it all worked out. In fact, he's already slipped into his new persona, Benjamin F. Talcott, American magnate. Needless to say, he isn't Benjamin Talcott, any more than he was George Everard. Nor is he British, as he's claimed for the past five years. He shifts in and out of identities and nationalities as easily as another man might shed a business suit for the weekend. One of his talents. Of which he has many.

Everard Sureties was his biggest con yet. So simple, really. Buying international reply coupons in Italy, where the exchange rate is low, and cashing them in England, where the exchange rate is high. Too small a return for an ordinary man who thought small. But no one could accuse him of thinking small. Or being ordinary. He saw the potential, enticed investors who were so enamored of their paper returns that they never cashed out and then encouraged their friends to invest. The newcomers feeding in from the bottom, he taking it all off the top. Child's play.

Marks are everywhere, and they have only themselves to blame when disaster befalls them. Maybe he'll find another comely, rich girl like Paulien Mertens to help with Talcott Reserves. Too bad she didn't want to leave with him. Such a live wire. Smart and sexy and good in bed, if naive. From her reaction to him in Paris, still crazy in love with him, if a little angry at the moment.

He's guessing Paulien will be accompanying Edwin Bradley when he returns to Philadelphia. The two have been working well together; she appears to be in awe of Bradley, while Bradley appears to be completely infatuated with her. Now won't that be nice? A ready-made conduit to one of the wealthiest men in America. Just as she was a conduit to one of the wealthiest men in Belgium. Philadelphia is right around the corner from New York.

6

VIVIENNE, 1922

For over three weeks, Vivienne scouts for Dr. Bradley. She visits studios and galleries, roams the city and its outskirts, searches for pieces by both known and unknown artists. Some of these places are from the list Dr. Bradley gave her, and some she's discovered by asking the artists and dealers for names of others doing exciting and original work. Papa always said this was the best way to find the most promising art before anyone else did.

It takes all her time and all her thoughts, which is good, as it keeps her from tormenting herself over her parents' renunciation and George's deceit. Being in a world swirling with new ideas and boundless talent, eating and sleeping and breathing it every day. The sharp odor of paint and turpentine; the artists, clothes and hands and faces splattered with color; canvases scattered about, finished, unfinished, primed and abandoned; listening to them talk about their work, their influences, their hopes for the future. It fills her with delight and unremitting sadness.

She pretends she isn't doing this for Dr. Bradley, that she's searching for unheralded masterpieces to add to the Mertens Museum of Post-Impressionism. She imagines the marvel of living with André Derain's *The Drying Sails*, which he painted in the Mediterranean village of Collioure during the summer he spent there with Matisse. Or the deep cobalt embedded in fragments of red, orange, and white in *Woman in Blue* by Fernand Léger. She's particularly fond of the paintings of André

Masson, who, like Vivienne—or more precisely like Paulien—grew up in Belgium and took classes at the Académie Royale des Beaux-Arts in Brussels. The line between playacting and reality grows indistinct.

She's heading to her rooming house after a long day of touring, ruminating about adding more Belgian artists to the Mertens collection to increase its distinctiveness, when a furry shiver worries its way up her spine. Someone is following her, and she's afraid to look. She speeds up, steals into a recessed doorway. If only she were still in London, where dusk takes possession much earlier than it does in Paris.

The narrow alcove lends little protection, and she can't stay where she is. There's an alley to her left. She slips into it, crouches behind a pile of trash, pushes her nose into the elbow of her coat in a failed attempt to mask the smell. Shame fills her. For what she allowed to be done to her and for what she allowed George to do to her family, to Alexandre's brother, to so many others.

Maybe she should just stand up and take what's coming. There's an appeal to this thought, to surrendering to her fate, to ending what will surely be a life of vigilance and remorse. A life pretending to be someone she isn't, of never allowing anyone to get close because she can't trust her ability to judge another's character. A putrid waft of rotted fish assaults her nostrils. She takes off at a run.

The sorry, shuttered storefronts, the crumbling bricks of the facades. There has to be somewhere she can hide. But the buildings are pressed too tightly together, too miserly to provide deliverance. He's catching up. His footsteps are closer. His shadow falls on her shoulder.

A hand grips her arm. "Paulien, it is—"

Vivienne pummels him with her fists, tries to twist out of his grasp, but he's larger and stronger than she is.

He grabs her hands, presses them together. "Stop. Look at me. Stop. It is me. It is Franck."

Franck. Her baby brother. How could she not have recognized his voice? Terror. She hugs him tight. The sight of his crooked smile, the feel of his narrow waist, the smell of him. At seventeen, he towers over her. She presses her face into his chest and breathes him in.

Franck awkwardly extricates himself. "Paulien, please."

"Vivienne," she corrects. "Vivienne Gregsby. That's who I am now."

"I cannot stay long," he says, his tone oddly vacant, cold. "We need to talk."

"Come," she says. "I know a place." She takes him to a small café that opens onto the alley behind her rooming house. It's moldy and smoky, and mice scamper in one corner—far different from anywhere she and Franck have ever been together. But it's hidden and shadowy and almost completely empty. They take seats at a table that backs up to a greasy brick wall and pull their chairs close together.

"Tell me," Vivienne begs. "Tell me everything. How are you? How are Papa and Maman?"

Franck hesitates and then says, "Papa has been stoic. Even after losing the estate, the mills, all the money, even after turning over most of the art collection to the Royal Museums. He is a strong man."

"Everything?" she whispers.

"There are some paintings left. The ones in the colonnade. But not—"

"Oh. Thank God he has them. At least . . . at least he has them. At least he has . . ." What has she done?

"The Royal Museums would not take them, and no other museum wanted them either. Something about standards, I think."

"So he'll be able to keep them?"

Franck looks around. "I do not have much time. We must—"

"Please tell me he can keep them."

He sighs the sigh of a much older man. "There is one potential buyer who wants them for his private collection. He is willing to pay only a fraction of what Papa is asking, and Papa has refused. But the courts will force him to accept the offer if a better one does not come soon."

"Oh," Vivienne moans. "How will he bear it?"

"He has given up many things far more valuable, and I do not understand why this is so trying for him." Franck's voice is thick with bitterness. "He says the paintings must be seen, that the public is finally ready. That the price is an insult to the paintings. An insult? After everything that has happened, this is what he sees as an insult?" He spits on the cobblestones. "They are nothing."

She covers her face with her hands. "This is all my fault. I've destroyed everything Papa loves."

He runs a fingernail along the edge of the wooden table, not bothering to contradict her. "This is not what I was sent to tell you."

Vivienne jerks her head up. "What?"

"There are rumors of arrest warrants. For you and Papa."

"But Papa did nothing. I did nothing."

"There are people who say you are guilty of fraud. They claim they have proof Papa was taking what I think is called 'a sweetener.' That you and Everard were working together."

"Working together? This is madness."

"They say if you were not, why would you both disappear at the same time? At the same time as all the money."

"What proof do they have? There is no proof. Papa and Maman sent me away days after George left. You know that. Who are these people?"

"Monsieur Lavigne—you remember, he is, was, one of Papa's largest distributors? He has been the most outspoken. Threatened that he and the others would take the law into their own hands if the police did not act. He has been speaking to the newspapers."

"You just said Papa was forced to sell the estate, that there is no money. How can—"

"This is what Papa's lawyer argued. But Monsieur Lavigne says he has evidence that Papa is only pretending to be poor. That he has hidden the money outside the country and will claim it when he meets up with you and Everard."

"I'm not with George. I hate him. I detest him and—"

Franck stands. "Please do not do this. You are my sister, but I cannot listen to your lies."

"What . . . what lies?" Vivienne sputters. "There are no lies."

"A friend of Léon's saw you embracing Everard outside of Café de la Rotonde a few weeks ago. This friend said he heard you talking of love, heard you speaking each other's names."

"That wasn't what it was!" She stands and grabs the lapels of his coat. "It's a misunderstanding. I sent George away. I told him I never wanted to see him again. You have to believe me."

He shakes her off. "Papa had almost convinced Maman to let you return. But then . . . then this news came and—"

"But it isn't true!"

Franck takes a step back, stares at his shoes. "Papa said that you must never contact anyone from before, never tell anyone your real name." His voice cracks. "He said it is the best way to protect the family—and to protect you."

Vivienne also stares at her brother's shoes. Papa is assuming the worst of her, yet he cares enough to send Franck. He worries for her and her future, yet he's casting her into permanent exile. She whimpers softly.

Franck drops an envelope on the table. "Tante Natalie sent this for you. She said to tell you that she thinks of you often. And fondly."

He walks away, shoulders heaving, and Vivienne is undone. When she discovers that the envelope is filled with francs, she begins to sob. Tante Natalie is the only family member who didn't invest with George. The only one who can still think of her fondly.

VIVIENNE STUMBLES BACK to her room. She doesn't know what to do and knows that there is nothing she can do. She wishes she had someone to talk to, but she's told none of the girls about her family, confided in no one at any of her jobs. Her own dear papa has been forced to tell her, his only daughter, they can never meet again, forced to save his family by tearing it apart. Because of what she did.

She lies down on her cot. All those hours she and Papa spent discussing art and artists, collecting and curating, how he used to laugh at her intensity, how proud he was of her aptitude for the work. She begins to cry again, or perhaps she never stopped, remembering how he would tease that she was attracted to Matisse and Picasso because their notions fit with what he affectionately called her irrepressible nature.

And now it's all gone, the last pieces of all they shared soon to be dispersed, virtually stolen at far less than their worth. Hidden from public view, breaking her father's heart, possibly breaking her father. *An insult to the paintings*, Papa had said. Franck didn't understand, but Vivienne does.

She closes her eyes, and she's back at the estate. She's standing in the great foyer with its branching staircase and double-high ceiling. The fresh flowers exquisite to the eye and nose, the thick carpets and carved furniture fashioning a comforting hush, the sun from the large mullioned windows throwing parallelograms of light over it all.

There are shipping crates in the foyer with her. Each holds a single painting. Each is addressed to Aldric Mertens. They vary in size, and she knows exactly what's in each of them. The tiny Cézanne. The large Seurat. She's waiting for her father to return from his offices, standing in the shadows to watch his response.

When he finally arrives, he steps briskly through the front door, fine looking and confident. Then he stops, his eyes riveted to the cartons. Slowly, as if in a trance, he approaches them, drops to his knees. He places his hands gingerly on the top of one. Then he reaches his arms out and touches each of the others, his expression flashing from confusion to wonder to exhilaration. He presses his forehead to the first box and murmurs, "You have come home to me."

Then he stands and takes her into his arms, full of gratitude and forgiveness. "As have you. Thank you, my darling girl. Thank you. All is forgiven."

Vivienne shakes off the dream, climbs from the narrow bed. If only there was something she could do to spare her father this final loss. She hits her head on the sloping ceiling, stoops, and stares into the cloudy mirror hanging next to the door. Her reflection is wavy in the old glass and only slightly resembles the face of the girl who once lived on the handsome estate she just saw, who once curled on a couch rapturously soaking in the paintings of Matisse and Picasso.

And then it hits her. The colonnade seven are perfect for Dr. Bradley. Matisse, Cézanne, Seurat, and Picasso are all artists he greatly admires. He would pay a fair price, keep them together, hang them in his museum for the world to appreciate. And if she can persuade Dr. Bradley to take her to America, she'll be able to be with them, watch over them. Maybe even find a way to bring them home, a gesture of restitution to her father.

It works out better than she could have hoped. She tells Paul Guillaume that another dealer mentioned an estate sale somewhere outside Brussels that includes works by some of the post-Impressionists. She doesn't go into specifics—for how would she know?—and is nonchalant about the whole affair. It doesn't take long for Guillaume to discover who's selling and what's for sale. He's intrigued by the possibilities.

The day after Dr. Bradley returns from Italy, Guillaume whisks him off on a quick trip to Belgium. They return triumphant. The price was high but what they negotiated was fair, and all parties seem satisfied with the result. Seven paintings are on their way to Philadelphia, each a true masterpiece according to Dr. Bradley. He's particularly pleased with *The Music Lesson* by his friend Henri Matisse.

7

VIVIENNE, 1922

The colonnade seven are boxed in a bulky crate, rolling with the waves, sailing thousands of miles to the west, and Vivienne needs to be headed in the same direction. Since Dr. Bradley's return she hasn't had the opportunity to talk to him about a position in Philadelphia, and his invitation to join him at a dinner party at the home of the Americans Gertrude Stein and Alice B. Toklas appears to be her last chance.

Still, she hesitates to accept. Even though Léon's friend identified her only because she was with George and they called each other by name, someone from her past knows what she looks like now. And he may have told others. But her misgivings are vanquished when Dr. Bradley mentions that Henri Matisse is also invited.

How can she miss the opportunity to meet the man whose work touches her like no other? Who pushes beyond everything that came before him, turning color into so much more than just a hue, drenching it with substance and sensation? Using it as structure. What will it be like to stand in the same room as a man who can create such magic?

She splurges on a silk dress she finds in a shop next to the millinery where she used to work. It's secondhand, possibly third, and has a long rip at the back and waist, but at the rooming house Adélaïde easily mends it and the dress looks almost new. Rachelle and Odette admire Adélaïde's handiwork as well as the way the dress hugs Vivienne's trim figure. They tease her about how sexy she looks and wonder what man she has her eye on. Vivienne blushes, and her friends tease her even more.

As they ride to "27," which is what Dr. Bradley and apparently every-one else calls Gertrude Stein's home, Vivienne can barely sit still. She's heard all the stories. Over a decade ago, Gertrude and her brother Leo created what many consider the first museum of modern art at the house on the rue de Fleurus. But there was a falling-out—it's rumored the rift was because of Alice, whom Leo apparently referred to as "a kind of abnormal vampire"—and Leo moved back to America.

They divided their collection; she took all the Picassos while he secured most of the Renoirs and Cézannes. Apparently both were pleased with the distribution, and now they're best buddies again. Vivienne can't wait to see Gertrude's artwork. And she can't wait to meet Henri Matisse.

It's raining hard when they arrive, as it often does in Paris in December, and she doesn't want to get her new dress wet while Dr. Bradley pays for the carriage, so she walks quickly up to the house and knocks on the door.

Gertrude Stein yanks it open, looks her up and down, and demands, "De la part de qui venez-vous?" Who is your introducer?

Vivienne wasn't aware she needed an introducer, and she's surprised by both Gertrude's appearance and her question. This small woman with the huge reputation is shorter than she is—and a good bit wider. Gertrude looks like a miniature rotund man, with her large nose, cropped hair, and corduroy jacket.

"Je m'appelle Vivienne Gregsby," she responds. "Although I'd like to tell you I need no introduction, I suppose I do." She turns to look for Dr. Bradley, who's talking with the carriage driver.

"Vous êtes française?" Gertrude asks. Are you French?

"À moitié," Vivienne answers, hoping Gertrude won't press for details. Her narrative is that she has a French mother, an English father, and was raised outside London. But she's hoping to use it as infrequently as possible.

"And British?" Gertrude asks in English.

"That's the other half," Vivienne responds with a strong London accent.

Gertrude's eyes are welcoming, but they grow cool when she sees Dr. Bradley come up behind Vivienne. "You've come with Bradley?"

"I'm his translator. I'm helping him find art for his new museum."

Gertrude actually says, "Harrumph," then ushers Vivienne into the house. "Entrez, Vivienne," she adds. Dr. Bradley tips his hat and follows.

Twenty-seven, rue de Fleurus, a house on a narrow street off the boulevard Raspail near the Jardin du Luxembourg, is a common enough Parisian building from the outside—white limestone with double wrought-iron doors topped by a carving of a bearded man—but inside it's a riot of colorful people and paintings, filled with conversation and the scent of cigarettes, clove, and cinnamon.

Vivienne stands in the entrance and gapes. She immediately snaps her mouth shut. Even with all her studies and travels, her museum and gallery visits, her work with Dr. Bradley, she's never seen anything like this. She doesn't want to appear unworldly, but she can't stop gawking.

The whitewashed walls are awash in paintings, alongside, above, and below one another, almost touching, reaching from the floor to the tall ceilings. This arbitrary jumble wraps around her and holds her tight. Gauguin, Toulouse-Lautrec, Cézanne, Matisse, Picasso, Renoir, Manet . . . if only Papa could see this. It's what they imagined the Mertens collection might someday become, although not displayed in such a haphazard manner.

Then she steps back into the foyer. She can't merrily walk into a party like this. Anyone could be here. For a moment it seems that the rooms are filled with people she knows. Family friends, classmates from the Slade, cousins, even her Tante Natalie. But as she looks more carefully, she sees that it isn't Bernice or Antoinette or Lannie or Scotty, and the woman she took for Tante Natalie is at least twice her aunt's age.

Dr. Bradley comes up behind her and points toward the back of the room. "I assume you'd like to meet my friend Henri."

Vivienne follows his finger. Henri Matisse is sitting in an armchair, talking intently with two men, one of whom Dr. Bradley tells her is the playwright Thornton Wilder. Matisse bursts out laughing, as does his audience.

"He looks so . . . so boyish," she says. And Matisse does, with his mussed hair and generous smile, his hand resting casually on Wilder's arm, the sleeves of his jacket a tad too short. An irrepressible man-boy. "I thought he'd be more serious. Much older."

"Henri is only serious about his work."

As they walk toward Matisse, the artist breaks off his conversation and jumps from the chair. "Edwin!" he cries. "I did not know you had arrived." He and Edwin pound each other on the back.

Vivienne is amazed that Dr. Bradley comes so close to embracing Matisse. He usually conceals his emotions, and she often wonders how many he actually has. This is the first time she's seen him touch another person other than to shake a hand.

When Matisse sees her, he smiles widely, and she feels his delight in the pit of her stomach. He looks more like a handsome professor than a painter: full beard and round glasses, intelligence and good cheer writ large across his face. Henri Matisse is standing in front of her, taking her in with apparent interest. Vivienne can barely breathe.

He kisses her hand and asks, "What kind of secrets have you been keeping from me, Dr. Edwin Bradley?" But he's looking at her.

As their eyes meet, a searing heat rises to Vivienne's cheeks. She's embarrassed by her reaction, which causes her face only to redden more. "Monsieur Matisse," is all she can say. Her hand is holding the hand that created *The Music Lesson. The Joy of Life.*

"Henri," he corrects. "Please. Monsieur Matisse was my father, long dead."

"H-Henri," she manages to stammer.

"Meet Vivienne Gregsby," she hears Dr. Bradley say in the distance. "My translator."

"Excellent choice." Henri doesn't release her hand. "You are stunning in that shade of red."

Dr. Bradley says something about their work, how she's translating and assisting him, but it's gibberish to her.

Henri doesn't appear to be listening either. He murmurs in her ear, "Enchanté."

She's heard rumors that he's a ladies' man—a true French husband, who, as they say, is "faithful to his wife in the fashion of Montmartre," meaning not faithful at all.

Before she can respond, Dr. Bradley looks at the two of them and frowns. "Come, Miss Gregsby," he says, taking her arm. "There are others here for you to meet."

Vivienne allows Dr. Bradley to lead her to the other side of the room. She dares a quick glance back at Henri, and he winks at her. It's all she can do to keep from swooning.

"This is Alice Toklas." Dr. Bradley bows slightly toward a small, stooped creature almost lost within the upholstery of a large chair. "She lives here with Gertrude and watches after the girls brought here by the men. Why don't you sit with her for a while? She'll keep you occupied." He turns to Alice. "This is my translator, Vivienne Gregsby." Then he walks away.

Alice and Vivienne look at each other. "Arrogant, isn't he?" Alice remarks dryly.

"He can be." Vivienne lights a cigarette in an attempt to calm herself. Henri Matisse winked at her. Winked at her. She takes a long drag, struggles to remember Alice's question, and then says, "He has his uses."

Gertrude swoops down and perches on the arm of Vivienne's chair. "Frankly I can't imagine what those might be."

"He pays well and introduces me to people like the two of you."

"Bradley waves his checkbook around too much," Gertrude complains. "He and his kind are part of the reason I left the States. Maybe more than just a part."

"He's got a great eye for art," Vivienne points out. "I've learned so much working with him over the last two months. He's smart—and charming when he wants to be."

"Those who are charming only when they want to be aren't charming at all," Gertrude grumbles.

"All charming people are charming only when they want to be," Vivienne says, knowing how true this is. "That's why they're so charming."

Gertrude looks at Alice and grins. "This young lass," she says, grasping Vivienne's hand and pulling her out of the chair, "is coming with me."

THE DINING ROOM is lined with books, almost library-like, but its most astonishing feature is the Picasso sketches that cover its double doors. Perhaps two dozen of them, pinned willy-nilly to the wood as if they were children's drawings instead of the work of the next great master. The room is small, though the high ceiling keeps it from feeling oppressive. As does the company: French intellectuals, English aristocrats, German students, American expats, Thornton Wilder sitting next to a young writer named Hemingway, Henri Matisse sitting next to her.

Dr. Bradley is at the end of the table, alongside an older woman with a perfectly round face underscored by half a dozen chins, and he looks none too pleased with the arrangement. Although Vivienne had hoped to talk with Dr. Bradley about accompanying him to America, she's more than pleased with her dinner companion. There will be time later.

Henri fills her wineglass from the bottle on the table. "Hélène is an exemplary cook and you have many delights ahead of you."

"The evening has already been full of delights."

"I do hope one of them was meeting me."

Vivienne takes a sip of wine, luxuriating in the full body of the Bordeaux, a Château Latour that reminds her of childhood summers in Portofino. She rolls it around on her tongue, the taste particularly delicious after her months of penny-pinching. How could she ever explain to him what a delight meeting him is?

"I see you appreciate a fine wine. You are French, no?"

She gives him the answer she gave Gertrude. "À moitié," she says with a hint of wistfulness for Paulien.

"Why so sad, *ma chérie*? You have been away from France for a long time?"

She forces a smile. "Not sad, not sad at all. The opposite actually."

"Homecomings are often bittersweet, no? Our memories play tricks, and the good ones can hurt even more than the bad ones."

"Yes," she agrees after a pause to collect herself.

Henri takes her hand, turns it over, and runs his finger along the curved line in her palm between her forefinger and thumb. She shivers. Henri Matisse is holding her hand, speaking to her as he would to a friend. Flirting with her perhaps.

"You are too young and handsome to let the past haunt you," he says. "It is time for you to make a new future."

Definitely flirting. And a charming and flirtatious man is not to be trusted, even if he is Henri Matisse rather than George Everard. She pulls her hand from his and asks what he's working on.

He describes his work in progress, *Odalisque with Red Pants*. "I am trying to create areas of pure, bright color that reflect the way I see the subject, the way I feel her. Not as she might look through a photographer's lens."

"Like what you did in *The Open Window*?" Vivienne asks. "The red ships? The pink anchor and the patterned dots of the flowerpots?"

"Yes and no," Henri says thoughtfully. "I have moved away from the Pointillist dots. Too mechanical. I am working with the patterns of tapestries. Islamic designs. I want everything on all the planes of the picture to pull the eye equally. For the subject and background to have the same value so there's no principle feature. Only pattern is important."

"Beyond the Fauves? No more wild beasts?"

Henri appraises her frankly. "There is nothing more devastating than a beautiful woman with a great understanding of art."

"No," she corrects him. "There is nothing more devastating than a man who creates great art."

They laugh, delighted with each other, and dive into a discussion about the interplay of Fauvism, Cubism, and what Henri is trying to achieve that's different from the other two.

Not long after Hélène serves the crème brûlée, Dr. Bradley appears at Vivienne's side. She reluctantly breaks off her conversation with Henri. "Are you ready to leave?" she asks Dr. Bradley, remembering that she has a more pressing discussion to engage in this evening.

Dr. Bradley grunts in the affirmative and motions to Hélène. "Please bring Mademoiselle's coat."

There's nothing Vivienne would like better than to stay and talk with Henri, but she puts her napkin on the table. Perhaps there will be another time. But before she can stand, a woman's voice calls from the far side of the room, "Paulien! Paulien Mertens! Est-ce que c'est vous?" Is that you?

Instinctively, Vivienne turns, then immediately twists her face back to Dr. Bradley. It's Antoinette Lavigne, the youngest daughter of one of her mother's friends. Or more correctly, the youngest daughter of the woman who'd once been one of her mother's friends—and the youngest daughter of one of Papa's largest distributors, the man whom Franck said had threatened to take the law into his own hands if she and Papa weren't arrested.

She thought she recognized Antoinette earlier, but dismissed the possibility because of Antoinette's short skirt and heavy makeup. M. Lavigne wouldn't approve of either, and Antoinette always followed her father's dictates without a whimper of defiance. If the situation were different, Antoinette's rebelliousness would have increased Vivienne's appreciation for the girl who had finally stepped out of her father's shadow.

Vivienne tosses her hair in an exaggerated way and says to Dr. Bradley, "Just let me say good-bye to Gertrude and—"

"Pardonnez-moi." Antoinette is standing to Vivienne's left, squinting down at her. "You look so much like a girl I know . . ."

Vivienne shrugs. "They claim everyone has a double," she says, dropping her voice an octave and emphasizing the British vowels. Fortunately, at that moment, Hélène brings her coat, and Vivienne pretends to search for something in the pocket, keeping her head down, wishing her hair were long again. It was useful for hiding behind.

"C'est dommage," Antoinette finally says after a long, excruciating pause. "I can see now that you are not she." She laughs awkwardly. "And it could not be. Paulien is no fool, and she would know better than to be waltzing around Paris." Then she walks back to her seat.

"Paulien?" Henri asks archly. "What is this all about?"

"That she mistook me for someone else?" Vivienne opens her eyes wide, trying to appear unconcerned, but her stomach is a corkscrew of dread. "Hasn't that ever happened to you?"

Henri leans back in his chair. "I cannot say that it has."

Vivienne stands. "Shall we go?" she asks Dr. Bradley.

Henri stands, too, takes her hand, and kisses it one more time. "We will meet again, I am sure," he says. "Otherwise I will die of a broken heart."

"That would be a tragedy for the art world," she tells him as she removes her fingers from his. "So I do hope we see each other again." But she knows this is not going to happen soon. And definitely not in Paris.

THE RAIN HAS stopped, and Vivienne tries to still her trembling hands as they climb into the carriage. Had Antoinette been fooled? Or is she on her way right now to the police station? Or to report to her father what she discovered? To tell him he should oil his shotgun?

Dr. Bradley doesn't appear to have taken any notice of her conversation with Antoinette, which is good, although strange. But she has no time for idle speculation. She's been recognized, and Dr. Bradley is leaving within days. "I have a question for you," she says.

"And I have one for you. May I go first?"

"Of course," she says, wishing it were otherwise.

"What would you think about a permanent position?"

"A permanent position," she repeats. Did he mean here or in the States?

"I need a secretary," he explains. "But more than a secretary, an assistant. Someone smart with an eye for art, someone to help me get my museum off the ground. I'm also going to start a school. To teach people how to appreciate art. I'll need someone to help me plan and run that, too."

"In America?"

"The salary is good," he says quickly, as if her question meant she was opposed to the idea. "Very good. I'll pay for your travel and anything else that you might need to get settled."

THE TRIAL, 1928

Edwin, it would astound you how much a judge's facial expressions can change the tenor of a courtroom—as well as, I fear, the minds of the jurors. Everyone knows the legal system is corrupt, but this has to border on judicial misconduct.

The judge smiles at the district attorney and frowns at my lawyer. He cocks his head and listens attentively to Pratt but rolls his eyes and stares upward when Ronald makes a request or offers an objection. He often glares down at me like a malevolent Old Testament god disappointed by the behavior of one of his minions.

And I don't believe for a moment that the fact that I'm sitting before this particular judge is a coincidence. It's the work of Thomas Quinton, whose motivations for wanting me convicted are as clear as they are chilling. And whose power in this city is the most disturbing of all. Just as he and Ada are certainly the masterminds behind the entire charade, from my arrest to this trial.

"I'm going to prove you killed my Edwin," Ada railed at me during your funeral. "Just sit back and watch me!" When Quinton tried to silence her, she turned on him and screamed, "Don't shush me—you promised to help me prove it!" Need I say more?

Perhaps Quinton is the one who hired the truck driver. What could be more perfect? He sets me up for your murder, finagles my conviction, and then gets your collection for his museum and your wife for his bed. I'm sorry to be crass, but you have to admit those are the two things he's been fighting for all these years.

First up today was Jacob Gusdorff. Pratt took him through the usual set-up questions: his extensive credentials, how many wills he had prepared in his career, how long he had been your personal attorney, et cetera, et cetera, et cetera. Then Pratt asked him to read specific parts of the will to the court, particularly those sections pertaining to "Miss Gregsby's complete control of the assets, including use and divestment."

When Jacob finished reading, Pratt asked, "Do you know if this was still Dr. Bradley's intention at the time of his death?"

"It was not." Jacob glared at me.

"It wasn't?" Pratt's face was awash with false incredulity. "Could you please clarify?"

Jacob checked his notes. "On Thursday, January twelfth, 1928, I received a call from Dr. Bradley directing me to draw up a new will. He instructed me to remove Miss Gregsby as the beneficiary and appoint his wife, Ada Leggett Bradley, as his legal heir. We had an appointment on the following Monday, January sixteenth, for him to sign the new documents."

"And did that meeting occur?"

"Unfortunately, no. Dr. Bradley died on Sunday, January fifteenth."

"So, correct me if I'm wrong, but because the new will was never signed, Miss Gregsby remains the beneficiary even though that was not Dr. Bradley's intent?"

"That is correct."

"And if Dr. Bradley had not been killed during those short few days between your telephone conversation and your meeting, who would be the beneficiary of his estate?"

Again the glower in my direction. "His wife, Mrs. Bradley, who is currently his contingent beneficiary."

It all sounded so harsh. Ronald promises me that this means nothing without evidence of opportunity. Both are needed in murder-for-hire cases, which he claims are notoriously tough to prove. Why doesn't this give me more confidence?

8

VIVIENNE, 1923

Vivienne tells Dr. Bradley she's seasick and stays in her cabin for the entire crossing. The steward brings her tea and biscuits but little else. This is fine, as she has no appetite and wants to stay as far away from the other passengers as possible. Although she will soon be reunited with her cherished paintings and is putting thousands of miles between herself and her mistakes, she struggles to work up enthusiasm for the new life ahead. This is what she wanted, what she prayed for, but to be exiled to America, on her own in that vast land, is far from what she ever envisioned for herself.

She curls herself into a ball, hollow and aching for loving arms to hold her. But there's only the ocean to rock her to sleep. She's as untethered as the waves outside her tiny porthole, adrift, severed from her family and friends, from who she is. Or more correctly, from who she was.

Because of George, a depraved man without a whiff of empathy, who purposely shattered countless lives for his own greed and self-aggrandizement. A man so narcissistic that he assumed she had recognized and accepted his scheming, that she would come with him when he called.

It's going to be a long time before she's able to trust a man again. If ever. Or trust herself. She fell so hard for George's lies, believing them because she wanted them to be true. *Wanted him*. But he didn't want her. Had never wanted her. He managed her like a puppeteer manipulates his dummy. Which is exactly what she was, never suspecting anything was amiss.

But he was also her first love, her only love, and God help her, sometimes she finds herself yearning for him, for the life they imagined together. For the light touch of his lips as they grazed the inside of her wrist, for his breath in her ear, for those sweet, sweet nights. She presses her limbs even more tightly together in an attempt to take up as little space as possible.

She will get justice for herself and her father and everyone else George swindled. He will be punished, forced to his knees. He'll come looking for her again—that night in Paris he all but promised he would. And when he does, she'll encourage him, scam him right back, edge him out into the open and make sure he's locked up for the rest of his life. Her contribution to George's demise will finally exonerate her in her father's eyes. Even if she will never be exonerated in her own.

She visualizes George being led into a grim-looking prison, handcuffed and shackled, one burly guard hovering close at his right and another at his left. He's pale and haggard, a crushed man, and he stares at the sidewalk as he shuffles along. He will be staying in the boxy brick building topped with turrets and barbed wire for the rest of his life. And she's the one who put him there. A bevy of flashbulbs pop as a policeman shakes her hand.

A FEW DAYS before they left France, she told Dr. Bradley that she'd lost her passport, and he miraculously handed her a new one the next day. So now, as she disembarks in New York City, she's Vivienne Gregsby, permanently, irrevocably, her fictive name now official. It's an odd feeling, to be herself and yet not to be herself, to stand essentially naked, unformed.

If Dr. Bradley is startled by the small size of her suitcase or how quickly she was able to divest herself of a life, he doesn't mention it. He and his wife, Ada, live in Merion, Pennsylvania, a suburb of Philadelphia, where the Bradley Museum is nearing completion. The couple presently resides in a rented house on the other side of town, but they will soon move into their new home, which is attached to the museum. Vivienne feels sorry for Ada Bradley, a delicate slip of a woman, pretty in an old-fashioned way, of whom Dr. Bradley clearly thinks little. He barely speaks to her, barely acknowledges her presence.

With Dr. Bradley's generous moving provision, Vivienne takes two rooms in a widow's house a block from the new museum. Even with the large number of francs she left under Adélaïde, Rachelle, and Odette's pillows, she's feeling flush. She saved in Paris, and her new salary is high. For the first time since leaving Brussels, she's not afraid of running out of money. Although she's never been to America before, which is unfamiliar and daunting, she's far away from Paulien Mertens, and this makes her feel safe. If unsteady.

Dr. Bradley brings her to the construction site her first day on the job. It's mid-January, well below freezing, and a sharp wind whips around her. It's much worse than anything she's experienced in Brussels or Paris, even London. He offers her his coat, which she takes; it's too big and she keeps tripping over the hem. She heard it was cold in America but never imagined it would be this bitter. She needs a warmer coat. Wool gloves, definitely wool gloves. More socks.

The exterior of the building is complete, a classical Beaux-Arts structure of creamy limestone, which surprises her, as she expected it to be more modern. They walk up two planks of wood, through what will soon be the front door, and into the main gallery, which is crawling with carpenters and plasterers and painters and every other conceivable kind of workman. But the walls are up and the windows installed, so it's easy to see what it will become, which is breathtaking.

Vivienne gazes up at the towering ceiling, at the open railing of the second floor, at the arches that crown the three two-story mullioned windows, at the wide doorways leading into rooms to the left, to the right, and straight ahead. "It's so open," she says. "So light. So big."

"That's why I need all that art."

From the size of the outside of the building, it's clear there are at least two dozen more galleries. "It's going to take you forever."

"A lifelong project," Dr. Bradley agrees. "Especially because I'm going to hang the pictures in groupings. Many groupings. Eight, ten, perhaps twenty paintings on a single wall, four walls in every gallery. I also have a large collection of metalwork—keys, hinges, padlocks, escutcheons, ladles, scissors—which I'm going to intersperse around and between the paintings."

She thinks of Gertrude Stein's salon and winces at the idea of her paintings being one among many. Each deserves its own wall, its own space with room to breathe. Hinges and scissors?

"Mine will be completely different from Gertrude's compositions," he explains as if reading her mind. "They won't be haphazard and lackadaisical—they'll be symmetrical and purposeful. I'm going to position the artworks in a different way. A new way. Not so much by century or school or artist, but by color and light and subject matter. Juxtapositions that show off the similarities and differences between them."

In every museum Vivienne has visited, the paintings are hung according to their chronologies: Greek and Roman in one gallery, Medieval in another, Renaissance and Baroque in the next. It was the same at the estate. She's in awe of Dr. Bradley's daring, if skeptical of its effect. It's almost as if he's an artist rather than a curator, developing new approaches to self-expression.

He shows her the rest of the building. There are twenty-three galleries, thirteen on the first floor, ten on the second, one flowing into another in a ring of rectangles. It's going to be a truly marvelous museum. If she has to be in exile, this isn't a bad place to be banished.

The next day, she accompanies him to his factory. She had no idea he owned a factory. But this is how he made, and is still making, his money. He explains that he grew up in a part of South Philadelphia called The Neck, one of the toughest neighborhoods in an area of tough neighborhoods. His father was often out of work, and the family was well acquainted with poverty and hunger. But Dr. Bradley went to Central High—the examination school of choice for the clever poor—did well, entered Penn, and received his MD when he was twenty. But that isn't how he got rich.

He quickly abandoned medicine for chemistry, then realized what he really wanted was to be a businessman. Along with another chemist, Ben Hagerty, he developed the formula for a drug they named Argyrol, which when put into the eyes of newborns protected them from blindness. Soon hospitals all over the world were using it, and Edwin Bradley was a multimillionaire.

For a number of years, he put all his energies into running Bradley and Hagerty, Chemists, the company and factory that produces Argyrol. But soon that, too, lost its luster, and as his interest in his business waned, he tried his hand at painting. When this was less successful than he had hoped, he turned his attention to collecting and curating. He still spends most of the week at the factory, because it is, after all, the way he supports his obsession. Although once the Bradley Museum his open, he claims he plans to split his time between the two.

"Remember I told you that in addition to a museum, I'm going to create a school?" he asks as he leads Vivienne past rows of workers at long benches. He points toward a room that appears to be a classroom, half a dozen rows of chairs facing a podium. "To teach people how to appreciate art. Not to tell them what to think about a piece, but to give them the tools to decide for themselves."

"Yes," she says, although she doesn't remember any such thing. She's finding that her memory is fuzzy about much that happened between July and December of the previous year. A blessing, she supposes.

They enter the room, where a painting by Modigliani sits on an easel to the left of the podium, and one by Rousseau sits on the right. The Modigliani is a picture of a redhead in a polka-dot blouse, flat and foreshortened but potent, taking up most of the canvas. The Rousseau is also of a lone woman, but she's tiny, dwarfed by fantastical trees and plants.

Each painting is striking in its own way, but seeing the two next to each other makes them even more so: one woman calm and comfortable, the other clearly out of her element; the colors of one tranquil and muted, the other rich and lush; the focus of one on the human, the other on the natural.

Vivienne never thought to look this way before, seeing what one artist included and what another left out, highlighting the choices taken and raising questions about why and why not. She's astonished by the insight, and she wishes more than anything that she could discuss this with her father. Maybe Dr. Bradley's curatorial ideas have more merit than she appreciated.

"The contrast between the two is so persuasive," she says. "Amazing to see them together like this."

"These two paintings are instructive," Dr. Bradley tells her. "Modigliani's painting style is freer." He points to a spot where the canvas shows through. "The opposite of Rousseau's tight control of the outline of every leaf."

"So you've begun already?" she asks. "Your school. The students are coming here until the museum building is finished? Then you'll move them over there?"

"I've started the classes, but no, the students aren't going to switch to the museum."

"I don't understand."

"I've been holding classes for my employees."

"The factory workers?" Most of the workers she's seen are Negroes, and she would guess none of them—including the white ones—have much education. "You're teaching them about art?"

"Twice a week for two hours. For two years now."

"They stay after work?"

"The classes are held during the workday," he tells her, as if there's nothing unusual about the arrangement. "I bring in new pictures and close the plant down. Everyone comes in here and we discuss what we see."

"You pay them?"

"Same as if they were on the floor."

She watches as the workers file into the classroom. "Another Modigliani," a tall Negro man says as he sits down. "I like how she's looking right at me."

VIVIENNE IS SETTLED into her temporary office, a bedroom in the Bradley's rented house. It's across from Dr. Bradley's office, another bedroom. When the museum is completed, the staff will be relocated there, and the Bradleys will take possession of their new home. She's handed piles of papers and files and letters and receipts and order forms. It's her job to file them, organize them, answer them, follow up on them, and then start boxing them up for the move.

At first she's overwhelmed, but she's naturally organized and takes to the tasks better than she would have thought, although her typing skills lag. Fortunately, Dr. Bradley is more concerned with the details of getting his museum off the ground than with her typing errors. He's also arranging to exhibit a number of his paintings at the Pennsylvania Academy of Fine Arts, and the academy show is the first time she gets to work as his assistant rather than as his secretary. She helps him to choose the paintings, to write the introductory essay, to hang the artwork.

Dr. Bradley is convinced the upcoming show will open conservative Philadelphia's eyes to the future of art. He acknowledges that a decade earlier, some of Manet's and Van Gogh's later paintings were included in an exhibition, and a well-known Philadelphia psychiatrist derided them as degenerate. The doctor claimed the men who created them were insane, and the art establishment agreed. But Dr. Bradley insists times have changed. Europe began to shift after the 1918 Paris show. Why not the United States?

When she cautiously points out that the pictures in the new show are even more radical—not only Impressionist but post-Impressionist, not only Cubist but Abstract—he dismisses her concerns. "The cultural icons of Philadelphia jeered at the first performance of Schoenberg's *Kammersymphonie*, and five years later the audience gave the same work a standing ovation. All they need is education. They did it for Schoenberg, and they'll do it for Matisse."

The evening of the opening is rainy, cold for April. The piano softly plays "By the Light of the Silvery Moon," as hors d'oeuvres are passed throughout the soaring gallery and the guests absorb the even more soaring paintings. There are several Picassos and Modiglianis, a couple of Cézannes and Soutines, a Mondrian, a Klee, as well as Matisse's *The Joy of Life*.

Vivienne misses the champagne that would have flowed had they been at a Paris opening, involuntarily wrinkling her nose at the overly sweet ginger ale she's forced to sip because of the crazy American Prohibition. She lights a cigarette and watches Dr. Bradley bustle about the room. He's striking in his tuxedo, his broad shoulders held straight and proud, impervious to the dampness. He's gracious and charming to all, clearly proud of his paintings. Ada is nowhere to be seen.

Dr. Bradley introduces Vivienne to Celeste Lee, an art critic for the *Philadelphia Investigator*, then draws the two of them toward *The Joy of Life*.

"*Le Bonheur de vivre*," he says to Celeste. "Come see my friend Henri at his best."

Vivienne watches as Celeste, her stride long and confident, walks to the picture. A positive review by a journalist of her prominence could set the tone for everyone else's.

The Joy of Life is nearly six feet high and eight feet wide, overpowering the regular-size paintings that flank it, sucking all their light. It's a wild and raucous scene of over a dozen nudes dancing and indulging in erotic pleasures, set against a background of luscious greens, oranges, and yellows, a slice of blue water receding into the background.

Celeste steps closer, takes a half-dozen steps back, then comes forward again and looks intently at the picture without moving for a good two or three minutes. "Bold," she finally says, her eyes still glued to Matisse's work. "The color, the action, the curves. The landscape like a stage . . ."

This sounds promising. *The Joy of Life* has been ridiculed as impenetrable, its colors garish and tasteless, its subject matter too sensual, perhaps even homoerotic, its perspective amateurish. It's none of these things. It's a brilliant work. A bridge from Van Gogh's and Monet's plein air brushstrokes to Cézanne's mediation between nature and the painted surface.

"Paradise." Celeste removes a small notebook from her pocketbook and begins to scribble. "Arcadia on the canvas," she touches a spot between her breasts, "and in here." Then her eyes shift to the paintings to its left and right. Derain, Utrillo, Modigliani, Soutine's *Woman in Blue*. She approaches the Soutine.

Celeste stands at least two feet farther from the painting than she did from *The Joy of Life*. "Soutine," she says as she reads the signature. "New to me. To you, too?" she asks Dr. Bradley.

He nods but doesn't say anything. Soutine isn't easy to appreciate; Vivienne's father was never fond of his work and neither is she. The woman in the picture is frightening, with her distorted, arthritic hands and unfocused black eyes. But given time, it's possible to detect intent in her awkward stance, a sense of moving through tragedy, triumphing over it, strength. This gives a hint of beauty to her homeliness. Although Vivienne still doesn't like it.

A slender man with a thick mane of dark hair follows his jutting chin toward them. "Bradley," he says crisply. "Celeste."

"Hi, boss," Celeste says.

Dr. Bradley ignores him.

Vivienne immediately understands that this is the infamous Thomas Quinton. He's the owner and publisher of the *Philadelphia Investigator*, the largest newspaper in the city, and he sits on the board of directors at the Philadelphia Museum of Art. Some say the has more power than the mayor—referring to him as Mr. Mayor—others say he has more than the governor.

According to Dr. Bradley, Quinton loathes him. Vivienne assumed this was an exaggeration, but the man is scowling at Dr. Bradley with such undisguised contempt that it's clear there has been no overstatement. Ada was to marry Thomas Quinton, but when she met Dr. Bradley, she called off their engagement. This apparently broke Quinton's heart—he's never married—and fostered the long-running enmity between the two men. Although it's unkind, Vivienne finds it hard to imagine Ada at the center of a passionate love triangle. But she acknowledges that Ada's delicate and feminine prettiness could appeal to a certain type of man.

The four of them silently examine the canvas, and then Quinton says, "You can't tell me you actually like this painting, Bradley."

"I most certainly can." He pulls himself to his full height, which is substantial, and adds in his most patronizing tone, "Appreciating art and the artist isn't necessarily about *liking* a painting, it's about understanding the artist's intent, how he uses his skills and tools to achieve his vision."

"I don't want any part of this man's vision," Quinton declares.

"Soutine is showing us life as he sees it," Dr. Bradley continues with a supercilious toss of his large head. "As he's experienced it. Felt it."

"But why do we have to look through his eyes?" Celeste asks. "What if we don't want to see that kind of suffering?"

"Because using just light and color and line and space, he's brought the pathos of this woman's world into full expression, into an emotion you can feel just by looking at it."

"And that one." Quinton points at *The Joy of Life*. "Matisse shouldn't be allowed to call himself an artist if he doesn't know the difference between foreground and background."

There's disdain in Quinton's eyes, sympathy in Celeste's. Celeste touches Dr. Bradley's shoulder and walks over to a waiter holding a tray of canapés. Quinton is in lockstep, whispering in her ear. Unfortunately it's Quinton's newspaper, and he's the one who decides what will and won't get printed in Celeste's review.

"Thomas Quinton is a narrow-minded piece of sod who believes only the work of dead artists has merit," Dr. Bradley sputters. "He's a Neanderthal, but the rest of the people here aren't. He's on the wrong side of this."

"Soutine isn't for everyone," Vivienne says.

"But what about Matisse? Cézanne? Picasso?" Dr. Bradley demands. "These artists are the toast of avant-garde Paris. And the citizens of Philadelphia will surely see why."

"Maybe they just need more time," she suggests. "Like Schoenberg."

Dr. Bradley's shoulders stiffen. "If that's the situation, they don't deserve more time."

"THESE RABID MODERNISTS lack subtlety, delicacy, or finesse." *The North American.*

"Debased art." *The Public Ledger.*

"Nonsensical clumps of nonsensical color." *City Paper.*

"Could have been done by a child." *Daily News.*

"Most unpleasant to contemplate." *The Post.*

But it's Celeste Lee's review in the *Investigator* that stings the most. Although she focuses mostly on Soutine, her condemnation of many of the other artists is equally strong. She talks of "seemingly incomprehensible masses of paint" and declares many of the paintings to be "portraits of the dregs of humanity created by the dregs of humanity."

There's no mention of her admiration for *The Joy of Life*. The work of Mr. Mayor's red pencil, Dr. Bradley is sure. And Vivienne agrees. She saw Celeste's reaction to the painting, how Celeste touched her heart, obviously touched in her soul.

People often reject what's new and different, but it's the depth of the antipathy that makes these responses so disappointing. Vivienne expected better. These are connoisseurs in a major American city, after all, people whose job it is to study and write about art. And this is what they think? "Nonsensical clumps of nonsensical color?" They are the ones without sense.

She feels for Dr. Bradley, who, like any poor boy made good, was looking forward to the respect of his hometown. But he overestimated the artistic sensibilities of the inhabitants of the City of Brotherly Love, and she can see that he's more upset than he's willing to admit. It's ignorance and intolerance, to be sure, but Philadelphia is his home, and Vivienne suspects he's also ashamed of his city.

9

PAULIEN, 1920

Paulien was supposed to spend the summer traveling with her family to their usual haunts: the apartment in Portofino on the Italian Riviera; the Bären in Saint Moritz; a month in Paris at Le Meurice, hotel to kings and sultans and maharajas with whom her father dined and often did business. Instead she stayed in London with George.

When her father heard of her plan, he threatened to come to England to bring her home. Although her mother maintained that he just wanted everyone to be on holiday together, Paulien guessed it was because he still hadn't forgiven her for turning down Maxence Van de Velde, his closest business associate's homely son, and he probably never would. But she'd been seventeen years old at the time and more than capable of making her own decisions.

Papa had tried to bribe her into accepting Maxence's marriage proposal with promises of lavish wedding gifts, including a new home. When she turned it all down, he resorted to threats of disinheriting, of putting her brothers in control of the Mertens collection instead of giving it to her. She didn't believe he would follow through on either—which he didn't—so she stuck to her guns, and now she was over the moon that she had.

George was the most exciting man Paulien had ever met. She wasn't even put off when she discovered he owned a securities company—Everard Sureties Exchange—on the same block as the National Westminster Bank. She'd been surrounded by men in business since she was a child and always imagined herself with a wilder, more artsy type.

But George wasn't like her father's friends and colleagues. He didn't work incessantly. He didn't think making money was the most important thing in the world. He laughed all the time—including at himself—and was spontaneous, loving, and generous. And then there was the way he made her feel when they were alone at night.

At first she'd been nervous, both about having relations and about getting pregnant. Although she'd had three different boyfriends and spent considerable time kissing each of them—one of whom, after six months, she allowed to touch the outside of her corset—she was uninitiated in what George called "the fine art of love." He was twenty-five, seven years her senior, and much more knowledgeable than she. He was also an excellent teacher.

Once her friend Bernice showed her how to soak a tiny sponge in quinine and place it correctly, she threw herself into this new and exquisite world with abandon. Now, as Paulien lay in bed, she ran two fingers up the inside of her thigh and pressed them into the place between her legs that George had brought to life. She shivered, then removed her fingers, wanting to keep the hunger for when she was with him.

She stretched her arms high and wiggled her fingers, allowed the sheet to drop to her waist, and lit a cigarette. George had stolen out in the middle of the night, as he always did, and was at his office, but he'd promised to meet her for lunch.

Her flat in a townhouse in Belgravia—a white stucco building with lovely terraces in the center of the city—had the benefit of a private back stairway, which they took advantage of. Even though they had been together almost every day since that afternoon at the Princess Louise, the thought of seeing him in a few hours electrified her.

Everything he did was perfect. The way he charmed her friends. The way he played tennis. The way he was willing to lend a hand or a few pounds to anyone who asked. The way he knew without being told exactly what she wanted—and then made sure she got it. She had found her man. This was for life.

The past weekend was just one example of his largesse. George had over a hundred employees at Everard Sureties/London—managers, brokers, runners, bookkeepers, secretaries—and at least another fifty at Everard Sureties/Rome. Once a year he threw a party to celebrate them. Their families were invited, and this year he'd rented out an entire wing of the Langham Hotel for the gathering.

The Langham in London rivaled Le Meurice in grandeur and history—Napoleon spent part of his exile from France there—and bested it on one important account: air-conditioning. It was the only place she knew where you could escape the mugginess of a London August. Or a Parisian one.

George spared no expense, maintaining that the employees deserved all this and more. Outings to lakes and museums, shows for the children, lavish meals, and an extravagant Saturday evening dinner-dance in the hotel ballroom with a twelve-piece band. Everyone enjoyed the party immensely, and everyone adored Mr. Everard. Especially Paulien.

She wasn't particularly interested in business or finance, but after the weekend, her curiosity was piqued. "Tell me exactly what it is, what you do." They were in her apartment on Sunday evening, having just returned from the Langham. It was hot and muggy, and the windows were thrown open. Still they snuggled close together on the settee, she drinking sherry and he scotch.

Paulien brushed back the lock of hair that fell into his eye, pressed her finger to the cleft in his chin. "I want to know everything about you."

George didn't demur or claim this wasn't a girl's concern; he took her seriously. "It's actually quite simple," he said. "Our secret is that we think big."

"About trading IRCs?" She knew he was involved in buying and selling international reply coupons, but she wasn't sure exactly what they were. Something about postage you put inside a letter for the recipient to use when they replied. But she thought it worked only if you were sending mail internationally. She'd never known anyone who used them, but apparently it was a common practice. A politeness.

"Basically, I buy IRCs for less in one country and redeem them for more in another."

"That's legal?"

"Absolutely."

"Why doesn't everyone do it?"

"They could if they wanted to. Probably some do, but it's a matter of scale."

"I don't understand."

He leaned over and gave her a quick kiss on the lips. "I have a weakness for an inquisitive girl—especially when she's fearless about getting to the answer."

"So explain it to me."

He laughed and kissed her again, this time longer and deeper. Paulien sank into it, as she always did, but then pulled herself back. "Don't distract me when I'm being fearlessly curious," she said.

"Yes, ma'am." George gave her a snappy salute. "You know how you buy IRCs in your country and then whoever you send them to redeems them in their country?"

"For stamps?"

"Exactly. The price of an IRC is tied to the price of a first-class stamp—on both sides of the transaction. Usually the cost of postage doesn't vary that much from one country to another, but when it does, there's the opportunity to make money in the exchange."

"And that's what it's like now?"

"In Italy it is. The country is a mess. Inflation is killing them, so they've discounted the price of their stamps—and therefore the price of IRCs. We Brits, on the other hand, are in the midst of a boom, so our postage costs a lot more. What Everard Sureties does is buy the cheaper IRCs in Italy—which is why we have an office in Rome—and exchange them for stamps in London, which are worth four times what they are there. Stamps are like currency, so we sell them at face value, and voilà, an enormous profit."

Paulien thought about this. "I still don't understand why everyone doesn't do it."

"Each transaction, in and of itself, doesn't make that much money—stamps here cost only a penny apiece. So for an individual to take advantage of this, he'd have to travel between the countries himself, go back and forth to the post offices to buy and redeem the coupons—then sell the stamps. This wouldn't be worth all that trouble unless he had a lot of money to invest."

"And that's where you come in? You supply the money?"

"Not the money, the manpower and equipment. The brokers, the runners, the ships, the lorries. A customer buys shares in Everard Sureties—so he's actually supplying the money—and we do everything else. All he has to do is watch the profits roll in."

"What kind of profits?"

"Gross profit after the transaction is four hundred percent."

"Your customers make that kind of money?" she asked, incredulous. "How can that be? It's like pound notes hanging on trees. Too good to be true." She paused, stricken by a wave of doubt, of wariness. How well did she actually know this man? "Is it too good to be true?"

George threw back his head and laughed delightedly. "Naturally that's not the actual return—not for them and not for me. After expenses, which are significant, we're down to about eighty percent net. I guarantee my investors fifteen percent in forty-five days, twenty-five percent in ninety days, and thirty percent in a year. Haven't missed any of those benchmarks yet."

"It was all your idea?" Was there anything this man couldn't do?

"The idea's been around forever," he said modestly. "What I came up with was the notion of creating a company to take advantage of it."

Paulien thought about the awkward position she'd put her father in when she refused Maxence. Although she wasn't sorry she said no to a loveless marriage, she was sorry she had upset Papa. What if she were to bring him an opportunity like this? "My father might be interested in that kind of investment. He's got a little money." She'd never told anyone in London about her family's wealth. Including George.

"I can't take on any new investors right now, doll. Probably not for the foreseeable future. We're all backed up. Even with our size, we run into problems with logistics. It's hard to find trustworthy brokers and runners, especially in Rome, and the sheer volume and weight of the actual IRCs is a transportation nightmare."

Paulien pulled a pout and fluttered her eyelashes in an exaggerated manner. "Even for me?" she asked coquettishly.

George lifted her onto his lap and nuzzled her neck. When he kissed her, her disappointment—and everything else—vanished.

10

GEORGE/BENJAMIN, 1923

As he lounges on the deck of his rented yacht, bobbing on the green-blue Mediterranean, champagne glass in one hand, cigar in another, he recognizes he's a cliché. And he basks in it.

The caterers are setting up for the party he's hosting that evening. There are many wealthy vacationers on Majorca this time of year, and he's asked some of the most distinguished to join him for a sunset cruise off the coast of Palma. Everyone is more than happy to accept an invitation from the mysterious and charming Benjamin F. Talcott, an extremely successful Wall Street broker. They're hoping for stock tips on the booming American market, and he's planning to pass on some investment advice to a few. A select few.

It's early in the venture, and these things take time. A confidence game can't be rushed. His last effort, his most profitable thus far, had been three years in the making. But he's a patient man and enjoys the slow setup almost as much as the fast kill at the end.

After he cleaned out the Everard Sureties Exchange offices in London, his suitcases full of money, he went to the United States and settled in New York City. He purchased a company that made ball bearings called Steel Bearings, Inc., and, after an infusion of cash, took it public. Once Steel Bearings was trading, he began buying up his own stock under various aliases, raising the share price in slow increments. Then he purchased three other companies and did the same thing.

He let it be known around town that his holding company, Talcott Reserves, used a highly sophisticated, mathematical set of rules to invest in the market and consistently returned a 15 to 20 percent profit. When a number of men expressed an interest in investing with him, he allowed only a few to open accounts. A select few.

Needless to say, no investments were made with the money these men tendered. He used the growth of his own companies to show paper profits—profits that his account holders almost always reinvested with Talcott and hardly ever cashed out—and kept all their money for himself. It's the possibility of being accepted as an account holder with Talcott Reserves that he'll be whispering into hungry ears that evening.

His Majorca guests are an international crowd, and word will spread after the one or two men he takes on as investors begin to see the promised returns. Soon everyone will be clamoring to invest with Talcott Reserves, which has two floors of prime office space on Wall Street and a reputation for both exclusivity and profitability.

But alas, Mr. Talcott will be forced to refuse almost all requests, which will only inspire more requests. This was how it worked for Everard Sureties, and this is how it will work for Talcott Reserves. It's impossible to underestimate the recklessness of a man who thinks he's getting in on a special deal.

People desperately desire what's denied them, and the longer it's denied, the more they want it—and the fewer questions they ask when it's ultimately in their hot little hands. Once he finally allows these men entrée to the Reserves, they'll throw every last penny they have into their long-sought-after accounts. And then brag about it to their friends, who will come clamoring . . . who will tell their friends, who will come clamoring. . . . Greed makes fools of even the smartest and richest of men.

And those are exactly the types he's searching for. When he gets back to America, he's got his eye on a lineup of potential investors: Charles Schwan, the steel titan; Howard Hopson of Associated Gas and Electric;

Arthur Cutten, the most successful grain speculator in the world; Edwin Bradley, multimillionaire and art collector.

As he predicted, Paulien Mertens left Paris with Bradley. And now she's his assistant, soon to be ensconced within the Beaux-Arts splendor of his new museum. Once again, she's in the lap of wealth and power. It appears it's time for him to make a visit to Philadelphia.

11

VIVIENNE, 1923

Dr. Bradley is so infuriated at the response to the academy show that if Vivienne didn't know better, she'd think he was the creator of the artworks rather than just their owner. He stalks through the nearly vacant rental house, his fury echoing off bare walls of rooms emptied of furniture, yelling to no one, raging at the stupidity and small-mindedness. Vivienne stays in her bedroom office. She's never seen behavior like this. It's as if he's gone mad.

When he stops yelling, he turns to browbeating. He sends letters to every publisher and editor of every magazine and newspaper that had the audacity to pen a negative review of the show. He seethes at them all: the wealthy who use art to social-climb; the academics so set in the old that they can't see their way to the new; the newspapers and museums too concerned with making money to take a risk.

The Philadelphia art establishment is laughing at him, and Dr. Bradley cannot accept being taken for a fool—especially when he believes it's his adversaries who are the fools. A more even-keeled man might have waited them out, smugly anticipating his I-told-you-so moment, but as Vivienne is rapidly learning, even keeled is not a description that applies to Dr. Bradley.

She's heard people talk—Gertrude Stein among them—about how mulish he can be, and he's living up to that side of his reputation. Although Vivienne agrees with his sentiments, she doesn't believe flinging personal insults in answer to comments based on artistic taste is the way to respond to criticism. She expected more of him.

He calls her into his bedroom office about a week after the show. "They're all going to pay," he declares, waving his cigarette at her. "And I've just figured out how."

She waits.

"If they refuse to see the virtuosity of Matisse and Picasso, then they won't get to see them at all." He stabs the cigarette into the ashtray and immediately lights another one. "I've decided there will be no museum. Not now, not while I'm alive—and not after I'm dead. Perfect, don't you think?"

"But what about your artwork? The new building?"

"That's the best part. I keep it all."

The expression on her face must be one of complete bafflement, because he starts to laugh. "It's going to be a school. And only a school. A private school, closed to the public."

"Closed to the public?"

"This way I get to choose who sees my art. Handpick an audience who will appreciate what I have here."

"But I thought you wanted the museum to introduce the people of Philadelphia to the future. That all they needed was some education."

"There will be no Bradley Museum. But there will be a Bradley School of Art Appreciation. With limited and restricted admission—each student's acceptance subject to my personal approval."

Vivienne is so upset by the thought of all these glorious artworks being squirreled away that she makes the mistake of adding, "How will you persuade anyone to change their minds if you don't let them see the paintings?"

His face reddens, and he slams his fist on his desk. "The academy show proved to me that they are all too bullheaded to change. It's not worth the effort."

They move into the new building at the end of April. Vivienne can now walk to work instead of taking two buses as she did to Bradley's rental house, and she has an actual office. It's small, to be sure, but there's a wide window with a view of the massive gardens Ada has already begun to plant. She calls it the arboretum.

Dr. Bradley's office is next to Vivienne's, large and commanding, and there's another small one with a connecting door for the secretary he hasn't yet hired. The remaining space is open, filled with desks for the teachers—who also haven't been hired—to work on their lesson plans. Ada is down the hall, closer to the double doors that lead into their private quarters. Vivienne isn't sure why she needs an office.

It takes well over a month to hang all the artwork. Dr. Bradley's ensembles, as he's calling his groupings, are radical, challenging hundreds of years of tradition in art exhibition. They ask the viewer to interpret the works in a completely unique manner, a grand manifestation of the classroom at Dr. Bradley's factory, where he asked the students to look at how differently Modigliani and Rousseau had approached the same subject. Instead of two paintings to compare and contrast, the ensembles include twelve or fifteen or twenty works on a single wall, organized not by chronology or geography or school but by the design elements of light, line, color, and space, sometimes subject.

As she wanders the galleries, she stops at the south wall of Room 6 and laughs out loud. The ensemble is composed of a triangle of five Renoirs enclosing a central Gauguin and two Prendergasts, with a Seurat and a Manet on the fringes. The amusing part is the positioning of a set of double Windsor chairs, each with a curved seat resembling a pair of buttocks. The chairs sit directly beneath two oversize Renoir nudes who face away from the viewer, their fleshy bottoms positioned just above the chairs. Who knew Dr. Bradley was such a card?

Although he might be a brute when confronted with disapproval, there's no denying the breadth of his ideas and his ability to move beyond what came before to create something completely novel. A true visionary.

Vivienne steps into Room 19. For the first time in over a year she stands in front of *The Music Lesson*, Matisse's oversize family portrait, her favorite of the seven post-Impressionist paintings her father used to own. She had no idea that her last glimpse of it—the day before George vanished—was anything other than a casual visit to the colonnade. Now, rather than hanging on its own wall, it's surrounded by thirteen other paintings, eleven metal objects, two chairs, and a bench holding five pieces of pottery; two andirons stand guard at its feet.

Her fingers curl into fists. She longed to be reunited with her *Music Lesson*, pined for it for months, and here it is. Diminished. Insulted. Humiliated. She bows her head. Doesn't Dr. Bradley understand that this seminal painting is a whole unto itself?

She forces herself to look again. Now that one of her own is encased within an ensemble, her appreciation for Dr. Bradley's groupings shifts. The gallery wall suddenly feels claustrophobic, its exacting symmetry painful to the eye, limiting to the mind. Matisse's masterpiece is dwarfed, forced to play handmaiden to an assortment of lesser actors. Dr. Bradley not only bullies people, he bullies art.

She wants to rip every other painting from the wall, wrench out the ridiculous metal keys and cookie cutters and door knockers, clear away each jug and vase. *Music Lesson* must be freed, as well as her other six. She can't allow them to be held hostage by Dr. Bradley's rigidity, imprisoned within his suffocating ensembles, unavailable to the world. To her. To her father.

She quickly leaves the gallery and tries to calm herself by visualizing how these walls would appear if she were the collector and curator, if she were able to transform the Bradley into the Mertens Museum of Post-Impressionism. Hers would be a singular collection, honed and finely tuned, focusing on the arc of European and American painting between Impressionism and Abstraction. She would sell everything that didn't fit within this model, buy more of what did, create space around each piece of art, liberate them all. No ensembles, no metal works, no pottery, no furniture, no Titian, no El Greco.

Her pruning would provide the elbow room the works deserve, refine the collection to its truest self. And most importantly, she would throw the doors open seven days a week. For unlike Dr. Bradley, who wants to secret his art away, she wants to be its custodian, preserving and protecting it for future generations, sharing its greatness with the world. With the exception of the colonnade seven, which she would send to her father.

Vivienne recognizes her inconsistency—some might say hypocrisy—but Papa deserves a small bit of recompense for all he lost; it's the least she can do. It's an impossible dream, an arrogant one that's a betrayal of Dr. Bradley's own vision, but she can't shake it.

WHEN THE TEACHERS have been hired and trained, the students vetted and granted admission, classes begin at the Bradley School of Art Appreciation. There are no classrooms per se; rather, the entire building is the classroom. The teachers and students roam from gallery to gallery, standing or sitting on collapsible chairs, always looking. Dr. Bradley is teaching a number of courses, and Vivienne takes all of them.

He's far from the finest lecturer, the most articulate or the best prepared, but when he starts pulling painting after painting from the gallery walls, moving them from one room to the next, showing the class how the works are simultaneously the same and completely different from one another, she's mesmerized by the novel connections. She winces when he touches one of her paintings with that ease of ownership, but still it's clear that he has great passion for his subject. She's a person of passion, and she responds to this. Maman used to complain about all the nannies who quit because she wouldn't mind them—and the tutors who were infuriated when she refused to do her lessons or respond to their calls because she was lost amid her paintings.

Although Dr. Bradley's curatorial ideas may differ from hers, it's obvious that he, like she, is animated by great art. He says he sees this in her, too. In the way she sits forward in her chair, the way she doesn't stop looking, the way she hardly ever takes notes with her pencil but always takes notes with her eyes. Sometimes it's as if she's with her father.

But other times, he doesn't act like her father at all. "There are only three types of line," Dr. Bradley tells her sternly one day. "That's what is in my notes, and that's how you'll type it up for the lesson." They're in his office, working on a new class based on his notion that the only way to understand an artist's intention is by analyzing his work through the four design elements of light, line, color, and space.

Vivienne has spent time thinking about this and believes he's missing something that will make the course better. "Doesn't it seem like there's an expressive type of line? The way a long, flat line feels calm and a series of sharp, slanted ones feel angry? More—"

"That's not a different type, it's a subcategory of the other three. Lines are actual, implied, or psychic. That's it."

"When you think about it, though, doesn't it seem more than just a subordinate?" she persists, warming to the argument, remembering how she and her father used to discuss their different views, weigh the pros and cons, synthesize their ideas into something better than either one of them could have come up with alone. How much fun it was.

"Like maybe it should be considered a type all its own?" she continues. "You keep telling us to look, to think for ourselves, to ferret out what the artist—"

"That's in the classroom, Miss Gregsby," he interrupts again, frowning. "Not when you're working. Your job here is to help organize what I tell you into a lecture, not to contradict ideas I've developed over many years of critical thought."

Vivienne is annoyed by his tone but blames herself for causing his irritation. By now she's learned that the way to get Dr. Bradley to think differently is for him to believe that he came up with an idea himself, never to attempt to instruct him.

A few days later, as they're walking past *The Joy of Life* hanging on its own in the large stairwell, dominating the space, the viewer, she tells him that she's going to stay there for a while. "Of course," she says as she settles on the top step, "I've looked at this many times before, but you're right about seeing more each time you contemplate a great work of art."

"I'll join you." He sits down next to her, closer than she would have expected.

They contemplate the painting in companionable silence.

"Are you enjoying yourself here?" Dr. Bradley asks.

"How could I not be, with all of this surrounding me?" she answers, her eyes fixed on the painting.

"You're not homesick? I wouldn't want you to be sorry you came."

He rarely talks about personal things and has never asked about her private life. She thinks about the letters she writes to her father and to Tante Natalie, of the responses she doesn't receive, although her return address is included in every missive; clearly they still believe she was in on the con. That damn George is going to pay. "Sometimes," she finally admits. "But not so much that I want to go back," she lies.

"That's good to know."

She says nothing and then points to the voluptuous bodies, the arched tree trunks, the wavy clouds. "I'm taken by the way Henri uses curved lines here. Their softness and richness draw you in like an invitation. To a place so full of delight that the viewer can do nothing but feel the same."

"Well put."

She brushes off the rare compliment but is encouraged by it. "And there in the far background, behind the dancing and frolicking, is the only straight line in the composition. The horizontal. The blue-and-purple sea, soothing and tranquil."

"You're doing well here," he says, touching her shoulder with the briefest of gestures. "And listening to you makes me even more pleased that you aren't homesick."

Vivienne glances at him, and when their eyes meet, she sees a softening in his. She places her elbows on her knees, rests her chin on her fists, and once again they contemplate *The Joy of Life* in silence.

Over the next couple of months, Vivienne and Dr. Bradley grow closer as they work together on hanging the artwork, developing course curricula, and handling the day-to-day details of running a school. She hasn't broached the possibility of allowing the public to view the collection. They've been getting on well, and she's seen his reaction to criticism. She's biding her time, which isn't easy.

She's also taken on a project of her own—a game, really—propelled by her musings about the Bradley collection as the Mertens Museum of Post-Impressionism. It makes her feel closer to her father, who drifts further away with each day Vivienne Gregsby moves forward. She hopes that he reads the letters he doesn't answer, that he knows she's with their colonnade seven.

She and Papa used to talk endlessly about what post-Impressionism was and what it wasn't. They agreed that the later works of Cézanne, Van Gogh, Gauguin, Matisse, Seurat, Vuillard, and Derain all fit within the school, but they never came to a satisfactory conclusion about how each one fed into the other, nor which other artists should be included in the group. She argued for Picasso, but Papa believed that Cubism and Abstraction were outside the frame.

The Bradley contains many works that definitively fall outside the frame, but she's using the paintings that do—or might—to create a map of the connections and influences to fashion her imaginary museum. She has free run of the galleries and spends hours with a notepad and pencil in hand, roaming and thinking and sketching. When she gets home at night, she reworks her ideas, and although she's absorbed by the pursuit, she's flummoxed by the many contradictions and gaping holes.

She stands in the main room in front of Cézanne's *The Red Earth*, painted in 1892, which is surely an Impressionist painting. It's a representational landscape, painted plein air, focusing on how light falls on the scene. Then she steps into Room 2 to view his *Still Life with Skull.*

Although Cézanne completed *Skull* only six years after *Red Earth*, it rejects traditional perspective, flattens the picture plane, and plays with the illusion of foreground and background. These characteristics, plus the odd juxtaposition of a skull and fresh fruit, a slash of red creating folds in the white tablecloth, and a pear precariously defying gravity, are not within the Impressionist canon. But it's a still life, a mainstay of traditional painting, and although a slightly oblique depiction, the painting remains a representation of what Cézanne saw before him.

Dr. Bradley steps next to her. "What are you thinking?"

"I'm wondering if this is Impressionist or post-Impressionist. My gut tells me it's post, as it speaks to me the way only the post paintings do, but my head isn't quite so sure."

"Perhaps that's because he's crossing from one to the other."

"But where's the demarcation?" She shows him the latest version of her map. Scribbled all over the page are boxes containing artists' names (Cézanne, Van Gogh, Gauguin, and Seurat) and others edging the names of schools of art (Impressionism, Pointillism, Symbolism, the Nabis, Fauvism, Divisionism, Cubism, Abstraction). The boxes are connected by arrows and lines penciled in and erased, crisscrossing, going nowhere. "I'm trying to figure out where the circle defining post-Impressionism would go. Who's in and who's out?"

He studies her map closely, studies her closely. "I was right about you, Miss Gregsby."

She laughs, as his praise is expressed as a compliment to himself, not to her. "Then I'd say it's time for you to start calling me Vivienne."

"Edwin." He bows slightly. "And if you have any interest, I believe you would make a valuable addition to our teaching staff."

After that, Edwin loosens up, allowing his sense of humor to surface, and their laughter drifts from his office. They have dinner together once in a while, which at first was uncomfortable but is growing less so. He's also helping her with the mapping project. His insights and knowledge are deep, and he's becoming less insistent that he's right—although their discussions are far from the open dialogue she and Papa shared.

They're laughing one morning about the antics of one of the students when Ada strides into Edwin's office and demands that they stop making so much noise. "I've got work to do," she declares. "An important proposal to import some English roses. All this racket is keeping me from getting it done."

"Why don't you go work in the house, then?" Edwin suggests.

Ada's face flushes with anger, but she doesn't move or take her eyes from her husband's.

Vivienne stands. "I've got things to do in my office. I'll just leave you two—"

Edwin motions her back into her chair.

Vivienne looks from one to the other, uncertain what the wisest step might be. But before she can make a move, Ada throws her a look Medusa would envy and stomps down the hall to the house.

Edwin lights a cigarette. "She'll get over it," is all he says.

THE TRIAL, 1928

After yesterday's constant drone of motive, motive, motive, I was more than a little shaken when we arrived back in court this morning. But Ronald reiterated that the evidence Pratt presented is circumstantial. Ronald says that as long as there's nothing to tie me directly to the accident, it means little.

Unfortunately, my first lawyer, the senior partner who succeeded in securing my bail and then dumped me into Ronald's unproven hands, had explained to me how a clever prosecutor, which clearly Pratt is, tries a circumstantial case.

The thinking goes that, even though a juror might not give much credence to an individual piece of evidence, when lots of these pieces are placed before him, his mind searches for patterns. Because the human brain is designed to unearth linkages, it tends to find associations even if they don't actually exist. It's the connecting of these seemingly disparate facts that creates the illusion of a preponderance of evidence—and leads to a guilty verdict.

I can't help wondering why the partner didn't explain this to Ronald. Perhaps Thomas Quinton told him not to. As you can tell, I'm growing more paranoid with each passing hour. Although I'm not sure it's called paranoia if what you suspect is true.

We knew the focus today would be on demonstrating I had the opportunity to kill you. Something we believed the facts would not support. First up was one of the teachers at the Bradley, Nathan Milner, who started just a month or so before your death—do you remember him? He testified that he and I had discussed how you always ignored that stop sign at the intersection of Route 29 and Phoenixville Pike.

"The site of the crash?" Pratt pressed, as if everyone in the courtroom wasn't aware of this fact. "The one in which Dr. Bradley was killed?" Ditto.

Even though Ronald's cross-examination revealed that many others also knew of this proclivity, it did little to mitigate the fact that I was aware you were going to drive right on through it. Ah, Edwin. Despite the seriousness of the moment, I had to smile at how consistently cantankerous you were. Only you would refuse to honor a stop sign because you opposed its installation.

Next was the Bradley cleaning woman, Blossom Sinclair. She reported overhearing a conversation between the two of us on the Thursday before the accident in which we made a date for dinner at six o'clock on that Sunday, thereby establishing my knowledge of the time you'd be leaving Chester County to return to Merion.

The manager of the Merion Savings Bank followed Blossom. He stated that I had a total of $18,033.43 in my savings account, which Mr. Pratt pointed out was more than enough money to "procure" anything I wanted— for example, a hit man. Although the judge sustained Ronald's objection after a long pause and an excessively long eye roll, the damage was done.

When we recessed for lunch, Ronald admitted he was a little concerned about one of the afternoon's witnesses, a supervisor at Empire State Transport, the trucking company that employed the driver who hit you. He asked me for the third time whether I was sure I'd never had any contact with Empire State or the driver, a John Johnston.

I didn't have any recollection of either name. But as I don't have access to the Bradley's records—Ada and her lawyers are contesting Ronald's right to review them—I can't be sure. Working as your assistant over the past six years, I must have had contact with thousands of vendors.

And so it was: Exhibit 33, a receipt dated November 14, 1925, signed by me for delivery of three parcels shipped from Amsterdam to New York City to Merion. The truck driver who transported the parcels and countersigned the receipt was none other than Mr. John Johnston.

12

VIVIENNE, 1923

Credentials are unimportant for the staff at the Bradley School of Art Appreciation, which is fortunate because Vivienne has none. Her degree from the Slade is in studio painting, and she has no experience teaching. All Edwin demands is loyalty to the school's principles, an enthusiasm for the artwork, and a willingness to deliver lectures that strictly adhere to his dictates.

His only concession to a teacher's personal preference is to allow him or her to choose the specific artwork to which they will be applying his directives. Vivienne can't bring herself to teach *Music Lesson*, or any of her other paintings. So for today she's chosen a much less loaded *Joy of Life*. Plus, it's not within an ensemble.

Her father would be proud that she's expanding her knowledge of art while also sharing it with others, and she wishes she could tell him about it. It's been almost a year since the split, and the pain has barely lessened. She thinks of the dream in which she returned the colonnade seven to him, of his happiness and the feel of his arms around her.

Vivienne opens her closet door. She needs to choose an outfit that best reflects the subject of her class. This is a game she likes to play, and she believes her students appreciate the lightheartedness of it. What's the right choice? Green and pink are the dominant colors in *Joy of Life* and therefore too obvious. As is anything mirroring the curves that swirl through the picture. What else did Matisse do to make the painting so alluring?

As in *Music Lesson* and the odalisque painting he told her about in Paris, Henri used perspective—or more correctly, lack of perspective—to play with the viewer's eye, simultaneous depth and flatness. Vivienne pulls a black-and-white herringbone skirt from the hanger; it, too, plays with the eye, popping first black and then white, pushing forward and pulling back. She puts it on with a black blouse and clips a pink flower surrounded by green leaves in her hair.

She's growing completely infatuated with the work and the mind and the method of Henri Matisse. She remembers how he traced the line on her palm. How she shivered. She wonders if he ever thinks of her.

"I KNOW COLOR is the first thing you notice in this painting," Vivienne says after the students, who are sprawled out on the stairs, have spent a silent ten minutes appraising *The Joy of Life*. She begins every class with this type of quiet looking. The students are a varied bunch: older men and women who want to learn for learning's sake, younger artists hungry for the secrets of the masters, Edwin's workers who have advanced beyond the factory classes.

Today she's going to talk about her concept of an emotional line, something she's been developing while looking at Matisse's paintings in particular. Edwin is at the factory, as he is every morning, so he won't be around to contradict her. Although he's willing to consider some of her ideas, he refuses to discuss anything that disputes his established notions. It's likely that some of the students may agree with him, and that's fine. At least they'll be willing to reflect and converse, not close their minds to an idea just because they didn't think of it themselves.

She leads the class through a discussion about the strength of the verticals, the tranquillity of the horizontals, the actual lines that define the edges of the nudes, the implied lines that draw your eye into the painting, the psychic line that isn't actually a line but a direction the viewer's eye follows when something or someone points in a particular direction.

When she asks them for their thoughts, she's disappointed that no one mentions the power of line to convey emotion. "What about the emotion in the picture?" she finally asks. "What does it make you feel? How does Matisse use line to enhance these feelings?"

"All the curves enclose this perfect and imaginary world? It reminds us that this is a place that doesn't exist except in our minds?"

"Good," she says, although it isn't what she wants. "What else?"

"There're no jagged or sharp lines?" a student offers, his answer formed as a question. "Nothing that's jarring? He wants to express smoothness, happiness, sexuality—and he chose curved lines to do this?"

"Yes," Vivienne cries. "That's exactly right. He uses lines to express emotion." She hesitates. "So is this expressiveness another type of line or is it a subcategory of the other three?"

There's a long silence, and then someone says in a tentative tone, "I think maybe it's . . . its own category . . ."

"And why is that?" Vivienne prompts.

"Because, I think—I could be wrong, but I think it's because it's what the line does, it expresses, like actual lines define or implied lines—"

"That's quite enough!" a voice roars from behind them. "Class dismissed!"

Vivienne spins around, although she knows exactly who's speaking. Apparently he left Bradley and Hagerty early. He never does this.

As the startled students descend the stairs, Edwin glowers at her. "What the hell do you think you're doing?" he demands, loud enough for the students—and anyone else within a mile radius—to catch every word. "The outline I gave you clearly stipulates that you are to discuss three types of line. Not four. Not five. Three! You purposely defied me, you—"

"It just came up," she counters. "A student—"

"Don't give me that horseshit, Vivienne! You knew exactly what you were doing. I heard you. You were leading them where you wanted them to go—where you knew I didn't want them to go."

The fact that he saw through her infuriates her almost as much as the way he shut down the class. "That's not what I was doing at all!" she yells, so incensed she almost believes she's telling the truth. "And it's unfair for you to think that, or talk to me like this, or dismiss my class early!"

"It's not your class," he hisses through clenched teeth. "It's mine and mine alone. You're just a conduit—and not a very good one at that!"

A conduit? This is how he sees her? Fury obliterates all reason. "Forget it, Edwin!" she cries. "All of it. I'm not a conduit of anyone's—and certainly not yours. I quit."

"You can't quit, because as soon as I heard you at the top of the stairs, your position ceased to exist!" He always has to have the last word.

She grabs her notes and, head high, walks down the stairs. As her parents, nannies, and tutors were fond of pointing out, she doesn't take direction well.

VIVIENNE MAKES IT home in half the time it usually takes, rage propelling her onward. It's a cold and wet September day, and the wind lashes her face. The man is so insecure that he can't bear anyone questioning him. Such a child that he flies into a tantrum at the first sign of a flaw in his thinking. So controlling that he's willing to turn his back on anyone who doesn't show complete deference.

She stood up for herself, which would feel good if it didn't mean she also defeated herself. Damn him and damn him and damn him. She takes a corner, and the force of the storm shoves her shoulders forward. She's lost her job, and now the colonnade seven will remain imprisoned within Edwin's suffocating ensembles, his collection unavailable to the world. "No!" she screams into the rain. The wind roars back at her.

By the time she reaches her small rooms, her anger has shifted inward. She flings her wet coat on the hook by the door and puts up water for tea. What is wrong with her? Who cares if there are four types of line—or seven or twenty, for that matter? Why did she need to be right about something so trivial? She knew it would lead to disaster if she clashed with Edwin, but in the end she succumbed to the hubris that she detests in him. She should have minded those nannies better.

Vivienne wraps her fingers around the warm teacup and stares out the window, imagining how George would laugh at her spectacular failure. He, who always succeeded, who always got what he wanted. He would never allow hubris—or anything else—to stand in his way. And if he did slip, he would use the mistake to his advantage. Devise a plan to make his mark beg for what he, George, wanted to give him all along. He would turn things around so that he ended up with an even greater gain.

The rain lashes the glass, and the drops merge into a rushing stream at the window ledge. Perhaps she could do the same. What was it that led to George's success? He paid close attention to detail, didn't skimp on what was necessary for the setup, and had the patience of a beast stalking its prey.

Despite Edwin's multitude of faults, he's a generous employer. Her original salary was high, and when she joined the teaching staff he doubled her remuneration, giving her the money, and now the time, she needs to emulate George. She can pay close attention and pay whatever is necessary, within reason, for the setup. Patience, on the other hand, has never been her strong suit.

Following George's logic, she needs to make Edwin beg to rehire her because he thinks she has a better offer. She'll tell him she's moving away, that there's no stopping her because . . . ? She paces the narrow space between the table and the couch. Because she's returning to Paris? Not strong enough, plus she just told him she didn't want to. Because she's taken another job? Too easily verified—or in this case, not verified.

She pours herself another cup of tea, running possibilities, absentmindedly stirring in twice as much sugar as she usually takes. It has to be something he'll believe she would actually do. Something that would force her to leave Philadelphia. She takes a sip of tea, wrinkles her nose at the sweetness, and then takes another sip.

School? How about graduate school? A degree in art history. A PhD. In New York City. That makes sense. Very believable. She'll send him a letter in the morning detailing her plans. Give him the opportunity to counter with an offer to get her to stay. On her terms.

Then she realizes that George wouldn't just tell Edwin about it, he would actually do it. She remembers the opulent offices of Everard Sureties bustling with busy employees, the elaborate parties, the years it took to put it all together. Authenticity is key.

The next morning she sends Edwin the letter and then takes the train to New York. She spends two nights at a ladies' boardinghouse that bears no resemblance to the one she stayed in in Paris, although it does remind her how much she misses Odette and the other girls, their warmth, their carefree company. She's very busy here, but she's as alone as she was as a child.

She goes to Columbia and New York University and speaks with the art history department at each. Unfortunately, Columbia doesn't accept women. The dean of admission suggests she apply to Barnard, the women's school, but although Barnard students are allowed to enroll in many courses at Columbia, art classes are restricted to men. New York University, on the other hand, is impressed with her work at the Bradley, her schooling in London, and her position at the Whitechapel Gallery. They have openings for the spring and encourage her application. So she takes the paperwork and scopes out an apartment for rent on Waverly Place, right near the campus.

As the train to Philadelphia sways and the backsides of narrow tenements rush by, she congratulates herself on the deftness of her plan. Now Edwin just needs to care enough to make it work.

WHEN SHE ARRIVES home and sees Edwin's car parked in front of the widow's house, it's all she can do to keep a grin of triumph off her face. But Edwin isn't in it, just his chauffeur, who hands her an envelope with her name on it and drives away. Inside is a note, short and direct: "Now that you have returned, I will visit tomorrow."

No signature. No request. No stipulated time. Just a statement of his intention. But his autocratic stunt will come to nothing. The grin she's been holding back bursts through.

She spends three days at the Philadelphia library studying art books and enjoys herself. If this doesn't work, perhaps she will actually go to graduate school. She won't have Papa's paintings and she won't be able to open the Bradley collection to the public, yet it could be a life. A good life. But she's not giving up so easily. It's time to stay home and have a little chat with Edwin Bradley.

At eleven o'clock the next morning, Vivienne hears the bell chime, followed by two sets of feet on the stairs. There's a knock on her door, and when she opens it, the widow and Edwin are standing in the hallway.

Her landlady frowns—male callers are not allowed—but Edwin is wearing a finely tailored suit, holds a new bowler hat in his hands, and is obviously much older than Vivienne. The widow is apprehensive about leaving the two of them alone, but Vivienne assures her that Edwin is her boss or, more correctly, was her boss.

The woman hesitates. "If you say so," she states in a way that clearly indicates she doesn't believe it. Then she heads down the stairs after giving Edwin a hard look of warning and telling Vivienne to leave the door ajar.

"Hello, Vivienne," Edwin says stiffly once they're alone.

"Edwin." She holds the door open for him to enter, but only a sliver.

He has to twist sideways in order to slide through the narrow opening. Once inside, he glances toward the small couch. When she doesn't offer him a seat, he stands, shifting from one foot to the other.

Vivienne doesn't say a word.

"How have you been?" he finally asks.

"I've been quite well, Edwin. And you?"

"May I sit down?"

It must have killed him to ask, so she takes pity. "Please," she says in the most distantly polite voice she can conjure. He sits on the couch, and she perches on the lone chair at the tiny table. He looks like a boy who's been sent by his mother to apologize for some misbehavior. And she intends to make him squirm until he does.

"What happened the other day . . ."

She purses her lips.

"I was hasty."

"Hasty?" she repeats. He's going to have to do better than that.

"That's the wrong word. What I mean is that I shouldn't have reprimanded you in front of the class."

"What you shouldn't have done is reprimanded me at all. I'm not a child whose knuckles you get to smack with a ruler. I'm a teacher. Presumably your colleague. And I won't be treated as anything less."

"You are a colleague," he concedes.

Vivienne doesn't respond. Is this supposed to pass as an apology? If she's to get the upper hand, he has to come out and say it.

"I want you to come back to the Bradley."

"I'm not coming back."

"Hear me out."

She shakes her head emphatically. "I can't work with you. I can't work under the constant threat of your anger. Being afraid I'll say something you don't like and then be subjected to your rage. To your humiliation."

"I never meant to humiliate you."

"Well, you did."

"It won't happen again."

"I don't believe you."

"The Bradley needs you."

"I've applied to go to graduate school in the spring. Art history. At New York University. I've already met with the admissions department, and they're certain I'll be accepted. I rented an apartment in New York," she lies. "Waverly Place. I'm moving at the end of the month."

"You can't mean that."

"You are who you are," she says. "And I am who I am. I'm always going to want to go my own way, think my own way, and you're always going to hate it when I disagree with you—and then get angry at me for it."

"That's not true."

Vivienne wonders how long she should protest. Hours? Days? Months? Or should she grab what he's proposing before he changes his mind? George would hold strong. "I'm sorry, Edwin, but it's just not going to work."

He runs the rim of his hat through his fingers, but he doesn't argue, and she goes cold. She's pushed too far. Edwin is too smart for George's tricks. He isn't going to fall for wanting what he can't have. He'll just go out and find someone else.

Then he says, "But it can. Your ideas are good, very good, and I believe that if we work together as a team, we can help each other come up with even better ones."

"So you want me to stick around so *I* can help *you* come up with better ideas?" His sort-of apology is as lame as it is self-centered. Clearly he just can't help himself.

"We'll be two parts that create a bigger and better whole," he offers. "Create what neither one of us would be able to do on our own. You'll be more than my assistant—you'll be my apprentice. And then who knows? We'll design curricula, travel to Europe to buy artwork. Together we'll mold the Bradley, build the school, the collection. Make it everything it can be."

She hesitates, knowing George would string him along for longer, wrestle for more. But she got her concessions, and from Edwin's obvious fear of losing her, it seems as if there might be more in the future. She isn't George. She has neither his patience nor his steel nerves. And she wants this too much. "No yelling," she finally says.

Edwin smiles. "No yelling."

It appears George is good for something after all.

13

GEORGE/BENJAMIN, 1923

This time it's a wealthy widow. Granted, she isn't as lithe and spontaneous as Paulien Mertens, but Katherine Clarendon handles middle age better than most, and she's proving to be an even more valuable channel to cash than Paulien was.

Katherine knows everyone in New York City with real money, and because both her own and her late husband's family have been blue blood since before the dawn of time, her connections stretch wide and deep, across generations and geographies. She has friends and relatives in Philadelphia, Boston, Miami, Chicago, and Beverly Hills—and they're all very, very rich. A veritable gold mine, the old girl is.

Katherine thinks he's only nine years her junior, as Paulien thought he was only seven years her senior. In truth he's thirty-five, fourteen years older than Paulien and fifteen younger than Katherine. These side games amuse him. People will believe anything you tell them, as long as it's what they want to believe. Especially women. They see what they want to see, what you guide them to see—and overlook what you guide them to overlook.

As always, this new project is protracted and tedious, but it's his business and he does it well. He imagines himself as a theater actor, playing essentially the same role in the same play every evening, whether he's Harold Berkeley or George Everard or Benjamin Talcott, whether he's in Toronto or London or New York. Every day and every night he delivers the best performance possible: he's witty and smart, charming and self-effacing. No one has an inkling of how much he hates them.

He's operating this business as he always does. Planning, patience, and an appreciation for the underpinnings of human greed do it every time. Not a single investor who came to him through Katherine has made a withdrawal. That's how much they trust him—and how truly moneyed they are. And although she's no randy young girl like Paulien, Katherine is better in bed than he expected. Another bonus.

Katherine runs with the art crowd, which makes his present game even more tiresome than usual. Although he actually does like art, all those gallery openings and museum fund-raisers and self-centered artists and even more self-centered collectors drive him up the wall. She was raised in Philadelphia, where most of her family still lives, and is a major patron of the Philadelphia Museum of Art. This means endless trips to the City of Brotherly Love, which he doesn't love at all.

Everyone there has New York envy and acts even snootier and more pretentious than the snooty and pretentious well-to-do inhabitants of the other cities he's visited. On the other hand, it's where Paulien lives. She has a hold on him none of his other marks ever had, which both displeases and intrigues him. He's seen her and Bradley around town, and he plans to see more of her. Much more.

Despite her protests in Paris, she must, at least at times, think of him tenderly. She thinks of their lovemaking tenderly, of that he has no doubt.

14

PAULIEN, 1920

Paulien brought George home for Christmas. On the train to Brussels they had a first-class compartment to themselves, and she told him about her family: her lovely but social-climbing mother; her driven father with a soft spot for art; her pompous older brother; and little Franck, now in public school and all grown up at fifteen. She also told him about the money.

He was amused. "Why all the secrecy? Did you think I wouldn't be interested in you if I knew you were of the landed gentry?"

It did sound foolish when he put it like that. "I just didn't think it was anyone's business," she said primly.

George began to laugh and gave her a hug. "Well, it's my business now." He pulled a valise from the overhead rack and began to rummage through it. "But since you've told me about your true social standing, I'm guessing you probably aren't going to think this gift is nearly as exciting as I'd hoped."

Paulien held her breath. A gift. Was he going to propose? *It's my business now.* What else could it be after a comment like that? He pulled out an envelope and handed it to her. Not a ring.

"Christmas isn't until Wednesday," she said as cheerfully as she could.

"I misspoke, it isn't actually a gift. It's more like an investment in the future."

An investment in the future? That sounded promising. She removed a single sheet of paper from the envelope and stared at it, confused. A bill? A bank receipt of some sort? Then she realized it was an Everard Sureties Exchange statement and that her name was on the top. She looked at George.

"For you," he explained. "I opened an account for you back in September. Five hundred pounds. I want you to share in what I'm doing, to prosper along with me."

Paulien tried to appear pleased. If he really wanted her to prosper with him, he'd ask her to marry him. She smoothed the creases in the paper to gain some time. "Thank you," she said finally. "It's very sweet. But I thought you weren't taking on any new investors."

George seemed oblivious to her disappointment, which was odd for a man so acutely attuned to her moods. "You're not just an investor, my darling. I'm in love with you."

They had been speaking of love for months now, and there had been a few oblique references to a possible future together, yet something about this gift felt like a repudiation of those declarations. It was so business-like, so unromantic, so unlike George—and so deeply disappointing.

The words rushed out before she could rein them in. "If you love me so much, why don't you want to marry me?" Her hands flew to her mouth.

But George, being George, just laughed. "Can we have a big party?"

"A big party?" she repeated, stunned at the turn the conversation had taken.

"For the wedding—a big wedding party."

Now Paulien was laughing, too, with relief. "Yes," she managed to say. "A very big party."

"Well then." George dropped to one knee and pulled a small box from his jacket pocket.

Paulien held her breath. He'd planned the whole thing to play out just as it had, the clever man. Such a jokester. He was going to ask her to marry him. And she was going to say yes.

The ring was yet another example of George's taste—and his

understanding of hers. He easily could have bought an ostentatious diamond, but that wasn't what he placed on her finger. The stone was neither large nor small, a carat and a half at most, a flawless thing that threw prisms of light throughout the compartment when she admired it. The simple platinum setting was perfect. As was the fit.

HER PARENTS WERE aghast at the news. Who was this British whippersnapper with a surname no one knew? Lacking the courtesy to ask a father's permission before proposing marriage to his daughter? Giving her a ring before there had even been a proper introduction to the family? But within a couple of days, George had charmed them all, as Paulien knew he would.

He played tennis with her brother Léon—who George claimed wasn't pompous at all—and always let him win after what appeared to be a close game. He took Franck shooting and riding, played bridge with her mother, and discussed the textile business with her father. Even the extended family approved. Tante Natalie whispered one night that George was far more accomplished than Maxence Van de Velde and much more handsome. Both of which went without saying.

George played poker with the boy cousins well into the night but was always up to share an early breakfast with her. It was unseasonably warm, and they took long walks together on the trails that wound through the estate. She showed him the barn on the backside of the lake where the Mertens Museum of Post-Impressionism would someday be housed, and he heartily approved of her plans and resourcefulness. The barn was also private and secluded and the perfect place to make love.

There was endless talk of the wedding, which George was more interested in—and involved in—than Paulien. She would have preferred they go to the local church and marry the next day, but her mother and George would have none of it. And she had promised him a big party.

Their original plan was to host it at the estate in August, when all Mertens weddings were held, but it quickly became apparent that there wasn't enough time to organize the kind of extravaganza George and her mother had in mind, and it was pushed back to the following summer. This seemed an awfully long time to wait, but Paulien was overruled.

What did she care? She was going to marry a man she adored, spend the rest of her life with him, laugh with him, have children with him. So what did another year matter? They would be together in London, and they had the vast future stretching ahead of them. It was all too wonderful and heady. She wasn't about to bother herself with trifles.

And she had to admit that it would be nice to have a wedding even better than her cousin Margaret's had been. Not to mention marrying a man far better in all ways than that boring Herbert.

Her father came and found her in the library one afternoon when George was off with Léon. "I'm very pleased for you, Paulie," he said, sitting down in a chair near her. "He's a fine young man."

"Thank you, Papa." She closed her book and put it on the table. "Finer than Maxence Van de Velde?" she teased.

For a moment he looked surprised. They hadn't spoken of Maxence since she'd refused his ring and left for London, over a year ago. But her father quickly recovered himself and said, "It's obvious that you care very much for George."

"Yes." She smiled at his backhanded acknowledgment of defeat. "I love him, yes. Very much."

"I've looked into his Everard Sureties Exchange. Asked around. And I like what I hear. He's apparently a very clever lad, a boy with ideas who's also able to run a business. Quite successfully, I'm told. I'm also told his investors are pleased with their returns."

"Ah, checking up on him, were you?"

"Unquestionably. You're my daughter, my only daughter." He looked at her with affection. "I'm not about to let you run off and marry some scoundrel."

"Well, you don't have to worry about that, Papa. George even opened an Everard account for me in early September. With five hundred pounds. Just a few short months later, it's worth almost six hundred—almost twenty percent more."

"You gave him five hundred pounds?" he asked suspiciously.

"He used his own money, but the account's in my name. A gift." It amused her that what she'd initially considered an insult she now saw as a declaration of devotion.

"So you're the exception. He told me he isn't taking on any new investors."

"Integrity is crucial to him. He's been turning down even his biggest longtime backers because he wants to make sure he can deliver on his promises." Her voice cracked. How lucky she was. How very lucky.

"That is an important mark of a man. A fine thing in a husband—and in a son-in-law."

"Did you want to invest? Is that why you asked him about it?"

"No, I was just curious." He pulled a mock frown. "I am not sure how much extra cash I am going to have, now that it appears I have a very expensive wedding to put on. Your mother cannot constrain herself. I worry that she is going to invite the entire world."

"Maybe that's why you should invest," Paulien said, laughing. "You could make back the cost of the wedding in no time."

Her father stood, then leaned over and kissed her forehead. "I wish you both a lifetime of happiness, my dear."

"Thank you, Papa. I have no doubt that's just what we'll have." As he turned, she added, "You should really think about Everard Sureties. As you said, George is a clever lad, and I'm sure I can persuade him to open an account for you. We're all family now."

PART TWO

15

Less than a year after her run-in with Antoinette Lavigne at Gertrude Stein's, Vivienne returns to Paris with Edwin. It's far too soon, and as they travel around the city hunting artwork, she searches everywhere for hostile faces. She also shuns anyone in a uniform, although she doubts the police are still looking for her—if they ever were—and hopes the same is true for her father.

Edwin is confused by her behavior. "What's wrong?" he asks one day as she stands outside the plate-glass window of Petit Robert scrutinizing the diners seated within. He pulls the door open. "It's late. Aren't you hungry?"

"I feel a headache coming on," she says, her eyes still on the dining room.

"What does a headache have to do with lunch?"

She has no answer for this, so she goes inside with him. Fortunately no one glances their way.

She agreed to come to France, against her better judgment, because of Henri. Edwin had published a book called *The Art in Painting* a few years earlier and asked her to coauthor his next, which he wants to focus on Matisse. The first task is to secure Henri's consent, but now that they're in Paris, Edwin thinks it best to wait for just the right moment. Any moment will be the right moment, as far as Vivienne is concerned, as she and Henri have fallen into an easy camaraderie on this trip. For reasons she's not quite sure of, she doesn't mention this to Edwin.

Whenever she and Henri find themselves together, he pulls a chair alongside hers, gazes deep into her eyes, and asks her opinion on the news of the day. Or they discuss Chaim Soutine, who, after Edwin paid him for sixty paintings, hailed a cab to the French Riviera, over five hundred miles away. They discuss Gertrude's idea of writing her auto-biography told from Alice's point of view. And they discuss the rumor that the artist Maurice Utrillo is the illegitimate son of the model and painter Suzanne Valadon.

Just the other day, they had a conversation about whether Signac's expansion of Seurat's Pointillist dots into thicker lozenge-shaped brush-strokes is a breakthrough or just the pilfering of Seurat's idea. Vivienne is starstruck, far more so than if Henri were Lon Chaney or Buster Keaton. She can't believe she's in the presence of the great master or that he appears to have an interest in talking to her.

As she does often, she thinks about how excited her father would be if he knew she was having exchanges like this with Henri Matisse, potentially writing a book about him. She imagines the finished volume on the blotter of Papa's massive desk, the pride and pleasure beaming from his eyes as he reads her name on the cover, runs his finger over the embossed gold lettering. But if Papa did see the book, he would have no idea who Vivienne Gregsby is. And she's certain he doesn't have his massive desk anymore.

HENRI'S APARTMENT IS enveloped in fabrics. Silk curtains are gracefully swagged at the edge of the windows; Persian carpets lie side by side on the floor. The upholstery is of the finest brocade, and pillows in riotous colors are scattered everywhere. Embroidered screens, African wall hangings, decorative cushions. Swatches of magnificent textiles flung on chairs, couches, even tables.

Henri watches her. "I am a descendant of generations of weavers," he explains. "The devotion to color comes from my mother, who was also a painter, although she chose to paint on porcelain, while I prefer canvas."

It's a splendid spectacle in and of itself, but it's also a Matisse painting: the vibrancy, the rich hues, the textures and patterns. It's all there. "I feel like I'm standing inside one of your pictures," Vivienne says in a hushed voice.

"I have been collecting fabrics since I was an art student. Here, there, wherever I travel." He points to a wall hanging. "Algeria." To a narrow swatch that lies along the middle of a long table. "Tahiti." To a drapery on the far window. "A bargain I found at the end of the season at a haute couture sale here in Paris."

She wants to tell him that she, too, comes from a textile family, but she says nothing. He shows her his bookshelves, laden with an odd assortment of items: vases and urns and an egg cup, African masks and Chinese porcelain, glass vitrines with mirrored backs. Some banal, others exotic. "The tapestries are my backdrops," he says. "The objects are my characters. A good actor can have a part in ten different plays. An object can play a role in ten different pictures."

She's seen the anthropomorphic green vase in his *Still Life with African Statuette* and *Vase of Flowers*, recognizes the stylized chocolate pot from *Dishes on a Table, Still Life with Blue Tablecloth*, and *Bouquet of Flowers in a Chocolate Pot*. How had she missed this commonality in his paintings?

"This is the working library from which I choose my actors," he says. "How I arrange them in relation to one another—a casual meeting or a romantic liaison—imbues them with my emotional reaction to them, which I hope to inspire in the viewer."

"Astonishing." She wishes she could be more articulate, but the experience is so overpowering she's almost speechless.

"Everything is inspiration." He motions for her to follow him. "Especially a beautiful woman."

They enter his studio, a large room filled with sculptures and drawings, watercolors and oil paintings. If there's a heaven, this is it. Even on this dreary Paris morning, sunshine and warmth radiate from every wall, every corner, every easel.

The paintings are almost a light source, so clear and strong are the colors, so fierce their luminous glow. Women, clothed, half-dressed, or naked, standing, sitting, or reclining. Vivienne recognizes the jewel tones of the silk swag in the front room, the decorative patterns of the embroideries, the harmony of color and line in the haute couture drapery. She moves slowly around the room, taking her time to drink in each one.

"You look at a painting the way an artist does," Henri observes.

"I like to try to understand the experiments, the risks the artist is taking. The discoveries he or she's making. What's left out, what's included, and why these choices were made . . ." Self-conscious, she lets her words drift off. "Sorry," she says. "I didn't mean to get so—"

"Do not apologize." Henri's eyes are filled with respect. "What you have just said is exactly what I hope for, but rarely find, when I watch someone looking at one of my pictures."

Vivienne doesn't know how to respond, so she focuses on a horizontal canvas depicting a partially naked woman wearing a pair of exotically detailed harem pants, lounging, her arms raised. Bold greens, blues, yellows, and reds, even bolder textures and patterns, the planes flattened, the verticals true.

"*Odalisque with Red Pants,*" he says. "Do you remember? I was telling you about this painting the night we first met at Gertrude's. It is to be the beginning of a series. Do you like it?"

She reluctantly tears herself away from the picture. "One can't *like* a Matisse painting."

"So you do not like it?" He pulls a long face, but she can see he's joking.

"Are you trying to get a compliment out of me, sir?" she teases. He's so down to earth and forthright that, although being in his company awes her, she begins to calm.

"You must have spent enough time around artists to know that we never weary of compliments."

"I have, but I'd have guessed that by now you would have tired of them."

"Beyond a small circle of fellow artists and collectors, I am a virtual unknown." He bows slightly. "You overestimate me, *ma chérie*."

She grins. "So you say."

Henri takes her hand and leads her back to the front room. "I have had the housekeeper bring us some café au lait, unless you would prefer wine?"

"Café au lait is fine." She settles on a couch upholstered with a nubby linen of green and yellow. "This is a business meeting, after all."

"I would much prefer to consider it a social one." He offers her a plate of croissants and a seductive smile.

Vivienne takes a croissant. The man is indeed an incorrigible flirt.

"If you insist on business," Henri says, "can we at least deem it a social visit as well?"

She considers him carefully. He's a brilliant artist, a fascinating conversationalist—it appears he knows everything about everything—and he's an extremely sexy man. But he could be playing with her, just as George had, and she can't trust herself to accurately gauge. Still, she finds herself saying, "Let's see how it goes."

"In that case," Henri says as he takes a seat on the couch next to her, "let us get the business part over as quickly as possible."

Vivienne opens her notebook. "Have you read Edwin's *The Art in Painting*?" she asks, hoping she sounds professional.

Henri sits up straight and places his feet firmly on the floor, his hands in his lap, an imitation of a proper French schoolboy. "Yes, Mademoiselle Gregsby, I have."

"And what did you think of it?" she asks, joining in his game.

"It was extraordinary, mademoiselle. Extremely eloquent."

She narrows her eyes. "What in particular did you find so extraordinary?"

"The way in which he discussed the art in painting."

She puts her notebook down, frowns at him, and asks in her best schoolmarm voice, "Did you or did you not read Dr. Bradley's work?"

"I own a copy of the book. Dr. Bradley gave it to me himself. Autographed it. But it has so many pages . . ."

Vivienne can't help herself and starts to laugh. Henri does the same, and soon they're both howling. "You get a zero on the assignment," she finally manages to say.

"Please do not tell Edwin."

"Your secret's safe with me."

They beam at each other, and then Vivienne quickly sobers. This was how George pulled her in, with laughter and repartee. "Seriously, Henri, would you consider working with us on a book about you and your art?"

"I feel privileged that you would consider such a thing, but as you can see, I am immersed. This past winter in Nice had such a powerful effect on my paintings—and now Paris is following suit. I am sorry, but I cannot see how I will be able to give up the time."

"Please, just hear me out. We'd call it something like *The Art of Henri Matisse*, a comprehensive analysis of your work to date: your creative use of traditions, treatment of color and light, thematic variations, shifting perspectives, and—"

"I would be happy to do this with you and Edwin." He winks. "With you especially. But I am afraid it would interfere too much with my painting."

"We can be flexible," she presses. "Do the interviews around your schedule. Travel to wherever you are. I'm sure we'd be able to find a way that wouldn't be too intrusive."

"How many hours do you think you will need?"

"As many as you can give us. As few as you can give us. I'll take whatever I can get, but you'd be in charge."

"In charge? Before, when you said 'working with us,' did you mean working with you or with Edwin?"

"Both of us. We're coauthoring the book, so we'll each be involved in all aspects of the project."

"Edwin can be such a bore at times." Henri's sigh is theatrical. "What if I told you I would consider your proposition on the condition that all the personal interviews be conducted by you?"

"He'd never agree," she says, although she's already running through ways to convince Edwin that this was his idea. "You know how he is."

"I am confident you can make this happen without his ever being aware of it." Henri's expression is full of mischief, and their eyes meet, hold. He leans over, cups her chin, and kisses her.

Vivienne supposes she shouldn't be surprised, but she is. She keeps thinking: I'm kissing Henri Matisse, I'm kissing Henri Matisse, I'm kissing the great artist Henri Matisse. She catches a whiff of paint and turpentine and that wonderful, intangible smell of a man. It's been a long time, and it feels so right. She opens her mouth to his.

When he kisses a line down her neck to the hollow at its base, the pull of desire is so strong it actually hurts. It's been over a year since she's been touched, really touched.

Vivienne jerks away, moves to a chair across from the couch, takes a shuddering breath. Henri makes her feel the same way George did: excited, alive, and full of wanting, but also impulsive, careless, and, she now realizes, vulnerable. Plus he's a married man, even if he's faithful in the fashion of Montmartre.

"I hope this doesn't mean that you won't agree to my condition?" Henri appears more amused than annoyed. "Just you, no Edwin."

"I, ah, yes. Yes. I don't think that will be a problem. The interviews, I mean. But I, ah, I don't think this . . . that this is a good idea."

He gazes at her tenderly. "And why do you think that? Do you have a lover?"

"No, no," she says quickly, then wishes she hadn't. Another man might be the one explanation he'd accept.

"Well, if that is the case, my dear Vivienne, I shall not be discouraged," he declares, and kisses her hand as if they'd just met. "There is no need to rush. We have time. And after I return from Barcelona next month, we shall spend much more of it together."

Vienne and Edwin begin to outline the book. She's impressed by the agility of his thinking, his talent for simultaneously seeing the big picture as well as the small, the way his creativity sparks her own. He seems to feel similarly, and their friendship and mutual respect deepen. She doesn't argue when they have a difference of opinion, she just gently nudges him over to her way of thinking. And sometimes he nudges her to his.

When he wants to arrange the book chronologically—which she believes will be boring—she suggests they apply Edwin's own brilliant concepts of light, line, color, and space to unlock the meaning of Henri's paintings. When he wants to focus solely on the work rather than on the man—which she believes will be limiting—she suggests that they use his own friendship with and insight into Henri to bring both the artist and his work to life. She's becoming deft at the art of managing Dr. Edwin Bradley.

Once the general outline is complete and they begin to assign tasks, Vivienne proposes that he be the one to interview Henri. "You've been friends for years and you're so familiar with his work that you'll be much more efficient." She hands him the piece of paper on which she's written the number of hours that will be necessary. Perhaps exaggerated the number.

He studies it.

"I'm thinking about at least forty hours of interviews—maybe more—and then there's the organizing, editing, rewriting, revising. . . . It's a one-person job, too many redundancies otherwise, and you'll be able to complete it much faster than I will."

He carefully studies her figures, makes a few notations in the margin. "I have too many things to do to take on this large a task. And given all the time I've spent with Matisse and how well I know his work, you'll be less biased."

16

VIVIENNE, 1923

A few days after Henri leaves for Spain, Gertrude's brother Leo comes to Paris. Although Leo and Edwin had a falling-out a couple of years before, Edwin agrees to meet Leo for lunch and asks Vivienne to come with him. Edwin explains that their disagreement involved *The Art in Painting*, which was published to almost universal acclaim. The "almost" is because Leo wrote a review in the *New Republic* that was less than glowing. Edwin was livid at the affront, and a flurry of heated letters left them, as Leo put it, "on unspeaking terms." But now Edwin has decided to forgive him.

She and Edwin are already seated when a well-dressed, lanky man approaches their table. It doesn't seem possible that this could be Leo or that he and Gertrude could have sprung from the same loins. Where Gertrude is short and stocky, Leo is tall and thin. Where her features are large and prominent, his are fine. And where her movements are straightforward and almost masculine, his are graceful. It's almost as if Gertrude were meant to be the man and Leo the woman.

Leo shakes Edwin's hand, then Vivienne's. "Ah, Gertrude won't stop talking about you," he tells her. "She said you're great pals."

"Your sister is an amazing woman," Vivienne says. "She's been wonderful to me, taken me under her wing."

"The feeling is mutual," Leo says. "Gertrude told me that 'strength attracts strength' and that you have plenty. Also that you don't try to hide your intelligence from men. Her highest praise."

"Please," Edwin says. "Join us."

There are two empty chairs at the table and Leo pauses, looks from one to the next, then at each of them. Finally he sits in the one next to Vivienne. He lifts the napkin from his plate, fusses with it, hesitates before extricating it from its ring, and carefully places it on his lap. She assumes he's nervous, which he probably is, but she later learns he has difficulty making decisions, even ones as inconsequential as what to do with his napkin.

For all his indecisiveness, Leo is knowledgeable on all manner of subjects, including art, education, psychology, and aesthetics. The three of them finish off a bottle of wine, and Edwin orders another. Perhaps because he's grown up with a sister like Gertrude, Leo treats Vivienne as an equal, speaking directly to her, listening attentively when she speaks. This isn't her usual experience while dining with Edwin's male colleagues.

After dessert is served, Leo clears his throat. "I, ah, I need your advice, Edwin. I've got some paintings I need to sell. Mostly Renoirs. Sixteen to be exact. I know the prices have gone up, but I don't know how to balance what I might ask with the fall in the franc . . ."

Renoirs. Vivienne lights a cigarette and glances at Edwin. One of Edwin's dreams is to buy enough strategic pieces of Renoir's oeuvre that not only will he possess the largest collection of Renoirs anywhere, but visitors to the Bradley will be able to view the entire arc of the master's career in a single setting. He already owns more than one hundred Renoirs, but there are holes to be filled.

"I, ah, I also don't know if this is the best time to sell," Leo continues. "If, given Renoir's rise in popularity, it might be best to wait it out to take advantage of the increasing value . . . even though waiting might prove problematic." He drums his long fingers on the table. "And then there's the matter of a possible auction. Would I get a fair return? Or would another method be more profitable?"

"Is this something you need to do right away?" Edwin asks.

Leo plays with his napkin ring. "There are also a few Cézanne watercolors, a Delacroix, a Daumier, and a Matisse bronze . . ."

"Are they in Paris?" Vivienne asks.

"I brought some of them with me. They're at twenty-seven."

"I'd like to see what you have." Edwin says. "I can give you my thoughts. Maybe find you some buyers. Even buy a few myself."

"I'm afraid you're thinking they're more important than they are. Most of them are small and slight. I cracked one enchanting nude by foolish handling and—"

"Let me be the judge of that," Edwin says.

The next morning the three meet at Gertrude's. They stand in the atelier and survey what Leo wants to sell.

"You're right," Edwin tells Leo. "Some of this has little merit, but some are quite fine. I might be able to find you buyers in America for the more major pieces, where a few collectors, although not many, are beginning to appreciate modern art."

"You think so?" Leo sounds doubtful.

"I'd also like to see the others," Edwin says. "Particularly the rest of the Renoirs."

"I think maybe I could do that, but it might—"

"Ship the whole lot to Merion," Edwin interrupts. "We'll be back there by the beginning of December, and that will give me time to make some inquires before everyone leaves the city for Christmas."

"Maybe this isn't the right time, then," Leo says. "The sales will take longer to complete because of the length of time it will take to get the paintings there. Especially if everyone is on holiday. And what if the collectors are less sophisticated than you think? Then I'd have to pay to have them shipped back and—"

"Leo, stop." Edwin points to a small Renoir nude. A woman stands in front of what appears to be a waterfall, her back to the viewer, wavelets lapping at her thighs. Not as lush as some, unfinished around the edges, but still lovely. Vivienne guesses 1890s, a period from which the Bradley has only a few Renoirs.

"I'll give you five hundred francs for it right now," Edwin says to

Leo's astonishment. It's a lot of money for a painting that size, but it's more valuable to Edwin than most.

Vivienne is taken with the study, with the colors and the curves of the woman's body against the water. But she hates to think about it as part of an ensemble, within which it will be swallowed up, barely noticed. If the collection were hers, she would find a small alcove somewhere, a narrow spot near a bench or a chair, where its diminutive character could be truly appreciated.

"Use that money to ship the rest," Edwin is saying. "And I'm sure I'll be able to find you some buyers by the spring." He scribbles a check and hands it to Leo.

Leo looks from Edwin to the check in his hand. "Thank you," he says. "This will help a lot." Although he makes an attempt at a smile, it's clear from his eyes that it isn't going to help enough. Edwin mentioned gambling debts.

Edwin takes back the check, rips it up, and writes another. This one causes Leo's eyes to water; he pretends to sneeze so he can use his handkerchief. Then he throws himself at Edwin and gives him a bear hug.

Edwin stands stiffly and awkwardly pats Leo's back.

When Vivienne and Edwin leave 27, he's exuberant. "I know he's got a few more Renoirs in that batch that will work for me. The man may have fallen on hard times, but no one has an eye like Leo Stein."

She touches his arm. "It was generous of you to help him out like that."

Edwin briefly puts his hand over hers. "It seems that I'm a more generous person when I'm around you."

THE NEWS OF Edwin's munificence spreads quickly, and even Gertrude warms to him, praising his discernment and the breadth of his growing collection, inviting Vivienne and Edwin on her boating excursions down the Seine and to almost all her parties. Things are going so smoothly between Gertrude and Edwin that Vivienne isn't surprised when Edwin decides to stay at Gertrude's beyond dessert one evening.

He usually complains about this latter part of the dinner parties, when the guests retire to Gertrude's atelier; he claims it gets too raucous and goes on too late. Plus it's raining that night, and Vivienne knows he hates getting his shoes wet walking between the house and the atelier. She assumes his new rapport with Gertrude has changed his opinion. She and Henri, along with Gertrude and Alice and Zelda Fitzgerald—who is a hoot—are having too much fun to worry about Edwin's change of heart.

Henri returned from Barcelona just the day before, and he's even wittier and more handsome than Vivienne remembers. Despite the fact that his arrival means they can now begin the interviews for *The Art of Henri Matisse*, Edwin keeps shooting the two of them sidelong glances. Annoyed, she tears herself away from Henri and walks across the yard with Alice.

When all the guests are in the atelier, Gertrude seats herself next to the cast-iron stove—the only source of heat in the room and therefore the center of activity—in a high-backed Italian Renaissance chair, and everyone clusters in small groups around both her and the warmth. As Vivienne edges her way toward Henri and Scott Fitzgerald, Edwin grabs her arm.

"Come look at this," he says, dragging her toward an oversize Picasso. "What do you think?"

It's from Picasso's Rose Period, and Edwin has been looking for a piece from this era. "It's magnificent," she tells him, "but you know as well as I do that Gertrude never sells her paintings. And—"

"I think it is some of his best work," Henri says, joining them.

Edwin twists his shoulders and takes a step to his left, positioning himself between Vivienne and Henri.

Vivienne inspects the painting. "With a nod to you," she tells Henri.

"Why, thank you, Mademoiselle Gregsby." Henri steps around Edwin and kisses her hand. "I appreciate that. Especially coming from someone with your discerning eye."

"Just because he's using simple forms and bright colors?" Edwin's voice is scornful. "Perhaps it is you, my dear friend Henri, who is nodding to him."

Vivienne is even more annoyed now. Edwin knows Henri and Pablo Picasso have a love-hate relationship, and he's purposely antagonizing Henri.

"If we have a positive effect upon each other's work," Henri retorts, "I can only believe this is a good thing. Artists do not stand alone. Pablo and I share an appreciation for many earlier and contemporary artists, and we use their work as a starting point for our own. Unlike in many other professions," he adds, looking from Gertrude to Edwin, "painters are not always in competition with each other."

"In every profession, and in every situation, there is competition," Edwin declares. "Winners and losers." Then he calls out to Gertrude, "How much to buy this one?"

Silence fills the room, and Gertrude says dismissively, "Not everything in this world is for sale."

"For the right price it is," Edwin insists.

"Perhaps you mistake my home for a gallery, Dr. Bradley."

Vivienne grabs his arm. "What's wrong with you tonight? Don't do this."

He shrugs Vivienne off and pulls his checkbook from his pocket. "I'll give you a thousand francs right this minute."

Gertrude turns to a young man at her right, an aspiring painter who looks at her worshipfully. "Monsieur—"

Edwin smirks at Henri. "Fifteen hundred," he calls to Gertrude.

"You work in oils, don't you?" Gertrude asks the artist.

"Most of the time I—" the boy begins.

"Two thousand."

"Most of the time you work in oils?" Gertrude prompts.

"Three thousand."

Vivienne hisses in his ear, "You're not going to win." Is this grand-standing because he's jealous of the notice she's been giving to Henri or because Gertrude, a rival collector, is the center of attention?

"Watch me."

"Pastels, actually," the boy says. "But I—"

"Four thousand!"

"Vivienne," Gertrude calls, "is there nothing you can do to silence this madman?"

Vivienne gives Edwin an imploring look. "There are other Picassos out there."

Edwin holds his checkbook high in the air. "I'll give you ten thousand francs," he declares. "In cash!"

For a moment Gertrude hesitates, and as soon as Edwin sees this, he chortles. "See, Mademoiselle Stein, everything *is* for sale at the right price." He bows to Gertrude and turns to Henri. "As I said, winners and losers." Then he walks toward the door.

"Out!" Gertrude bellows. But Edwin is already gone.

Zelda, quite drunk—as is her usual state at this hour—starts to gig-gle. Scott, also drunk, throws his arm around her and joins in. Then the snickers begin. The guests try to hold themselves back, but it's impos-sible. Soon everyone, with the exception of Gertrude and Alice, are exploding with laughter. The hilarity is contagious, and Vivienne col-lapses into Henri's arms, hooting along with the rest of them. Edwin has indeed made his point.

Gertrude stands, pulls herself to her full height, and in her deep, booming voice declares, "Go! All of you! Go!"

The merriment immediately abates, and everyone shuffles out into the rain like chastised children sent to their rooms.

THE NEXT DAY, Vivienne schedules a series of interviews with Henri. And to spite Edwin for his antics at Gertrude's, she goes out and buys a velvet dress for their first meeting. It's a luxurious shade of forest green, a color she knows Henri likes because he uses it so frequently in his paintings. Perhaps the purchase is not just to get back at Edwin.

But she doesn't get to spite Edwin or to go to Henri's apartment. The day before the first interview, Edwin receives a cable from his lawyer in Philadelphia. The district attorney general's office is bringing a lawsuit contending that the Bradley should be opened to the public, and Edwin must return immediately.

So instead of sitting on Henri's Matisse's green-and-yellow couch in her new dress, Vivienne finds herself in Marseille, boarding a ship bound for New York.

THE TRIAL, 1928

My life is a roller coaster, Edwin. A hackneyed metaphor perhaps, but true. After the last two sessions, in which my motive and opportunity were on broad display, Pratt petitioned the court to revoke my bail, and the judge took it under advisement. For two long days, I huddled in my bed, praying to be allowed to continue spending my nights there.

When sleep finally came, it was full of nightmares of being stalked or held in a cage with no doors. Once in a while there were pleasant dreams in which I freely wandered the back fields of the estate in Belgium, a young girl still, but these dreams became nightmarish when I awoke to my true situation. Yet you know nothing about that young girl or those fields, do you? Odd to think how much we shared and how much we withheld from each other.

Fortunately the judge rejected Pratt's motion. That's the top-of-the-roller-coaster part. The rush downward was due to the meeting I had with Ronald to discuss his strategy. We met in his office, a small, windowless room at the end of a narrow corridor, far from the opulence of the marble-sheathed lobby. Ronald stared into his coffee cup and mumbled, "Hello."

"What's your overall plan?" I asked, as any reasonable client on trial for her life might. "Pratt seems to be positioning his pieces for a quick checkmate. What's our next move?"

"Reasonable doubt."

"Specifically . . . ?"

"There are three prongs: other potential suspects, the implausibility of someone choosing to stage a car crash as a viable murder technique, and the likelihood it was an accident."

He did have a plan. With three prongs. "So all the others he promised the collection to and then reneged?" I asked hopefully. "The Philadelphia Museum of Art, the University of Pennsylvania? And there are tons of people who disliked him." Sorry, Edwin. "Thomas Quinton for starters. Ralph Knight at the PMA. Clifton Sherman at Penn."

"They're all on the prosecution's list of potential witnesses."

"Wouldn't they be our witnesses?"

"They were going to be."

"But not anymore?"

"No."

His cryptic answers revived my irritation, and I demanded that he explain exactly what was going on.

"Pratt is trying to head us off at the pass."

I wasn't encouraged by the cowboy reference either. "We're talking about a goddamned murder conviction!" I cried. "You tell me how you're going to make sure that doesn't happen or you're fired."

This seemed to get his attention, and he explained that he'd deposed each of Pratt's witnesses and determined their testimonies were going to hurt us more than help us.

Apparently they were all eager to express their dislike for you, Edwin. To describe the fights and the insults. But one after the other, every man and every institution's representative insisted that he never believed you'd leave the collection to anyone but me.

"But that's not Quinton's only possible motivation," I explained as calmly as I could, trying to keep from screaming. "Thomas Quinton hates Edwin with a passion. Blames him for stealing his true love, Edwin's wife, Ada. The man is still holding a torch after all this time. And Ada told me he was going to help her prove that I killed Edwin."

For the first time Ronald appeared interested. "When did she say this?"

"At Edwin's funeral."

"Who else was there?"

"Just Quinton."

"*Nobody else?*"

"*No, but she could have told someone at another time.*"

"*Not good enough.*"

My voice rose a few notches. "*Thomas Quinton is on the board of directors at the Philadelphia Museum of Art. For years he and Ralph Knight have been cooking up ways to move Edwin's collection to the PMA. They both know that if I inherit it, I'd never give it to them. And I'm sure Ada promised them that she would—probably part of her deal. Quinton helps her get revenge on me, and she hands over the collection. Sounds like a lot of damn motive to me.*"

Ronald waited patiently through my tirade, and then said, "Suggesting men of their stature and gravitas are setting you up for murder wouldn't be good for us."

"*Not good for us?*" *I argued. "How can it make it any worse?*"

"*Thomas Quinton owns the* Philadelphia Investigator,*" Ronald informed me, as if that was all that needed to be said.*

"*That doesn't mean he's not orchestrating this debacle!*"

Ronald shrugged. "That would be difficult to prove."

"*So apparently you have only two prongs,*" *I pointed out, my voice dripping with sarcasm. "Your third one doesn't appear to actually exist.*"

He glanced at his watch. "I suppose that's true."

"*What about Ada? Mrs. Bradley?*" *I'm sorry, Edwin, I appreciate how you always protected her, but all I need is reasonable doubt. "She's an heir, too—and the spouse is always a suspect, right?*"

"*Problematic to go after the grieving widow,*" *Ronald said. "Especially when they were married for so many years. And in this case, his will didn't stipulate that Mrs. Bradley was to get anything beyond what Dr. Bradley had already agreed to give her—in writing, I might add—before he died.*"

"*But that isn't the—*"

"*It's not going to work, Vivienne,*" *he interrupted. "Ada Bradley didn't stand to inherit anything she didn't already own, so it'll be hard to convince* the jury she had cause." His implication was that there would be much less difficulty in convincing a jury that I did.

"What about the fact that she believed Edwin and I were having an affair? The scorned wife?"

"But you told me you and Bradley weren't involved in that way." He spaced his words as if he were talking to a slow child. "It would have more merit as a motive if you'd had an actual affair."

"She didn't know that!" I wanted more than anything to tell him, as you would say, what a horse's ass he was. But I don't know any other lawyers, and my inheritance is being held in escrow—if I'm found guilty of your murder, I can't claim it—so I don't have the money to pay someone to start all over again. Actually I barely have the money to pay Ronald's firm. "I want you to go after her anyway."

He looked at his watch again and sighed. "I didn't want to tell you this, but I've been looking into alternative theories and other possible suspects— including Ada Bradley—and so far I've come up empty. The firm told me just the other day that I've charged too many hours, and they won't give me any more money to investigate further."

17

VIVIENNE, 1924

Once Vivienne and Edwin arrive back in Philadelphia, Henri corresponds frequently with both of them, mailing letters about the book to the Bradley, posting personal ones to her home address. Some of his notes to her are friendly and chatty: tales of Saturday evening opium smoking at Gertrude's, descriptions of the weather in Nice, talk of his progress on the odalisques, his latest disagreement with Picasso. Others are more intimate.

In February: *I cannot stop thinking of you standing so still in my studio, taking in* Odalisque with Red Pants *with your painter's eye, striving to see what I had done and what I had found, crawling into my soul. It was a moment more intimate than if we were making love. When will you return?*

In March: *I sat on my yellow-and-green couch today and conjured you there next to me. For a moment it was so real I could feel your arms around me, the softness of your skin, the warmth of your lips. Then you were gone, and it nearly broke my heart.*

In April: *Paris in the spring is the most exquisite place on earth for lovers, if only you were here to become mine.*

He sounded just like George: the compliments, the longing, the enthralling language. And he's a ladies' man, also just like George. She will not allow him to ensnare her. But she keeps the letters in a shoe box in the back of her closet, rereads them often.

Perhaps not surprisingly, she begins to imagine she sees George around town. She could swear he was standing in the lobby at the symphony last month, but when she looped around to come from behind, he was gone. The same thing happened at a restaurant in March, and in Atlantic City a few weeks later.

When he told her in Paris he might be going to the States, she assumed he was headed for New York City. Philadelphia seems too much of a backwater for his type of grand enterprise. Yet George's logic is far different from everyone else's because he's always playing a chess game ten moves out, or more correctly, a con game. And he might very well be coming after her.

She hopes he is, wants him to be. She won't act the way she did that night outside the Café de la Rotonde. She's no longer simple, gullible Paulien Mertens; she's Vivienne Gregsby, far wiser and craftier than that naive girl.

If he's watching her, stalking her, it's because he's sizing her up as a mark. And the way to enact her payback is to pretend that that's just what she is. She'll play him the way he played her, the way he played so many others. And when she's convinced him that she's going to let him walk all over her again, when he allows himself to let down his guard, maybe while he's in her bed—she'll bed him if she has to—she'll call the police. Justice will be hers, as will revenge, but most of all, his arrest is the calling card that will bring her home to her family, to forgiveness. Come on, you chump. Come get me.

On her way to work early one morning, she notices a tall, broad-shouldered man in a linen jacket heading in her direction. He's a couple of blocks away, too far to see his face, but the assured way he carries himself and his purposeful yet sauntering gait scream George. This is it. This is her chance. What's her best move? Should she walk right up to him? Pretend she doesn't recognize him? Wait for him to confront her? Should she be happy to see him or is she still angry?

Before she can decide, the man turns at the next intersection. As she watches him travel away from her, she realizes that it isn't George. The man is too old—his hair's completely gray—but more importantly, there's something about his demeanor, his lack of interest in his surroundings, which speaks of someone who's on his home turf, comfortable and familiar, no evil intent.

EDWIN BELIEVES THAT Thomas Quinton is behind the district attorney general's lawsuit. The owner and editor of Philadelphia's largest and most powerful newspaper can conceivably influence judicial events—and has done so before—but Vivienne can't believe this would be worth his trouble. Nor can she buy that it's revenge for stealing Ada decades ago. But when a number of editorials and opinion pieces run— one written by Ralph Knight, Quinton's close friend and the director of the Philadelphia Museum of Art—supporting the public's right to view the Bradley artwork, this gives her pause.

It's part of her job to help Edwin win the suit, which is awkward, as she wants him to lose. The litigation is based on the contention that the Bradley, which is a tax-exempt institution, is neither an accredited school nor a museum, and therefore Edwin must pay taxes or allow the public to view the collection on a regular basis. Edwin is unlikely to agree to shell out the tax money—with the exception of purchasing art, he's tight with a dollar—and therefore, if the suit succeeds, he'll be forced to open the doors.

Vivienne accompanies him to meetings with the lawyers, writes letters, collects materials, plots strategies, but if she makes a mistake now and then that might undermine their case, she lets it go. It's not as if she's hurting anyone. On the contrary, her efforts are a gesture of generosity.

Late one fall afternoon, or more correctly early one evening, Edwin pops his head into her office. "Got a minute? There's something I want to ask you."

Vivienne looks up from her post-Impressionist mapping. "Just fooling around here, boss. Whatever you need."

He looks over her shoulder, rocks back on his feet. "I'd say that's a lot more than fooling around. That's scholarship."

"Except I'm not getting too far." She points to the mess of crisscrossing and intersecting lines. "It's the links between the artists who started out as Impressionists and then created all the schools that came after. Is Gauguin a Symbolist or a Nabi? Or both? And did the Fauves emerge at essentially the same time as the Pointillists and the Symbolists? Or are they a later derivative of the other two? Perhaps three, including the Nabis?"

Edwin's forefinger follows the lines in her chart. "One of the problems is that you're representing each of these movements as single entities," he says. "Enclosing them within individual boxes. But the reality is more fluid. Maybe it's more like a bunch of wiggly amoebas overlapping and dripping into one another." He laughs. "Although I think I'm mixing my metaphors."

"Mixed metaphors or not, you're exactly right," Vivienne says, impressed, as always, with his ability to rapidly conceptualize and verbalize complex issues. "The problem is that I'm trying to break it down. To understand it. I want to know, to be able to explain to my students, what the parameters of post-Impressionism are. Where it starts and where it ends."

"Then you must oversimplify. You need to allow yourself to make choices that might not be one hundred percent correct but will get at the deeper truth you're trying to understand and teach."

She crosses out the boxes for Futurism, Divisionism, and German Expressionism, holds it out to him. "That streamlines it, but it leaves out these three important pieces, important influences . . ."

Edwin beams at her with pride. "You've come a long way since that morning in Paris two years ago, Vivienne Gregsby. Very far."

"I have a good teacher."

"Indeed you have." He steps toward the door, then turns and says with an uneasy casualness, "I was wondering if you might accompany me to dinner on Saturday evening. There's something important I want to discuss with you."

"I would be honored," she tells him.

THE NIGHT OF the dinner is cold for October, and Vivienne burrows inside her coat as Edwin drives them to a French restaurant she's heard of but never visited. A full-throated fire burns, throwing both heat and surges of orange light around the small room. The food is excellent and the service impeccable, but Vivienne can't relax. What does he want to talk to her about?

They drink an illegal but lovely French wine—Edwin drinks far more than she, as she's purposely taking small sips—and discuss the Matisse book, what to do with the sixty Soutines that just arrived, and their next visit to Paris, the timing of which depends on the court date for the lawsuit. He's in high spirits, and as the evening progresses he gazes at her with increasing fondness.

Over dessert, he says, "I was thinking about your post-Impressionist map, about what you're trying to achieve with it. To oversimplify, if the Impressionists broke with European tradition by focusing on light, then maybe the post-Impressionists broke with the Impressionists by emancipating color from its primarily descriptive role."

"That's all true, but somehow it seems too . . . too academic. What draws me is the pure and unnatural color, the rejection of perspective. The way the world is depicted as slightly oblique, askew, both more and less than it actually is. . . . How this . . . this somehow makes it all feel more real, more present. As if the artist has put himself and his feelings between what he sees and—"

"I love you."

Vivienne stops speaking. "What?"

"I have since that very first day I met you in Paris. When you told me what different colors smelled like."

"You have?"

"I know I'm much older than you, but I was hoping you might return my feelings. That we could be together."

"I . . . I had no idea. I don't know what to say . . ."

"Say what you think."

"I do care for you," she assures him. "Very much. You know I do. But this is so sudden. . . . And what about Ada?"

"This has nothing to do with Ada. She has her life and I have mine."

At least he isn't talking about divorce, and this gives her a gracious way to refuse him without insult. "I'm sorry, Edwin, but I can't get involved with a married man. I won't. It's not how I was raised."

"I'll get a divorce. I'll speak with Ada tonight, and then you and I can—"

"Divorce?" Vivienne interrupts before he can go any further. "That's . . . that's such a big step. Drastic even. I can't let you do this. You and Ada have been together for so many years. She's your wife. What would she do without you? Who would she be?"

But as she says the words, she wonders whether she's being too rash. Edwin is a handsome and accomplished man. Yes, he is much older, but he is vital, his intelligence prodigious, and he has great affection for art, as does she.

"There hasn't been anything between Ada and me for a long, long time," he says, interrupting her thoughts. "If ever."

"This is . . . is so much." What if she did marry him? She thinks of Henri, but he can't factor into her decision because she will never be a factor in his. She would become Edwin's wife, his heir. Perhaps she could persuade him to give her the colonnade seven as an engagement gift, to send her family money, maybe move them all to the States. Her mother would consider a marriage of convenience to a rich man a great accomplishment.

"What are you thinking?"

"I don't know what I'm thinking," she says truthfully. "It's so fast. And I'm flattered. Of course I am. I'm overwhelmed. Have to think. I think you should take me home now. Could you please take me home?"

He immediately signals the waiter for the check.

"I need to be alone," she adds quickly, afraid he misunderstood her request as a proposition. "It's so much so fast. So overwhelming," she stammers, and realizes she's repeating herself. "I never imagined. Never expected. I . . . I can't quite believe it."

When she reaches home, she closes the door behind her and slides to the floor. *Merde.* Married to Edwin Bradley. Obviously she doesn't love him, but she respects him, enjoys his company, and he has much to offer: companionship, safety, protection, the collection. . . .

The Mertens Museum of Post-Impressionism. Or perhaps, to be fair, the Bradley-Mertens Museum of Post-Impressionism. She, the owner and curator, a collector and philanthropist, known for her support of the arts. The twenty-three galleries simplified and streamlined, warm and engaging, filled not only with light and color and coherence but with people.

THE NEXT DAY, Edwin comes into her office looking both angry and nervous.

"What's wrong?" she asks.

He sits down on the corner of her desk, stretches his hand toward her. "Vivienne—"

She takes it, presses it between her own. Overnight she'd weighed the pros and cons and decided she's going to marry him. It's best for everyone: Edwin, herself, her family, the colonnade seven, the collection. If not for Ada. But from the look on Edwin's face, it appears this may not be her decision to make, which is simultaneously a blow and a reprieve.

"I'm not giving up."

"Giving up?"

"It's Ada." He falters. "She won't agree to a divorce. The Catholic thing. She claims it's impossible, that she'd be excommunicated, which I suppose she would."

Ada is meek and docile in most things, but Vivienne figures there's little chance she'll change her mind about this; a practicing Catholic is not about to mess with her immortal soul. "Wouldn't you be excommunicated, too?" she asks, because she doesn't know what else to say. Because she can't untangle her conflicted emotions.

"I converted for her and her goddamned mother. I don't give a rat's ass about their church. How the hell can you take a religion seriously when it's run by men who wear dresses?"

Vivienne bursts out laughing, glad for the release. "You've got a point there."

Edwin doesn't smile. "Once when we were having a quarrel, Ada told me if she had the opportunity, she'd sell off every piece of art to a different place because that would destroy what she called 'my fixation.' And now she says if I try to divorce her, she'll demand half the artwork—and then who knows what she might do with it."

"But she claimed she doesn't believe in divorce," Vivienne says. Then more tentatively, "You could call her bluff."

His face releases a bit. "Once again, we've come to the same conclusion. Soon we won't even need to speak."

The day after Edwin calls her bluff, Ada files for divorce on the grounds that he committed adultery. Even though there's obviously no concrete evidence, it will be a problem for Edwin to prove a negative. Ada also contends that Edwin has caused her to "suffer indignities." These indignities include denial of marital rights, mistreatment, and humiliation.

Ada's lawyer sets out the parameters of the compromise they're willing to make: in lieu of pressing the suit, Edwin and she must remain married and he will cease all "adulterous activities." Edwin will legally place the house and grounds in Merion as well as their country estate, Ker-Feal, in Ada's name. And she will receive half of everything Edwin has earned or acquired during their marriage in cash.

Edwin is fuming. "The 'in cash' piece," he explains to Vivienne, "would mean selling Bradley and Hagerty, the Bradley building, and at least half of the collection. Not acceptable!"

"Can she win?"

"It's possible. My lawyers say that even if she doesn't go much further, the cost of starting the litigation would be prohibitive."

"And?"

"We countered by accepting all her conditions except the cash demand."

"And?"

He hangs his head. "She agreed. I know we wanted to marry, but we'll still have the Bradley, our time together."

Vivienne inspects her fingernails. She'd come so close to fail this spectacularly. Gone in a flash. The colonnade seven, restitution, the collection. The Bradley-Mertens Museum.

"We can still continue our work." Edwin kneels, takes her hands. "The Bradley. The book. The school. It will be almost as if we're married. If you're willing to consider the . . . the other thing, it, well, it could be a good life for us."

Vivienne shakes him off and goes to stand at the window, her back to him, thinks about what George might do to recoup his losses. She watches the gardeners put the beds to sleep for the winter. It's melancholy work, pulling out ailing plants, slicing off yellowed leaves and browned flowers, covering bushes to protect them from the coming cold. "I will not be your paramour."

"You would be more than that."

"If that's what you think, you don't understand the meaning of the word." She faces him. "This is . . . it's . . . it's all so very awkward now. How can we continue as we were? Working together so closely? I . . . I can't be with you like that. I don't know anything about it. I've been saving myself for marriage . . ." She looks away from him. "Maybe . . . maybe it would be best if I leave."

"We'll go back to how things were," he protests. "Just as they were. I respect your choices, very much so, respect you for them. I won't push you, I promise. We'll let it be. But you can't leave. What would the Bradley do without you? What would I do without you?"

She turns to the window again. The gardeners rake the dead leaves and branches onto a large tarp, drag the load off to an already looming pile of the season's demise, return to fill it yet again. The days are growing short, the shadows of dusk leaning in by midafternoon.

"Please, Vivienne, tell me you won't leave us."

She doesn't respond. Just because they can't marry doesn't mean that she can't inherit the collection.

"Vivienne," he pleads.

She's silent for another full minute. Then she says in a throaty whisper, "How could I leave either you or the Bradley?"

18

GEORGE/BENJAMIN/ASHTON, 1925

Damn the bitter losers. Damn the jealous liars. Damn the mealymouthed investors with their lack of confidence and misplaced suspicions. None of his businesses have ever failed. He's always been the one to close them down—on his own terms. This is a slap in the face. Sudden, sharp, and surprising.

He slams his empty scotch glass down hard on the table and walks to the window, gazing out at Central Park from a tenth-floor room in the hotel where he registered under yet another assumed name. He has also washed the gray out of his hair, bought a pair of spectacles, and begun to grow a beard.

The park is denuded, harsh, and barren. The few walkers are hunched over, pushing against the wind into the deepening shadows of winter's early dusk. He'll find whoever started the rumor that Steel Bearings, Inc.—the largest company held by Talcott Reserves—was on the verge of bankruptcy. And he'll make him pay. The stock market is rising and the economy is booming, so why would anyone believe that one of the largest manufacturers of ball bearings in the United States is in financial trouble? Damn it all to hell.

But all his damning changes nothing. It happened. It's done. Talcott Reserves is gone—and so are the millions of dollars he poured into the business, not to mention the millions more in profits he expected to reap over the next two years. He has barely enough stashed away in Switzerland to start a new venture.

Talcott Reserves had grown more slowly than he anticipated, and he wasn't able to pull out as much money as usual. He was obligated to leave a sufficient amount of cash in the New York account for those clients who might want to take some profits. An amount that would have been adequate if he'd had the additional time he needed to recoup the early losses.

And that's exactly what would have happened if someone hadn't egged on his four biggest investors, who began sniffing around and then all showed up at his offices last week demanding their money. Of which there wasn't nearly enough on hand. What was, in all his previous endeavors, a sufficient reserve was suddenly not sufficient at all.

Betty, his fetching secretary, poured each of the investors a glass of twenty-year-old scotch while he happily wrote hefty checks against a balance that couldn't cover them. Then he walked the men out, joking about how sorry they were going to be to lose the forecasted Talcott Reserves profits and chitchatting about the trips they all needed to take to the Caribbean or Monaco for respite from the winter weather. As soon as the men disappeared behind the elevator doors, he nonchalantly picked up his coat, told Betty he would be back in an hour, and left. For good.

Now they're all looking for him: the investors, the banks, the police, and, needless to say, Katherine, the unfortunate jilted lover. In truth, except for the financial losses, his situation is exactly the same as it was when he walked away from Everard Sureties or any of his other businesses. He's a master at eluding the law and reinventing himself. He'll just disappear and start a new enterprise somewhere else. He's done it before, and no one has caught him yet.

Although he won't have the ease of unlimited funds, he has more than enough for the setup, and there are many possibilities: the gem scam involving tourists and fake jewels, veneer salting involving bricks covered with a thin layer of gold, a wire swindle involving fake bookies and casinos. But he's partial to the type of scheme he's had so much success with. It worked for Wesson Investments and Everard Sureties and Talcott Reserves, the latter's failure having nothing to do with him or his management skills—just some jerk with an ax to grind. All he needs to do is find the right setup to make it work again.

He watches a little girl, wearing a ragged coat far too large for her, lift her mouth to the sky and stick out her tongue to catch the snow that has started to fall. Her mother tugs on her arm, forcing her forward, and the child begins to cry. The mother lifts her, snaps her onto her hip, and proceeds briskly down the sidewalk. Rushing home to make a paltry dinner of potatoes and a few scraps of meat? To a tiny apartment and a husband who has a lousy job and drinks too much? A life he escaped and has no plans to return to.

This time he'll go for something tangible. Not cash or stocks. Diamonds are an option, as is gold, but these are too common and don't interest him. Perhaps paintings? He's learned a little about art from both Katherine and Paulien, and it would be fun to develop yet another area of expertise. He'll create a company that buys up fine art and then sell shares of its future value. He can already see himself whispering in a few select ears that art is an investment far more solid than putting money in the stock market or in a bank: its value always goes up.

He'll rent a warehouse and fill it with art, invite prospective customers to verify the many major pieces he has there. But even at bargain-basement prices, that much artwork will be excessively expensive. Below him, a couple of men stagger down the street, obviously drunk, probably from that bootleg whiskey that rips out stomach linings and leaves the poor bastards blind. He stares after them. What if the paintings are fake?

Forged art costs far less than real art, a fraction. He flips on a few electric lights and draws the curtains, enclosing his elegant suite in a cozy glow. It could work. He'll hire quality forgers—there are more than enough hungry artists to choose from—purchase supplies, rent spaces for work, storage, offices. He strides through the rooms, consumed by the energy a new idea always brings.

He'll go to Paris, scope out the prospects. Everyone in Paris thinks they know and appreciate good art, although few actually do. Paris is perfect, and his French is impeccable. He sits in an oversize wing chair, rests his feet on the ottoman, and lights a cigarette.

He will need to buy some genuine paintings first, some by the old masters, some by the post-Impressionist and Abstract artists who are becoming all the rage: Cézanne, Matisse, Picasso. The ones Paulien is so keen on. The purchases will establish his credibility and contacts as well as provide the artwork to display to his marks. The fakes will be stored in an area of the warehouse where the lighting is poor, but their sheer numbers will impress. Brilliant.

Now, who should he become? He's been British, American, and Canadian, preferring English language countries even though his gift for languages and accents is remarkable. Australian. That would work. An Aussie, hard to trace. An art collector and businessman, scads of inherited money.

Australians, like the British, have solid surnames as well as given names, and this appeals to him because they are nothing like the name on his own birth certificate. Lots of Smiths and Joneses and Robinsons. King is a common Australian name, and he likes what it implies, especially paired with a virile first name like Cooper or Ashton or Braxton. Ashton King has a nice ring. He'll become Ashton King, well-to-do art collector known for his excellent eye.

He thinks of Paulien Mertens, or more correctly, Vivienne Gregsby. She's now Edwin Bradley's highest-ranking employee and lives just outside Philadelphia. He saw her at a performance of the Philadelphia Orchestra last year, then again at the Statler while dining with Katherine's family. He's gone to Merion a few times, followed her to the Bradley, and then followed her home. She used to be an artist, was raised by an art collector, and is now working for one. He's good. So damn good.

He decides he'll stick around the States a little longer, shadow Paulien for another few weeks, prepare for their accidental meeting and figure out how to make the best use of her.

19

PAULIEN, 1921–1922

Paulien was completing her final studio project at the Slade. It was a series of London street scenes in pastels: one from the east-facing window of her flat in the morning; one from the south-facing windows at midday; the third from the west in the late afternoon; and the fourth a north view she worked on at night, dragging her easel to the roof.

She was trying to create works like Matisse's and Cézanne's, full of color and somewhat abstracted and flattened, a different way of seeing the usually gray and cloudy city. The paintings weren't nearly as good as she had hoped, although her teacher was vaguely encouraging. It would have been fun to have more talent, but becoming a painter wasn't her ambition. Becoming an extraordinary art collector was.

"I've been thinking that taking over the Mertens collection isn't going to be enough to keep me busy at first," she told George as they shared dinner at a bistro near her apartment. "Not until my father is ready to sell some of the traditional artwork so there's money to start the museum. He seems reluctant—although that's what we'd always planned—and now that school is almost over, there's going to be a big hole with nothing to fill it. I need to do something else."

"How about being my wife?" George asked, pretending to be wounded. "That's not filling?"

She leaned over and kissed him lightly. "That's a very full future, but I want to be more than my mother with her vapid parties and endless changing of clothes. Something more challenging. More interesting."

"I like your mother."

"That's because you both like vapid parties."

"Are you calling our wedding vapid?"

"Maybe not vapid, but you've got to admit the preparations are end-less—and all the costume changes will be, too."

He grazed the inside of her wrist with his lips, and the facets of her engagement ring threw prisms of light. "Do you want to elope, doll? We could do it tomorrow if that's what you'd really like."

Paulien did. More than she would let him know. Another year seemed both interminable and unnecessary. But she'd promised him a big party, and she wasn't going back on her promise, especially when she saw a trace of worry cross his eyes. "No, my darling," she said. "Let's do it your way. Let's do it up right."

George leaned back and lifted his wineglass. "To long engagements."

They gazed into each other's eyes, smiling, and resumed their dinner.

"What about curating?" he asked. "For a museum."

"Because I studied studio art, I don't have the right training. It would be years before I'd be able to do anything interesting . . ."

"You could go back to school for a degree in art history."

"I thought about that. But I want to do something more active, more participatory."

"So what are you thinking, my little minx?"

"What about an art gallery? I'd be buying and selling and finding new talent. It's just what I need to prepare, to get ready to build the collection." She hesitated. "Would that be all right with you? To have a wife who works?"

"Of course it would. I'm proud of you for wanting more. And you'll be wonderful at it."

"Nothing too fancy or expensive," she continued. "No one too established, up-and-coming would be the best. Where art is going, not where it's been. Where the post-Impressionists are pushing new artists to go."

"We can rent space on the edge of a nice neighborhood," George suggested. "Not too highbrow, not too lowbrow. A place all kinds of people will feel comfortable visiting. Where there aren't a lot of other galleries. But maybe where there are a lot of artists. Where do the teachers at the Slade live? We could—"

"No. Not yet. I can't get ahead of myself. I'm not ready. I've got to learn more. I have no idea how to go about setting up a gallery—let alone how to run one."

"I could find someone to help you. Someone with experience in the business. I'm sure I must know—"

"I think I need to work in a gallery first. See all sides of it for myself— the things that turn out well and the things that don't. Get my hands dirty." She looked at the paint under her fingernails. "So to speak."

He pulled her toward him, kissing her longer and harder than could be considered appropriate in a public place. "You're the most amazing girl I have ever met."

She pushed him away. "Let's skip dessert."

Two weeks after graduation, Paulien had a position at the Whitechapel Gallery in Tower Hamlets. George, naturally, had a friend on the board of directors who was more than happy to find a place for her. Everyone was more than happy to do a favor for George Everard.

It wasn't the type of business she had in mind. The Whitechapel was publicly funded, and in that sense it was more like a museum than a gallery. But it had no permanent collection, only temporary exhibitions, the way a private gallery would. And it was turning out to be a grand training ground, especially for learning how to find and nurture artists, which was exactly what Paulien needed to learn. Along with almost everything else.

Their plan was to marry in August, now only five months away, honeymoon through September, and return to London at the beginning of October. She would work another year or two for Whitechapel and then open Mertens Everard Art.

Life couldn't have been more glorious and became even more so after her parents' visit. On the last evening of their stay, Papa hosted a five-course dinner just for the four of them in his suite at the Langham. Paulien was already bloated from a week of rich food and champagne, but she dressed in the new gown she'd bought with her mother that afternoon, and she and George, so handsome in his tux, glided across the hotel's ornate lobby and took the elevator to the penthouse.

Over scotch and cigars, her father presented George with a list of his business associates and friends, including himself, who wished to invest in Everard Sureties. George scanned the names while her father explained the background of each man, each one more successful and influential than the last. Paulien listened with only half an ear to her mother, who was catching her up on a scandalous piece of Brussels gossip that she'd learned from a letter she'd received that afternoon.

When Paulien looked over at the men, George was shaking his head. "I'm sorry, but it's not a good time," he was saying. "I have more money than I can make use of at the moment. It's frustrating, but I can't seem to find enough Italian runners who can be entrusted with what is essentially a cash business. And without them, I can turn over only a limited number of IRCs."

"Having too much money is an uncommon situation for a businessman," Papa said, trying for a joking tone.

"As you know, we're a volume venture," George explained. "The greater the amount that goes in, the greater the amount that comes out. I could make more money for everyone, including myself, if I could just hire more hands."

"Maybe I can help," her father offered.

Paulien listened more carefully.

"I have a number of associates in Rome," Papa said. "In textiles and other areas as well. How about if I ask them to help you find men who could be trusted with such a job?"

George's face lit up. "If you mean it, I'll take you up on it right this minute."

"I absolutely mean it." He turned and looked at Paulien affectionately. "Why wouldn't I want to help the man who's going to marry my beautiful little girl?"

"And why wouldn't I want to help the father of the beautiful girl I'm going to marry?" George countered. "I'll accept whatever monies you'd personally like to invest—and as soon as we find a few more men in Italy, you can tell your friends I'll welcome their investments as well."

20

VIVIENNE, 1925

Edwin's lawyer's motion to continue is granted, and the trial is postponed until spring, which allows Vivienne and Edwin to return to Paris in early February. It's grand to be away from Ada, whose hostile vigilance weighs heavily, and it's just as grand to be away from the Bradley, whose demands are equally daunting. Although Edwin agreed they would return to their earlier relationship, he's overly concerned with her comings and goings in ways that befit a lover rather than an employer. But she must step carefully if she's to convince him that she's the only one who can bring his plans for the Bradley's future to fruition.

She's not surprised when Edwin tells her he's coming to the first interview with Henri. Henri is gracious when they arrive, although it's obvious he's disappointed. So is she. Henri keeps shooting her meaningful glances, which she dodges as best she can. Becoming Edwin's heir is more important than flirting with a ladies' man, but Henri isn't easy to resist. The three of them spend the afternoon sitting close together, reviewing the outline and pages she's already written. At one point, Henri throws his arm casually over the back of her chair. She pretends she doesn't notice.

It gets even more knotty when Henri shows them some of his new work, most of it from his series of oil-on-canvas paintings of odalisques: *Odalisque with a Green Plant and Screen*, *Odalisque*, and *Odalisque with Magnolias*. Without realizing what she's doing, she reaches out and touches his shoulder. "They're magnificent," she breathes.

Edwin turns from the paintings and gives her a sharp look.

Vivienne drops her hand and steps away from Henri. She can feel the heat of him as she can feel the heat of his paintings. Although inspired by the more staid nineteenth-century works depicting maids and concubines of Turkish royalty, these are pure Matisse: a touch of flatness and abstraction, full of color, bursting with eroticism.

How could anyone not be drawn to such a man? She remembers their kisses, lingers on what might have been, on what still might be. What George awakened cannot be put back to sleep.

A WEEK LATER, Gertrude sends a note asking Vivienne to join her for lunch at La Fermette Marbeuf, one of the finest restaurants in the city. Vivienne has no idea what prompted the invitation, but from the formality and the location she guesses her friend has more than a sociable meal on her mind.

Gertrude, her face obscured by a massive menu, is already seated when Vivienne enters the famed room with its mirrors and stained glass, its immense ceiling a tapestry of wrought iron supporting painted windows. She'd come here often as a child on visits to Paris, and these windows were always the highlight. As usual, she carefully checks the room before entering, although her apprehension has lessened. It's been three years, and most people are more concerned with themselves than with the long-ago lapses of others.

When she reaches the table, Gertrude lowers her menu. "You can't fool me, Vivienne Gregsby," she declares. "I want to know what's going on, and I want to know it now."

Vivienne sits and gazes guilelessly at her friend. "What are you talking about?" She throws in a laugh that sounds awkward to her ears—and must to Gertrude's.

Gertrude crosses her arms over her chest and looks at Vivienne with her unwavering gaze. "Fess up, sister."

Vivienne lights a cigarette. "I don't know what you want me to confess to." Gertrude found out about Paulien. *Merde.*

"How about that you and Bradley aren't just boss and assistant anymore?"

Vivienne is concentrating so hard on acquitting herself in the Paulien situation that it takes her a moment to realize what Gertrude is referring to. "Oh, of course we are." She laughs. "Why? Do you think I've been fired?"

"You can deny it all you want, but I know something's going on." Gertrude gives the hovering waiter a crisp nod. "I don't want to spoil my appetite, so let's eat before we talk about it."

Two bowls of consommé appear, and they discuss Scott Fitzgerald's latest novel, *The Beautiful and Damned*, through that course as well as the oysters and pâté that follow.

"It's all about him and Zelda," Gertrude declares. "A woman who only wants to marry a rich man, and an alcoholic man waiting around to get rich—now who does that sound like to you?"

"Perhaps," Vivienne says. "But I think it's more than that. A morality tale about love and decadence, don't you think? It seems like he's showing us there's no running from the past. That it always follows you." She winces as she articulates this thought. "That you need to come to terms with it before you can move into your future."

"Hmmm." Gertrude's eyes narrow. "So there's something you're running from? Something from the past that's got its snares into you? That won't let go until you beat it back?"

Vivienne shrugs. "Why should I be any different from anyone else?"

Gertrude gives her a look that implies she'll return to this topic at another time. "So is that why you're with Bradley? Is he going to help you shed your past? Or maybe protect you from it?"

"I'm not 'with him,' as you well know," Vivienne says. "I work for him. It's a good job."

"There's more to it than that. He's got some kind of hold on you."

"He's my boss, and being here is an oppor—"

"Horseshit," Gertrude declares. "He fawns all over you and you let him. What does he have that you want so much? Money? Art? Not to mention that he's way too old for you—and as sexless as a rock."

"You make him sound so appealing. Which in many ways he is."

"Really? Are you going to claim that's why you're having an affair with him?"

"Edwin and I are not having an affair."

"So you say." Gertrude shoots her a peevish frown. "But what I want to know is why you're lowering yourself to his level."

"Lowering myself? Given Edwin's many accomplishments, I'd say that he's the one who's lowering himself to mine."

"Aha!" Gertrude's eyes glint. "If you're not having an affair, how could he be lowering himself?"

"You're twisting my words."

"Just because he's managed to buy himself into prominence doesn't mean he's accomplished."

"Are you kidding? That man is a visionary. He started out with nothing. Became a doctor, a chemist, a successful business—"

"How about the way he treats people?"

"As I'm sure you're aware, people are more complicated than they seem. I bet you don't know that Edwin gives his factory workers, mostly Negroes, two hours off every day—paid, I might add—five days a week, to learn about art, do you? That he's a big supporter of rights for—"

"You should be with Henri."

"He's married."

"So is Edwin."

"I'm not—"

"Henri's in desperate need of a companion," Gertrude interrupts. "Fulfilling his greatness is more important than giving Negroes art lessons, wouldn't you say? And what you get from Henri will be far better than anything you believe you're going to get from an old man like Bradley. Mark my words, in the end you'll get nothing from him. You should take up with Matisse."

"Henri's older than I am, too."

"Not nearly as much—and no one would ever say he's sexless."

Vivienne thinks back to the soft give of Henri's lips, to the trail of kisses down her neck.

"Do you find him attractive?"

"I'm guessing any woman he flirts with finds him attractive. And that number has got to be in the hundreds, probably thousands."

"True." Gertrude chortles. "But you'd be perfect for him—and maybe he could help you with that past you're running from."

"I'm not running from anything."

"The wife's not as important as she used to be. They're hardly ever in the same city at the same time anymore."

"That doesn't—"

"He told me you have the soul of an artist, the mind of an intellectual, and the face of an angel."

"I'm sure I'm not the only woman he's described that way," Vivienne says. The great Henri Matisse said that about her? Henri said that about her. She concentrates on carefully slicing her chicken to avoid looking at Gertrude.

Gertrude barks a loud laugh, clearly enjoying both Vivienne's discomfort and what that discomfort confirms. "He wants you, he told me so. I've known him a long time, and I can see how lonely he is. I worry it's going to affect his work—you wouldn't want that to happen, now would you? He needs stimulation, companionship, a muse."

"I'm not the muse type. I've got my job, and now I've got a book to write. Why would I give that up to have an affair with a married man who's a notorious playboy?"

"Just don't forget that you're not a straitlaced American," Gertrude cautions. "Or that he's Henri Matisse."

OVER THE PARIS winter, Vivienne and Edwin are busy working together on the book, buying art, developing new curricula, preparing for the Bradley's future. She's the perfect assistant: conscientious, supportive, a boost to his ego. If it weren't for his suspicions about Henri, she's sure he would be close to naming her as his successor.

One afternoon when they're working in the living room of Edwin's suite, which the hotel has turned into an office for him, Edwin receives a letter from Bill Glackens. Bill says he's heard rumors that both the University of Pennsylvania and the Philadelphia Museum of Art, along with Thomas Quinton, have been pressuring the district attorney general's office to pursue the lawsuit.

"I'm going to get them, and get them good!" Edwin declares.

Vivienne tries to pacify him, but he'll have none of it. "They're all going to be sorry they tried to mess with me!"

She waits.

"A ruse," he tells her. "I've been thinking about this for a while, and now I'm going to do it. When we get home, I'll have them all running around over nothing! Make fools of the whole pack of them."

"A ruse?" This didn't sound good.

"I'm going to tell Penn I'm bequeathing the collection to them when I die. And then when the university does something to annoy me—which I'm certain it will—I'll reverse myself and claim the museum is the beneficiary. And when the PMA backstabs me, I'll make it even more insulting and announce that I'm leaving it to you."

"Me?" she repeats, as if the idea had never crossed her mind. "You can't leave the collection to me."

"Why not?"

"I don't have the credentials or—"

"That will make it all the more insulting," he says triumphantly. "Not a school or a museum. Not a relative or even a man. Just some girl. An Englishgirl, to boot. And who knows what you might do with it? You could move the whole kit and caboodle to London." Then he adds, "Only you and I know what an excellent choice you actually are."

A very promising development.

Yet for all his hypothetical trust in her, he continues to come to the sessions with Henri. For the most part, Henri behaves himself, although it's clear his frustration is growing. He's luminous and fascinating, and the way he thinks about art is almost as amazing as the art he creates. Vivienne is completely smitten. Edwin watches them warily, subtly and not so subtly inserting himself between them.

On the day before their last interview, Edwin's art dealer Paul Guillaume insists that Edwin accompany him to Arles. An estate is being sold off by heritors in need of quick cash, and it includes some Derains, Vlamincks, and Renoirs. Edwin is reluctant to leave Vivienne alone with Henri, but his wish to obtain the paintings at a good price bests his jealousy.

"What is this nonsense Gertrude tells me?" Henri demands as soon as she arrives for the interview.

"And hello to you, too, Monsieur Matisse. May I come in so that the entire city isn't privy to this inquisition?"

"I am not at all certain that you should," he replies petulantly.

"And anyway," she adds, "I'm here to work, not to discuss my personal life."

He leads her into his colorful sitting room and motions her into the settee. "Is it true?"

"You sound just like your friend Gertrude with your enigmatic questions. What exactly are you talking about?"

He sits down next to her. "If you are aware I am speaking about your personal life, than you know what I am asking."

She can't help laughing. "Edwin and I are not having an affair. Never have. Never will."

"Gertrude doesn't believe you, and I am not sure that I do either. I see how he watches you, how he responds to me when you and I are together. Why would you get involved in such a thing?"

"I told you, I'm not."

Henri scowls. "He is too old for you."

"You're not all that much younger than he is."

"I am younger, but chronological age is irrelevant." Henri points to his heart. "In here is what matters. Bradley was an old man on the day he was born, and I have always been—and always will be—young."

There's no denying this—or that it's one of the things she finds so attractive about him. She compares the delightful messiness of the room with Edwin's fanatically symmetrical and perfectly aligned ensembles. "It's not that he's old, it's that he's serious minded. But not all the time. We laugh."

"I have known Bradley for far longer than you, and I do not understand why you would want to waste your youth on an old man with no sense of humor and the passion of a rock."

"I'm not wasting anything because I'm not doing anything! And anyway, Edwin has many qualities that neither you nor Gertrude know anything—"

"You naughty girl!" Henri hoots. "I had no idea he was so well endowed."

"That's not what I meant and you know it." Nonetheless, a flush rises to her cheeks, and Henri's hoot turns into full-throated hilarity. It's irresistible, and soon they're folded over with laughter in a reenactment of the first time she was at his apartment.

When they finally calm, he says, "I bet you do not laugh with Edwin like this."

She doesn't answer, because it's true. Instead she bends to get her notebook.

He reaches over and lightly presses his forefinger to a spot between her jaw and ear. She pulls her head back, but not quickly enough. She could do this, just a dalliance, just for fun, just because her body wants it. But she's afraid her feelings for Henri are more than a dalliance—and that she's just another potential conquest to him. She won't twice be made a fool.

"Not only will we laugh together, *chérie*," Henri whispers, his breath warm on her throat, "but I have many things to share with you that I know you will enjoy even more."

She moves to a chair across from the settee and clears her throat. "I'm working on the chapter about your time at Belle Île with John Peter Russell in the late eighteen nineties. Can you tell me how this affected your style?"

Henri gives an exaggerated sigh and says, "Russell explained color theory to me, and after that everything changed."

"Can you expand on that? Are you talking about his color wheel? Or do you mean his insight that the juxtaposition of a color and its complement makes the intersection sizzle?"

"You look very beautiful today." He picks up a sketchbook and a piece of charcoal. "Green suits you."

"I'm going back to Philadelphia in a few days. We've got a lot of ground to cover before I leave if we're ever going to get this book done."

"Turn your head a touch toward me," he orders.

She hesitates, then puts down her notebook and does as he asks. Henri Matisse wants to draw her. What else can she do?

"You have the coloring of a blond. So mysterious against your dark hair."

"Like your odalisques?" Vivienne asks quickly. She shifts in her seat.

"Do not move!" he cries. "Stay exactly as you are. The light across your right cheek is perfect."

The morning sun is warm on her face and shoulder, as is the intensity of his gaze. At first she's stiff, nervous even, but as in her days as a model, soon her concerns and self-consciousness begin to melt. She loses herself within a piece of silk thrown over the back of the settee; it's a purplish blue and shimmers like a school of fish in flight, alive and full of motion while remaining perfectly still.

After what might have been five minutes or fifty, Henri stands and comes toward her. He kneels, brings his eyes level with her. "I want you," he says.

Vivienne doesn't move.

He smiles, stands, and reaches out his hand to her. She takes it, allows him to pull her up. She's shaky and her thighbones are so weak she can barely stand. Henri's eyes don't leave hers, and neither of them says a word.

He leads her into his bedroom and they enfold themselves into each other's arms. This time, Vivienne doesn't pull away. Instead she helps him undress her, and he helps her undress him. They fit together perfectly, move together perfectly, understand each other's wants without speaking. Communicating with their mouths and their hands and their bodies. Their locked eyes.

21

VIVIENNE, 1925

May in Philadelphia isn't May in Paris, but it's still delightful, and the Bradley grounds are an eruption of color and new life. Horticulture is Ada's passion, and while she's planted the area surrounding the building with magnificent Japanese maples and clusters of painted ferns, what impresses Vivienne most are the southern plants Ada has coaxed into growing in Pennsylvania.

She imagines Henri beside her, his arm on hers. They breathe in the lemony fragrance of the creamy magnolias, the liquorish scent of the camellia blossoms, and the almond honey of the powder-puff mimosas. They stroll among the topiaries, the cascading roses, their conversation exhilarating, stimulating. Juxtaposing contrasting colors does make them sizzle. Pure and bright colors do produce passion. But her arm is empty, and she only has herself to talk to.

In the evenings she lies in bed thinking about him, missing him, wondering how long it will be before she sees him again. She relives their lovemaking, her body more easily aroused now than when she had gone three years without. She's only twenty-two and needs to be with a man.

She wonders if she means more to him than his usual conquests do, wonders how much he means to her, then scolds herself for the questions. Henri is a flirt and a playboy.

Words are easy, flowing glibly from the mouths of men who want far more than they're telling, willing to give far less than they're promising. She can't trust him. Can't trust herself. She isn't ready, doesn't know if she ever will be. The pain of George's desertion, the fictiveness of all she so foolishly believed, is too raw. And it happened because she fell in love, let herself go, which rendered her incapable of seeing.

THE HEARING FOR the suit to open the Bradley to the public is held on a sweltering day at the Montgomery County Courthouse in Norristown. The gracious building, fronted by Ionic columns and topped by a dome embedded with clocks, looks solid and serious, judicial and fair minded. Inside, however, it gives the opposite impression. The heat wave is stretching into its fifth day, and the air, weighted with moisture, reeks of age and despair. Despite the building's high ceilings and wide corridors, the temperature has to be hovering in the eighties.

Vivienne presses a handkerchief to her face as she follows Edwin and his lawyer, Jacob Gusdorff, along a circuitous route through the building. After working with Edwin on the case for months, she's still disconcerted to be rooting against him. But he's holding the wrong hand; art is meant to be shared.

They enter a small, windowless hearing room. A single fan sitting on the judge's bench pushes the hot air around, cooling no one. Edwin and Jacob settle at their table, and Vivienne takes a seat behind Edwin. Daniel Martin, the assistant district attorney, and his associate are at the matching table across the aisle.

The judge is overweight and sweating so profusely that Vivienne fears he might be ill. He mops his red face with a damp handkerchief and frowns at the lawyers. "Please begin," he grumbles. "And please get right to the point."

Martin stands. "The Bradley was awarded tax-exempt status because it claimed to provide a service to the good people of Montgomery County," he begins, his voice coated with disdain. "Unfortunately, Your Honor, this has not been the case.

"The so-called Bradley School of Art Appreciation is a privately owned building containing a private art collection. Both are controlled by

Edwin Bradley, who uses them solely for his own purposes. Dr. Bradley has perpetrated a fraud on the trusting, tax-paying citizens of the great Commonwealth of Pennsylvania, and he cannot be allowed to continue this charade!"

The judge wipes his face again and sluggishly moves his hand through the air. "No theatrics please, Mr. Martin. It's too damn hot."

Martin shoots his cuffs. "Your Honor, the Bradley is not a school, as it contends. It employs teachers without expertise in the field, does not award grades or diplomas, has no consistent curriculum, and uses an arbitrary admission process that has more to do with Dr. Bradley's whims than with any impartial standard. Our own esteemed University of Pennsylvania would not allow its students to study there, owing—and rightly so—to its inferior staff and lack of accreditation."

Martin pauses for effect, and the judge throws him an irritable glance. "But this is only one-half of our complaint," he resumes. "The Bradley is currently not functioning as a museum either. Only a small number of Dr. Bradley's friends are allowed to view the collection, and there has not been a single instance in which a person not favored by the doctor has been allowed entrance.

"It is the commonwealth's contention that, in order to maintain its tax-exempt status, the Bradley must function as either a school or a museum—if not both. As it fails to conform to the requirements for either, we propose that it be ordered to open its doors to the public for a minimum of six days a week. Either that, or Dr. Bradley must pay taxes on his property like every other law-abiding citizen of this great commonwealth!" He sits down and mops his own face.

"Mr. Gusdorff?"

Jacob stands and smiles at the judge. "I will keep it short and sweet, Your Honor. The Bradley School of Art Appreciation was awarded tax-exempt status because it meets the legal definition of a school, which is 'a place or establishment of instruction.'

"A variety of courses are offered to hundreds of students each year at the school. These classes are taught by trained and qualified educators who use the collection's artworks to aid in their instruction. No grades or diplomas are given because that is not, and never was, the school's mission. The objective of its educational curriculum is the acquisition of the skills needed to appreciate art, not the acquisition of a piece of paper. This was true from the first day it opened, and it will always be such."

Vivienne watches the judge's face, but his eyes are closed and his mouth clenched in a firm line, so there isn't much to give away his thoughts.

"As to Mr. Martin's contention that the Bradley isn't a museum," Jacob continues, "I completely agree: it is not a museum, nor was it ever meant to be. Dr. Bradley purchased the artwork himself, paid for and built a building to house the collection, and is the single benefactor funding its educational operations. There is no violation of the law here. Dr. Bradley is not committing fraud. He is running a school. Just as he promised he would. Just as the commonwealth expected him to do."

They *are* running a school. Jacob is too damn good.

The judge slowly opens his eyes and watches Jacob take his seat. The silence grows as oppressive as the heat. "Mr. Gusdorff," he finally says, "what's your response to Mr. Martin's contention that the Bradley School doesn't fit this criterion because it's unaccredited?"

Jacob smiles serenely. "Your Honor, when Mr. Martin refers to the Bradley School's lack of accreditation as outlined by the University of Pennsylvania, he's speaking of the university's contention that the school is not an accredited *college*. This is true, and I will add that the Bradley School of Art Appreciation never attempted to, nor wanted to, be such. As is clear from its name, it is a *school* teaching art appreciation—nothing more and nothing less."

The judge flips through a pile of files in front of him, presses his handkerchief to his face. "I've read the Bradley trust agreement as well as the papers granting it tax-exempt status." He pauses. "Nothing that's been said today convinces me that it is not in compliance with these regulations. It is clearly a school and therefore is under no obligation to either pay any additional taxes or open to the public." He languidly hits the gavel. "Case dismissed."

Vivienne closes her eyes in defeat. The only way the Bradley collection will ever be shared with the world is if she makes it happen.

EDWIN COMES INTO her office the following week. "Ada accused me of breaking our contract. She claims you and I were 'together' in Paris." His voice is as unruffled as if they were discussing the day's mail.

Vivienne lights two cigarettes, hands him one. "What did you tell her?"

"I told her no." He raises an eyebrow. "Not that I don't wish it were true."

"She didn't believe you?" Vivienne asks, ignoring his inference.

"She forgot all about it when I told her I changed my will and made you my beneficiary. Apparently this is more upsetting than being cheated on."

"Why lie about that?"

"No lie. I signed the papers last week."

Vivienne worries he can see her heart pounding through the thin cotton of her blouse. "You did?"

"I did."

"But . . . but why now?"

He blows smoke at the ceiling, coughs a few times, hesitates as if he has something difficult to tell her, and then says, "I could have an accident. A heart attack. Quinton's suit made me realize that I can't take the chance of the collection ending up with anyone but you."

"Thank you, Edwin," she says. "Thank you so much. I promise I'll live up to your expectations. But"—she smiles at him—"you're so damn cantankerous, you'll probably live to be a hundred. You'll probably outlast me."

"Cantankerous, am I?" he interrupts with mock indignation. "Take that back, woman!"

"I cannot tell a lie."

"Not even a little one?"

When Vivienne shakes her head, Edwin knocks on her desk and walks down the hall, whistling. She tries to keep her expression neutral in case he returns. She made it happen, albeit with a little know-how acquired from George. She's the beneficiary, the successor. The collection will be hers. She'll be able to return her father's paintings, focus the vision, open the Bradley and its multitude of masterpieces to the world community of art lovers. Of course, she'll have to wait for Edwin to die. She wonders how long this could take and hates herself for the thought.

EDWIN CALLS FOR a dinner for fifty to celebrate his court victory, and he taps Ada to oversee it. Although Ada is rarely involved in Bradley events, Edwin deems this more social than business, and he knows Vivienne dislikes lavish displays. Ada is pleased with both herself and the task, clearly believing it signifies Edwin's reliance on her and his loss of interest in replacing her with Vivienne.

The dinner party is far too excessive for Vivienne's tastes, reminiscent of the affairs orchestrated by George or her mother: the china and heavy silver; the harp and the flutes; the vintage wines; the gowned women and tuxedoed men, all overly impressed with themselves. She's glad she has her role representing the Bradley, which she much prefers to hovering over the chef and waiters. And she's basking in her new, if secret, status as heir.

Edwin appears happy with the proceedings, drinking scotch and mingling with his guests. He comes up to her often during the cocktail hour, introduces her to the few she doesn't know. Extols her virtues. "My esteemed colleague," he calls her.

"The Bradley wouldn't be the Bradley without her," he confesses to Bill Glackens, the post-Impressionist painter who introduced him to art collecting. Then he puts his arm around her shoulders. "I honestly don't know where I'd be without her."

As always, Vivienne and Ada studiously ignore each other, and Vivienne isn't surprised when she's seated as far from Edwin as possible. Vivienne is surprised, however, when Ada comes toward her just as dessert is being served, a man with a distinctly British air in tow.

"This is Mr. Terence S. Williamson," Ada says with a perky smile. "He's an artist. From London."

Vivienne stands and holds out her hand, wondering what Ada is up to. "I'm Vivienne Gregsby."

"Lovely to meet you, Miss Gregsby," he says with an accent that could come only from a childhood in Liverpool.

"You went to the Slade School of Fine Art, didn't you, Vivienne?" Ada asks sweetly. "You said from 1920 to 1922, if I'm not mistaken?"

Vivienne never told Ada anything about her life in England, but perhaps Edwin did. "Yes," she admits.

"Well, so did Mr. Williamson." Ada frowns. "And he claims he doesn't remember anyone called Gregsby there at the time."

"There were lots of students passing through," Vivienne says as smoothly as she can. "It would be tough to remember everyone— especially me, as I kept pretty much to myself."

"And I have got a bad noggin for names," Terence says, clearly uncomfortable with the situation. "Our mum was always saying."

A chill freezes Vivienne. Not because of what he said, but because she recognizes his voice: Scotty Williamson. He called himself Scotty then, not Terence S. A sculptor, if she remembers correctly, a good one. He dated her friend Bernice.

Scotty shifts back and forth on his feet.

"But it couldn't have been that big," Ada exclaims. "I can't imagine that you two wouldn't have at least run into each other."

Vivienne sits back down, picks up a spoon, and pulls her dessert toward her, hoping Ada and Scotty will leave before he gets a closer look at her face. But she senses he's studying her. Far too carefully.

"Paulien!" he cries. "I do know you. You're Paulien Mertens." He hesitates. "Aren't you?"

Vivienne tosses her hair in the same exaggerated manner she used when Antoinette Lavigne recognized her at Gertrude's. "Nope," she says, dipping her spoon into the parfait. When neither Scotty nor Ada responds, she smiles and adds, "I'm pretty sure I've always been me."

"And just who is this Paulien Mertens?" Ada asks.

Vivienne cringes at the curiosity in Ada's voice. At how repeating the name will most likely sear it into Ada's brain.

"She was mates with . . ." Scotty pauses. "No. You sound a bit like her, but her hair was blond. Pretty thing but with more meat on her. Got mixed up with the wrong bloke, Paulien did. A real mess she got herself into. Got to be in jail or dead by now." He chuckles. "Or maybe hiding out on some deserted island with a pile of cash."

Vivienne places a small bit of parfait into her mouth and manages to swallow it. "Guess she's not me then." She shrugs. "Seeing as I'm here."

Scotty apologizes again for not remembering her, and then for believing she was someone she isn't. Vivienne tells him not to worry about it, and he appears happy to let the incident go. But not so for Ada, who watches Vivienne carefully, her eyes narrow and her smile smug.

22

VIVIENNE, 1925

Henri is nominated to sit on the jury for the Carnegie International Exhibition in Pittsburgh and plans to visit Merion when the competition is over. He reluctantly gives in to Vivienne's pleas and promises to act as if they are nothing more than friends. But given his propensity for high jinks, she's far from certain he's going to keep his promise.

It's well over ninety the day of his arrival, and Vivienne can't decide what to wear. She rifles through her closet, which is stuffed with colorful dresses, and then walks to the closet in the second bedroom. Edwin keeps increasing her salary, and she's been able to buy a small house in Merion, about half a mile from the Bradley. It's a charming Arts and Crafts cottage, with deep mahogany floors and moldings, a fireplace, and a tiny garden out back, where she's planted some of Ada's best bulbs and bushes. It's nothing like the estate she grew up on, but she's proud of having purchased it by herself, using money she earned through her own hard work.

Vivienne's hand lingers over a mauve dress with tiny peach flowers, a couple of years old, a bit faded and not her best color. This is the safest choice, but she reaches for the orange one she bought in Paris with the low waist and short skirt. She'll pair it with a double string of long blue beads. Henri will appreciate her nod to complementary colors.

Henri has never been to Merion, and she and Edwin wait on the front steps of the Bradley for him. Edwin hasn't mentioned anything, but she knows he's nervous about Henri's reaction to the collection and the ensembles, especially the artist's response to how his own work is displayed. When the car pulls into the drive, she rests her hand on Edwin's elbow, a gesture that would be interpreted by anyone watching as that of an assistant keyed up by the arrival of a famous artist. A gesture that will remind Henri of his promise.

Henri leaps from the car and approaches them with a wide smile, spry and animated. She holds on to Edwin's elbow more tightly.

The two men slap each other on the back, and then Henri turns to her. Their eyes meet and she feels a warm thrill deep within her.

"Vivienne," he says after they kiss each other on both cheeks. "You look exquisite. Not many women have the eye or the gumption to pair orange with its complement."

She hurries up the stairs to the front door. "Come," she cries. "We want to show you everything."

Henri wants to see everything. She's almost forgotten how vibrant he is, so energetic, with no checks on his enthusiasm. Edwin's seriousness and composure pale in contrast. As does his vitality. She and Edwin bring Henri up the stairs to view *The Joy of Life* and stand silently on the landing while he appraises its commanding position. Alone on the large wall, lit by the skylight above. Henri's eyes glisten. "Thank you, my friend," he says to Edwin. "Thank you."

As they wander through the rooms, Henri bubbles with compliments. The splendor of the building. The brilliance of the art. Vivienne knows he finds symmetry dull, so she's not surprised when he doesn't praise the ensembles. But he does admire the rare combinations unrestrained by classical rules of chronological display. "You have created a home for the old masters of the future," he tells Edwin.

They complete the tour in the main gallery, where they started, and Edwin points to the south wall. "See that?"

Henri follows Edwin's finger. Two narrow walls—one holding Henri's *Seated Riffian* and the other Picasso's *The Peasants*—separate three twelve-foot-tall windows. An oddly shaped portion of plaster roughly forty-five feet wide and seventeen feet high sits atop the windows: flat at the bottom, separated about a quarter of the way up by two projecting masonry supports that buttress the vaulted ceiling and form three rounded arches. It's an awkward expanse, too high to be seen in its entirety from the ground, irregular, and horribly lit.

"I want a mural there," Edwin says, pointing. "Above the windows. Something that flows across the three spaces, but that's a single painting. Something active, continuous, that isn't stopped by the supports. I'm going to commission it."

Edwin has mentioned his desire for a mural before, but Vivienne had no idea he was planning to offer it to Henri. He may not have known it himself before this moment.

Henri follows Edwin's finger. "Are you offering it to me?"

"If you think you can do it."

"The light is impossible."

"Nothing's impossible."

"Look at it." Henri points upward. "The shadows from the ceiling vaults fall over at least a third of it—and the light from those windows obscures it from below."

"Are you saying you can't do it?"

"Is that a dare?"

"That's just what it is."

"I cannot do it here. I would have to create it in Nice."

"Take all the measurements you need now," Edwin instructs. "I'll have paper templates created based on your figures. Then I'll ship the cutouts over to France. You can work from them there."

"I will need complete control of the form and content."

"It's yours."

Henri ponders the irregular space. He walks along the north wall, inspects the other three, climbs the stairs, and stands at the open railing, eye level with where the mural will be.

"It may take years," Henri says when he comes down to rejoin them. "I refuse to rush."

"Is that a yes?"

"How much are you willing to pay?"

"Thirty thousand dollars," Edwin replies without hesitation. "In three installments. Before, during, and after."

Henri blanches, obviously taken by surprise at the amount proffered. It's a lot of money, probably more than he's ever been offered before. But he recovers quickly. "I think we should be able to work out the details in a manner we are both happy with."

ADA JOINS THEM for dinner that night, which has the effect of creating two couples: Edwin and Ada, Henri and Vivienne. Awkward, to say the least. Vivienne feels as if she's caught in some kind of bizarre double love triangle, although she supposes that Mme Matisse would have to be with them for that to be the case.

Ada is completely absorbed in Edwin, smiling up at him lovingly and hanging on to his arm, shooting Vivienne sharp glances of triumph. Despite his promises to the contrary, Henri is completely absorbed in Vivienne, repeatedly filling her wineglass, laughing at everything she says. It's obvious Edwin is uncomfortable with Ada's attentions and jealous of Henri's. They're only on the salad course, and Vivienne wonders how she's going to make it through to dessert with her status as the Bradley heir intact.

Henri says to Edwin, "You better get back to Paris as soon as you can, my friend. There is a new collector in town—although probably new only to us. Very wealthy. He is from Australia, a man named Ashton King, and he is buying up every Cézanne, Modigliani, and Picasso he can find. Many of mine, too."

"I'm sure there are enough for both of us," Edwin says, but Vivienne can see from the set of his mouth that he doesn't like the sound of this.

Henri recognizes Edwin's discomfort, and he lets the issue drop. He turns to Ada and compliments her on her delightful home and even more delightful gardens, and then lifts yet another glass. "To Edwin

and Ada," he cries. "To their many long years of marriage and to their
continued happiness together!"

When Henri's hand strays under the tablecloth and finds Vivienne's
knee, exposed by her short dress, she throws it off with the flick of her
leg. "I've hired a copy editor who's about halfway through the correc-
tions to the manuscript," she tells them. "We're hoping the book will be
published in the early spring."

"A triumph for all three of us," Henri declares, and runs his finger
along the sensitive skin on the underside of her thigh.

This time, Vivienne doesn't move. Because she can't move. Because
she doesn't want him to stop. Edwin is watching her closely. Without
looking at Henri, she jerks her chair beyond his reach. His hand drops
away, and she's filled with a hollow sadness that rushes in to fill the space
where the wanting had been.

HENRI IS STAYING at the house with Edwin and Ada, and
Edwin does everything he can to keep Vivienne and Henri apart. After
their dinner he requests Henri's advice on an addition to one of the
ensembles and shoos Vivienne home. The visit is for two days, and
Edwin is masterly in his scheming: lunch and dinner to which she isn't
invited; a museum trip in which she isn't included; late nights drinking
scotch and smoking cigars at Edwin's club, which doesn't allow women.
Plus a list of menial tasks, which she must complete immediately. Then,
in a final coup d'état, Edwin has his chauffeur drive Henri to New York
to board his ship so early in the morning that she has no chance to say
good-bye.

Vivienne is furious at Edwin, and even more so at Henri, who
flaunted rather than hid their attraction. She's sure he believed he was
amusing, and her only consolation is that now he's kicking himself for
his behavior. It's not much of a consolation.

Edwin is moody and bad tempered after Henri leaves, never acknowl-
edging the source of his anger, striking out at her at random moments.

There's too much at stake to provoke him, so she falls back into their usual routine, holding her tongue as they make the final edits to the Matisse book, taking day trips to New York in search of art, and complimenting him at every opportunity.

When she comes into work one morning, Edwin is fuming, and she wonders what she's done now. But it isn't her. "Bill Glackens just called and said a curator at the PMA told him Quinton and the district attorney's office are cooking up another lawsuit. Some fancy new legal maneuver to force me to open the doors."

Vivienne sits down on the corner of his desk.

"Three years ago he was denigrating my paintings to anyone who would listen," Edwin rages. "And now he claims they're so important that it's a crime to withhold them from the public?"

"It just goes to show how right you were. As you predicted, the art community in Philadelphia is becoming more accepting. Just like Schoenberg." She smiles at him. "I told Gertrude you were a visionary, and you've proved me correct."

"That's not it!" Edwin yells. "Quinton is unable to appreciate anything that isn't at least three hundred years old—he just wants to jump on the bandwagon after the Paris show proved him wrong. The mealy-mouthed hypocrite!"

"But the *Painters of Paris* show was—"

"What he's really after is me."

"So you think this is about Ada?"

"Damn straight it is. A sore loser, if ever there was one. He knows the last thing I want is a bunch of uneducated strangers wandering through my house and gawking at what they don't understand. And that's exactly why he's doing it! He's still looking for his goddamned revenge."

"He's got to be after more, don't you think? What if these suits are about getting your collection for the PMA? He's on the museum's board."

"My collection is never going to the PMA," Edwin declares. "The Bradley will never be a public museum!"

"Think about it. Quinton gets his revenge on you and gets your collection for—"

"It's my property, and I have my own board, and we're the only ones who decide what happens to it!"

"Your board . . ." Vivienne repeats. "The board of trustees," she adds slowly. "They have to give final approval on all your decisions, right?"

"It doesn't make any difference. I'm chairman, and the trustees will do exactly what I tell them to do." Edwin begins to cough and smashes his cigarette into the ashtray. "Plus, they all have the best interests of the Bradley at heart."

Vivienne watches the smoldering butt. A board of trustees that will go along with Edwin unless they believe he doesn't have the interests of the Bradley at heart. A board of trustees that, after his death, will never allow her to remove the colonnade seven or sell the peripheral pieces or open to the public.

"Don't look so worried," Edwin snaps. "We're going to win this thing—we did before and we will again. Even if Quinton has bigger plans, we're going to crush him, along with the rest of them."

Vivienne tries to smile, but her face is as brittle as a mask. How did she miss this? She was aware that the Bradley was a foundation—which meant it was held in a trust—but she hadn't followed this fact to its logical conclusion. She was also vaguely aware there was a board of trustees, but Edwin never mentioned them or seemed to consult them, so she hadn't given it much thought. Neither the Bradley's finances nor the intricacies of its management ever interested her.

But now they do, and the facts are clear: as long as the collection is held within a trust, the artwork doesn't actually belong to Edwin. And it won't belong to her either.

23

VIVIENNE, 1925

If you can create a trust, you have to be able to terminate one. A termination would make Edwin the true owner of the artwork, and then he could do whatever he wanted with it, no board of trustees to overrule him. The same would be true if the Bradley belonged to Vivienne.

"You know," she says to him the next morning, "this new lawsuit would fall apart if you owned the collection outright." She keeps her tone light, as if she's reflecting on something she's given little thought to.

Edwin grunts, only half listening as he peruses a stack of papers in front of him.

"There'd be no basis for it," she continues. "The suit is grounded in the fact that the Bradley is a charitable trust that doesn't pay taxes. Without that argument, the state has no vested interest."

"Hmmmm."

"So maybe you should just tear up the trust papers," she suggests, again very casually. "Throw the case in the trash along with them."

"Terminate the trust agreement?" he asks, turning his full attention to her. "I'll be damned if I'll pay taxes I don't have to pay." Although Edwin is a wealthy man, he doesn't like spending more money than he has to. As he always points out, this is how he's managed to stay rich.

"What about all that money you're paying the lawyers?"

"A pittance compared to the taxes. But it doesn't matter. I'm looking forward to the court's decision. Can't wait for Quinton to lose a second time."

"What if he doesn't?"

Edwin's chin juts out in annoyance. "He will."

Over the next weeks, she mentions the termination a handful of times and gets the same response. Then Edwin develops a bad head cold, which makes him even more grouchy than usual, so she backs off until he recovers.

"Can you imagine what would happen if Quinton did win?" she asks when he seems to be feeling better. "All those people in your house? Wandering through the galleries? They'll clog the building, smother the artwork." She shudders. "We might even have to close the school."

"Damn it, Vivienne. I'm sick and tired of your constant negativity."

"It's not negativity, it's planning for the future of the Bradley. I'm thinking through all the possibilities so we can figure out what to do if things don't work out the way you expect."

He begins to cough, spits into his handkerchief, scowls at her. "I suppose you're going to suggest your dim-witted termination idea again?" Apparently still sick, undeniably still grouchy.

"I'm not suggesting you do it this very moment, I just think you should consider it a possible option. Among others," she adds quickly.

"No! No! No! The answer is still no and will always be no!"

When Edwin gets this absolute, nothing will change his mind, so she goes back to her office, where her thoughts turn to George. If he were backed into this corner, he'd most likely convince himself that he was never interested in the collection in the first place, that he'd wanted something else all along. Perhaps just the colonnade seven? If so, then he'd steal them, declare victory, and get the hell out of town.

Vivienne hits the back of her pen on the desk. She would actually be emancipating the paintings rather than stealing them, bringing them home to a place where they can breathe free. A small recompense for all she caused her father to lose, the least she can do. Granted, no one except Papa would be able to enjoy them, but only Edwin and a few students can enjoy them now. A rationalization, but an apt one.

The thought of liberating her beloved paintings from their captivity, wresting them from Edwin's confining ensembles, is appealing. He likes to believe both he and his collection are invincible, so there aren't any guards or other safety precautions. And what are seven pieces of art to a man who owns thousands? Another rationalization, but also apt.

Of course she'll do nothing of the sort; that isn't how she was brought up, isn't how she sees herself. Yet she finds herself asking people in the art community about security, citing her concern about the Bradley's lack of it, as well as the fact that Edwin doesn't believe it's a problem. Do they agree with Edwin, or should she convince him that steps need to be taken? Do they know of any recent robberies? Instead of being given the names of nefarious criminals who brazenly commit well-plotted art heists, she's told how much better guards are than any of the crazy, highfalutin alarms and gizmos that are coming on the market.

There's that slimy truck driver who's always badgering her for a date when he makes his deliveries. A few months back, he said that if she were willing to turn a blind eye, he would be willing to "lose" one of the paintings in the back of his truck, and then they could "run off to South America together and live the high life." On a lark, she calls the company where he works, Empire State Transport. They tell her he's taken a leave of absence and have no idea when—or if—he'll return.

Once she thinks it over, she realizes she doesn't need an actual art thief—or even an experienced thief. She'll be taking care of unlocking the door and faking the forced entry, so he doesn't have to possess any particular skills. He just needs to be willing to take a risk, have a fondness for money, and little regard for the law. She can't believe she's thinking this way, but she can't let it go. It occurs to her that one place to find such an unsavory character is a speakeasy.

Vivienne has never gone to a speakeasy; it isn't something Edwin does or approves of, although he has no problem serving liquor at his own parties or accepting a fine bottle of wine from the owner of one of his prized restaurants. Obviously speakeasies aren't necessary in Europe, where there's no prohibition against alcohol.

She's been told there are hundreds of speakeasies all over Philadelphia, hidden in backrooms and basements, behind false facades and trick doors. A special password or secret hand signal are often necessary to get in, and these illegal saloons are a breeding ground for trouble. They're called speakeasies because of the need to reduce noise to avoid detection, hence "speak easy," but it seems they're very loud and known to everyone, including the police.

One, disguised as a tailor shop, was recently raided, and two prominent politicians were arrested along with all the other customers. Another, under the control of organized crime, was the site of a gangland-style shootout that resulted in three deaths. It's too risky to visit one—and unlikely to be successful—but when she overhears one of her students talking about the Red Fedora and laughing over how foolish the secret password is, she decides to give it a shot.

Armed with the password and address, she travels to South Philly, an area more destitute than the quarter where she lived during those awful months in Paris, also sadder. Flimsy, mud-splattered tents are scattered everywhere, filled with out-of-work men—and often their families. She takes a cab and asks the driver to come back for her in an hour. A girl cannot be out alone in this neighborhood.

When the door of Upton's Apothecary opens to her knock, she mumbles, "Rose," and a man in the white jacket of a pharmacist points to a hallway with a sign that says STOCKROOM. The corridor ends in a set of descending stairs. She follows them down toward the sounds of laughter and music, pushes the door open.

It's what she expected, but even more so. Noisier, more crowded, smokier, and more vivacious. Almost every girl in the house is decked out in flamboyant colors and an extremely short skirt, a powdered face and bright red lipstick. They're all smoking cigarettes and drinking cocktails, dancing with great abandon. The musicians are Negroes, as are many of the patrons, and the saxophones and trumpets are forceful and full throated—far from speaking easy.

It's as if she's standing on another planet, nothing and no one familiar.

Then she sees George standing at a tall table, talking with two other men. Someone she knows. Someone who'll help her navigate this alien world. But as she starts toward him, he turns and melts into the crowd, and she sees that, once again, it isn't George. She needs a drink.

Vivienne works her way to the bar and orders a sherry, as she doesn't know what the cocktails are called. She lights a cigarette, unsure what to do, then takes a seat across from the bartender. She finishes the drink quickly and asks for a second.

"New around here?" the bartender inquires. "You don't look familiar."

She gazes up at him and smiles. "New to the city," she says in an exaggerated Belgian accent.

"From Germany?" he asks. "Looking for some fun?"

She lifts her glass and takes a long sip. "Just a drink." What the hell is she doing in this place? What the hell is she thinking?

"You've come to the right spot for that, pretty German lady." He pours her another glass of sherry and places it in front of her. "Finish up what you've got. This next one here is on the house."

By the time Vivienne finishes the third glass, she's tipsy but no closer to finding her thief. If anything, she's closer to admitting that this is not the way to find one. Or more precisely, that there probably isn't a way, which is for the best. She might try to act and think like George, but she isn't George.

She grows much more loquacious, and she and the bartender, whose name is Tim, are now fast friends. She learns about his little son, who's a mama's boy, and how when Prohibition ends—which Tim knows will be soon—he's planning to buy himself a bar.

"So are there really people here involved in organized crime?" she asks in a stage whisper.

Tim nods to a table of five men. "Some of the biggest."

Vivienne tries not to stare. They're almost caricatures: big and beefy and very Italian looking, smoking cigars and talking intently to one another.

"Need someone knocked off?" Tim jokes.

She lights another cigarette and says nonchalantly, "Nah. Just looking for someone to commit a robbery for me."

He laughs. "Not their usual type of crime. Killing and bootlegging and gambling—sometimes prostitution—but that's about it."

Vivienne sweeps her arm grandly to indicate the whole crowd. "How about a petty thief who might need a few bucks? There's got to be one of those here, right?"

Tim's smile disappears, and he throws her a piercing look. He grabs a rag and starts moving down the bar, wiping it as he goes. "Not that I know of," he says over his shoulder.

THE TRIAL, 1928

I have no idea what you would make of this morning's session, Edwin. Obviously you would be surprised, as I never told you about Paulien Mertens or George Everard or the fact that I wasn't born Vivienne Gregsby.

Would you be horrified? Irate? Disappointed? Sympathetic? I really don't know. And that's probably why I kept the whole sad saga from you for all these years.

When Ronald told me that a Mr. Terence S. Williamson was to be Pratt's first witness of the day, I knew precisely what his testimony would comprise, as well as who informed the prosecution of the potential damage he could do to my status as an upstanding citizen without a single legal blemish on her record.

Ada is the only person who knew about the conversation at the party. She clearly didn't tell you, but she's just as clearly been talking about it to her boyfriend—sorry, Edwin—and Quinton has clearly been talking to Pratt.

I'm starting to think, as you always claimed, that this is more about Ada than about the collection. I don't know whether Ada believes I had you murdered and wants justice or whether she just wants revenge. Either way, Quinton is doing everything he can to part the waters for her—and to acquire both your collection and your wife. It wouldn't surprise me if they marry soon.

I spent enough time with Scotty at the Slade to know that he actually was an upstanding citizen—and that he would tell all he knew, even if he wasn't happy about telling it. He'd once tried to throw a surprise party for Bernice but ruined the whole thing because he couldn't lie to her about where he was going to be that evening.

When I explained to Ronald how disastrous Scotty could be to our case, he was unconcerned, assuring me that he would object based on relevancy. "The judge will have to exclude this Williamson's testimony," Ronald insisted. "The fact that you changed your name years ago has no bearing on the crime at hand."

The judge overruled his objection, and Scotty—excuse me, Terence S.— told his story. So much for Ronald's assurances.

Scotty explained, reluctantly, that we'd been in art school together and double-dated often, as he was courting a close friend of mine. I was a nice enough girl but had gotten mixed up with the wrong bloke, someone called Everhand or Evering or something like that. He wasn't quite sure of the name.

What he was sure of was that this guy and I had been part of a scam in which innocent people all over Europe lost millions of pounds. When everything broke open, the bloke and I both disappeared, along with all the money.

Ronald did get an objection sustained at this point, but the damage was done.

Scotty said he hadn't seen me until about three years after it all happened. When he went to a party at the Bradley in 1925 and recognized me. Under prodding, he finally admitted that at that time, I said I'd never heard of Paulien Mertens, claiming that I wasn't she and that my name was Vivienne Gregsby.

Although I did acknowledge that I'd attended the Slade School in London at the same time he had. At the same time Paulien Mertens had. No, he hadn't recognized me at first. No, he had believed what I'd told him.

"What exactly was it that changed your mind, Mr. Williamson?" Pratt asked.

Scotty hesitated, then whispered, "Afterward I realized that I recognized her voice."

"Please speak up, sir."

This time he said it louder. "I recognized her voice."

Pratt preened for the judge. "And do you see the woman whose voice you recognized as belonging to Paulien Mertens in this courtroom, sir?"

Scotty didn't look at me directly, but he did point.

"But that woman's name is Vivienne Gregsby," Pratt said with mock confusion. "Are you certain she's the same girl you went to school with? The one called Paulien Mertens?"

Scotty nodded, again reluctantly.

"Could you please give us verbal confirmation of your identification, sir?" Pratt requested obsequiously. "For the record, please."

"Yes," Scotty said. "It's her."

24

VIVIENNE, 1926

The winter is trying for Vivienne; her disappointments weigh heavy, her choices prove muddy, and the new lawsuit turns out to be no more than an idle threat. But her spirits lighten as she and Edwin head to Paris in the spring. She's sailing toward Henri, and there are a dozen copies of *The Art of Henri Matisse* by Edwin Bradley and Vivienne Gregsby in her stateroom.

She keeps picking up the book, flipping through the pages, pressing her nose to the binding, running her finger over the engraved letters of her name. With the reproductions and the appendices it's 464 pages. Four hundred and sixty-four pages. Over two years of work. But worth every minute. She's proud. Giddy, in fact. Except when she imagines her father coming across the book and not recognizing that Vivienne Gregsby is his very own Paulie.

The economic situation in France is much worse than in the United States. According to Edwin, the decline in textiles and the government's refusal to devalue the franc have thrown the country into stagnation. Even Gertrude's events aren't as lavish as in the past, and all the artists and writers, from Pablo Picasso to Ernest Hemingway, are complaining about the lack of commissions and contracts.

It's a source of embarrassment to Vivienne that Edwin is doing so well, but Edwin doesn't see it this way. Having pulled himself out of poverty, he believes that a man is who he makes himself to be, that blaming governments or economic situations or others' poor judgment is spineless and cowardly. She tries to keep him from voicing this opinion too loudly or too often.

There are many more artworks available for sale than there were on their earlier visits. Almost all at low prices. Edwin cheerfully prances through Paris scooping up bargains from those who have fallen on hard times. Although he often complains that an Australian named Ashton King is grabbing deals out from under him.

When Edwin secures another eight paintings from Leo Stein at far less than they're worth, Gertrude is beside herself and talks about canceling the party she's throwing to celebrate the publication of *The Art of Henri Matisse*, and Vivienne doesn't blame her. But rather than offending either Vivienne or Henri, Gertrude decides to downgrade from a dinner party to an after-dinner party. Since Hélène makes a fabulous sweet soufflé, no one protests. Criticizing Gertrude has the same result as criticizing Edwin: banishment from the premises. And no one in Paris wants that.

The party is larger than Gertrude's usual gatherings, full of guests who are both familiar and unfamiliar to Vivienne. After her encounter with Scotty Williamson, she's watchful again. Because the crowd is so big, it's difficult to see every face, but she tries to throw off her anxieties. She hopes Ashton King isn't in attendance. King beat out Edwin for two Modiglianis the day before, and Edwin is not known for his composure when coming face-to-face with a rival.

The celebration is for the book, and obviously for Henri, Edwin, and her, but from the start it's clear Gertrude hasn't cast Edwin in a leading role. Vivienne and Henri are seated at the head of the dining room table, flanked by Gertrude and Leo, while Edwin is relegated to the foot, flanked by no one of note. Vivienne is tickled to have Henri to herself but does feel for Edwin.

Henri arrived just before the party and is leaving immediately after to resume working on the mural. "If it were not for you," he tells Vivienne, "I would have stayed in Nice." He's buoyed by the commission and seems younger and spryer than she's ever seen him. Edwin's tight composure pales against Henri's enthusiasm.

She links her ankle with Henri's and whispers, "When we come to Nice to see the mural, we will have to stay overnight."

"Ah," Henri says, blowing a puff of breath into her ear. "And what shall we do then?"

Before she can respond, Gertrude hits a fork against her champagne flute. When the room quiets, she makes a toast to the book, followed by one to Vivienne and a third to Henri. As an apparent afterthought, she raises the glass halfway and mumbles Edwin's name. Even Leo, to whom the book is dedicated, only twice mentions Edwin when he reads the positive review out loud.

Vivienne is annoyed with Gertrude's underhandedness, so after the fruit and cheese course but before the soufflé, she stands and taps the side of her own flute. "Not enough credit has been given tonight to the true genius behind this book," she tells the crowd. "I don't mean to take anything away from Monsieur Matisse, but it's another man who conceived of the idea, persuaded Henri to join the undertaking, and worked long and hard to bring it to fruition."

She walks down to the other side of the table, puts her hand on Edwin's shoulder, and raises her glass. "So please join me in a toast to Dr. Edwin Bradley, collector, curator, and author extraordinaire!"

The applause isn't as extravagant as that which followed Gertrude's tributes, but it's strong enough not to embarrass. Vivienne nods to Gertrude, who tips her head in acknowledgment of Vivienne's point. Gertrude might be a bit callous, sometimes even cruel, but she also has a keen sense of self-awareness that is redemptive.

Henri surprises Vivienne by coming over and placing his hand on Edwin's other shoulder. "My dear friend Edwin has done me a great honor," he says to the guests. "I am humbled by both his belief in me and the depth of his consideration of my work."

Edwin stands and the two men hit each other on the back, then

Edwin turns to Vivienne, nods his thanks, and raises his own glass. "And many thanks to our gracious hostess, Gertrude Stein, who's always the first to recognize and herald the work of a friend."

There are a few coughs and a few snickers, but then another round of applause drowns them out.

HENRI HAS RENTED a large, empty garage at 8, rue Désiré-Niel, in Nice, where he's creating the mural he's calling *The Dance II*. He's been hard at work on it since he left Merion last year and seems guardedly pleased with his progress. At Gertrude's he explained that, based on the templates Edwin sent, he stretched three canvases the exact size of the arches and hung them adjacent to one another along a sixty-foot wall. The canvases are over twice his height, so he had a long bench built beneath the length of the mural, and he attached a stick of charcoal to a long bamboo pole to draw with.

"My bamboo pointer," he said, "is truly a magician's wand," giving it credit for performing the feat of completing the design, which he described as an amalgam of "color, shape, and movement—the materials that stir the senses."

He also developed a novel approach to make the work possible: he hired housepainters to cover massive sheets of paper with either gray, pink, blue, or black—the pigments he chose for the mural—which his assistants then cut into the shapes he draws. Using a few well-chosen lines, he roughs in the dancers on these cutout pieces of painted paper, which are then pinned to the canvases so he can assess the relationships among all the elements. More often than not, the cutouts are pulled down and refashioned.

When Vivienne and Edwin walk into the garage, two of Henri's assistants are on ladders pinning up an awkward section of gray paper. The cutout is about twelve feet tall and appears to be an abstraction of three or four dancers with over a dozen appendages.

A head, maybe two, five or six legs, and a swirl of seven or eight arms, most of which end beyond the mural's borders. Energy and movement and pleasure. The intertwined nudes, cavorting, dancing, surging beyond the edges into an imagined space. Reminiscent of *The Joy of Life*, it's more sophisticated, more compelling, owing to its size and simplicity. And it isn't nearly complete.

"Bravo!" Vivienne cries when Henri comes over to greet them. Even though Edwin is standing next to her, she gives Henri a warm hug.

Henri releases her faster than she would have liked, and she looks at him questioningly. But he only has eyes for Edwin, who is, after all, paying the bill.

Edwin studies the charcoal sketches of the slightly abstracted and slippery forms leaping across the canvases. He turns to the cutouts on the floor, then looks back up to the rounded gray bodies pinned against a background of elongated geometrical fragments of pink, blue, and black.

Henri dismisses his assistants, and he and Vivienne glance nervously at each other. The silence is thick, Edwin's expression inscrutable. She can't imagine he'll disagree with her—how could he?—but Edwin goes his own way.

Finally he claps Henri on the back. "I knew I was right to choose you."

Vivienne and Henri laugh, both from relief and from their shared amusement at Edwin's manner of framing everything in terms of himself. Then they dive into the details. Henri explains his times of despair and elation, his mistakes and victories, the intense strain the mural's complexities have caused him.

"Your solution to the problem of the support beams works well." Edwin points to the two recumbent figures linking the panels below where the beams will be. "Moving the eye across the dancers around and above them. Linking the pieces while remaining a part of the whole."

"It seems like it's the only way it could have been," Vivienne says. "The only way it can be." She counts the appendages. "Twenty-four limbs all gamboling together . . . I can't imagine how you conceived of such a thing. Or how hard it must have been to make it work."

"It drove me nearly mad," Henri confesses. "But I will tell you that when I finally saw the full mural in my mind's eye, when the expanse of it was inside me, it was like a rhythm that carried me along, erasing all the difficulties that came before." He pulls three chairs in front of the mural. "Please sit." He opens a bottle of wine, and they discuss the plans for the mural's installation, which is at least six months away.

"Where are the templates I sent?" Edwin asks. "The ones based on your original measurements."

Henri looks around the messy studio. "They are here somewhere. I admit I have not seen them since I began the design work."

"Find them," Edwin orders. "Then lay them on top of each other. I need to see what the largest dimension is in order to size the containers. To decide if we need to transport the three canvases together or separately." Although the rounded arches at the top of the individual pieces are the same size, because of the placement of the support beams, the width at the bottom of each varies slightly.

Henri begins pulling drawers open in the deep chests lining one wall. It takes him a while to come up with the templates. When he finally finds them in a far corner of the garage, Vivienne and Edwin help him spread the unruly pieces of paper on the floor. When they place the templates on top of one another, the middle section is longer by at least two feet.

"It will be less expensive to send them in a single crate," Edwin says. "But this is no place to cut corners. What do you think, my friend?"

"I do not see any reason why we cannot ship them together." Henri pulls the three pieces apart and lays them directly in front of their corresponding canvases. "The packing materials would be the same and—" He stops short, his gaze moving from the templates, to his mural, and back to the templates again. His face turns the same gray as the cutouts.

"What?" Vivienne cries. "Henri, are you ill?"

He grasps her arm, stumbles backward a few steps, and sits down hard in his chair.

She kneels by his side and presses her wrist to his forehead; it's damp and icy cold. A heart attack? A stroke? "We need to find a doctor," she shouts at Edwin. "Right now. Go!"

"No," Henri says, his breath coming in shallow gasps. "It is . . . it is . . . it is not that."

"Then what is it, man?" Edwin demands, also alarmed.

Henri points from the canvases to the templates. "The dimensions are wrong. They appear to be off by roughly a meter." His expression is that of a man who has just heard of the death of a loved one. "I have made a terrible error."

25

GEORGE/ASHTON, 1926

If he isn't the smartest man alive, he doesn't know who is. He set it up, waited for it to happen, and voilà, it did. There he is, at another one of Gertrude Stein's parties, perfecting his Ashton King persona as wealthy Australian collector and businessman, when whom does he spy? Little Paulien Mertens, a.k.a. Vivienne Gregsby. With her sleek hair and chiseled cheekbones, she's looking even better than when he last spied her in Philadelphia. Much better than in London. Losing that baby fat did her a world of good.

He didn't notice her at first. It's a typical evening at 27, noisy and crowded, replete with all manner of self-satisfied "talent" and their awestruck sycophants. Sycophants with lots of money whom he's spent the past six months charming, turning them into dear and trusting friends—potential investors all. Some of the talent also, but only those with money. There aren't many.

The party is a celebration for some new book about Henri Matisse, and he figured it would be the perfect place to begin the next step of his current project: the investment phase. The first stage of King & Associates, Inc., went just as planned, and the second will also. Intelligence, planning, and patience: three of his greatest strengths, the key to his continuous string of triumphs.

He's bought a number of authentic artworks by old masters as well as some by the current crop of artists touted to be the next old masters: Monet, Manet, Cézanne, Matisse, Renoir, and Picasso. He rented a warehouse, studios, and office space, set up the required company, and hired half a dozen artists who have begun forging the four hundred or so paintings he needs. Once he finds more forgers, he'll be on his way.

He's busy brewing up interest by whispering—to a select few—about the profits he's going to make buying quality art from those hurt by the current economic situation and holding it until the markets correct. When two of these men ask if he would consider taking on minor partners, he reluctantly refuses.

"It's just not profitable enough yet," he tells them sadly. "I wouldn't dream of bringing anyone in as a partner until I can guarantee at least a twenty or twenty-five percent return. But maybe when the earnings get more consistent . . ." He pauses as they wait, greed shining on their faces. He taps his forefinger to his chin as if he were just struck by an idea.

"Yes?" one of the men prods.

"Maybe if that happens, I might consider selling shares of the business. Not as a partnership per se, more like buying stock." He looks at them with wide, innocent eyes. "Would that kind of investment be of interest to you?"

Needless to say, it would.

In fact, he's so engrossed in one of these conversations that he barely hears the first round of toasts Gertrude offers to Matisse. But when she mentions that one of the authors is Vivienne Gregsby, he abandons the German nobleman he's speaking with and hurries to the dining room.

He feels a pleasant stirring as he eyes Paulien, remembering the months he courted her, her enthusiasm once he bedded her. She lusted for him then, and she lusts for him now. Your first is always your first.

He didn't know she was a virgin when he approached her that day in London. All he knew was that the Mertens family was one of the wealthiest in Belgium, with social and financial connections all over the world—and that a Mertens daughter was on her own in the city, ripe for the picking. The fact that she had never had sex before was an added bonus.

Even though he has a full beard, unstylishly long hair, a deep tan, and is wearing eyeglasses, he moves off into the shadows. This isn't the right moment to let his presence be known.

Aside from feigned spontaneity when it suits his needs, he never makes a move without prior thought and planning. Now that he fully understands Paulien's current situation and its resulting dilemmas, he knows precisely how he's going to turn it to his advantage. In a week, maybe two, he'll take his first step toward convincing her that what he wants is exactly what she wants.

26

VIVIENNE, 1926

"I cannot believe I did not notice before." Henri's hands scramble wildly over his disorderly worktable until he finds a tape measure. He kneels in front of the templates and lays the tape along the bottom. Muttering numbers to himself in French, he moves the measure beneath the canvases and then back to the templates.

Neither Vivienne nor Edwin needs to hear Henri's conclusion. It's obvious to the eye that the canvases are wider than the templates. By at least three feet.

Henri rocks back on his heels and closes his eyes. "The templates are 13.3 meters and the canvases are 14.4," he says in a monotone. "This is impossible, and yet it is so." He looks up at them. "I am sorry, Edwin. Vivienne. More sorry than you can ever know."

Without a word, she and Edwin take hold of the ends of the tape and double-check Henri's figures. There's no mistake, or rather, there's been a disastrous mistake.

"It must have been the inches and feet," Henri says. "The conversion to meters . . . when we cut the canvases. Somehow it was miscalculated . . ."

Vivienne leans over and puts her arms around him. "You'll fix it," she tells him. "You created it once, you can create it again. You can redo it, reshape it, fit it to the new volume. Who knows? Maybe it'll be better."

But even as she says this, she knows it will take much more than a simple reshaping. The mural he created is a product of the particular space it encompassed, or that encompassed it; they're one and the same.

If the space changes, then the mural must change with it. An artist with less integrity might attempt to simply reduce the size. But that artist is not Henri Matisse. For him, the new dimensions—which shorten the width of the three canvases relative to their height—will demand a completely new design. Vivienne's heart hurts.

Henri helps her to her feet as if it's she who has suffered a misfortune. He kisses her on both cheeks and sits her back down. "No, *ma chérie*," he says softly. "You know as well as I do that it will not be—how do you say? A quick fix."

She looks into his face, at the sorrow lining his every feature. "It won't be easy, but you've always excelled at difficult things—and made them seem effortless in their final execution."

"Damn it!" Edwin roars. "Will you two cut this lovey-dovey crap and take a look at this mess we've got to clean up."

Vivienne jumps in her chair, and Henri steps back. She was so lost in Henri's pain that she forgot about Edwin. It appears Henri did also.

"You've made an error of monumental proportions, Matisse!" Edwin bellows. "You're a fool. A reckless fool! And I never should have entrusted such an important commission to someone as sloppy as you."

Vivienne is speechless. Yes, Henri made an error, there's no doubt of that, but the personal insults are uncalled for. No matter what else Henri might be, he isn't sloppy.

"Those templates are correct," Edwin continues to rail. "I checked them myself before they were sent. More than once." He points a finger at Henri. "Which is exactly what you should have done on your end."

"I take full—" Henry begins.

"But no," Edwin continues, "you were too caught up with being an artist to be bothered with something as mundane as correctly converting feet into meters! Instead of exercising a modicum of care, you let the canvases go up and then lost the templates in a corner of some crummy garage and never thought of them again!"

"Edwin, you're not being fair to him. It's—"

Edwin swings around to face Vivienne. "Your precious Henri has painted himself into a corner, and now he's going to have to paint himself out of it." He glowers at Henri. "And I demand to know exactly how you propose to do this."

Henri pulls himself to his full height, which is, regrettably, inches below Edwin's. But even under these circumstances, Henri has a gravitas that lends him an air of dignity. "It is as you said, and I take full responsibility."

"As you should." Edwin's tone is terse, unrelenting. "But responsibility and completion of your commission to my satisfaction are two completely different things."

"Can you give him at least a few moments to digest what's—"

"This isn't your problem, Vivienne," Edwin interrupts her again. "It doesn't concern you. As a matter of fact, there's no reason for you to be here. You need to leave." He points imperiously in the direction of the door. "Now."

"It does concern me, as you well know," she snaps back at him. "I'm going nowhere."

"Edwin," Henri says warily, "I am as distraught about this discovery as you are. And I apologize for not holding up my end of the bargain. But at the moment I do not have the wherewithal to find a solution. I will need time to—"

"Time is something we don't have," Edwin roars, and begins to cough. "The mural is to be installed by the end of the year. The contract you signed stipulates that fact, and now you're not going to be able to meet your commitment."

Henri refuses to be cowed. "That is true. Up to a point. I will meet my commitment, deliver a mural that meets your standards. That exceeds them. Unfortunately, as you say, it will be late."

"I don't see how that's meeting your commitment," Edwin says disdainfully, wheezing slightly. "But I'm not going to argue semantics. What I will do is guarantee you that no more money will be coming.

You're going to fix this fiasco on your own dime. And you're damn lucky I'm willing to let you do this instead of demanding my deposit back!"

Vivienne gives him a withering look. Although Edwin is within his rights to withhold payment until the new mural is complete, he knows he's Henri's only source of funds at the moment. People don't buy art in bad economic times, and few collectors have the money to purchase a single painting—let alone offer commissions. Plus the name-calling is shameful. The man is acting like a tyrant of the worst sort.

"That is only fair." Henri's voice is calm, but she can see concern in his eyes.

Henri's wife, Amélie, is an invalid who lives in a separate residence with a full-time nurse, and some of his children still require his financial support. Then there's the additional cost of materials for the new mural, as well as the salaries of his assistants for at least an additional six months, maybe more—not to mention the value of his own time.

"You're acting as if Henri did this on purpose," Vivienne tells Edwin. "There were some miscalculations, unfortunate miscalculations to be sure, but hurling hurtful slurs injures you more than it does Henri. How's he going to create a new mural without money?"

"Vivienne," Henri says, "this is not necessary."

"Oh yes, it is." Her eyes don't leave Edwin's face. "You seem to want to punish him for punishment's sake. To penalize him for something beyond his control." As soon as the words are out of her mouth, she wishes she could call them back.

"It was most certainly within his control," Edwin corrects her. "He admitted it himself. And I don't see why I should compensate him for his mistakes—mistakes that wouldn't have occurred if he'd taken more time to make sure everything was in order. I did it on my end, why didn't he do it on his?" He turns to Henri. "The mural won't be completed in the time frame we agreed to, and therefore any lawyer will tell you I am on firm legal ground to withhold payment until it is."

"You make a valid point," Henri tells Edwin. "I will manage."

But Henri will have great difficulty managing. Although Edwin might have an argument from a purely business point of view, this is more than a commercial transaction; it's an agreement between a collector and an artist to produce a great work of art. For the ages, not for just one man—but this is something Edwin can't understand. To him, whatever he pays for belongs to him alone.

"I can't believe you," she says to Edwin. "You don't give a damn about Henri, about his disappointment, about all the work he's going to have to redo. He's your friend—has been for years—and he's producing a masterwork that's going to enrich the Bradley forever. Enrich the world. But none of this matters to you. You care more about being right than you do about people! And I feel sorry for you because that's a wretched way to go through life."

Edwin looks at her slack jawed, and Henri smiles for the first time since he found the templates.

VIVIENNE REFUSES TO speak to Edwin and takes the train back to Paris that evening. She slips a note to Henri explaining that abandoning Edwin might be the slap in the face that he needs to understand that he's gone too far. She also gives Henri the name of the hotel to which she'll be moving as soon as she arrives in the city.

As she rides through the darkness, the train tracks clicking beneath her, she exults in her willingness to risk what she most desires to stand up against a grave injustice. Edwin's insensitivity to Henri's situation surprises her less than she'd like to admit, although the viciousness of his invective is truly alarming. Calling Henri a fool? Such tirades are one thing when aimed at Thomas Quinton or the Philadelphia Museum of Art, but against Henri Matisse they're unconscionable.

She arrives as dawn breaks, checks out of the hotel where she and Edwin had been staying, and checks into another. She leaves no forwarding address. Then she goes to see Gertrude, whose first response isn't unexpected. "Oh, my poor Henri," she cries. "What a disaster this is for him. I must send a telegram immediately."

Nor is her second. "Bradley is a cold bastard," Gertrude declares. "Nasty and self-serving. You must leave him. Immediately."

Vivienne doesn't disagree with Gertrude's sentiments, but she has wrestled with the situation over the long, sleepless night, and now her feelings of virtue have ebbed and uncertainty has crawled in. She needs to rethink her position, talk it through. If anyone can help her with this dilemma, it's Gertrude.

"You should be with Henri right now," Gertrude is saying. "He needs you. But I suppose you already know that."

Vivienne looks at Gertrude miserably. "Edwin made me his beneficiary."

Gertrude's eyes widen. "Everything?"

"His wife gets the house and gardens, I get everything else."

"Ah." Gertrude leans back in her chair and rests her neck in her intertwined fingers. "That does gum up the works a bit now, doesn't it?"

"He won't let anyone into the Bradley to see the artwork. It's a crime."

"And you'd like the opportunity to correct that?"

"Right now there's a legal roadblock," Vivienne says. "But it's possible this won't always be the case."

"And then you would own the whole kit and caboodle?"

"You can't tell anyone. You have to promise me. This is in the strictest confidence."

Gertrude places her hand on Vivienne's arm, holding it there in a motherly way. "I may be known for my big mouth, but I also know how to keep a friend's secrets."

Vivienne isn't sure she believes Gertrude is capable of keeping that promise, although she believes Gertrude means what she's saying at the moment. "It's very important to me."

Gertrude lights one of her small cigars and gazes at a Picasso drawing on the door. "Now all we have to do is figure out how to get you what you want without losing what you have."

"Couldn't have said it better."

"Are you and Bradley having relations?" Gertrude asks. Although this is a highly inappropriate question, given the source it isn't startling.

"No," Vivienne tells her definitively. "Never."

"Good. So that's not part of the bargain."

"It's not a bargain. That's not how it is with—"

"Oh, don't fool yourself, child. It's a bargain. Everything in life is. Once you understand that—and admit it to yourself—you'll be able to navigate the world much more successfully."

Vivienne snorts. "So cynical."

"Do you want to have relations with Henri?"

Heat rises up Vivienne's face, and Gertrude shrieks, "And neither of you told me? I heartily approve."

"It could also be a problem."

"So you're willing to give up the man you love for a bunch of pictures?"

"I don't love him. It's just a fling."

"Pretend you do."

"Would you give up Alice?"

Gertrude looks around the art-covered walls, seriously considering the question. "I see your predicament."

"If Edwin finds out about Henri, it's all gone. My job, the books, the collection . . ." Vivienne hesitates. "Edwin claims he loves me."

"Damn."

"He wants to marry me."

Gertrude covers her mouth with her hands and pretends to gag. "Don't make me picture it. Don't do that to me!" she cries in mock horror.

"You'll be relieved to hear that Ada won't give him a divorce."

Gertrude uncovers her face. "You could continue with Henri and be very, very careful. As you know, people have gotten away with far worse."

"It's dangerous."

"When you want more than most people want," Gertrude tells her, "you've got to be willing to take more risks and make greater sacrifices to get it."

27

VIVIENNE, 1926

When Henri shows up at Vivienne's hotel room that evening, she lets him in and locks the door behind her. They undress in seconds, and as he presses into her, she throws her legs around his waist and draws him in. That powerful, wonderful warmth spreads out in waves from her center. She hears nothing and sees nothing, rides the wave until it explodes, until Henri explodes. They crumble together on the bed. Then they do it again, much more slowly.

No one knows where they are, no one even knows Henri is in Paris. He has to return to his mural in the morning, and she has to work things out with Edwin, so they stay awake, making love and talking deep into the early hours of the next day.

Henri speaks about his difficult father, his sick wife, his horror at his mistake. He's the first person to whom she reveals her past. Paulien and George, all that is and all that isn't, who she is and who she isn't. She cries when she tells him that Tante Natalie is the only one who might forgive her, but neither her aunt nor anyone else has responded to her letters. The relief is tremendous. Not only the confessing and Henri's sympathy, but because Henri views her as the innocent victim of a ruthless criminal.

"Where is this Everard now?" he demands.

"I've no idea. He mentioned Australia, New Zealand, America, but he's not the truthful type. He could be anywhere. Could be dead. Sometimes I think I see him, that he's following me. Coming back to ensnare me again . . ."

"Why would he do that? If you saw him, you would turn him over to the police. I believe this would be the last thing on his mind. He would want to find someone new."

She pulls his arms even more tightly around her. "You think that because you're not capable of thinking the way a man like George does. To him, I was a sucker once, so I'm always a sucker, a potential mark. I bet he believes I'm still in love with him. Narcissist that he is."

They also talk of art, and she tells him about her post-Impressionist mapping, about her tussles to align the puzzle pieces.

"This is because you are imposing categories on something that cannot be categorized," Henri says. "Making it all black and white when it is gray. Is Van Gogh an Impressionist or a post-Impressionist? He is both, a part of other groups also. I have been called an Impressionist, a Fauvist, a Nabi, and a post-Impressionist. What matters is the work, not the name."

"But it's a useful construct to understand influences," she argues, enjoying the back-and-forth of ideas. "Of all the things about art that fascinate me, I'm completely taken with the idea of who's standing on whose shoulders, who's got one foot in one school and the other in a different one, who creates something completely new from the combinations. If Picasso and Braque are Cubists, are they post-Impressionists or Abstract artists? It matters because of what comes from them as well as how they got there."

"All I can tell you is that Paul Cézanne is the father of us all."

"More than Van Gogh, Gauguin, Seurat?"

"Paul's concept that objects exist only in relation to one another sets him apart. I use this idea every day. If you surround the subject with white space, the subject disappears. This is why I use the same vase or fabric or piece of furniture in many works. The object is changed by what surrounds it."

"But what about color? Isn't that what's central? Wasn't he the first to say that sunlight couldn't be reproduced? That it could be represented only by color?"

Henri pulls her close. "You sound like a teacher."

"I am a teacher. But really I'm a student trying to understand the most magical of all magic. How with just a brush and paint and a canvas, you can make me feel what you feel."

"You are thoughtful and you are wise and I adore the way your mind works, but you are too damn serious." He begins to trace a line of kisses down her stomach. "Let me show you how I can make you feel what I feel."

AFTER HENRI LEAVES, Vivienne falls into a deep sleep and doesn't wake until late afternoon. She takes a shower and goes out to find Edwin. This isn't a problem, as she knows he likes to return to his hotel around seven to dress for dinner. She also knows his room number.

When he sees her at the door, his face creases with relief and he beckons her inside. "Where have you been? I've been looking everywhere for you."

A flash of guilt, until she remembers how furious she is with him. Or how furious she was. She's suddenly having trouble mustering up all that anger. "I moved to another hotel."

His features harden. "So I learned from the concierge."

"I was extremely angry at you."

"And I at you."

She grins at him. "Well, I'm glad we got that out in the open."

He frowns. "It's a crushing blow. And Matisse is responsible for it. Whatever I said to him, he deserved. It was a reckless error. One that an artist of his caliber and maturity should never have made."

"It was a mistake, Edwin. I suppose you've never made one?"

"Other than trusting Matisse with this commission? No."

Vivienne can't help it. She starts to laugh and sits down in a chair.

"I didn't mean that as a joke." He takes a seat opposite her, unsmiling. So different from what Henri's reaction would have been. "I'm serious."

"And that's why it's so funny." She offers him a cigarette, but he refuses it. She lights one and blows the smoke skyward.

He begins to cough and has a hard time controlling it.

Vivienne stubs her cigarette out and proffers her handkerchief, which he takes. When he stops wheezing, she says, "You saw Henri's mural. It's truly original, the perfect solution for an almost impossible space. It's a masterpiece—and I'm not using the word lightly. Are you willing to jeopardize his ability to create another?"

"He'll find a way."

"And you want to make this as hard for him as possible?"

"He brought it on himself."

Some of her previous anger resurfaces, but she has to let him save face. "It's such a disaster for everyone," she says. "You're disappointed. And so am I. But Henri is devastated. He knows it's his fault. And that makes it even more difficult for him. Not to mention that after he worked so long and so hard, he's going to have to put it all aside and start over from scratch . . ."

Edwin stands and moves some papers around on the desk in the corner of the sitting room. "I suppose I could foot the bill for some of the materials," he says grudgingly.

"That's generous of you." Another push could backfire, but what he's offering won't be enough. "And maybe you could add a few dollars to cover the salaries of his assistants? That way the mural will be finished in the fastest time possible."

He eyes her with a trace of amusement. "You drive a hard bargain, woman."

She acknowledges that she does, and that's that. It won't undo the hurt his words caused, but it's better than nothing, and she knows Henri will appreciate the support. She also knows this concession is as close to an apology—both to Henri and to her—as Edwin is going to get.

THE NEXT DAY, Vivienne goes to the Louvre to do some preliminary research on a book about Renoir that she and Edwin are planning to write. It's a pleasant spring day, the sidewalks filled with the typical

Parisian noonday crowd noisily enjoying the fine weather. But she's impervious to the day's glories.

She has no idea how Henri actually feels about her, or how she feels about him. She has no idea how she might persuade Edwin to terminate the trust and make the collection his own. And she has no idea how to return the colonnade seven to her father. If only she could see Papa's eyes light at the sight of his treasured masterpieces, as she did in her dream. The truck driver isn't the only person who can pull off a robbery. A speakeasy isn't the only place to find a thief. She gave up too easily.

A man is coming toward her with an expectant smile on his face, as if he knows her, almost as if they had arranged to meet. He doesn't look familiar with his glasses, long hair, and beard, his face bronzed and rough like a farmer's. But as he draws closer, she knows exactly who it is. The broad shoulders and strong chin, the sauntering gait, the clump of hair falling over his forehead.

He bows when he reaches her. "Ashton King," he says with a heavy Australian accent and a roguish grin. "Perhaps you've heard of me?"

Vivienne gapes. George is Ashton King. Of course he is.

"You've grown into a beautiful woman," he says, taking her hand. "It's a pleasure to finally meet you, Vivienne Gregsby."

It's as if she's watching a play: there she stands, her hand limp in his; he, full of confidence, his smile at full wattage. She yanks her hand back.

"I've never stopped thinking about you." His voice is warm and his eyes brim with sincerity. "I've thought about you every day for the past four years."

"And I've never stopped thinking about you," she spits at him, taking a step backward. "I haven't been able to. Not after you stole everything my family had—not after you stole my life!" How dare he reappear like this? Ambush her in the middle of the street? Pretend nothing happened?

"I'm sorry." He hangs his head. "More sorry than you can imagine."

"Right," she snorts. "Particularly sorry about enjoying all that money that doesn't belong to you."

"I'm sorry for hurting you. Sorry for what happened. But I've changed. That's all behind me now. I've come to make things up to you. Maybe even—"

She begins to stalk off, but he grabs her arm.

"Please, Paulien—"

"Don't you dare mention that name. Paulien is dead. And you killed her!"

"No," he begs. "Please don't say that. Don't think it. I'm here because I want to help you. To repay you for at least some of what I've taken from you."

"Then give me back the money you stole. Give my father—and everyone else—everything you stole. That's the only repayment I'll accept."

"I know you won't believe me, but at the moment there isn't any money. That's why I've come—to extend a proposal of sorts. Please hear me out."

"Right. No money. That's a laugh." Vivienne tries to shake him off, but his fingers don't give. "A proposal? Are you out of your mind? A proposal to invest in one of your con games? Or are you perhaps proposing marriage? I accepted proposals like these from you before—and you can be certain I'll never do anything like that again." She wants to knee him in the groin and would if she had the leverage. "Let me go!"

"It's not a proposal as much as an offer. An offer to help you get what you want."

"What the hell do you know about what I want?" she demands, then calls in her anger. He *can* get her what she wants. What she wants more than Edwin's collection or even the colonnade seven: justice, revenge, and her family's forgiveness.

28

PAULIEN, 1922

Paulien couldn't have been more pleased: George did exactly as he promised. Her father's associates in Italy found George some runners, and business picked up considerably because of it, paying all of Everard Sureties' clients, including her father, generous profits. And now George was planning to accept a dozen of her father's friends as investors.

"I know it sounds crazy, but it's as if your father was the catalyst who turned the tide," George said as they lay in bed after making love. "As soon as he got involved, got his business associates involved, there was a sea change. Where everything had been stagnating, now everything is booming."

"That's wonderful," Paulien mumbled, drifting off to sleep. "I'm glad."

"When I offered him his first month's profits, he said he wanted to reinvest the money—and add to it. I let him triple his initial share. But he'd like to invest even more."

She pulled into wakefulness. "Are you going to let him?"

"Things are running much more smoothly, and far more transactions have been completed. Profits are skyrocketing, so I suppose . . ."

She snuggled into his side. "I'm so proud of you. Helping him. All his friends . . ."

"I take it that means you'd like me to let them all buy more shares?"

"If you can. I wouldn't want you to do anything that would be bad for your business."

"I'd have to cut back on some of my original clients' requests. Even with the additional runners, there are only so many trades we can process at a time. The early investors wouldn't be happy about that—especially given their recent gains."

"He's going to be your father-in-law," Paulien reminded him, melting as she said the words. "His friends and business associates will become yours, potential Everard Sureties clients for life."

"Oh, this isn't going to last that long. The Italian economy is picking up, and the cost of their IRCs is going to rise and cut into our profits."

Paulien sat up. "When do you think that's going to happen?"

"Six months, maybe fewer. But unless something derails the country's growth, the price isn't going to stay this low for long."

"But what about Everard?" she asked, both confused and concerned. "How will you keep going if that happens?"

George pulled her close. "We'll stop taking in new money, pay all the clients their proceeds, tell them the run is over, and close down the business. They'll be disappointed, but they'll also have earned back three or four times their initial investment—and I'm betting every one will be ready to become a part of whatever new venture I come up with. Same with the staff."

"So this could be a once-in-a-lifetime opportunity?" Paulien asked slowly. "Investing with you? Something to jump on?"

"I'm not sure I'd put it that way," George protested. "But there are profits to be made now that may not be possible later. So, in that sense, I suppose, yes."

Paulien knew George always underplayed his potential, particularly when it came to Everard Sureties. He was consistently self-deprecating—about both himself and his business—and never promised what he couldn't produce. "Can his additional investment be my wedding gift?"

George laughed. "I have a far better wedding gift in mind for you than some investment."

As much as she wanted to hear more about her wedding gift, Paulien persisted. "I'm serious. Would you consider letting Papa and his friends give you however much they want? And let me invest my trust fund money? Maybe my brothers will want to do the same with theirs. How about my mother and her family?"

"I don't think it's a good idea, doll." He frowned. "What if it doesn't work out? What if I'm wrong and Italy's economy picks up more quickly than I think? I don't want my entire new family to be angry with me."

"Please?" she begged, wanting more than anything to share her good fortune with everyone she cared for. "If it's not your wedding gift to me, it can be our wedding gift to them."

"Is that what you really want, my sweet, generous darling?" he asked, nuzzling her neck.

"Yes," she replied happily. "That's what I want."

"Then that's exactly what you'll get."

PART THREE

29

VIVIENNE, 1926

Vivienne allows George to lead her down the boulevard to a small café. They sit inside, where there aren't any other customers; only crazy people or those with secrets would be willing to forgo the splendors of such a spring day. When they're seated, she looks around for a telephone.

There isn't one in the dining room, but there must be one in the back room. After an amiable tête-à-tête about how he proposes to procure whatever it is that he believes she wants, she'll excuse herself to go to the water closet, sneak into the kitchen, and call the police. Then she'll waltz back to the table and chat him up until they come to arrest him.

She puts her napkin on her lap and tries not to smile as she imagines the expression on his face when he understands what she's done. The waiter places two menus in front of them and asks if they want anything to drink. Vivienne asks for a glass of water. George does the same. The waiter bows and leaves them alone. She pulls her chair as far away from him as she can. Being this close enrages her. She would happily kill him if she could get away with it. Instead, and perhaps better, she's going to destroy him.

George smiles with a serene beneficence, as if all he wants in the world is to secure her happiness. Horseshit, as Edwin would say.

"So what exactly is Ashton King up to?" Vivienne asks more sharply than she intends.

"It's good to see you haven't lost any of your spunk," he says, maintaining his thick Australian accent. "I was always partial to that about you."

"Another scam in which you wreck people's lives?"

He throws back his head and laughs. She swears his laugh has an Australian accent. He's such a fake. Such a good fake.

"What is it you want from me?" she demands. "Haven't you taken enough?"

"My dear Paulien, it's like I told you before—"

"Vivienne. And I'm not 'your dear' anything."

He holds up his hands in mock surrender. "My proposal is to help you—I don't want anything in return."

"I don't believe you've ever done anything without expecting a return."

He tilts his head to the side, pulls a hangdog expression. "Like I said, I want to make up a little for what happened."

"There's no way you can ever make up for what happened. And there's definitely no 'little' way."

He maintains his wounded countenance. "I heard you were in need of a thief, and I just wanted to offer my services."

She feels her jaw drop.

"I was in a speakeasy in Philadelphia last fall and overheard you talking with the bartender," he says smoothly. "Aren't those Americans ridiculous? Banning alcohol and then allowing the gangsters to take it over? It's not as if everyone doesn't know what's going on."

Vivienne manages to close her mouth. "You . . . you . . ."

"I was doing some business in Philadelphia and happened to see you at the symphony one night. You looked so stunning, so confident—a woman, not a girl any longer. I was filled with such admiration that I—"

"That you followed me? Listened in on my conversations? How dare you?"

George isn't the least bothered by her anger. "What does it matter? It worked out for both of us: I discovered what you need and I'm here to help you get it." He leans in closer. "Now, tell me exactly what you want me to steal."

BY THE TIME Vivienne and Edwin leave for America a week later, she and George have worked out a deal. She'll leave a back door unlocked, and he'll find some thieves to fake a break-in. To disguise the purpose of the robbery, the men will grab at least two dozen paintings, including hers. She'll keep the colonnade seven, and George will dispose of the rest.

What troubles her—obviously there are many things that trouble her—is that it isn't an actual deal. George refused to accept any of the extra stolen paintings as compensation, claiming he wants to do her a favor, is happy and eager to do so, that he'll make sure the additional paintings find their way back to Edwin in a manner that casts no suspicion on either of them. Except George Everard doesn't do favors unless there's some payoff for him. Nor, she's sure, does Ashton King.

He explained that he needed to stay in Europe for at least another four or five months to get his latest "business" off the ground. When things are set, he'll come to Merion to, as he put it, "get the lay of the land." She's aware she's acting like a lunatic, taking a crazy risk, but it all landed in her lap, and she can't resist the opportunity to return at least a small portion of all she caused her father to lose.

Perhaps she should have called the police from the café, but she can have him arrested in Philadelphia as easily as in Paris. And George is the perfect man for the job, exactly who she was looking for: a risk taker who's fond of money and holds little regard for the law—and they don't come any more unsavory. It's simple and elegant, as the best solutions are. The paintings will be her first gift to her father; George's arrest will be her second.

AS PROMISED, GEORGE turns up in July. He's on her porch, rocking in her rocking chair, when she comes home from work. Although it has to be close to ninety degrees, he appears as cool and comfortable as if it were seventy. He stands and smiles at her, flexing those dimples, and she can't help but appreciate how handsome his chiseled, perfectly proportioned features are. He no longer has a beard or long hair, and his glasses are gone. He's shaved and trimmed and clean cut, and now his dark hair is graying at his temples. She guesses he's no longer Ashton King.

Vivienne swallows her loathing, her desire to grab a kitchen knife and drive it into his heart, and reminds herself that this isn't about retribution. Yet.

He comes down the steps, takes her hands, and kisses her on both cheeks. A European move. Definitely not Australian anymore.

"So who are you now?" Vivienne demands, again unable to control her visceral reaction to his presence.

"My name is István Bokor," he says with a faint Slavic accent, bowing. "Pleased to make your acquaintance."

"A Hungarian count, I presume," she says. He's disgusting—and so very proud of it.

"I hadn't thought of the count angle." There are those dimples again. "But now that you mention it, that is a nice touch."

There's nothing else she can do but invite him in.

He takes a seat on the couch as if it's his home instead of hers. She sits as far away from him as she can. Unfortunately the room is small.

"I've got some bad news," he says, dropping the accent. "I know we discussed carrying out our plan this summer, but I need to be in Paris longer than I expected. Business—you know how it is. So I won't be able to get back here until the fall. Probably September or October. Will that be okay?"

"But you're coming back? You'll still do it?"

"Absolutely." He looks at her fondly. "I'm here, aren't I? Just like I told you I'd be."

Vivienne is so relieved that it takes her a moment to realize what he's said. George Everard is expecting her, of all people, to take him at his word. From the expression on his face, it appears he's convinced he's worthy of this trust. And she realizes this is his secret: he actually believes his own lies.

Before she can respond, he comes over and kneels next to her chair. "But mostly I'm here because I love you," he says, "and I want us to be together. I want what my stupidity took from us." His face is stricken, his eyes raw with pseudosuffering. "I want to start a new life, just the two of us. I want you back, doll." He pulls her to him, pressing her close. He kisses her hard, then more gently.

Her lips soften of their own accord, meeting those she knows so well, swept up in the heady wonder that was George and Paulien. Then she recovers herself and breaks out of his arms. "Get away from me!" she yells, horrified by her body's response. "Get out of here!"

He stands, takes a step back, and looks at her with great tenderness, his smile so magnetic that even with all she knows, with all her bottled-up fury, she feels it in her core. "It's still there between us," he says softly. "You felt my love, and I felt yours. You know I'm telling the truth: how sorry I am, how much I want to set things right."

Telling the truth. His life is such a web of lies that he's incapable of differentiating fact from falsehood. How many people has he devastated since she last saw him? How very sorry is he for what he did to them?

He looks at her with those dark, liquid eyes. "I've changed."

He repulses her. She hates him, and wants more than anything to send him away, but she doesn't. God help her, he reminds her of how she once loved him, loved the feel of his lips on her body, his tongue. How she loved his smell. And for a flash of a moment, she wants it back. All of it. Youth and love and boundless optimism.

"I'll make us some tea." She flees to the kitchen. Once there, she fumbles with the match and burns her finger as she lights the stove. She sticks her finger in her mouth and tries to assess the situation. She doesn't know what's more absurd, his claims of shame or of love. In order to feel shame, you have to believe you've done something wrong, and George is unable to view his actions as anything other than reasonable and evenhanded. In order to feel love, you have to experience empathy, another impossibility.

She eyes the knife drawer but pulls two cups from the shelf over the sink, trying to figure out what he's really after. Obviously, allowing him into the Bradley under cover of darkness will give him the opportunity to take additional paintings, but that's too clean and straightforward. Does he plan to keep all the paintings his stooges steal, including the colonnade seven? Perhaps, but again it's too small a take for a man who thinks as big as George does. Last time, she was his entrée to her family and their wealthy friends. This time, she's his entrée to . . . Edwin. Or more precisely, Edwin's art and wealth.

George has his sights on the collection. That's why he stalked her, went to the speakeasy, insinuated himself with Gertrude, and agreed to participate in the robbery. Although some may suspect, few know for certain that she's Edwin's heir. Needless to say, a few are all that's necessary for George—or István or whoever the hell he is—to ferret out the truth.

He's a master at extracting information with charm and deception. No one's secrets are safe. But this time she isn't his dumb mark, following him around like a lovesick puppy. She'll entrap him while he believes he's entrapping her. The fact that he's embarking on this game means he knows nothing about the trust. And this gives her an advantage.

She arranges the teapot and cups on a tray and waits for the water to boil. First they'll have a nice "spot of tea," as George would have said when he was pretending to be a Brit, and then they'll have a heart-to-heart.

30

GEORGE/ISTVÁN, 1926

He didn't just arrive in the States, as he told Paulien. He's been here for four months, long enough to take three courses at the Arboretum School at the Bradley, all of them taught by Ada Bradley: Plant Materials, Soil Science, Cultivated Trees and Shrubs. One in the spring and two over the summer.

He walked miles through the acres of landscaped gardens in Merion and made two site visits to Ker-Feal, the Bradley's Chester County estate, where Mrs. Bradley has designed terraces of flowers and fruit trees and turned a quartz quarry into a botanical garden. He has no particular interest in horticulture, but he has a compelling interest in Ada Bradley, with whom he's now on a first-name basis. Actually he calls her "sweetheart" much more frequently than he calls her Ada.

She usually calls him István but sometimes shyly reverts to "dear." She believes he's a Hungarian count—yes, Paulien had gotten that right— who always wanted to be a landscape architect but was forced into the family's massive munitions business. Being a man of the earth, he hated guns and war and hated his job even more. He recently escaped from his family's clutches. Ada also believes he's in love with her.

Which is ludicrous. But as the soon-to-be owner of the Bradley, he can't leave anything to chance. Which means he needs to have an angle in reserve. More than one.

Ada fell in love with him easily, and now he needs her to divorce Bradley. Stripping her of her status as Mrs. Bradley will clear the path for Paulien to inherit without any legal interference from the bereaved widow. And then once he and Paulien are married—how convenient that she proposed the idea herself—the collection will be his free and clear.

"So here's my deal," Paulien told him when he first went to her house. "You give me my paintings after you steal them, and I'll make sure you get the collection. Edwin is old, and he's not well. After he's gone, the entire collection will belong to me. If you do what I ask, I'm willing to marry you and then I'll move back to Europe permanently. I won't take anything else with me. It will all be yours."

When he posed a hypothetical and asked what she'd do if he decided to abscond with her paintings, she said, "You want more than my measly seven—you want them all—and I swear if you don't give mine to me, I'll do everything in my power to make sure no part of Edwin's collection ever becomes yours." He doesn't believe she can or will do this, but all he needs is for her to believe that he does. Nor will she have him arrested; he controls what she wants, which is more protection than a crooked judge.

He's optimistic Ada and Paulien will both fall in line; they've each taken the initial steps. But he's less sure of Paulien. If by some long shot, things don't work out with Paulien, he'll dissuade Ada from divorcing, and when Edwin dies, he'll marry her. Either way, he wins.

Obviously, Paulien is his first choice. Gertrude was reluctant to part with the details of Paulien's situation, and it took him longer than usual to wrest the information from her. But as always when he pours on the charm, the woman succumbed and finally told him everything.

Ashton King's art forgery scam is moving forward, but he's surprised by how problematic it is to find artists who are willing to forge paintings. The half-dozen forgers he's managed to hire, whom he's using to scout for others, are also having trouble. It seems that even the most poverty-stricken artists feel a moral compunction about copying someone else's work. Even when it's explained that the paintings aren't going to be sold, they still shy away. Misplaced principles make fools of so many.

So he stored his authentic artwork in a warehouse on the outskirts of Paris, blackmailed a man to oversee his forgers, and told his friends and colleagues that Ashton King's father had just been diagnosed with tuberculosis and that he had to rush back to Australia. And now here he is in Merion, Pennsylvania, of all the godforsaken places.

The Bradley scam is different from his previous endeavors, and he welcomes the challenge. Especially a challenge that includes courting Paulien Mertens. Not only is she more appealing than ever, but despite her family's tumble from grace, she's managed to position herself quite well. Heir to the Bradley fortune. He's got to hand it to her.

Yet Paulien's standing is more tenuous than he would like. Her fortune is only on paper, and he's run into more than his share of clever lawyers who would be more than happy—and able—to wrest it from her. Then there's Paulien's rumored affair with Henri Matisse, which makes the whole arrangement even less secure. And he's troubled by Edwin Bradley's notorious volatility and fickleness. Too many unknowns for his taste, but there have been virtually no initial capital expenditures and the payoff is mammoth, far more than any of his cons have accrued thus far. Hence the new love of his life, Ada Bradley.

He was the perfect student in Plant Materials last spring, his first class at the Arboretum School. He listened carefully, took detailed notes, and, most importantly, smiled and nodded sagely at everything Mrs. Bradley said. After class he approached her and asked probing questions involving the finer points of nomenclature and the intricacies of plant identification. He never skipped a class and he always arrived early. No one doubted his status as teacher's pet.

Needless to say, there's the age difference. But as he'd done with Katherine in the Talcott Reserves scam, he added a touch of gray to his hair and told Ada he was forty-eight, which is ten years older than he is and only five years younger than she. By the time he began Soil Science in June, she was too besotted to question his age, and now that he's completed Cultivated Trees and Shrubs, she's so agog over him that if he told her he was twenty-five she would believe him. She sees what she wants to see, sees just what he wants her to see.

Fortunately, Ada doesn't seem interested in sex, although if he pushed she would undoubtedly succumb. He flinches at the idea, but he's performed more debased deeds in pursuit of his goals in the past. He just hopes it won't come to that. Paulien, on the other hand, is a whole different ball of wax.

It's clear she's never fallen out of love with him. He felt it in that kiss. As much as she tried to fight, there was a give in her lips, a moment of surrendering herself to him. Paulien is caught in his gravitational pull, the way the earth is fixed in its orbit around the sun. And like any planet, she's tethered to him, unable to go anywhere except where he leads her.

He isn't bothered by her threats. Frankly he admires her boldness, as he admires her for intuiting his true motives. She's been studying his methods, learning his moves, considering him a mentor of sorts, a real protégé. A worthy—or in this case, semiworthy—adversary makes the game all that much more fun. Her threat to keep the Bradley collection from him is based in her naïveté and inability to see the whole chessboard, but a few more years of studying at his feet and she might have been able to figure it out. Fortunately she's a freshman.

Nor does he have any worries in the unlikely event that Paulien has a change of heart. Locked in the safe of his hotel is her letter describing the enclosed map of the Bradley with an X marking the location of each of the seven paintings she wants him to steal.

THE TRIAL, 1928

When Ada took the stand, she was calm and composed and believable, much tougher than I thought she'd be. The grief-stricken widow, married for decades, her husband's life and vast wealth stolen from her by a gold digger. A gold digger with a past. A gold digger who had killed her sugar daddy because she couldn't wait to get her hands on the gold.

Ronald's objection to this depiction of me was sustained, but from the way the jurors were leaning forward in their seats, hanging on to Ada's every word, it seemed they were inclined to accept anything she said.

I can just imagine the fury in your eyes when she described me this way, Edwin. How you would have snapped at her to keep quiet.

Ada told the court that I ensnared you with brazenness and debauchery, lured you into making me your beneficiary. She explained how she begged you to fire me, to change your heir to anyone but me. Pleaded with you to see me for who I really was.

But you dismissed her entreaties, told her she didn't understand me or my value to the Bradley. Obviously the words of an older man smitten by a clever and provocative younger woman who was feigning adoration in order to get his money. A story as old as the Bible.

"Excuse me, Mrs. Bradley," Pratt said, "but I'm confused. If your husband was so smitten with Miss Gregsby and had already named her as his heir and successor, why would she have needed to take any other action?"

"Obviously she didn't want to wait until he died."

"Objection."

The judge, for once, shook his head at Pratt. "Rephrase."

"Do you know of any circumstance that might have caused the defendant to believe Dr. Bradley might want to change his will?" Pratt rephrased.

"That he planned to disinherit Miss Gregsby?"

"His attorney told me after . . ." Ada struggled to collect herself.

"Hearsay!"

"Please proceed, Mr. Pratt," the judge ordered. "This information is already part of the record."

Ada sniffed. "Afterward, Jacob Gusdorff told me Edwin directed him to disinherit her and change his beneficiary to me." She covered her face with her hands. "Just three days before she killed him!"

"Objection!"

But Ada, suddenly no longer the fragile, bereaved widow but an enraged woman scorned, didn't care about Ronald's objection. She pointed at me. "You murdered my Edwin to feed your own greed!"

"Objection!" Ronald roared again.

Before the judge could rule, Ada turned to the jury. "Please don't let her get away with it."

Ronald's objection was sustained, but it was a hollow victory. The jury heard what Pratt and Ada wanted them to hear.

During his cross-examination, Ronald did establish that Ada had also known what time you were leaving that day and that you never obeyed the stop sign, but when she saw the thrust of the argument, she addressed the jury again. "If I were going to kill anyone, I would have killed her!" she said, and began to sob.

The judge admonished her for the outburst, but it was clear that we had lost what little advantage we might have gained from suggesting that Ada had the same opportunity I did.

31

VIVIENNE AND GEORGE/ISTVÁN, 1926

Vivienne is the first to arrive at the Bradley on the day she and George have chosen for the robbery. The building is dark and shadowy, and she turns on the lights in the hallway, her office, and the main room. Then she saunters nonchalantly through the circle of rooms on the first floor, hands in the pockets of her dress. She makes another half circle and enters Room 10, which is the farthest point in the building from Edwin and Ada's residence.

The south wall of Room 10 holds four of Henri's paintings, including one of her favorites, *Reclining Odalisque*, and a door. The door is barely noticeable, painted the same warm beige as the walls, its hinges camouflaged by the metal works included in almost every ensemble. Behind it, a small anteroom and another door lead to the back garden.

She takes a pair of short evening gloves from her pocket, dons them, listens carefully, then opens the first door and steps into the anteroom. She disengages the insubstantial lock securing the second door and then steals back inside. She returns the gloves to her pocket and saunters just as nonchalantly to her office, where she puts in a normal day of work.

Now it's up to George.

THE NEXT MORNING she climbs out of bed just before first light. She gets dressed, throws down a quick cup of coffee, and heads for the door, a light jacket in hand. An envelope sits on the floor in front of the mail slot. George's handwriting. She grabs it, tears it open.

A thick note card capped by the embossed emblem of the Morris House Hotel is inside. "Sorry," the note reads. "Will be in touch when the commotion dies down." She clutches the coatrack to steady herself.

When she left work yesterday, she didn't check the door to the garden, as she was afraid it might call attention to Room 10; therefore it's possible someone found it unlocked during the day and locked it again. But no one uses that door. When she and George discussed this possibility, they agreed he would instruct the thieves to leave and try again another night; so maybe it's just a small hitch. But why would there be a commotion? She hurries to the Bradley.

The row of police cars parked on Latches Lane answers her question. There's no small hitch; there's a full-blown disaster. She stares at the ten-foot wrought-iron fence surrounding the building, a stylized letter *B* embedded in its crown, wraps her hands around the curved iron. Once again, George has ruined everything. She presses her fingers so tightly to the bars that the squared edges cut into her flesh. She relishes the pain, grips harder. When she finally lets go, fiery red indentations cover the inside of her fingers and palms.

Vivienne takes an unsteady breath and enters the building. Three policemen guard the opening to the main gallery; they ask her questions but refuse to answer hers. Finally they allow her inside. She hears the noise of raised voices and the clank of metal from the direction of Room 10, races up the stairs, and marches into Edwin's office.

He's speaking with two more policemen, who look as though they must be father and son. "What's going on?" she cries. "What happened?"

"A robbery," Edwin replies.

"What did they take?" she demands. "What's missing?"

"Nothing." He begins to cough, punches his fist into his chest, coughs some more. "They couldn't get in," he manages through his wheezing.

"Oh." She looks at the policemen and presses a hand to her heart. "Whew. Wonderful. Wonderful news. You had me scared there."

No one says a word.

"Did something else happen?" she asks, wide eyed with innocence and concern.

"This is my assistant, Vivienne Gregsby," Edwin explains.

"No, Miss Gregsby," the older policeman says. "There's nothing else. Dr. Bradley here is a very lucky man."

"Please. Tell me what happened."

"Someone tried to break into the museum through one of the back doors—"

"The school," Edwin interrupts. "It's not a museum."

The officer frowns. "The school, then. The incident took place at approximately one thirty a.m. Looks like he used a crowbar."

"Did you catch him?"

"No," the officer tells her. "But he couldn't have gone far. Seems there was some planning involved, so he might be local. Might even be known to us."

"Why do you say that?" Edwin asks.

"It appears he knew the layout of the . . . the school," the younger one explains. "We're guessing this because he tried to gain entrance through a door that was as far away from your residence as possible. One, from the looks of it, that's hardly used and had a flimsy lock. Probably would have succeeded if Dr. Bradley here hadn't heard him. As it turned out, he never even got it unlocked."

The door was locked. So it isn't completely George's screwup. It's hers, too. "You have no idea who it could be?" she asks.

"As of now," the older policeman says defensively. "But rest assured, we will find him—or them." As he summarizes the remainder of the details, Vivienne puts on a great show of shock and dismay. The dismay isn't nearly as difficult to conjure.

He's HAVING A scotch, his feet up on the ottoman in his suite at the Morris House Hotel, one of Philadelphia's finest, tucked alongside Washington Square. A little early in the day for a drink perhaps, but he has to toast his success. Another step completed. A small one, but an important one nonetheless.

Once you and a mark suffer a joint failure, especially when the mark believes that failure is partially his—or in this case, hers—a sense of attachment develops. A spirit of "we're in this together." When that connection is made, the mark will assume all your subsequent decisions are in her best interests, and after that it's smooth sailing. Which is exactly how the "robbery" had gone.

The night was cloudy and starless, the crickets causing a racket. He wore dark clothes and gloves, approached the building from behind a little after one o'clock, a crowbar at his side. Just as planned, the door was unlocked. He twisted the knob, pushed it in a few inches, inserted his gloved hand, locked it from the inside, and closed the door again.

Then he began smashing it with the crowbar. As loudly as he could. He hacked at the doorknob, scratching metal against metal. He thrust the curved edge into the wood, hacked some more. He kicked the door with his boot a few times just for luck and then disappeared into the darkness. From a neighbor's yard he watched a few lights come on, and then, chuckling, he made his way to his car.

After the entire brouhaha, the sirens and the lights and all those cops running around like a gaggle of Mad Hatters, no one will be lifting any paintings from Edwin Bradley's little fiefdom anytime soon. Which, once again, is just fine with him.

The best part, the reason for the entire escapade, is that Paulien will now believe he tried his damnedest to get her precious paintings. And because she'll also feel responsible for the failure, she'll agree to his next, infinitely more profitable suggestion.

WHEN VIVIENNE ARRIVES at the Bradley the next day, it's as if the turmoil of the last twenty-four hours never occurred. Edwin is in his office meeting with his bankers, and Sally McDonald, his new secretary, is busy typing. There's no sign of the police.

Vivienne sits down at her desk and pulls out the materials for a course she's been developing, but her eyes refuse to remain on the page, straying toward the window, the bookshelf, the ceiling. Just a few days earlier, she was consumed with ideas for a class on Renoir, which dovetails nicely with the book she and Edwin are writing—not to mention the over one hundred Renoirs in the collection. Now she can't work up any enthusiasm for figuring out the best way for the students to discover Renoir's groundbreaking insight that shadows aren't black or brown but the reflected color of the things around them.

She stares at her notes, but they look like a swarm of bugs rather than words. If the situation stays as it is, there's no hope of returning the colonnade seven to her father; Edwin will surely hire guards, and the trust agreement fixes the paintings in place as securely as the ensembles do. Her only hope is to convince Edwin that the benefits of terminating the trust are worth the money.

After he escorts the bankers out, Edwin comes to find her. "The Bradley is bleeding money." He lights two cigarettes, offers one to her. "The endowment is shrinking."

"Bleeding and shrinking," she says, taking the cigarette. "You make it sound like the Bradley is on its deathbed."

His mouth is a straight line, his voice gravelly. "It's not good."

"Bankers like to worry," she reminds him. "It's their job." How critical can this be? Edwin is a millionaire many times over, and the collection's value is mind boggling—and growing every day.

He stares at a spot over her shoulder and doesn't respond.

"Couldn't you buttress it with some of your own money?"

Now he focuses on her, and his eyes are cold. "I'm not particularly liquid at the moment."

This makes sense, given the amount of artwork he's been acquiring—and for how long. Bradley and Hagerty, Chemists, is doing well, but Edwin mentioned that sales have been slow lately. And although the stock market is booming, Edwin considers stocks too risky and invests only in bonds.

"Hermans said that without changes, we'll run out of cash in the next three to five years." He starts to cough.

Vivienne pours him a glass of water from the pitcher on her side table, hands it to him along with her handkerchief, tries to absorb what he's telling her.

The monthly bills for an endeavor of this size have to be staggering—for salaries, electricity, maintenance, and so much more. Edwin has begun only a small portion of the conservation effort needed to keep the artwork in decent condition and patched a few holes in the roof. Despite its young age, the building has suffered significant settling, shifting, and cracking—something about cement and the cold winter during construction—plus the collection is showing serious signs of wear as well. All this is going to worsen, necessitating more money for more repairs.

"So what did Hermans suggest?"

Edwin takes a long drink of water. "The usual. Allow paintings to go out on loan, sell color reproductions, open to the public, get rid of the bonds at a loss, and invest in the stock market." He pauses. "Deaccessioning."

Deaccessioning, selling off a portion of the art, is something Edwin will never consider, but perhaps he might accept one of the others. "And?"

"As you well know, none of it is negotiable." He scowls at her as if this is her fault. "Which is exactly what I told Hermans. No books. No stocks. No loans. And I refuse to allow random people off the street into my home!" He pounds her desk for emphasis and leaves the room.

Vivienne stares into the corridor. If Edwin doesn't have the cash to pay the taxes, the trust cannot be terminated.

ONCE A DAY, sometimes more, she goes into each of the galleries where the colonnade seven hang, visiting the paintings as one might visit incarcerated family members. Touching the frames, murmuring to them if no one's in earshot, trying to raise their spirits. To raise her own. She wishes George would show up so she could have him arrested. Now that he has nothing to offer her, she might be able to pull a success out of this debacle. But he's surely aware that this might be on her mind—and it's probably why he's staying away.

Although Henri is racing to finish *Dance II*, he writes more frequently than ever, but now his letters are less about missing her and more about the mural's progress. In one he boasts that the new dancers are looser and more lyrical than the earlier ones, and in the next he claims that images of the still-unfinished mural haunt his waking hours and torment his sleep. He grumbles that his willpower is completely depleted and that it's only his stubbornness that stands between him and abject failure.

Edwin is constantly bellyaching also: about the money, about Quinton, about the damn bankers, about his damn cough. It's not that she doesn't sympathize with both Henri and Edwin, but their peevishness is annoying, and it's not as if she doesn't have peeves of her own. This is what comes of being the loyal confidant to two men: two sets of grievances, two sets of placations, two sets of vexations.

As fall deepens, Vivienne spends as much time outside as she can, kicking up the red and yellow leaves that cover the sidewalks and grassy parks, roaming without destination. She's at a picnic table in Gladwyne Park one afternoon, finishing off a sandwich and watching a mother teach her little girl to play hopscotch, when she feels someone sit down too close to her on the bench. She twists around, annoyed at the presumption.

"Paulien," George says.

"George."

"Sorry about the robbery. The guys screwed up."

"You hired them." She scours the park for a policeman, a ranger, anyone with authority.

"It wouldn't have happened if the door hadn't been locked."

Their eyes engage in battle. A tickle at the corner of George's mouth, a matching one at Vivienne's. Why does she find it so hard to stay angry with him? Even though he's the most contemptible man she's ever met.

"Touché," she says, trying to control her smile. "I guess I should also apologize."

"Apology accepted." He leans back into the bench. "So now we need to come up with an alternate plan to get your paintings."

"I thought you always have an alternate plan," she says dryly. "Or three."

"I do know that forcing Bradley to terminate the trust agreement is the way to begin."

She stares at him. How on earth could he know this? But George is always a few steps ahead of everyone else. "Do you have any thoughts on how this might be accomplished?"

"I understand there are some financial issues."

"Which is why Edwin will never terminate it. He doesn't have the money to pay the taxes."

George watches a wave of leaves roll along the sidewalk, pushed by the wind. "Is there anything that could happen that would make the termination worth the money to him?"

"Highly unlikely."

"There must be something," George presses. "What is it that would enrage him the most?"

Now it's Vivienne's turn to watch the twirling leaves, which remind her of Henri's dancers. "If someone was going to take the collection away from him . . . ," she says slowly. "Especially if they were going to turn it into a public museum."

George beams.

32

GEORGE/ISTVÁN, 1926

Once Ada explained that the Bradley was held in a tax-exempt trust, his next steps were plain. Whether the beneficiary is Paulien or Ada, the trust must be terminated. As it stands now, after Bradley's death, neither woman would actually inherit the collection; they would only gain pseudocontrol of it, their hands tied by a board of trustees. And if they don't own it, neither will he.

After the attempted robbery—well, the not-really-attempted robbery—he takes a month-long train ride to California and back. Going west through Chicago, east through Texas. The idea is to let any investigation of the break-in cool down, and for both Vivienne and Ada to heat up. He finds that absence works just as the sages say it does.

When he gets back to Philadelphia, he continues where he left off. He spends a day at Ker-Feal with Ada, encouraging her to fall even more in love with him than she already is—if that's possible—and milking her for information on the Bradley. She's shrewder than he believed at first, but unfortunately she's got little interest in or knowledge of her husband's business affairs. "If it were up to me," she told him, "I'd burn the whole place down—with the girlfriend inside."

The next day he follows Paulien to the park. Even after the "bungled" burglary, she's clearly pleased to see him—and more than pleased to collude with him to get her hands on her colonnade seven. She's still willing to marry him, even if she claims it's only for the purposes of their bargain, which it isn't. It's because she loves him, has always loved him. He knows how to play her, has always known how to play her. Which is useful because, unlike Ada, she does have a lot of interest in and knowledge of Bradley's business affairs.

33

VIVIENNE, 1927

Vivienne is in Edwin's office trying to find the files he left for her documenting his Renoir purchases. His desk is a mess, and it takes her longer than she expects. She finally finds what she's looking for under a pile of opened mail and is just about to return to her own office when she catches a glimpse of a letter from Edwin's physician, Dr. Tauber. She pulls it out.

It is with great regret that I inform you that Drs. Evarts Graham and J. J. Singer of New Orleans, Louisiana, have refused to take on your case. While they have attempted surgical remedies for carcinoma of the lung in the past, none of these interventions proved successful, and the doctors are reviewing their procedures prior to making another attempt. In the meantime, they recommend, as do I, morphine for the pain and shortness of breath, ginger tea and alfalfa seeds for loss of appetite and fatigue.

Vivienne allows the doctor's message to flutter to the desk. Carcinoma of the lung. Edwin has lung cancer. This explains the coughing and wheezing, the cold that never went away. Cancer. The word no one speaks out loud.

"Edwin must have known about this for a while," she tells George. "Long enough for the doctor to contact the surgeons. For them to write back. And he's been sick a lot longer than that." She thinks back to when she first noticed his coughing fits. "Over a year, I think. Maybe two." Her eyes widen. "Which is just about when he made me his beneficiary . . ."

George strokes his chin as if he still had Ashton King's beard. "Can't have much time left."

"Which means we have to get this done." It isn't that she's completely coldhearted; she's shed more than a few tears over Edwin's diagnosis, and she's concerned about how tough his last days might be. What she and George are doing doesn't have anything to do with Edwin's illness. They'd begun moving forward before she found the letter.

"Building trust takes time," George says. "Especially with a fish as big as Thomas Quinton. He and I—or to be exact, he and Copper Robinson—have had a number of dinners, cigars, et cetera, but it's only been a couple of months, not long enough. He has to believe, really believe, not only that Robinson is a highly regarded Australian architect, but that I'm his friend."

"What if Edwin dies before—"

"Trust is key," George says calmly. "Without it you lose, and I don't plan to lose."

"I understand that," she protests. "But it's not only the cancer. The Bradley's finances are getting worse. We need to move faster if Edwin is ever going to agree."

"No, my dear Paulien, we need to move slower if Edwin is ever going to agree."

Vivienne hesitates. It goes without saying that George has more experience conning people than she does, but she knows Edwin better. "He's a stubborn old coot, and once he's made a decision, he feels it's a sign of weakness to change it."

"Which is exactly why this setup is so important." George's voice is confident. "If done correctly, once the new information is added into the equation, he'll convince himself that changing his mind will make his position stronger. Or he'll fail to recall he ever made the first decision."

"This is making me nervous."

The laugh is full of warmth and affection. "Okay, okay. Fine. Let's gather all the information Robinson is going to need to persuade his good pal Thomas Quinton to help us, then I'll see what I can do to speed up the action."

The next night, Vivienne brings George to the Bradley after hours. They walk into the main room. "The engineers told Edwin the building itself is structurally sound," she says. "But because of problems when the footings were poured, there's been a lot of settling." She points to cracks that run down the west wall. "And the roof leaks."

George strolls around the room, a notebook and pen held behind his back. He looks carefully at a picture of three nudes by Seurat. "Is this warped?"

She looks at the tiny ripples he's pointing to with the back of his pen. "I'm afraid it is."

He writes this down, and they continue into Room 2. A water-damaged wooden German chest, a Manet stained in one corner, Van Gogh's *Postman* covered with a visible layer of dust. She brings him to the utility closet and shows him the dozen pails they use when it rains.

"There hasn't been nearly enough conservation work, so some of the undamaged pieces need repair—and almost all of them need cleaning." Vivienne points to a Renoir. "See how the varnish is darkening here?" Then to another Seurat. "And all that along the bottom there? It's dirt. Varnished paintings collect it like a magnet."

George follows her, scribbling in his notebook. "I'm going to have my work cut out for me after we close this deal. It's going to take a hell of a lot more know-how and money than I thought to get this place in shape."

She stops abruptly and eyes him warily. Is he going to change his mind?

He laughs. "Don't worry. You've got plenty of know-how, and after this is over, I'll have plenty of money."

They walk into Room 19, stand in front of *The Music Lesson*. "I remember this in your colonnade," George says reverently.

"My favorite, my father's, too," she says wistfully. "It's this very painting that brought us together when I was a little girl." The very painting George stole from them, tearing them apart.

"I'm sorry, Paulien." George reaches out to pull her to him. "I'll get them back for you. For Aldric, who I always liked. I promise I will."

For Aldric, who I always liked. She wants to spit at him, but instead she points to the next gallery. When the robbery failed, she lost her stick; there's nothing to hold over his head if he goes for a double-cross. It occurs to her that he might have planned it this way. But even George can't be playing that many moves ahead. Ultimately it doesn't matter; she'll destroy him in the end. And if this all works as she hopes, she'll get the collection, too.

She begins explaining how canvases and wood panels need strengthening, how injuries from age or transportation or inattention pile up. "And the restoration process can also be complex. Come see this."

She brings him to a large painting in Room 6. "Some artists use different materials in a single painting. This one is made from oil, glue tempera, pastels, and a bit of gold leaf. Each of these elements ages and degrades at a different rate, and each requires a different technique to recondition it."

He inspects the picture. "Fascinating."

"It gets worse," she says. "The collection contains artworks made with all kinds of substances: egg, wax, house paint, even chocolate. And they're on all kinds of backings: canvas, wood, linen, paper, metal. So again, different rates of decay and different techniques for restoration."

He raises his head from his notebook and beams at her with admiration. "We're going to make a great team."

VIVIENNE BEGINS SPENDING time with George, who claims he's a new man and that they can now have the life they planned six years ago, live happily ever after with the Bradley collection as their family. Although this is not her vision of the future—where he rots in prison for eternity—she's lonesome. So she lays out the ground rules: they'll see each other no more than once a week, they'll be circumspect, and there will be no physical contact.

Every Tuesday night they drive into Philadelphia in his Pierce-Arrow convertible roadster and dine in fine restaurants. Although not the famous ones. He knows of these hidden gems, which would be puzzling, given his relative newcomer status, if he weren't George. And this fits Vivienne's needs. She doesn't want anyone telling Edwin that she's been seen dining with a strange man.

The worst part about being with George is that she actually enjoys his company. When she's with him, she can loosen up in a way she can't with anyone else. George knows her past and her present, so it isn't necessary to be on guard, worrying about saying the wrong thing, tripping herself up. Often she finds herself laughing with him or absorbed in an interesting conversation about art, which she had no idea he knew so much about. And he's the only one with whom she can speak openly about the state of Edwin's health.

One night they go to a tiny bistro, which appears to be the parlor of the chef's house. There are only eight tables, each discretely separated from the others by latticed room dividers and potted plants. Over salad, George says, "Tell me about Matisse."

"What do you mean?" she asks. Could he be reading her mail? She wouldn't put it past him.

His expression is guileless. "I mean, what's he like in person? You must have had a lot of contact with him when you were writing your book."

"Why this sudden interest in Matisse?"

"I've been thinking about *The Music Lesson* since we looked at it the other night. He's one of my favorite living painters."

Sure he has. Sure he is.

Vivienne wonders what George knows about her relationship with Henri, and says, "Henri Matisse the man is almost as fascinating as Henri Matisse the artist."

They discuss Matisse and his work through most of dinner. Then to Vivienne's regret, George switches to Picasso over dessert. "You know that Henri and Pablo hated each other's work at the beginning?" she says, not wanting to let go of Henri.

"I get the impression they still do," George says. "That they don't like each other much either."

"Partially true, partially playacting. Pablo once told me that no one has looked at Henri's paintings more carefully than he—and that no one has looked at his paintings more carefully than Henri."

"Really?" George is clearly surprised. "I was at Gertrude's one night, looking at Henri's *Blue Nude*, and Pablo came over and asked if it interested me. I told him I didn't really understand what Henri was doing. Pablo agreed and said something like, 'If he wants to make a woman, let him make a woman. If he wants to make a design, let him make a design. This is a muddle somewhere between the two.'"

Vivienne laughs. "They're two ambitious men competing to be the one to make the cleanest break with the past. To take the biggest step beyond what other artists are doing. Beyond what he himself is doing."

"Allied in the fight against the status quo," George says. "Comrades and opponents both."

"Exactly," Vivienne agrees, noting the similarity between the artists' relationship and hers with George. They continue to trade inside stories, and she's impressed with how much he's been privy to during his short stint as Ashton. Once again, she finds she's enjoying herself.

When George drops her off after dinner, he holds her hand a moment longer than usual. "Do you think that someday you might speak of me with as much admiration and affection as you do of Henri Matisse?" he asks wistfully.

She searches his face for signs of disingenuousness. Finding none but knowing that means nothing, she says lightly, "Perhaps when you produce a painting as grand as *The Music Lesson*."

His laugh is full of mirth and warmth, and for a moment she wants to stay in the car with him.

QUINTON'S CLOSE FRIEND Ralph Knight, the director of the Philadelphia Museum of Art, lobs the first broadside in Vivienne and George's war on the Bradley trust. Knight requests the loan of *The Joy of Life* for an upcoming show, and as expected, Edwin informs him that under no circumstances will he lend *The Joy of Life* or any other piece he owns to the museum.

Then suddenly, as if out of nowhere, rumors begin to spread about the Bradley's financial problems—and Edwin's inability to adequately maintain the artwork because of it. These are followed by an editorial in Quinton's *Investigator* in which the "wretched state" of the Bradley is described, citing the precise location of leaks, buckling floorboards, and crumbling stairs as well as "an appalling lack of conservatorship and preservation of the priceless artworks, which belong to all of mankind."

The thrust of Quinton's argument is that if Dr. Bradley is unable to maintain the collection, the state must take it over because it's a public treasure. Therefore the *Investigator*, in conjunction with the Philadelphia Museum of Art and the University of Pennsylvania's School of Fine Arts, has asked the attorney general's office to do just that.

Edwin strikes back with a letter to the editor, that is, to Thomas Quinton, reminding him that only a couple of years ago—it's actually over five, but Edwin is not one to be overly concerned with the facts—Quinton stated, in reference to the exact painting the PMA is now requesting, that Matisse "shouldn't be allowed to call himself an artist if he doesn't know the difference between foreground and background."

Which, as Edwin put it, "proves that Thomas Quinton is both a fool and a hypocrite." He also accuses Quinton or one of his staff of breaking into the Bradley. "How else would his paper know the exact location of the leaks? The specific damage?" How indeed.

As is Edwin's custom, he sends copies of his letter to all the newspapers in town, and many publish it. This, predictably, sparks an onslaught of negative Bradley articles, op-ed pieces, and letters to the editor. Edwin is irate, apoplectic actually. His coughing and wheezing increase.

As Vivienne and George planned, she's at Edwin's side throughout the onslaught, encouraging his anger, supporting him in his savaging, salting his wounds. She's eager to move ahead, but George cautions patience. Finally they agree she can take the next step.

She sits down in the chair across from Edwin's desk. "I know you don't want to hear this, but as long as the Bradley claims a tax exemption—"

"You're right. I don't want to hear it."

"Please, Edwin, please just think about it. It may be the only way out of this mess. If you terminate the trust, all the property reverts to you personally, and neither Quinton nor Knight nor the state will have the right to tell you what to do with it. You told me Jacob said that as things are now, the state could contend it has a compelling interest in how the facility is maintained. So it makes—"

"If I don't have the money to fix the roof," he roars, "how the hell am I going to find the money to pay the damn taxes?"

"You can easily get a loan based on the value of a few of the paintings, and—"

"Great idea," Edwin says sarcastically. "Then I'll have to take out a new loan every April. Year after year. Not a good long-term financial plan."

She tries to keep her voice low and reasonable. "Once you do the necessary repairs and restorations, you can pay the loan back by lending out some of the paintings or—"

"I refuse to break up the collection—even temporarily."

Vivienne bursts into tears, which is easy, given the precarious state of her nerves. "We've got a potentially calamitous situation on our hands," she sobs, pulling her handkerchief from her pocket. "And I'm afraid if you pretend we don't, it's going to make it worse. You could lose it all," she wails.

"I'm not paying all that money for nothing," he says through clenched teeth, although he's clearly upset by her tears.

"It's not for nothing," she tells him, wiping her eyes. "It's for everything."

A LAWSUIT IS filed within a month arguing that "in order to protect one of the state's greatest cultural assets," it is necessary for the Commonwealth of Pennsylvania to place the operations of the Bradley School of Art Appreciation in receivership. Although Jacob Gusdorff warned him this was likely, Edwin is hit hard by the news.

"I'm worried that this time it's not going to turn out the way the last suit did," Vivienne tells him.

"They're not going to win."

"You can't know that."

"I do."

They're standing in the Bradley's main room and Edwin says, "These are my possessions. Bought and paid for by an American citizen—and as such the government cannot take them. No judge is going to rule against me on this," he adds. "Private property. The United States of America."

His intractability is so blinding that she pushes her fists into her armpits to keep from screaming. Then she hears George in her head: *You're an actress in a play, speaking a character's lines, a playwright's lines, not your own.*

"Edwin, please," she says, "please listen to me. The Bradley isn't your private property until you make it private. If you leave things the way they are, you could jeopardize it all."

But again he refuses. "We'll see how it plays out."

She begs Jacob Gusdorff to talk some sense into him. Jacob tries, explaining that the state's argument has validity and that he can't guarantee a positive outcome. In fact, if he were to predict, he'd predict defeat. Edwin is unmoved.

She's stunned when George remains optimistic. They strategize, and a few days later Edwin receives a letter.

My dear Edwin:

It is my understanding that the Bradley is currently suffering financial difficulties, and that these difficulties are the underpinnings of a lawsuit to place it into state receivership. I am also aware of the majesty of the Bradley's art collection, so I feel it is my duty, and also my honor, to offer to assist you in this extremely grave matter.

As a fellow art lover, I cannot bear the thought that those who share neither your passion nor your expertise will be placed in charge of the handling and potential deaccessioning of these precious paintings and sculptures. Therefore, my proposal is this: I am willing to fund all necessary restoration of the artwork in the collection, which would cause the state to drop its lawsuit. In exchange, the collection will be moved in its entirety, without deaccessioning, to Philadelphia and installed in a new building to be erected for this purpose, or perhaps in a new wing of the Philadelphia Museum of Art.

The details of such a structure have yet to be determined, but I have no issue with creating an exact replica of your current galleries in which the remarkable ensembles you have created would be duplicated in precisely the manner in which they are currently displayed in Merion.

I look forward to working with you to ensure that the priceless artifacts you have collected are properly maintained and protected and that the fine citizens of Philadelphia will be able to appreciate them for generations to come.

Your friend,

Thomas

"My friend Thomas!" Edwin explodes as he strides into Vivienne's office and thrusts the letter at her. "What horseshit!" He continues to rant as she reads it. "'The fine citizens of Philadelphia,' my ass," he rails, struggling to breathe. "'A fellow art lover'? The bastard has one hell of a nerve!"

"Don't forget about Ralph Knight," she eggs him on. "Both of them have finally figured out a way to move your collection to Philadelphia. To turn it into a museum!"

"Steal my collection is more like it!" he wheezes. "And that is never, ever going to happen!"

Vivienne waits.

"I'll get him to give me the restoration money, and then I'll arrange it so nothing can be moved."

"Quinton is no fool," she argues. "He's not going to pay you anything without a written contract allowing him to move the collection."

Edwin rips the letter into little pieces and throws them in the trash can. "I'll make it work. I'll find a way."

"Don't do it," she implores him. "It's a bad idea and it's not going to work."

"And you've got a better one?"

She just looks at him.

"I'm not taking out a loan to pay taxes I don't have to pay."

"So then what?"

He doesn't yell at her, which is what she expects. He just stares off into the distance. "You really think we might lose?"

"And so does Jacob."

"Damn fucker's got me over a barrel." Edwin has never spoken that word in her presence, which is a clue to the depth of his despair.

"I'm sorry," she lies.

Edwin raps his knuckles on her desk. "I'll have Jacob get started on the paperwork this afternoon."

"Paperwork?" she repeats to make sure he's talking about what she hopes he's talking about. After all their years together, she shouldn't be surprised at the swiftness of his decision, but she is.

"Quinton is not getting his hands on my ensembles," Edwin growls. "No matter how remarkable he says they are."

THE TRIAL, 1928

I despaired at the beginning of the trial because Ronald refused to give his opening statement until after the government rested its case. Well, I was wrong. It was an excellent move, and he did a commendable job.

He rebutted almost every argument Pratt made against me over the past week. And as far as I'm concerned, he nullified more than enough of them to establish reasonable doubt. He started with motive and named all the people—aside from me—who might have had reason to want you dead. I'm sorry to say that the list was long and included Ada. Cruel but effective.

So what if I'd once signed a receipt presented to me by the truck driver who hit your car? I'd signed thousands of receipts in the years I worked for you. And said driver had presented receipts to thousands of other people during the years he worked for Empire State Transport. How was I supposed to remember his name?

Ronald pointed out that, at various times, you'd appointed Ada, the University of Pennsylvania, and the Philadelphia Museum of Art as your beneficiaries, insinuating that each of them might have had reason to believe they were the current heritors to "one of the greatest private art collections on earth—a feather in the cap of any college or museum."

"And you must remember," Ronald said, "that Ada Bradley also had knowledge of precisely when her husband would be leaving their country home for the city. As did the cleaning woman, Blossom Sinclair. And it was a universally known fact that Dr. Bradley never obeyed that stop sign."

He went on to explain to the jury that you and I had been working together closely for years. That we had traveled together, written books together, purchased artwork together, taught together, and that together we'd made the Bradley and the educational curriculum what they are today. He emphasized that there were many more projects lined up to further expand our vision—projects that I needed you to help complete, including a half-finished manuscript on Pierre-Auguste Renoir.

But this wasn't the only reason I wanted you alive. Ronald hesitated, appeared to be reconsidering what he planned to say next, then plowed ahead, admitting that we had been having a longtime affair—and pointing out that many others, including Ada, were aware of this fact. That I was very much in love with you—and you with me. He told me that it didn't matter if this wasn't true. It served our purposes.

And then there was my character, the lies I'd been forced to tell to put Paulien Mertens behind me. "A youthful transgression," he assured the jury. "A teenage girl taken advantage of by a much older and seasoned con man, exiled from her parental home at nineteen, penniless and left to find her way alone in the world."

Ronald shook his head with great sadness. "I hope none of you thought, for even a minute, to hold this against Miss Gregsby. I say the fact that she has created such a successful life for herself indicates her character is strong—and that she should be admired rather than denigrated for all she has accomplished."

Take that, Ada. Take that, Pratt. Take that, Quinton.

And as for opportunity, well, Ronald pointed out that anyone could pay a truck driver to crash into a car, couldn't they?

But here is where Ronald really excelled. He approached the jury box and asked, "If you wanted to hire someone to kill your wife, your husband, your father, or your lover, how would you suggest the hit man go about doing this?" Then he answered his question with more questions. "A gun? A knife? Poison, perhaps?"

Ronald's voice was laden with sarcasm. "No, those are all too simple, too straightforward, too certain to be successful. I say there's got to be a better way."

He paused as if he were thinking what that way might be, then brightened. "How about getting a great big truck to wait at a stop sign, hope your potential victim won't stop at the sign, and then have the truck driver ram his car if he doesn't! Yes, that's it. That's what we'll do. It's clearly the best and surest way to get rid of someone!"

The jury remained stoic, but there were chuckles from the spectators. Ronald had warned me against it, but I couldn't help smiling.

"Under no circumstances does this make any sense," he continued. *"No one, especially a woman as accomplished and intelligent as Miss Gregsby, would be this stupid. Moreover, there's no doubt in my mind, and there shouldn't be in anyone else's, that Edwin Bradley was not murdered. That he was the unfortunate victim of an accident. Pure and simple. Nothing more and nothing less."*

Ronald turned to the judge. *"Although I have promised to present witnesses who will corroborate my assertions, I hope this will not be necessary. Instead, I offer a motion to dismiss, based on the fact that the prosecution has failed to produce any real evidence in support of a guilty verdict against my client."*

Ronald had cautioned me that judges almost always deny a request to dismiss, that he considered it a long shot at best, but his arguments were so persuasive I found it impossible to believe the judge wouldn't agree.

But he didn't, and despite Ronald's warning, I was crushed.

Edwin, there is no doubt that the result of this trial is guaranteed by Thomas Quinton's money and arm-twisting, his quest to move the collection out of Merion, which he knows I won't allow and Ada will. This has all the markings of shady deal making: Quinton gets me out of the way for Ada, and Ada turns her collection over to him and his buddy Ralph Knight at the PMA. Not to mention that Ada, the love of his life, will be so filled with gratitude for sending her nemesis to the electric chair that she will surely agree to marry him.

I fear that whether I'm innocent or guilty isn't going to matter, that the evidence isn't going to matter, that logic isn't going to matter. That I'm a dead woman.

34

VIVIENNE, 1927

After the trust termination papers are signed, Edwin begins to lose weight and his skin takes on an unhealthy sheen. He's listless, coughing and wheezing, getting next to no work done. He stops going into the factory, sleeps late in the morning, and often naps in the afternoon. Vivienne watches his decline with horror and self-loathing and, yes, grief. She can't believe she finds herself in a position where she's anxiously anticipating the death of a man who, for the most part, she respects and cares about.

Nor is it just the cancer that's eating at Edwin. Although he managed to best Quinton, avoid state takeover, and is now in full possession of the collection, he construes the termination as a failure. Vivienne tries to convince him this isn't the case, but he refuses to accept her arguments, and she worries that at any moment he'll renege on the decision he believes he was coerced into making.

George may have underestimated Edwin's stubbornness, but he was right about everything else. She is now the rightful heir; soon the Bradley building and every piece of art in it will be hers, to do with as she pleases. Loath as she is to admit it, this good fortune is, in large part, due to George.

He's a complicated man, and her feelings for him are just as complicated. If she were a better painter she could bring her conflicted emotions to life in a portrait of him: cool blue for friendship, dark crimson for revenge, vivid green for respect, high red for passion, black for hatred.

Plus a slash of orange for frustration: now that she's finally free to call the police, George has disappeared. But he'll be back to collect his spoils.

Months pass and George doesn't return, while Edwin's moods grow even darker. One morning, Vivienne is staring out the window instead of working on the curricula on her desk when Edwin stomps into her office. "I can't believe that now that you've got exactly what you want, you're moping around like a sick puppy," he gripes. "What the hell's wrong with you?"

Vivienne picks up her pen. "Just under the weather, I guess."

"Then take some aspirin," he says, unimpressed. "You're the one who got us into this predicament—and you're the one who has to figure a way out."

Edwin still hasn't told her about his diagnosis—nor does she believe he's confided in anyone else, including Ada—but it's clear he's taking some kind of new medicine, and it seems to be working. Over the past few weeks, he's pulled out of his lethargy, gained a few pounds, returned to the factory, and the naps have ceased. Unfortunately, whatever is in the drug is also making him extremely irritable. For a man who's already perpetually bad tempered, this is a disaster for everyone around him.

While she's growing accustomed to his venom, it worms its way into her. He's now completely soured on the termination, and she's to blame for everything that's followed: the absurdly high tax bill, the absurdly high estimate for the conservation work on the collection, the absurdly high interest rate the bank is proposing on his loan. It's all her fault because she was the one who pushed him into signing the papers—not his fault because he signed them.

Her aggrieved musings are interrupted by a knock on her door. It's Sally McDonald, Edwin's secretary, a plump, clever woman about ten years older than Vivienne, who started working at the Bradley about a year ago. "Stop daydreaming," she orders cheerfully. "Don't you have work to do?"

Vivienne makes a face. "No," she says. "Nothing to do at all."

Sally laughs. "Don't let the grump hear you say that."

They've become friends of a sort. When Vivienne found Sally crying at her desk after a vicious and unwarranted attack by Edwin, Vivienne comforted her, sharing Edwin stories of her own. Now they surreptitiously roll their eyes at each other when he's being an ass, giggle and console one another when he's at the factory. Sometimes they have lunch together, but Sally usually eats at her desk so she can go home earlier to her husband and three children.

Sally surveys Vivienne's face. "He up to his usual?"

Vivienne rolls her eyes.

Sally holds a stack of mail. "This should perk you up," she says. "A letter from your favorite artist." She hands Vivienne an envelope with a French stamp and Henri's unmistakable handwriting.

"Thanks." Although Vivienne has never spoken with Sally about her relationship with Henri, the older woman often teases her about him.

"Then I'll leave you to it," Sally says, closing the door behind her.

Vivienne rips the envelope open. "The end is near," the first line reads, "win or lose." Henri goes on to explain that he's finished cutting out the pink, blue, black, and gray paper shapes—as well as trimming them and pinning them to the canvas. After more than a little rearranging and reshaping, he released his assistants and booked passage to the States. He expects to arrive in Merion, along with the crated canvases, by the first of the year.

It does perk her up.

THE DAY HENRI arrives is bright and clear, although cold. She and Edwin rush to the front door when Sally tells them a car and a large truck are entering the drive. Vivienne reminds herself to remain attentive to Edwin. To avoid looking directly into Henri's eyes. To keep as much physical distance between herself and Henri as possible. To be friendly yet businesslike—until they can be alone.

For the first few days of his visit, she manages to do just that. She's a paragon of virtue: helpful and solicitous to Henri, as any hostess would be to an important guest; responsive to Edwin's needs, as any good assistant would be to her boss. But this grows more difficult. It's as if every nerve in her body is buzzing, inflamed. Seeing Henri, being with him, laughing with him, fuels her longing, and she worries that her craving is for more than just sexual release.

Classes have been canceled from Monday through Wednesday, and *Dance II* is being installed in the four days between the end of the last class on Saturday and the beginning of the first class on Thursday. This would be more than enough time if it weren't for the glue. Outside temperatures don't usually affect the inside of the building because of its thick plaster walls. But because of a weeklong cold snap, the glue is taking an overly long time to dry. This is frustrating for everyone, but Henri suffers the most.

Vivienne finds it remarkable that a man of Henri Matisse's stature and talent can be so unsure of the merit of his work. He watches uneasily while a small army of laborers climbs ladders, spreads the glue, places the first canvas, and begins to smooth it down with long, oversize brooms. Then he paces, muttering to himself as he walks the first floor's thirteen galleries, climbs the stairs, and walks the second floor's ten, stands mute behind the railing facing the mural. He then returns to the main gallery and does it again.

Midafternoon on Tuesday, Vivienne sends Edwin to get Henri some whiskey to still his nerves. This gives them a few minutes alone. They step into an alcove near the stairs and press together until there's no space between them. "When can you get away?" she asks, trying to keep her voice soft, but the deep throatiness of the words sends them bouncing against the walls.

"Tomorrow night," he whispers. "I have to go to a party with Edwin tonight. But tomorrow after you finish work, I will come to you. There is something important we must discuss."

"Yes," she breathes, feeling his heat and his hardness. "So many things to talk about."

There are footfalls on the floor above, and they spring apart. Henri resumes his pacing, and Vivienne stands against the wall, staring at the incomplete mural, trying to still her breathing before Edwin comes down the stairs.

A few hours later, when the last of the laborers climb from their ladders, Henri stares up at the first third of his mural, fixed in its place. A radiant smile spreads over his face. He turns to Vivienne. "It is good, no?"

"Far more than good," she assures him. "Stupendous."

Edwin is equally pleased. "I can't imagine how magnificent it's going to be when all three canvases are together."

She takes this opportunity to give Henri another hug and then steps quickly away.

35

GEORGE/ISTVÁN, 1927

It's an opal, round and full but not ostentatiously so, fiery with pink and turquoise, surrounded by a circle of tiny diamonds set in platinum filigree. Thirteen diamonds, a quarter carat apiece. The ring is tasteful and timeless, and he has no doubt Ada will adore it. He's been trying to develop more of an appreciation for her, to focus on her intelligence and quiet passion, her faded beauty, instead of her age and neediness. It's best when he warms to his marks, as it enhances his apparent sincerity. But she doesn't make this easy.

He's at Ker-Feal for the weekend, and as is always the case, Bradley has remained in Merion. In the course of his mock courting of Ada, he's surprised himself by developing an interest in botany and horticulture. Remarkably, he enjoys getting his hands in the soil.

He's particularly fond of Ker-Feal, especially the botanical gardens Ada created at the edge of an abandoned quarry on the property, where he sits. In the fall, he planted bushels of daffodil, tulip, and hyacinth bulbs, but now he's bundled in a heavy coat and there are few signs of life. After the bulbs winter over and the spring sunshine warms them, there will be a riot of color where the edge of the quarry climbs to the trees. This juxtaposition of flowers and water and rock will be soothing, and he wishes it were like that now.

Although he's pleased with his steady progress on the Bradley scam, there are a few areas of concern. He's frustrated that after more than a year of plying Paulien with his most reliably seductive moves, she's still holding herself back, unable or unwilling to let go of her grudge. Every once in a while she forgets their history and allows her true feelings to ignite, but then she remembers and snuffs them out.

The long-distance affair she's having with Henri Matisse might be a factor. But Matisse is a notorious playboy and has had many dalliances in the past, of which she must be aware. Paulien has learned a lot in the past five years and won't be the easy prey she once was. It's the glow on her face when she speaks of Matisse, who is currently in Merion installing a mural at the Bradley, that concerns him.

Plus, with the termination of the Bradley trust a fait accompli, she no longer needs anything from him, and she will surely try to have him arrested. Which is why he's disappeared from her sight. Although the American police would have difficulty developing a charge that would stick, any contact with criminal authorities is to be avoided. She also plans to renege on her promise to give him the remainder of Bradley's collection—she would have to be dim witted to do anything else—but he's taken precautions to ensure this won't occur.

There's also the small problem of Edwin Bradley, who, regrettably, must die. And soon. According to Ada, who knows nothing of the real cause of Edwin's maladies, he's been feeling better of late. But all scams call for strategic adjustments along the way, and fortunately he's an expert at this, agile and quick thinking, open to alternatives. He's overcome a myriad of problems in each of his previous undertakings and had wild success with each at the end. The end is all that matters.

His toes are numb and despite his thick gloves, his fingers are, too. He stands and begins the hike back to the house. He calculates that Bradley's collection is worth somewhere between $20 million and $30 million. A hefty take indeed. Made even greater because of the low cost involved in the initial preparations. He didn't even need to bribe Thomas Quinton.

It's always easier when you find a tool who wants exactly what you want. Quinton's eyes lit up when Cooper Robinson suggested that the disrepair of the Bradley building and collection could be used to show the need for a state takeover. And if Quinton wished, Cooper, Quinton's young, brash, and blond poker buddy, would be happy to provide any specific details that might be useful in verifying the claim. Quinton wished.

As he walks over the rocky expanse, he calculates a number of scenarios that will put Bradley—and, if necessary, Matisse—out of the picture. Some are more promising than others; some are more depraved than others. Being squeamish is no way to win. Especially in a game this big.

AFTER DINNER IS over and the maid clears the plates, he and Ada stay at the table, sipping a vintage port and discussing an expansion of the beds to the west of the house.

"I'm in correspondence with a horticulturist in England," Ada is saying. "He's a master at designing these types of—"

He presses his finger lightly to her lips and smiles so that his dimples flex and his eyes shine.

"What?" she asks flirtatiously.

"You are so lovely."

She blushes. "You make me feel like a young girl again."

"Would you like to feel that way all the time?"

"Wouldn't everyone?"

He drops to one knee and takes the ring box from his pocket, flips it open. "Marry me."

Ada gasps. "You can't be serious."

"But I am." He takes her left hand in his, removes her wedding band, and slips the opal on her finger. It fits perfectly, as he knew it would; he sized it from one of her other rings.

"Oh," is all she says, staring at the stone and moving her hand back and forth to catch the light. "Oh, István, you didn't."

"I want to spend the rest of my life making you feel young," he declares, forcing his eyes to moisten. "I love you."

"It's . . . it's astounding," she stammers. "It's perfect, and I adore it. But you know I'm married. A Catholic. I don't understand."

He sits back in his chair and takes both her hands in his. "Do you love me?"

"I do. Yes. You know that. And I want to marry you, but I can't just . . . I can't walk away from my vows—"

"You can do whatever you want, sweetheart."

"It's not that simple . . ."

"If you love me, then that's all there is. We must be together."

Ada dissolves into tears, and he moves to the chair next to hers and holds her while she cries. "It's all right, my darling," he murmurs into her hair. "It's going to be all right."

She lifts her tearstained face to him, and there's no loveliness there; she's sad and anxious and reminds him of his aunt Selma, his mother's older sister, which isn't a compliment. "As much as I long to, want to, I can't do it." She takes the opal ring off her finger and tucks it into his palm, closing his hand around it. Then she returns her wedding band to its place. "I'm so sorry to disappoint you—and me—but it goes against everything I believe in. And without that, who am I?"

He opens his hand and looks sadly at the ring, blinks as if holding back tears. "I had so hoped . . ." He allows his voice to trail off. There's nothing else to say.

His contingency plan is in place.

36

VIVIENNE, 1928

A warm front comes through overnight and the temperature jumps from twenty degrees to over sixty. Because of this, the remaining two panels go up more easily and faster than the first. *Dance II* is better than anyone, including Henri, expected. It frolics and leaps, sings and gambols, leads the eye across the great expanse and loops it back around again. This mural is simpler than his earlier flawed attempt, lighter and more carefree, the colors perfect. It's hard to imagine anything else in that space.

"Oh, Henri," Vivienne breathes, incapable of expressing the impact his mural is having on her. "It's . . . it's . . . it's just, well, it just is."

Edwin is far more articulate. "The way the radiant light streams through the gallery," he says in a hushed voice, "like a rose window in a cathedral."

They stand in reverential silence until Sally hurries in and approaches Edwin. "It's Mr. Hermans," she tells him. "From the Bank of Philadelphia." Sally looks from Vivienne to Henri and then back to Edwin. She lowers her voice. "He sounds upset."

Edwin pulls himself from *Dance II* and follows Sally to his office. Vivienne knows his casualness is a sham and that he isn't happy Sally mentioned trouble in front of Henri. Despite Gertrude's allegations that he's always waving his checkbook around, Edwin is very private about the state of his financial affairs.

But the Bradley's money problems aren't Vivienne's priority at the moment. "After such a long day inside," she says to Henri with great propriety, "I'm sure you'd like to stretch your legs, Monsieur Matisse. How about a walk, now that it's turned balmy outside?"

"What an excellent suggestion, Miss Gregsby," he answers with equal decorum. "Shall we?"

As they follow the paths winding through the grounds closest to the house, they keep a proper distance between them and talk in platitudes in case they're overheard by one of the gardeners, who even in winter are always roaming the premises.

"How was your dinner party last night?" she asks him.

"How is the Renoir book coming?" he asks her.

When they determine that all of Ada's staff has left for the day, they steal into an area of evergreens and towering rhododendron bushes that are hidden from the house. They seize each other, their lips crushing, and within seconds they slide to the ground.

Vivienne knows it's crazy, that Edwin's phone call could end at any minute, that Henri will be at her house in only a few hours, but the heat flooding her body is far more persuasive than any logic. Their clothes form their bed, and within moments they're making love. And it's even more intoxicating than she remembers.

"I love you," he says when he's deep inside her, their eyes fastened on each other.

She kisses him deeply. "And I love you."

Afterward, as they lie coiled together, she presses a finger to each bone in his back, places a flurry of kisses along his arm, and throws his coat over them. "So I guess this means we're in love," she says.

He smiles. "Indeed it does."

"So what do we do now?" she asks, not really wondering, because at that moment she doesn't care what comes next; she wants only this.

Henri lifts himself on one elbow. "I want you to come to France and live with me. For us to be together. This is what I wished to talk to you about."

"Live with you?" she repeats. She isn't just another lover to him, another conquest. He wants her with him.

"Is not that what people in love do?"

Before she can respond, the sound of scraping branches and the crunch of footsteps reaches them. Edwin. She freezes, gropes for a possible explanation but knows there is none. She clutches Henri's coat to her chest in a vain attempt to hide her nakedness. Holds her breath. Maybe he'll walk by. Miss them completely.

But it's not to be. And it isn't Edwin. It's Ada, which is just as bad.

ADA RUNS TO find Edwin, which gives Vivienne and Henri time to dress hurriedly. The four of them converge as Vivienne and Henri step onto the back patio.

"What the hell do you think you're doing, man?" Edwin demands of Henri. He doesn't look at Vivienne.

"Taking a walk," Henri replies with a straight face. "The mural is complete, is it not? Why the concern?"

"Vivienne is my concern," Edwin sputters. "She's in my employ, and she's currently at work. So what she does on my time is my business."

"If you must know," Henri explains calmly, "I was asking her to move to France and live with me."

"That's impossible," Edwin declares. "I won't allow it."

"Edwin . . . ," Vivienne begins, but stops when she realizes she doesn't know what to say.

"I do not understand," Henri tells him. "As you said, you are her employer. So that is surely where your interest stops." He pauses. "Does it not?"

"It's exactly where his interest stops," Ada says.

"Don't speak for me." Edwin scowls at Ada. "I'm standing right here."

Ada pales. "I told you already, I will never allow you to divorce me to marry this . . . this harlot."

"You are not to speak of Vivienne in this way," Henri orders.

"This is my home, and I will speak of anyone in it in any way I please."

"Stop this, Ada," Edwin snaps. "That's quite enough."

Ada glares at him. "Given your part in this charade, I'd say that *I'm* the one who should be telling *you* to stop—not the other way around."

"You seem to have forgotten that you found Vivienne with Henri"—Edwin winces as he says these words—"not with me."

"It could just have easily been you," Ada yells at him. "You think I don't have eyes? That I don't know what's been going on here?"

"You've seen nothing, because there's been nothing to see." Edwin's voice is hard and flinty.

"There is no reason to continue this discussion," Henri interjects. "Vivienne will be returning to France with me."

"That will be just fine with us," Ada says.

"Speak for your goddamned self!" Edwin commands.

Vivienne looks from one man to the other, at a loss. "But we . . . we . . . we haven't settled anything yet," she says to Henri.

"After everything that just happened, you'd allow her to stay here?" Ada demands of Edwin. "Are you out of your mind?"

"You do not wish to come with me?" Henri asks.

"You know how I feel about you," Vivienne tells him. "About us. It's just that we need to talk about it. I . . . I can't just pick up and go . . ." She looks over at Edwin, who still isn't willing to meet her eyes. "I think . . . I think we should all leave now. Let everyone cool down."

WHEN VIVIENNE GETS home, she closes the door and presses her back to it. What a disaster. But even in the face of the consequences, that rush of desire and the sweetness of its consummation were just too delicious to wish away. To finally hold him, be held by him, to have him inside her. To be loved by him.

She surveys her comfortable bungalow: the beamed ceilings, the stone fireplace flanked by built-in cabinets and benches, the way the living room opens into the kitchen, her bedroom tucked to one side, another smaller one nestled behind it. She's so fond of this place and enjoys living by herself: the privacy, the quiet, the way things remain exactly where she placed them. If she goes with Henri, she will have to leave her sweet home.

She throws open the windows that ring the house, letting in the spring-like air. She's grown to like it in America. She even became a citizen, believing this would cement her as Vivienne, allow her to finally lay Paulien to rest. But that's just metaphor.

Henri will never leave France; she's sure he hasn't given it a thought. And she's just as sure that if she suggests it, he won't consider a move. He has his career and his home, and she will be expected to adapt to his world. Which is right, she supposes. He is, as Gertrude once pointed out, Henri Matisse.

She walks into the kitchen, the white cabinets warm under the glow of the lamplight, the tiny yellow flowers dotting the wallpaper pretty and soothing. She pours herself a glass of wine and sits down at the table. She drinks slowly, following the intersecting lines of the blue-and-yellow checked oilcloth with her fingernail.

She wonders what Edwin will do. Will he fire her? Order her out of the Bradley? Or worse, change his will? And what will her response be? If Edwin allows her to stay, she will stay, at least until the Bradley is hers. She can't abandon the collection, the opportunity to improve it, to share it, to return the colonnade seven. And what of George? If she leaves, she'll also be leaving behind her chance to crush him, to exonerate herself.

She pictures a sunny kitchen in a house sitting on a rocky outcropping overlooking the Mediterranean, sipping coffee with Henri, both of them still mussed from their morning lovemaking. She's always adored southern France, and Nice is particularly charming.

WHEN HENRI ARRIVES, she leads him to the couch. They sit close together, silently holding hands. She rests her head on his shoulder.

"You understand that now we must leave immediately," he finally says. "We will go to New York in the morning, and I will book passage on the first ship to Europe. We can come back another time to settle your affairs."

"I can't leave that quickly, my love. I need to talk to Edwin, figure out how to handle all the repercussions."

He frowns. The first time she saw him, she thought he looked like a college professor; now he looks like a college professor facing a student who's performed below his expectations. "You want to stay until he finds someone to fill your position? Is this necessary?"

"It's . . . it's a little more complicated than that. . . . Remember the George Everard story? I need to return the seven paintings my father lost because of him, to make amends. They meant so much to my father, to me, to us. . . . Three of them are yours."

"The paintings are here? Bradley has your father's paintings? How can that be?"

"I'll tell you some other time, but the important—"

"I will paint more for you. I will do another version of my three. I will make copies of the others."

"Thank you," she says miserably. "It's a generous offer, but it wouldn't be the same. I'm Edwin's heir, and I have to stay here until I can send the real ones back for my father. Until I can open the collection to the public, free the paintings . . ." Her voice trails off as she realizes how absurd it all sounds. "But mostly I have to stay until George comes back. So I can have him arrested."

"George will come back? To Philadelphia? Again, I do not understand."

"That's complicated, too. But—"

"You say you are Edwin's heir?" He's clearly struggling to grasp all that she's telling him. "Does this mean you cannot leave the States until he dies? That could be years."

"No, no, it's going to happen sooner than that."

Henri's eyes narrow. "He is ill?"

"Lung cancer." She throws herself into his arms, terrified that her ruthlessness will push him away. "I know it sounds awful, but he's . . . he's going to die whether I stay or not, whether my father gets his paintings, whether, well, whether anything."

Henri holds her and rocks her. "Let us make love."

They go into her bedroom and undress each other with painful slowness; it's exquisite and it's heartbreaking because they both recognize that not only will he leave for France in the morning, but she will remain here.

Henri pushes deep and whispers, "Can you feel how much I love you?"

She arches her back, holds him in tightly. Afterward, she rocks her hips gently to keep him close. "And I, you," she says, and begins to cry.

He kisses her forehead, blots her tears with the edge of the sheet. "I do not want to waste the time we have in argument. I am going home tomorrow, and although there is nothing I want more than for you to come with me, I now understand that you will not."

"I want to be with you, you know that. More than anything. But I've come this far. I'm getting so close to—"

"Hush," he interrupts. "We make our choices because they are our choices. You have made yours and I have made mine, and they do not end in the same place. There is nothing else to be said."

"This is only for a short time," she protests. "You make it sound as if it's forever. I'll be back in France before you know it. We'll be together every minute after that. He . . . he can't last all that much longer."

Henri sits up. "I cannot to wait around for Edwin to die. I cannot live like this."

The harsh reality of his words, the shame.

HENRI IS GONE in the morning. They have each come to a personal decision that makes their separation inevitable, however temporary. Most likely, hers is wrong and his is right. If only she were more like Edwin and George. If only she could find someone besides herself to blame.

She drags herself to work and waits at her desk, chain-smoking. She has no idea how Edwin is going to react. Yesterday he appeared more hurt than angry, but he could feel completely different in the light of day. More times than she can count, she's seen his fury erupt when he believed he had been wronged. But just as often, he pretends a disturbing situation doesn't exist.

When he storms into her office, he leaves little doubt. "You lied to me, you betrayed me, and you made a fool of me!"

"Edwin, please." She stands and touches his arm. "None of those things were ever my intention. It was—"

He takes a step away from her. "I could never be with a married man," he mimics her. "*I'm saving myself for marriage.*"

Vivienne hangs her head. She forgot she'd said those things to him. "I'm sorry. I never meant to—"

"I don't care what you meant—all I care about is what you did."

"But you have to look at it in perspective. It wasn't—"

"I don't have to look at anything in any way other than how I want to look at it," he corrects her. "If the Bradley didn't need you so much, I'd fire you in a second."

Vivienne closes her eyes so he won't see the happiness in them. He's going to let her stay.

"But there will be other changes. If I can't trust what you say—which I clearly can't—then how can I trust that you'll carry out my wishes as you promised? Your word means nothing, and therefore I no longer believe you are qualified to take over the Bradley. You've forced my hand, Vivienne. I've already spoken with Gusdorff. He's going to revise my will."

Her head snaps up. Although this possibility had crossed her mind, she hadn't seriously considered it. "Who else can do it? You've trained me to be the one. Who's qualified besides me?"

"Ada."

"Ada? You can't be serious. She knows nothing about the collection and clearly can't run the Bradley. She doesn't have the knowledge or the skills or the wherewithal. And you told me she hates the artworks, that she would sell—"

"There's no reason to talk about my wife that way. I'm sorry this choice distresses you, but you see, Ada is a woman who keeps her word. She would no sooner lie to me than she would lie to a priest. I will find people to teach her. I will teach her."

"I'm sorry. I didn't mean to be insulting, but I just don't see how she's an appropriate choice."

"Take the rest of the week off," he tells her curtly. "We'll discuss the transition on Monday. Ada and I are going up to Ker-Feal for a few days."

Vivienne waits an hour and then goes into his office. "Edwin," she entreats. "Please look at me."

He pretends to read a letter in front of him.

"We have too much history, too many connections. And too much is at stake here. What happened with Henri has nothing to do with the Bradley. With its future. What we're building here is what's important. Not some failing of mine."

He signs the letter and places it in his out-basket. Then he takes another and pretends to read that one as well.

"Edwin, please. After all we've been to each other, can't you try to find it in your heart to forgive me? To accept my apology so we can move forward with our work?"

He raises his eyes, and they're so cold that she almost shivers. "I thought you were moving to France?"

"I'm not. Henri left this morning, and I'm still here. Doesn't that say something? Show you my commitment to the Bradley? How sorry I am?"

"Apologies are easy, and coming from you, how could it mean anything? Words. Just words."

"But they do. It does. In this case in particular, an apology matters a lot. Are you really willing to take a chance with the Bradley's future, with everything you've spent your life creating, because you're angry at me?"

"The Bradley will survive," he says, but his voice isn't as adamant as it was earlier.

"Please give me another chance," she begs, sensing a weakening. "How about Saturday night? I'll make dinner and we can talk. Remember how much fun we had the times you used to come over? I'll cook that pot roast you like so much."

"I doubt talking will make any difference."

"But maybe it will. And isn't it worth the try? We need to try for the collection, for what it can be, for what we can make it together."

Edwin hesitates. "I told you I'll be in the country this weekend."

"Sunday then," she says. "Come when you get back. Six o'clock. At my house."

He grunts his acquiescence and returns to his papers.

WITHOUT WORK, VIVIENNE is filled with nervous energy and dives into an explosion of spring cleaning in January. She pounds rugs and launders draperies, scrubs cobwebs from every corner of the house. Anything to keep busy. To keep from thinking about Henri and Edwin, about the collection.

On Sunday afternoon, she cooks Edwin's favorite dinner of pot roast, green beans, and mashed potatoes, sets the table, and chills the wine. Then she waits. But she doesn't know whether she's waiting for him to arrive or waiting for him not to.

It's six, then seven, then eight o'clock, and Vivienne understands he isn't coming. She's on her third glass of wine, much more than she usually drinks, and it goes to her head. Blessedly so. She grabs a blanket from her bed and wraps it around her shoulders, leaving her hand free for the wineglass. She falls asleep on the couch.

She wakes to the chime of the doorbell and the first rays of light edging the curtains. Disoriented and fuzzy, she stumbles to the door, her face and clothes creased with sleep.

A policeman stands on the porch.

Vivienne blinks at him. "May I help you?"

He shows her his badge and asks to come inside.

"What?" she asks as she leads him into the house. "What is it?"

He looks around the room, at the table still set for dinner, at the almost empty wine bottle, at the disheveled blanket, at her disheveled self. He clears his throat. "You are Miss Vivienne Gregsby? Employed by Dr. Edwin Bradley?"

"Yes," she croaks. "I . . . I . . . yes, I am."

"Dr. Bradley has been involved in an accident."

"Is he hurt?"

"A car accident." He pauses, watching her closely. "I'm very sorry to tell you that it was fatal."

"Fatal," Vivienne repeats, because it seems that he expects a response. And she has none.

THE TRIAL, 1928

After the judge denied the motion to dismiss, Ronald and I met to discuss our strategy moving forward. I suggested he could use my knowledge of your terminal cancer to create some reasonable doubt, and he exploded. Although I'm sure I'd told him about this at the beginning, he claimed he'd never heard it before and was infuriated with me. Perhaps it was the first attorney to whom I gave this information. Not Ronald at all.

Yes, Edwin, I was aware of your secret. I wish you had trusted me enough to confide in me, but I respect your right not to have done so.

Ronald immediately contacted Dr. Tauber, who, after some hesitation, confirmed your diagnosis and grim prognosis. Ronald was ecstatic until I told him that I was pretty sure I was the only one who knew you were sick, a fact Dr. Tauber again confirmed. Then there was no more ecstasy, for without verification of my knowledge of your impending demise, the diagnosis has no relevance.

Henri and George could verify my knowledge, but I didn't bother to mention this to Ronald. Ah, but you didn't know about George either, did you? So much you didn't know.

We were once again left with Ronald's two prongs: the absurdity of a car crash as a viable murder plan and the likelihood it was an accident. So that's what we went with, along with some additional padding from character witnesses: your old friend Bill Glackens, two of my students, and our secretary, Sally McDonald.

This all went well enough at first, with each claiming I was completely devoted to you, but when Pratt brought up Henri, they all admitted that I appeared to have been besotted with him. And, according to Bill and Sally, he with me.

Oh, Edwin, besotted is one thing, murder is quite another.

Then it was time for the big climax: the accident argument, our strong suit. Ronald called a "forensic crime-scene expert" and two policemen who had been there that night but hadn't been prosecution witnesses.

Yes, all three testified, it did appear to have been an accident.

Yes, it would be difficult to stage such a thing.

But once again, our victory was short lived. On cross, Pratt asked each man a series of questions and each gave the same answers.

Yes, he had seen staged crashes before.

Yes, the truck driver had a clear view of your car coming down the hill, which was particularly unobstructed because there were no leaves on the trees.

Yes, if the truck driver turned off his lights, you wouldn't have been able to see him.

Yes, it was a cloudy night and there was no moon.

Yes, given the angle and his time to prepare, the truck driver could have purposely hit the driver's door.

Yes, the configuration of the collision would support this explanation.

Yes, it was possible it wasn't an accident at all.

37

VIVIENNE, 1928

The policeman continues to stare at Vivienne, and she at him. "Maybe you should sit down, Miss Gregsby," he suggests. When she doesn't respond, he takes her arm, leads her around the couch, and gently urges her into it. Then he reaches down, picks up the blanket from where she dropped it on the floor, and wraps it around her.

She pulls the soft wool tight across her shoulders and curls herself into a ball until all but her head is shrouded. Then she begins to shake, her hands tremble, and her teeth chatter. Edwin is dead. All that energy gone? To where?

The policeman glances toward the kitchen. "Is it okay if I get you some water?"

Vivienne doesn't remember telling him it was okay, but he suddenly appears before her, offering a glass. She's afraid she'll drop it on the floor and doesn't want to remove her hands from underneath the warm blanket, so she doesn't move. She's disoriented, perplexed. Can Edwin really be dead?

The policeman sits down next to her. "I'm Detective Westford, Miss Gregsby. I can see this has been quite a shock, but you really need to drink the water. We don't want you fainting away on me, now do we?"

To please him, she holds up her blanket-cloaked hands and takes the glass. It wobbles as if she's an elderly woman unable to control her tremor, but she manages to get it to her mouth. She tries to drink but instead spills water down her chin and all over the blanket.

"Never mind," the detective says, taking the glass from her. "Why don't we just sit here for a moment? You take some deep breaths."

Vivienne tries to do as he asks, but her breathing is quick and shallow. The Bradley collection is hers. She'll be able to return Papa's paintings. Restructure and share the collection with the world. Put George in prison. Reconcile with her family. Go to Henri. But for any of this to be possible, Edwin has to be dead. She knew this was coming but feels as if she didn't.

Detective Westford picks up the almost empty wine bottle from the floor, puts it on the coffee table, and surveys the room. "Expecting some-one for dinner?" he asks conversationally, nodding to the table.

She realizes that she hasn't said a word since he told her about Edwin. She clears her throat, clears it again. "I . . . I guess."

He raises an eyebrow. "Looks like more than a guess."

"Yes," she manages. "Yes, I am. I was."

"Dr. Bradley?"

"Dr. Bradley?" she repeats, not following him.

"Was Dr. Bradley to be your guest?" His words are clipped, formal.

"Why . . . why do you say that?"

He shrugs, but his eyes sear into hers. "Mrs. Bradley told me that he sometimes comes here. She's the one who asked me to tell you what happened."

Ada asked him to come tell her. The grieving widow asked the police-man to tell the woman she believes is her husband's girlfriend that her lover is dead.

"You're surprised she sent me?" he asks.

"Yes," she says. "Yes, I am."

In all her imagining about Edwin's death, she never thought about how it would affect Ada—she thought only about how it would affect herself—and she's ashamed. But Ada will still have her arboretum and her school and Ker-Feal. Vivienne doubts Ada will mourn much for a man with whom she had no meaningful relationship. In fact, Ada will probably like it better this way: no Edwin to worry about, no Vivienne to worry about, no pretenses.

"Was Dr. Bradley here often?" The detective's voice has a slightly different ring to it, harsher, more demanding.

Vivienne wraps herself even more tightly inside the blanket. She doesn't like his tone. This isn't an interrogation. No need to interrogate suspects when there's been a car accident. No need to interrogate her when it's clear that she's been here all night fast asleep and is now hung over from disappointment and too much wine.

"Miss Gregsby?"

"Yes," she says from somewhere inside the groggy fog surrounding her. "Yes, I was expecting Dr. Bradley. We're colleagues, close friends. We sometimes have dinner together. Or used to. Not so much lately. That's why . . . that's why I'm so upset."

Detective Westford stands and walks around the small table, taking in the fine china, the linen napkins and silver cutlery. The unlit candles waiting to add ambience to a romantic dinner. "I can see that you must have been *close* friends."

Vivienne wants to tell him to shut up, to mind his own business, but he's a policeman, and she supposes that in some ways it is his business. It's time to cry, time to get him to leave. So she does, and he does.

THE SKY SPITS sleet on the day of Edwin's funeral. The church is so packed that one might have thought they were burying a much-loved man instead of the person who had been vilified in the Philadelphia press as "The Bad Tempered Dr. Bradley." The priest's eulogy is full of accolades for Edwin's brilliance and generosity, for the contribution Bradley and Hagerty, Chemists, has made to both the community and the world. All of which is true.

Vivienne rides with Sally and two Bradley teachers to the cemetery. Sally holds her hand in the backseat, but no one says much, although the teachers keep casting curious glances over their shoulders. Vivienne stares out the window, her face impassive. When they reach the cemetery, she looks into the stark rectangular hole in the ground, at the heap of dirt at its head, pulls her coat close. It's taken almost a week for her to grasp the fact that Edwin is gone. That everything is going to change.

Yesterday when she came home from work, George was standing in front of the glowing fireplace. He apologized for letting himself in but claimed it was too damn cold to sit on the porch.

Vivienne shrugged off her coat and went to stand next to him. He didn't have a key and she didn't ask him how he'd gotten in. She held her hands toward the flames. "Thanks for the fire."

They were silent for a long time.

"So," he finally said.

"So," she replied, transfixed by the flickering logs.

"I didn't have anything to do with it," he told her.

She watched the flames darting and shifting. "Neither did I."

George took her shoulders and turned her toward him. "Then something very fortuitous and wonderful has happened to us." He pulled her to him.

Vivienne twisted away. She longed to be held, to be consoled, but his callousness made her feel dirty, guilty. "It's too soon to think about it that way."

"Why, you little hypocrite!" His laughter boomed through the room. "After all this finagling, you're pretending to be sorry Bradley is dead? When you're finally going to get your father's paintings? I don't believe you haven't been thinking this very same thing since the moment you found out." Which, of course, she had.

But now as she stands next to the grave, tiny pieces of ice sticking to her hair, she wonders. She has the right to feel more than one way about Edwin's death, doesn't she? She may have been looking forward to becoming his heir, but that doesn't mean she can't be sorry he's no longer alive. They were friends, worked together for years, and he taught her much, gave her opportunities few men would offer a woman. She'll miss him in many ways.

But she's also glad, as George so crassly put it, to get her father's paintings, the collection. To be with Henri, free and clear. Even when the dirt begins to rain down on Edwin's coffin, she has a hard time dredging up the grief she professes to feel. That damn George has always been able to read her.

"You have a lot of nerve to smile at a moment like this," Ada hisses. The crowd is beginning to disperse, and Ada is standing in front of Vivienne, arms crossed, her chin quivering. Thomas Quinton is standing next to her. "You're a little harlot—and a murdering one to boot!"

Vivienne wasn't aware she was smiling, but given her thoughts, it's not impossible. "You think I drove a truck into his car? How could I have done that?"

"A conniving woman like you could devise a way," Ada says with a sneer. "I wouldn't—"

"It was an accident. Nothing more and nothing less. It was nobody's fault—except the truck driver's." Vivienne doesn't mention that it was Edwin who drove through that stop sign because he disagreed with its location. Even harlots and murderers have a sense of propriety.

"An accident?" Ada repeats. "An accident that just happened to hand you everything you ever wanted? It was no accident—and you know that as well as I do! Mark my words, I'm going to prove you killed my Edwin. Just sit back and watch me!"

"Ada, please." Quinton places a protective arm around her shoulder. "There's no reason to start this now. It's not the—"

"Don't you shush me!" Ada shouts at Quinton. "You agreed. You promised to help me prove it."

"Come on," he says forcefully. "Let's get you home." Then he deftly turns Ada around and leads her to the line of waiting limousines.

Vivienne is taken aback by the loathing in Ada's eyes, by the disgust on Ada's face as she looked at her. Did Ada actually believe she, Vivienne, murdered Edwin? Did Quinton? Could they persuade other people to believe it? *You agreed. You promised to help me prove it.* What the hell did that mean?

There is no doubt that both Ada and Quinton have reason to stop her from becoming Edwin's heir. Ada out of spite, and Quinton because if Ada controls the Bradley, he'll be able to persuade her to turn it over to the Philadelphia Museum of Art. Edwin's ultimate horror, Quinton's ultimate payback.

Vivienne doesn't know much about criminal law, but she does know that if you're convicted of killing a man, you can't inherit his property.

THE READING OF Edwin's will is postponed twice, probably the work of Quinton and Ada's lawyers, buying time to contest it. Before the episode with Henri in the garden, Edwin had always been adamant that Ada would never get the collection, convinced that she, as she'd threatened, would sell it off piecemeal. He'd assured Vivienne that the language was written in such a way that it would be impossible for Ada to break the will. Except now Ada has powerful friends. Powerful friends with a vested interest in her stake.

Vivienne is also worried that Jacob Gusdorff might have had time to incorporate Edwin's adjustments, although it's unlikely Edwin had time to sign the new will. Still, there were three days between Edwin's death and his threat to disinherit her. It wouldn't have been enough time. It couldn't have been enough time.

She doesn't worry as much about Ada's contention that she murdered Edwin. A car accident is a car accident, and there's no way to prove otherwise. George isn't as certain of this as she is. For a man who never appears to be bothered about anything, this strikes her as odd. She's eager to have him arrested, but given Ada's threats, now isn't the time to get involved with the police. So she agrees when George suggests that they not see each other until things are settled.

Finally the will is certified, and despite Ada's attempts at interference and Edwin's late change of heart, Vivienne becomes the sole owner of the Bradley and all its contents. A tremendous, yet bittersweet, victory. Her first order of business will be to send the colonnade seven to her father. Her second will be to let Henri know she'll be coming soon— even though France won't be her permanent home for a while.

For she's going to transform the Bradley into the Bradley-Mertens Museum of Post-Impressionism, and it will be housed in Nice. Her museum will be everything she's imagined, and so much more: the greatest private collection of post-Impressionist works in the world. Her vision will be focused, sharp, and pointed, telling the tale of the sweep of European and American artistic innovation over the past fifty years— and hopefully the next fifty.

An ambitious project, yes, but one she's grateful to be able to bring to fruition. She'll hone and streamline, and then she'll erect a modern building that reflects the art it encloses and allows her new collection to breathe. She'll throw the doors open, welcome all, and share the wondrous gift she's been given. The gift of overseeing grand masterpieces, orchestrating them, and protecting them for the generations to come. What an honor it is to be their custodian, for this to be her life's work. Just as she's always hoped.

TWO MONTHS AFTER Edwin's death, Vivienne is still in her own tiny office. She hasn't felt comfortable moving into his yet, although she could use the space. Her workload is heavy; she has to do both her job and Edwin's, as well as manage all the issues a transition in leadership brings. She's so overwhelmed that she hasn't had the time to do anything about the colonnade seven, although she has written to Henri, who's anxiously awaiting her arrival in France. This, unfortunately, doesn't appear to be imminent.

One afternoon, there's a knock on her door. "Do you have a few minutes, Miss Gregsby?" Detective Westford asks.

"Detective." She stands and smiles as if there's no one she'd rather see. "Please. Come in and sit down." She scoops up a number of folders that are resting on the chair next to her desk. "If you can find a free spot."

"I'm fine standing." He scrutinizes the cluttered room, scrutinizes her. "A lot of work?"

Vivienne runs her hand through her hair and drops back into her chair. "More than you can imagine."

"I understand you're the boss now."

She lights a cigarette and inhales the smoke deeply. "Chief cook and bottle washer, too," she says in an attempt to keep the conversation light.

"Must be especially hard without your *close* friend to lend a hand."

"I do miss him," Vivienne admits, pretending not to notice the sarcasm in his tone. "Very much. All the time, actually. As a friend and a colleague—and even as a boss."

"And yet, you've accrued many advantages from Dr. Bradley's death."

So much for light. "I'm learning that there are advantages and disadvantages to just about everything in life."

"Yes," he says, nodding his head appreciatively. "That's true enough."

"How can I help you, Detective? I'm guessing you didn't just drop by for a friendly chat." Stop it. Do not antagonize. "I'll be happy to answer any questions you might have."

"Did you know that just three days before his accident, Dr. Bradley instructed his lawyer to modify his will?"

"No," she says, opening her eyes wide. "I didn't. What kind of modifications?"

"He wanted to remove you as the beneficiary."

"I don't believe that," she says as her stomach plummets. "He trusted me implicitly. He said that aside from himself, I was the only one capable of running the Bradley."

The detective scratches his cheek. "Apparently he reconsidered. Tens of millions of dollars is a lot to leave a relative stranger."

"And who exactly did he want to appoint?" she asks scornfully. *Stay in character,* George always cautioned. In this case, that of an innocent person.

"His wife."

Vivienne snorts. "Now I know this can't be true. Ada knows nothing about the collection—she doesn't even like art and told Edwin she'd sell it off if it were hers. Something he would never have wanted to happen."

The detective looks thoughtful. "Perhaps she reconsidered also." He nods crisply. "I'm sorry, Miss Gregsby, but I've got to run. Just wanted to keep you abreast of the changes in the case."

After he leaves, she stares into the empty doorway. So Ada has moved beyond accusations and into action.

DETECTIVE WESTFORD RETURNS three weeks later, accompanied by two uniformed policemen. He knocks politely, but the three of them enter Vivienne's office without being invited.

She stands, notes the guns sitting in the policemen's holsters, the handcuffs the taller one is pulling from his pocket. This can't be happening. Even Thomas Quinton doesn't have this kind of power. Or does he? Her throat closes up, and all she can do is stare at the detective.

"Miss Vivienne Gregsby," the detective says, placing a piece of paper on her desk, "we have a warrant for your arrest."

"For . . . for what?" she manages to gasp, although she knows what his answer is going be.

"For the murder of Dr. Edwin Bradley."

"It was an accident!" she cries.

The detective glances at the two policemen, raises an eyebrow. "You say it was an accident? That you did it by accident?"

Vivienne backs up until she hits the bookshelves behind her desk. "That's not what I meant and you know it." But even in her horror-struck state, she understands she's just said something these policemen can use against her. "It was a *car* accident," she adds. "Edwin was hit by a truck. That's not murder."

"I'm sorry, Miss Gregsby," the detective says again. "Proving guilt is the prosecutor's job. Ours is to arrest you."

One of the policemen pulls her arms behind her back and closes the handcuffs around her wrists. Sally, who is now Vivienne's secretary, comes out of her office and demands that they stop immediately; she places herself between Vivienne and one of the policemen. But the officers order her to step back, along with the teachers clustering around the door. The staff watch, slack jawed and wide eyed, as Vivienne is escorted down the hallway.

Her feet move and she continues to breathe. She's aware of her surroundings, but it's as if this is happening to someone else. She knows she's being arrested. That these men believe she's a murderer. That they're going to bring her to the police station, take her fingerprints, and lock her up in jail. But she also knows it isn't real. Can't be real.

As they pass Henri's *Joy of Life*, she takes in the colorful paradise, the sumptuous nudes, the splashes of purple and orange and green, the entwined lovers. She'll be back, she silently promises them. Soon. It's a mix-up. Everyone has it wrong.

She turns her head, and there's *Dance II* directly across from her. The frolicking dancers, the graceful curve of the arches, of their bodies, the ribbons of black and pink and blue, the jubilant expansiveness. You, too, she tells the dancers, tells Henri. This is a mistake. A momentary lapse. She'll be back.

And then they're down the stairs and out the main entrance.

38

GEORGE/ISTVÁN, 1928

Bradley is dead, and Paulien has been arrested for killing him. Owing to a law, referred to in the vernacular as the slayer statute, if she's found guilty, she can't inherit, and Ada is the contingent beneficiary. Sometimes he amazes even himself. Not only is his backup plan in place, but with the exception of having to marry Ada, it will work out just fine.

This doesn't mean he isn't shaken up about Paulien. Whether she's convicted or not, it's going to be a terrible ordeal for her. Her motive is abundantly clear, but Bradley was widely disliked, and there are many people who also had motive.

Ada told him that Paulien posted bail. Apparently she put up her little house as collateral, and because of that, her clean record, and her United States citizenship, the judge decided she was neither a flight risk nor a danger to the community. Although Ada is incensed at the ruling, claiming a murderer is now loose on the streets of Philadelphia, the judge's assumptions seem reasonable to him.

Paulien must have a good lawyer to avoid jail while awaiting trial for murder. He's glad for that, glad for her. Unfortunately he can't take the risk of going to see her, even though he needs her to believe he's on her side, behind her all the way. He continues to hold out hope that she, not Ada, will be the one to hand him the Bradley.

It's been almost three months since Bradley's death, and Ada hasn't yet recovered from the shock. Frankly he's surprised she's taking it so hard; it isn't as if she liked the man. When she got word of Paulien's arrest, she cheered up, but after a few days she fell back into despair. Women.

It appears unlikely that Paulien will be convicted. Beyond all the other potential suspects, there's the whole accident angle. If her lawyer was good enough to secure bail, the man should be good enough to establish reasonable doubt. Although there is Thomas Quinton, who, according to Ada, handpicked the judge and is prepared to use his influence and fortune to smooth every bump in Ada's way in exchange for the collection and Ada's undying gratitude.

Won't Mr. Quinton, a.k.a. Mr. Mayor, be surprised to discover that no matter who his friends are or whomever he bribes, he's going to come up empty? No artwork, no museum, and unless Paulien walks, no Ada.

It's a magnificent spring afternoon, and he and Ada spend most of it in the botanical gardens, silently and companionably working side by side. The daffodil bulbs he planted last fall are in full bloom, and the riot of yellow as well as the warmth of the sun on his back fills him with optimism.

Ada seems to be coming out of her winter doldrums along with the weather, and he almost hopes for Paulien's conviction so that Ker-Feal, which Edwin bequeathed to Ada a few years before he died, will belong to him. He always wanted to own a grand country estate, to be lord of the manor, which is the least he deserves after all his hard work. Bradley had an accident; perhaps Ada will also.

Ker-Feal or no Ker-Feal, it will be far better if Paulien is acquitted. It's possible she'll try to have him arrested, but he's got the letter outlining her plans for the robbery, and that should dissuade her. Ultimately he knows she'll forgive him for everything, let go of her anger, and allow herself to bask in the affection she's always had for him. Especially after they consummate their marriage. She can be a wild woman in bed, and he knows exactly how to please her—and how to keep her wanting more.

Perhaps when it's all over he'll slow down for a while, enjoy the fruits of his labor for a few years. Enjoy Paulien. After Bradley's death, he let it be known in Paris that Ashton King's father remained very ill, so there's no rush to return to Europe. On second thought, a vacation is probably not in his future; he has enough self-awareness to recognize that he'll never be truly happy unless he's in the game. Because it isn't about the money—that's only how he keeps a running tally—it's about coming out on top.

He and Ada sit on the veranda sipping sherry, which he detests, and eating the tasteless hors d'oeuvres the maid brings, discussing the new plantings they're preparing to install the next day. As they talk, he grows more distant, stares at the sky, frowns wistfully, and begins to answer her in monosyllables.

"What is it, dear?" Ada asks. "Are you feeling unwell?"

He doesn't look at her. "I'm fine."

"István Bokor," she says sternly. "I've known you for almost two years, and you are definitely not fine."

"Ah, sweetheart," he says, smiling at her sadly. "I guess there's no fooling you."

She reaches her hand over and rests it on his arm. "Tell me."

He sighs. "I don't want to upset you, but . . ."

"Upset me?" she asks. "What will upset me?"

"It's just that, oh, I don't know, I just don't know how much longer we can go on like this."

"On like what? Didn't we just have the loveliest afternoon? Are you unhappy with me?"

He takes her hands in his. "No, no. Just the opposite."

"Then what do you mean?"

Another heavy sigh. "I don't want to push you, and I know it's been only a few months since . . . since . . ."

Ada disengages her hands from his and stiffly places them in her lap. He swallows his irritation at her seemingly endless anguish over a man whom she surely wanted dead. He draws the small box from his pocket and flips it open, revealing the opal ring. "I've been saving this for you. I never wanted it to happen like this, but I still want to marry you. And now that you're . . . you're . . ."

"Oh, István." She takes the box from him and begins to cry.

"Does that mean no?"

She tries to speak, fails, and begins to sob even louder.

"This is exactly why I didn't want to bring it up." He doesn't reach out to comfort her, allowing her to feel his distance, how empty her life will be without him. "I didn't want to—I don't ever want to—make you unhappy."

"I'm . . . I'm not unhappy," she wails. "I just don't see how it can happen."

He grabs the box and snaps it shut with a loud click. "Never mind," he says, dropping it back into his pocket and adding a touch of annoyance in his voice. "I see you're still in love with Edwin, and I can't compete with a ghost." He stands. "I'm going for a walk."

"No!" she cries, jumping up and throwing her arms around him, just as he knew she would. "I'm not in love with Edwin. I don't know if I ever was. I'm in love with you."

He untangles himself and takes a step backward. "The time isn't right, Ada. And I'm guessing it never will be. You've suffered a great loss, one I can't begin to fathom. The best thing for both of us is for me to go back to Hungary. My family's been begging me to come. My father said my job is always open."

"But you hated that job," she protests. "And you have such a gift for horticulture. A munitions factory is no place for you."

He shrugs. "I hate the idea of being with you but not really being with you more."

She closes her eyes, and a shudder runs through her. Then she squares her shoulders and wipes her tears with a handkerchief. "I'll marry you. I want to marry you, to be with you. But . . ." She hesitates.

"But what?"

Ada looks up at him, her face blotched, a wad of mucus visible in one nostril. "I . . . I . . . I've been Mrs. Bradley for so long. It doesn't feel right, no matter what my feelings are for you. I know it shouldn't be like this, but it's as if I'd be cheating on—"

"You're Bradley's widow, not his wife. So even though you're still calling yourself Mrs. Bradley, that doesn't mean you're still married to the man."

"I know that, but—"

"I can't wait around forever for you to figure this out," he says sternly. He needs her to agree to marry him, and then he'll postpone the wedding until after Paulien's case is decided. If Paulien is acquitted, he'll leave Ada and marry Paulien. But if Paulien is found guilty, Ada will be there to step into her shoes.

Ada swallows hard. "Do you think we could put it off for a while? Just a little while longer. Be engaged, but keep it a secret?"

"I don't want to put it off." He pouts.

"Please, István," she begs. "For me?"

He frowns but allows his eyes to warm.

"I just need a little mourning period," she babbles. "To make my peace with what happened, to show the proper respect for Edwin. Maybe a year from now? And then I'll be ready, happy to become Mrs. Bokor."

He wraps her in his arms and kisses the top of her head. "Yes, sweetheart, yes. That's just what we'll do." Then he picks her up and twirls her around, both of them laughing. "Thank you," he murmurs into her hair. "You've made me a very happy man."

THE TRIAL, 1928

Ronald says we won't have to wait for the foreman to deliver the verdict, that we'll know as soon as the jury files into the courtroom. All I have to do is scan the faces. If eyes meet mine, I'm free. If not, things haven't gone as well. Simple as that, he tells me. Simple.

They've been deliberating for two days. Apparently this is a good sign. It means there's no consensus, that at least one juror isn't convinced beyond a reasonable doubt that I killed you. Which is all we need.

But the trial took seven days, and now it's been another two. Jurors have jobs and families. They're tired, put out, want to settle things and go home. That kind of pressure can make even a tough dissenter reconsider.

Then there's the human brain searching for links, which my first lawyer explained could be a defendant's downfall in a case based on circumstantial evidence. And Pratt laid out those circumstances in nice little rows, the connections all too easy to make.

But it could also be the other way around. Maybe the dissenter is the only one who thinks I'm guilty, and all the rest are convinced I'm innocent. If he's the one who's being forced to reconsider, there's hope.

I've sat through the testimony, the opening and closing statements, the judge's instructions. And honestly, Edwin, I have no idea what they might decide. The way Pratt twisted the facts—from my relationship with that damn truck driver to my lies about Paulien Mertens—is concerning. Even Ronald looks at me oddly more often than I'd like. I wonder how you would look at me.

I'm sitting on a bench in the lobby of the courthouse when Ronald comes to get me. There's a verdict.

I fidget at the defense table while we wait for the jury to return. I don't *know what to do with my hands, my legs, my eyes, my muddled thoughts. My heart pounds, and sweat drips down the back of my neck. Yet I'm freezing cold.*

The door opens, and the jury files in. Not a single one of them meets my gaze.

PART FOUR

39

VIVIENNE, 1928

Riverside Prison allows visitors only for an hour on Sunday afternoons, which matters little to Vivienne, as she has few. Ronald comes once to see how she's doing. He tells her how sorry he is and that he's in the process of filing an appeal. Then, being Ronald, he has to add that the decision will most likely go against them, says he's sorry again. She waves his apologies away, waves him away.

Sally McDonald shows up one Sunday with flowers and candy, saying she doesn't believe for a moment that Vivienne killed Edwin, that she'll do anything Vivienne needs her to do to rectify the situation. Vivienne would be touched if she were able to feel anything but terror. They don't let her keep the candy or the flowers.

Sometimes she imagines she's a turtle living within a carapace that protects her from the world—as well as from her own judgments and fears. The longer she wears it, the stronger and tougher the shell grows, and the more impervious she becomes to both external insults and those of her own making. She longs for the time when it will thicken enough to cut her off completely. She withdraws into it as often as she can.

The fear of one possible visitor penetrates her shell. Henri has been insisting that he's coming to Philadelphia. His last letter indicated he should be here soon. As much as she longs for him, longs to see his face, to be with someone who cares about her, she can't let this happen. She loves him too much.

She begs him to stay in France, warns that if he comes she'll have the guards turn him away. Her life is over, and there's no future for him with her. The sooner he accepts this, the better off he'll be. This is all she has to give.

For weeks after her incarceration, she bangs on the bars of her cell until her knuckles bleed. She screams out her innocence, insists she be let free, demands a review of the evidence, a new trial.

"Look into Ada Bradley!" Vivienne cries. "She did it."

"It was an accident! A goddamned car crash!"

"There's a man out there named István Bokor. Ask him what really happened to Edwin Bradley!"

"The judge is crooked!" she howls. "He was paid off."

The guards ignore her. It's obvious they've seen this behavior before, heard many false claims of blamelessness, and know it will end on its own. And they're right. As the days pass, both her quest for answers and her drive for vengeance begin to abate. Vivienne finally falls silent as the impossibility of the situation becomes unambiguous. There will be no colonnade seven for her father. No Bradley-Mertens Museum. No Henri. No family. No punishment for George. No life for her.

She covers her face with her hands, huddles in the corner of her cell, curls into a ball, rocks back and forth, gestates her shell. She does this for days, maybe months. She's losing track of time. The terror begins to recede into a distant ache, and she lets the days drift from one to the next. It's better this way. She wonders whether she's also losing her mind. But it's just an idle thought. She doesn't actually care. She just rocks.

She's confined to a grimy cell with two cots, but the other one remains empty. There are few women at Riverside, and she's told she's the only convicted murderer. She figures the warden wants to keep her away from the other prisoners, perhaps believing she'll turn them into killers, too. Again, she doesn't care where she is—or who is or isn't with her.

It's a relief to succumb to her fate, to be free from the constant agonizing over the jury's possible judgment. Now there's no hope and no wondering, which is liberating. As Ronald so callously told her, Pennsylvania performs more executions than almost any other state in the country, and that's what they plan to do to her. It will probably be two or three years before they get around to it. She wishes it were tomorrow.

One afternoon, Tony, the weekend guard, who has the face of a choirboy and the empathy of a pin, yanks open the door to Vivienne's cell. "You've got a gentleman caller, Killer Girl." He always calls her Killer Girl.

Henri. She doesn't move.

"Come on, KG," he orders. "Up!"

She looks into Tony's pretty green eyes and wonders what she should do, but it's as if she's wondering about someone else, a friend perhaps. Henri needs to go home. Back to the beaches of Nice. To the sunshine. To a life free from her. But it's as if he, too, is someone else, not the man she once loved so passionately. Does she still love him? she wonders, woozy from so much thinking. A twinge of something akin to pain twists through the numbness that buffets her.

The inmates are allowed only two showers a week, but Vivienne hasn't had the energy lately, turning her back to the door when the one female guard comes to get her, holding that mean little sliver of soap. Or lye. Or whatever that nasty, smelly thing is made of. Her hair is lank and uncombed, and she can smell her own stink. She slowly pulls herself to her feet.

This is the way to make him go away. To keep him away. To save him. She'll let him see her exactly as she is. Dirty and malodorous, with no light in her eyes. Exactly as she'll be for the rest of her short life. He'll be horrified and run back to France as fast as he can. Her parting gift.

Vivienne staggers as Tony drags her down the corridor, holding her arm so tightly that there will certainly be bruises by morning. What do a few bruises matter? She doesn't recognize the hallways or the turns they take, but that doesn't mean she hasn't been here before. So much would be confusing if she cared enough to let it to be. She's content to slip in and out. Sleeping, waking, drifting, it's all the same: fractured and fragmented, making little sense.

Tony pushes her into a low-ceilinged and cramped VISITORS' LOUNGE, as the sign on the door proclaims it to be. It seems familiar, but she isn't sure. Inside, there are a few small tables and a bunch of wobbly chairs. A guard whose name tag reads "Moses" stands in a corner, arms crossed, glaring, waiting for someone to commit yet another heinous crime, such as patting the hand of a loved one.

Henri is already there, and when Vivienne enters, he starts toward her, his arms spread open. But Moses catches him by the elbow and spins him around. "No physical contact!" Moses growls, pointing to his chair. "Do that again and you'll be out of here before you say boo."

She tries to locate herself in this new place, in this new situation. It feels odd to be somewhere that isn't her cell.

Henri sits down, his eyes wide with alarm. Vivienne idly wonders whether this is due to Moses's words or whether it's a reaction to the way she looks and smells. Probably both.

Tony indicates the chair across from Henri. "Fifteen minutes," he snaps.

"I was told we would have an hour," Henri protests.

"Not with her you don't," Tony tells Henri. Then he turns back to Vivienne. "Killer Girl," he adds in a snarky stage whisper.

She gives Henri a weak smile. "Life on the inside."

Henri's face crumbles, and he covers it with his hands. He's crying.

"Don't," she begs, the world suddenly shifting into clarity. "Please don't."

He presses a sleeve to his eyes, pulls himself together. "You did not do this, and—"

"It doesn't matter."

"It matters very much. You knew Edwin was dying of cancer. There was no need. And that is why I have come. I must tell—"

"The jury has already decided."

"I will not allow you to take the blame for something someone else did—or that no one did. I have spoken to many people. To a lawyer in France who talked with one here. I also have pledges of money. I will go now to the powers-that-be and tell them that this is an impossible thing. I will—"

"There's no one to tell. No one to hear. They all believe I'm a murderer, and that's all they will ever believe."

"I do not accept that," he says fiercely. "Not now and not ever."

She decides it's time to go under, to withdraw into her shell.

Henri must sense this, because he begins talking very quickly. "I am adding a new dimension to my portraits," he tells her. "With the odalisques, too. Do you remember that mask from the Congo I showed you in Paris? The one with the pearls and the seeds?"

Vivienne wonders if she does remember, but not enough to try to do so.

"I thought I might integrate ideas from African culture into my work. I want to make use of the simplifications, the abstractions, and the geometric designs to add distinction, to convey individuality. What do you think?"

What she thinks is that he's trying to pull her into his world, to reclaim her. But there's no one to reclaim. No one is there.

"You would like these very much," he continues when she doesn't respond. "They are full of the deep colors you adore but are also mysterious. One in particular, *Woman with a Veil*, I want very much for you to see. And"—he leans as close as he dares—"it will fit into your map. Definitely post-Impressionist."

She has a feeling this is supposed to be a joke; there's something in his expression that tells her this. But she doesn't get it. Or maybe she does and just doesn't remember.

"Vivienne, please," Henri says, his eyes filling again. "Please come back to me. I will get you out of this place. We can live as we once planned. You will be my model, my muse, my love. We can start a museum, you can continue your work, and we—"

Vivienne stands, presses her fingers to the table to steady herself. "I don't love you," she says, as clearly and coldly as she can, her voice unexpectedly even. "I'm not sure I ever did. You need to go home. There's nothing for you here."

"You are lying," Henri says softly. "And as much as I appreciate the gesture, you and I both know the truth."

Vivienne turns her back on him and nods to Tony, who stayed to enjoy the show. "I'm ready to go now."

40

GEORGE/ISTVÁN, 1929

As always, he's jubilant after a big score: that swell of well-being and confidence, the drive to rush out and execute another even greater triumph. There's nothing, nothing, nothing like winning. The sheer power of it. He never gets enough. The best feeling ever. Better than the finest champagne or twenty-year-old scotch. Better than sex.

His biggest con yet is a dazzling success: the Bradley is his. The day after the wedding Ada signed it all over to her handsome husband, and now everything of hers belongs to him. Granted, it took time to persuade her to renege on her promise to Quinton and the Philadelphia Museum of Art. But the woman is like a schoolgirl with her first crush, giggly and so besotted that hoodwinking her is embarrassingly easy. Thomas Quinton is hopping mad, as is to be expected. Not only did he miss out on Edwin's collection, but he missed out on Ada. Quinton is particularly enraged with her new husband, who he has no idea is the same person as the rakish and blond Australian architect Cooper Robinson.

But even with all his jubilation, something feels off. He wonders whether this is because there weren't as many marks to best in this scheme. The larger the number of fools he dupes, especially those who pride themselves on being smart and savvy, the greater the kick. There's Bradley, but he's dead. And Ada, neither smart nor savvy, isn't a worthy opponent. He did trounce Thomas Quinton, a worthy adversary indeed. But somehow it doesn't seem like enough.

There's also the dispiriting happenstance of marrying Ada. She's always clinging and staring up at him, her doe eyes full of wonder, and it irritates the hell out of him. He suggested separate bedrooms, and thankfully she didn't object; apparently this was her agreement with Bradley as well. He did have relations with her on their wedding night, a necessary part of the job. He needs her to believe he loves her, to develop complete trust in him, until he works out exactly how he's going to extricate both himself and his windfall from her. The act was distasteful, but the prize is worth the unpleasantness, as it always is. So this probably isn't what's bothering him.

He was incredulous when he discovered Bradley's finances were in significantly worse shape than he had feared. The idiot invested in bonds while the stock market roared, and he spent extravagantly on artwork without any concern for how much reserve he had. It appears that his partner, Ben Hagerty, handled the business end at Bradley and Hagerty, and that the Bradley board of trustees had rubber-stamped Edwin's every whim. This wouldn't be as grave if the collection and the building weren't in need of costly repairs.

While this fact was expedient when he used it to encourage Quinton's lawsuit, which brought about the trust's termination and thus cleared the way for Ada's unencumbered inheritance, now it's working against him. A relatively small inconvenience. He'll sell some of the pricier items he isn't fond of, which will give him the cash he needs to start the restoration work on the paintings he plans to take with him when he leaves.

But he keeps putting off both the sales and the repairs because he's fond of roaming the silent galleries by himself, luxuriating in the fact that each and every one of these masterpieces belongs to him. To him. He owns them, all of them. A collection only a man of prodigious discernment could call his own. A man of greatness.

He runs his fingers over the canvas of a Modigliani, feels the brushstrokes rise and fall under his touch. His. He can pour paint on it if he wants. Set it on fire. Neither of which he would do, but if he did, no one could stop him. He picks up a sixteenth-century bronze sculpture, throws it back and forth between his hands. Then he sits on a hope chest hand-carved by John Bieber. Just because he can. Heady and intoxicating. So this probably isn't what's bothering him either.

He isn't a man of abundant empathy—a talent he values, as it gives him an edge over those who succumb to this weakness and are therefore rendered vulnerable—so it takes him a while longer to figure out that he's upset about Paulien. That he's concerned about her and feels bad about what happened to her, even though her situation has nothing to do with him or his life.

He has to resist the urge to visit her at the prison, to talk to her, to console her and let her know she has a friend. It's too risky. No one can connect him with her—or him with Edwin's death. Now that he's Ada's husband, his motive to knock off the old guy is glaring. He supposes this type of thinking proves he isn't Paulien's friend after all, and he's relieved by the thought.

As the months pass, Ada makes him so crazy that if he doesn't unclench himself from her clingy fingers he knows he will go out of his mind. When he discovers that preparing for deaccessioning—getting estimates on the value of the individual works, the cost of restoration, sizing up institutions and individuals as potential purchasers—is ridiculously time consuming, he decides not to do it. There will be no repairs to the building or the collection. He'll ship the paintings he wants to keep for himself to Europe and have them restored there. Then he'll hire an agent in Philadelphia to sell the rest as they are. He may lose a few dollars in the transaction, as the artwork won't be worth as much in its current state, but his sanity is at stake.

The paintings he takes with him will be useful in the Ashton King scam, and when that's successfully completed, he'll hang his entire collection in the massive waterfront estate in Monaco he has his eye on. He can already imagine how his three favorite Picassos will look against the

long whitewashed wall in the living room, how perfect *The Music Lesson*
will be for the dining room.

In a moment of weakness, it crosses his mind that he could send
Paulien's seven paintings back to her father. But that's ludicrous. They're
his, not Aldric Mertens's. Bradley purchased them from Aldric in a
straight-up transaction, and now they legally belong to Ada. To him.
Mertens probably has no idea where Paulien is or what's happened to her,
and it'll be better for him to remain ignorant of his daughter's situation.
Better for everyone.

But before he can proceed with his plan, he receives notice of a public hearing at which the Commonwealth of Pennsylvania will argue
its right—under its power "to protect and maintain one of the state's
most valuable artistic assets"—to confiscate the contents of the building
located at 300 North Latches Lane, Merion Station, Pennsylvania, all of
which are in "immediate danger owing to lack of maintenance to the
building and deferred restoration of the artworks."

It contends that Mr. István Bokor, the owner of this property, has
refused to take any action to improve either circumstance, and therefore the commonwealth has no choice but to undertake and oversee the
actions necessary to correct the situation. Thomas Quinton is clearly up
to his old tricks, trying to best his current rival, Ada's second husband,
just as he tried to best her first.

A letter accompanies the notice. It states that according to federal
law, when a governmental entity takes possession of personal property
under eminent domain, just compensation must be paid to the owner of
said property. "The value of said property, located at 300 North Latches
Lane, has been established by commonwealth assessors at $5 million, to
be paid to Mr. István Bokor at the time the property is transferred."

He throws the papers on his desk. None of this makes any difference.
Their attempt to steal his artwork is as unworkable as it is ludicrous.
Eminent domain involves the government seizing property in order to
build something like a railroad or a courthouse; it can't possibly apply to
a private art collection.

And $5 million? A fraction of what his collection is worth. It's a preposterous maneuver, and if they think he's going to buckle under, they have another think coming. He immediately calls his lawyer, who doesn't believe the measure is unreasonable and warns him that he's at a disadvantage because the hearing is being held in two weeks.

"What difference does that make?"

"There's no time for you to address the maintenance and restoration issues," the lawyer explains.

"Can't you argue that we're planning to do them?"

"We can try, Mr. Bokor. But it looks bad that you haven't done anything in the year or so you've owned the property."

"I've been getting the money together."

"Do you have it in an account we can point to?"

"No, not exactly, but I can get it. I just have to sell a few paintings."

The lawyer hesitates. "I'm not sure that's going to be a winning argument."

"How can they presume to walk in and seize my personal property? It's un-American."

"I'll give it everything I've got, Mr. Bokor, but as it stands now, I'd be remiss if I didn't tell you that I believe your position is weak."

"EDWIN WOULD BE heartbroken," Ada says at dinner the night the decision comes down. "This is absolutely the last thing he would have wanted. It goes against everything he stood for, his . . . his life's work." Then she starts to cry.

It happened just as his lawyer predicted. The state is going to confiscate his collection, build a museum next to the Philadelphia Museum of Art, and move his personal possessions there. Quinton and Ralph Knight are elated, as is the entire population of the city of Philadelphia.

He throws his napkin on the table and begins pacing the oversize dining room. He came by it fair and square. It's his private property, and the state has no right to take it from him. Steal it from him. Ada, who lawfully inherited it from Bradley, is now his wife, and she gave it to him.

No one is going to take what he's worked so hard to acquire, what he was forced to marry an old woman for, what's legally his.

He wants to strangle Ada. He can feel the tiny bones crunching under the pressure of his fingers. She was the one who wanted to get married, the one who promised she'd turn the collection over to him. And now she has nothing to give. Snap, snap, snap.

41

VIVIENNE, 1929

After Henri's visit, Vivienne falls into a deep stupor, sleeping as many hours a day as she can. She stops rocking because it's too much effort. When she's awake, she lies on her cot, staring at the ceiling and making pictures out of the water stains. They all look like vicious animals—or, at their most benign, frightened children.

She eats what's slipped through the slot in her door, takes the twice-weekly showers, stands listlessly on the muddy or dusty or snow-covered ground next to a basketball court without nets. She goes along, doesn't make a fuss. It's as if the piece of her that she recognizes as her true self has succumbed ahead of her body, leaving just that carapace behind. When they finally get around to executing her, she'll already be dead. Perhaps she already is.

Henri writes letters, many letters, but she doesn't read them. She leaves them unopened on the metal tray, along with the trash from her meals. All she has left to give him is permission to forget her, as she's forgetting herself. She was Paulien and then Vivienne and now she's Killer Girl.

Sometimes she remembers killing Edwin. Other times she thinks she didn't. But mostly she doesn't trouble herself with the question. It makes her tired.

Tony comes into her cell one day and tells she has a visitor, a woman, he says. Vivienne has no idea how long it's been since Henri's visit, but she thinks it was warm, then cold, and now it's warm again. So at least a year. Or is it two? She also has no idea who it could be, even less

curiosity. She goes with Tony just as she does everything else, sleepwalk-
ing, not there.

He brings her to a room labeled VISITORS' LOUNGE, where she's never
been before. It smells like the mold that crawled up the walls of some
cellar in a previous life. She forgets for a moment why she's here. Turns to
Tony, notices another guard. A visitor. Right. An older woman is seated
at a lopsided table, drumming her fingers nervously. But she's a stranger.
The woman's face falls when Vivienne enters, and it's clear Vivienne is
not who she's waiting for.

Then the woman gasps and presses her hand to her heart. "Paulie.
Oh, Paulie. Oh, my dear Lord."

Vivienne's knees buckle, and she falls into a chair. "Is Papa dead?" she
demands, then wonders who Papa is. Her father? Does she have a father?

"No, child," the woman says soothingly. "No one is dead."

"H-how . . . ?" Vivienne begins, not quite sure whether she's awake
or dreaming. Or maybe hallucinating. The word *tante* comes into her
mind. Is that who this is, sitting across from her? An aunt from a long
time ago? How many seasons? How many years? No. She's dreaming.
She has to be. Dreaming is sometimes interesting. So she goes along with
it. "How did you get here?" she asks.

"By ship," the woman says with a wry smile. "But I think what you
are asking is how I found you. The answer is that your friend Henri came
to see me."

"Henri," Vivienne repeats. Definitely a dream. If she had an aunt,
this aunt wouldn't know Henri. People are always getting mixed up in
dreams.

The woman places her hand over Vivienne's, and because it's a dream,
the guard lets her. It's been a long time since Vivienne was on the receiv-
ing end of a gentle touch. It feels nice. She's glad she decided to go along.
It's good to be in a happy dream.

"No one but your uncle knows where I am," the woman says. "That
you are . . . are in this place."

The woman does seem real. Maybe it isn't a dream. "What are you doing in my dream?" she asks to try to trick her.

But all the woman says is, "I wanted to tell you that you are forgiven."

This makes even less sense. "The appeal was denied. It's final. There's no chance of a pardon."

The woman winces and then catches herself. "No, Paulie, that is not what I meant. It is your father who has forgiven you."

Vivienne narrows her eyes. "Paulie?"

The woman tilts her head, a vaguely familiar gesture, and looks at Vivienne with great compassion. "He is brokenhearted over what happened. He does not care if you were involved with Everard or not. He recognizes that you were a child who was duped either way. He blames himself for not understanding this sooner."

It crosses Vivienne's mind that this might have been important to her at one time, but now it means nothing. She's Killer Girl, and this Paulie and her concerns are many lifetimes ago. If they ever existed. "I'm sorry he's sad," she says, because the woman is nice and it seems like the right thing to say.

"Do you want me to tell him where you are?"

Vivienne thinks about this, but there's little she wants anymore. "I'm going to be dead soon," she says. "So it's probably not worth the bother."

42

GEORGE/ISTVÁN, 1929

After the court's decision confiscating the Bradley, he did everything he could to get it countermanded: cajoled and bribed and blackmailed, switched attorneys, even made Ada go begging to Quinton. But the appeal failed, and the Commonwealth of Pennsylvania is claiming his collection for "the people." They've already taken steps to wrest it from him. His new lawyer, no better than the old, informed him that the state has been authorized to begin crating the art as early as next week. He has to work fast.

He sends Ada to Ker-Feal, explaining that he'll be consumed with cleaning up the aftermath of the litigation and that she should stay in the country until he's able to join her. Which will be never. Ada will be so sad when her handsome young count disappears.

He calls in some favors, and three men arrive late one afternoon. They begin packing up the forty-two artworks he's marked: the most valuable, the ones he's most partial to, Paulien's colonnade seven. There isn't time to grab more than that, so he's grabbing the best. The men need roughly six hours, and he's arranged for a truck to be parked at the back entrance at eleven o'clock. The truck will bring the crates to a dock in New York, where they'll be loaded onto a ship heading for Marseilles. Upon landing, they'll be driven to the estate he just purchased in Monaco.

As soon as the paintings are on their way, István Bokor will vanish. When the staff arrives on Monday morning, they'll find forty-two holes in Bradley's ensembles, and he'll be long gone, taking with him at least

$10 million worth of artwork. No one beats him. He always wins in the end. Always.

And there's a bit of frosting to sweeten the take. He knows where Ada keeps her cash and jewelry—and where she keeps the key to the box that holds them. It would be imprudent to leave such easy pickings behind. In her room he takes the key from the small glass dish on her dressing table where she foolishly leaves it. Then he pulls the box out from under the bed. Also foolish.

It's large and solid, stuffed with money and jewelry and papers. Bradley didn't believe much in banks, and apparently Ada doesn't either. There has to be at least $10,000 in neat stacks. Perfect for his traveling needs.

He's never seen her wear any of the jewelry. She adores the opal ring he gave her and claims it's all the adornment she'll ever need. These delightful trinkets were inherited from her mother and grandmother, much too large and gaudy for Ada's taste and diminutive size. He, on the other hand, finds them much to his liking.

He goes to his room to retrieve a valise and begins scooping money and jewelry into it. When he completes this pleasant task, he flips through the papers: letters from her brother; a few from Bradley as a young man; a packet from a niece in England; an old photo of four unsmiling children, all with the same unfortunate, weak chin Ada sports; her father's will; the deed to Ker-Feal. He's about to return them to the box when he sees a postcard covered with large handwriting that looks like a child's. A child? Ada never mentioned a child.

Mrs bradlee take big risk to my self and breakin the law. not enuf $. 1000 more or I do not do u no what on sunday. U hav a lot but not me. Tomoro or elce nothin. U no where. JJ

He has to read it three times before he understands what it's saying—and what it means. Ada was being blackmailed. Hit up for more money. For some crime she commissioned to be executed on a Sunday. By someone with the initials of JJ.

This can't be what it appears; Ada isn't that cunning or devious. After yet another read, he realizes that there's nothing else it can be. JJ was the truck driver—and Ada has a hell of a lot more pluck than he gave her credit for. He laughs out loud. The woman was too good a Catholic to get a divorce, but she was fine with committing murder.

The more he thinks about it, the more sense it makes. She knew Bradley always went through that stop sign. She knew he would be returning to Merion late Sunday afternoon. She knew it would be dark and his headlights easy to spot, that a truck waiting with its own lights off would be invisible to Bradley as he came down the hill, the driver's door an easy target. She also knew Vivienne, as Edwin's beneficiary, would be the prime suspect.

A suspect Ada must have pressed the police to investigate and the state to prosecute—with the help of Thomas Quinton, the man who'd been pining for her for decades, whose loyalty she would reward with Edwin's collection and, Quinton believed, her hand in marriage.

Ada once told him that until the trial, she had no idea Edwin was going to disinherit Vivienne or that he had cancer. So she saw endless years ahead of her in which Vivienne would rule the roost while she, Ada, would be the woman scorned and disregarded.

It's a plan worthy of him. With one fell swoop, Ada got rid of the cheating husband and his girlfriend, freeing herself to marry her dashing young count. So that was what all the tears and carrying on were about. She wasn't grieving for Bradley. She was feeling guilty because she had killed him.

43

VIVIENNE, 1929

It had taken the jury in Vivienne's murder trial two days to return with a verdict. On both mornings of those terror-ridden days, she'd left the house spotless before she went to court, not a dish in the sink or an ashtray dirty. She did this to ward off disaster; if she acted as if she expected to be found guilty, then maybe it wouldn't happen. Either that or she knew in her heart what the outcome would be. Whichever it was, when she turns the key and opens the door almost a year and a half later, everything looks calm and tidy, if dusty.

Being free is as unsettling, in its own way, as being locked up was. A blurry and wavering bubble has replaced her shell; she's unable to see clearly through the undulating haze or to feel the edges of the world, but she isn't completely cut off any longer. Which is good. It's been very much very fast, and she still needs padding. She's terrified that a policeman with handcuffs will come by at any moment and snap her reprieve out from under her.

When Ronald first came to the prison to tell her what had happened, she refused to believe him. It must be a trick—although she had no idea why Ronald would want to pull such a mean-spirited stunt. She always claimed Ada could have staged the accident just as easily as she herself could, but she never believed Ada ever would.

As she waited through the two weeks it took Riverside to complete the process of releasing her, she finally came to accept that Ronald was telling the truth. Ada had been furious at Edwin and furious at her—and

Ada figured out a way to punish them both while enhancing her own standing. By killing Edwin and setting Vivienne up for his murder, Ada got rid of them both, kept Vivienne from inheriting, and became the beneficiary herself, thereby leaving herself free to marry some much younger man, who was probably only after her money.

Vivienne places her coat on the back of the couch and opens all the curtains. She wanders through the house, running her fingers along the mantel, the kitchen counter, the bathroom sink, her bureau. She sneezes from the dust this disturbs and is delighted by it all.

She flips on the radio, and a song called "Orange Blossom Time" fills the room. The piano trills happily, and it's as if the words are meant just for her: "Everyone's happy and gay . . . Nature is smiling today." She looks in the closets and there are her dresses. Her shoes. Her scarves. So many of them. She presses her nose to her bathrobe and breathes in. Her own scent still lingers between the threads. Vivienne's scent, not Killer Girl's.

The events that led to her release are as incredible as those that led to her imprisonment. Apparently the new husband found correspondence between Ada and the truck driver, John Johnston, indicating that Ada was behind the so-called accident. When the police approached her with the evidence, Ada immediately broke down and confessed; she was arrested straightaway. A cop who was there told Ronald that Ada was obviously relieved. Vivienne knows this relief will quickly dissipate in the face of Ada's new reality: Riverside Prison.

Which is no longer her own reality. She's free. She isn't a murderer; she's an unjustly imprisoned victim. With Ada's conviction, she's once again Edwin's rightful heir, and the collection would be hers if there were a collection to inherit. All the artwork is now controlled by the Commonwealth of Pennsylvania and is headed to Philadelphia to become the Bradley Museum. Such irony. But she's free, and that's better than all the paintings in the world.

She feels for Edwin. Killed by his wife and bested by his worst enemies. Sure, he could be trying at times, hard nosed and stubborn, but he was a visionary who saw the future of art before almost anyone else did. He was also kind to her in his way, perhaps even loved her in his way. And perhaps she loved him a little, too.

She's glad Edwin isn't around to witness Quinton's victory, to see everything he wanted for his collection foiled. A museum with little white cards and guided tours, most likely a gift shop. Vivienne shudders at the thought of his fury. But at least the collection will now be open to anyone who wants to see it, even if it's not hers.

Vivienne goes into the kitchen and heats water for tea. She's heating water. She's drinking tea. In her very own house. Ronald's firm paid for the upkeep from her accounts while she was in prison; the plan was to sell it after she was executed. Whatever meager monies remained were to be given to Sally McDonald.

After she was executed. Vivienne shivers and traces the crisscrossing lines of the blue-and-yellow tablecloth. After she was executed. If not for Ada's husband, she'd still be rotting in Riverside, waiting for the electric chair to end her misery.

She would like to thank him, but she heard he left town immediately following Ada's arrest, apparently grabbing a few dozen Bradley paintings and all Ada's jewelry on his way out—just as Vivienne thought, only out for the money. She looks through the window, at her bedraggled garden, at the road heading east. Now she can go anywhere she pleases. No one can stop her from doing whatever she wants to do.

She opens the front door and peers down the street, searching for police cars. There are none.

VIVIENNE SPENDS A month in Merion, mostly sleeping and eating and taking lots of baths. She's grimy and skinny and weak, and she doesn't want anyone see to her until she's regained herself. She doesn't visit anyone; there's no one to visit except Sally, but she can't bring herself to go near the Bradley. Nor does she write either Henri or her aunt. Her prison meetings with them are foggy at best, and she needs to be clearer, stronger, before she does.

In early November, she boards a ship and sets sail for Marseille, from where she'll travel to Brussels. She sends Tante a telegram with her arrival date but asks her not to tell anyone else. Vivienne wants a few days alone with her aunt to catch up on everything that's happened during the years she's been away, to prepare herself for what's to come.

She has a vague recollection of Tante saying something about forgiveness, but she can't be certain. She'll contact her father when she understands more about his possible reaction to her homecoming. If only she had the colonnade seven for him. If only she had the proof of her innocence that George's arrest would have provided. These failures aren't easy to accept, but berating herself will get her nowhere. Facing a death sentence changes your perspective, shifts your priorities. She will move forward, not wallow in regrets over the past.

Vivienne doesn't let Henri know she's coming either. As much as she longs to see him, she worries about his reaction to her reappearance, too, and wants to take one tumultuous reunion at a time. His letters stopped coming about six months ago, and she'd been relieved. She hoped he'd found a new life, perhaps a new love.

She feels differently now, but she's prepared for him to spurn her. She was awful to him: claiming she didn't love him, ordering him to forget her, never answering his letters. It will break her heart, but her battered heart has been through much and will somehow find a way to recover. She has been given a second chance, and she's going to embrace it no matter who rejects her, no matter how many paintings she's lost.

As the ship pushes closer to Europe, Vivienne finds herself wondering about George. She never heard from him after her arrest, nor had she expected to. He was in Philadelphia for only one reason, and once their deal went sour, he had no more use for her. He wanted the collection, and if she couldn't get it for him, there was no reason to dally.

Unless he had someone else waiting to step into her shoes. Vivienne prowls the narrow wainscoted corridors of the ship, trying to pull the pieces together. Ada married a younger man, a man who ultimately turned on her. A man who left his elderly wife and disappeared when his plan failed. A man who snatched valuable paintings and jewelry while he had the chance. She grips the handrail for support. How had she not seen this before?

Her mind races along with the ship, and she steps out onto the deck. George's scheme to use Quinton to pursue the lawsuit worked in his favor whether he married Ada or her. Marrying for money wasn't one of his usual scams, but this reeked of him all the same: thinking many moves ahead of everyone else, an understudy in the wings, raking in millions of dollars that didn't belong to him.

Vivienne stares into the churning waters. If George was Ada's husband, then he was the one who found the correspondence and used it to free her. It doesn't seem possible that a man with no feelings for anyone but himself could do something so selfless. But it's difficult to argue with the fact that she isn't in Riverside Prison, that there's no longer an execution hanging over her head.

She vomits over the railing. She doesn't want George to be the one who saved her. She doesn't want to be grateful to him. Yet it was a remarkable gesture, especially given his nature, and it warms her to think that he cared enough about her to do such a thing.

But this doesn't mean she doesn't despise him, that she's not devastated to have missed her chance at revenge. She wipes her mouth with her handkerchief, closes her eyes, lets the wind blow her hair back. Here she is, seven years after he walked away and left her with nothing, still loathing him, still deeply connected to him.

VIVIENNE PLANNED TO take the train from Marseille to Brussels by herself, but when the ship docks, Tante Natalie is at the bottom of the gangplank. It's November, yet the weather is mild, and Tante waves her hat as Vivienne comes down the ramp. They run into each other's arms and both start to cry. Holding tight to Vivienne's shoulders, Tante pushes her back, inspects her face. "You look wonderful, Paulie. Like yourself but even better." She crushes Vivienne to her again. "Oh, oh, you feel so good."

On the train ride across France, Vivienne tells her aunt everything that happened on her side of the ocean, and Tante Natalie explains what happened on hers. Tante can't believe that such a travesty of justice could have taken place in America. Vivienne can't believe that Papa has regained his financial footing. Although he isn't nearly as wealthy as before, he and her mother are living in Germany in a charming home outside Stuttgart.

Léon is married, with twin boys. Franck is working with Papa and courting a pretty girl from Munich. And although the Mertens name still raises a few eyebrows in England, Belgium, and France—George apparently confined his Everard con to those three countries—after almost eight years, the affair is mostly forgotten. Or so Tante claims.

The air grows colder as they continue north, and the closer they move to Brussels the more nervous Vivienne becomes. Tante assures her that her father is no longer angry with her, that he and Franck will be ecstatic to see her, but adds that although her mother and Léon may take time to warm, eventually they'll be a family again. Or so Tante claims.

She forgot that her aunt met Henri, that it was he who prompted Tante's visit to Riverside. Vivienne had apparently mentioned Tante to him, and he'd found her, come to her house, begged her to talk some sense into Vivienne. Tante was enchanted by Henri, impressed with the depth of his feelings for Vivienne. Vivienne tells her she feels the same way about him, and she and Tante discuss what might be the best way to approach him. Should she send a telegram or a letter? Have Gertrude be the emissary? Or maybe she should just show up unannounced at his studio in Nice?

It's splendid to have another woman to talk with. Outside of Sally, Vivienne didn't have any real friends in America—well, maybe Edwin, but he wasn't exactly the kind of friend you could pour out your heart to. What a strange time it had been. Telling Tante her stories, listening to herself as she speaks, she understands what she hadn't fully grasped while she was living through it: she was a very lonely girl. No wonder she'd enjoyed George's company in Philadelphia.

When they reach the train station in Brussels, Oncle Liam is waiting for them. He greets Vivienne with a warm hug and arranges for her bags to be sent to the house. Then they walk through the streets of the Old Town, Tante's hand resting on Oncle's left arm and Vivienne's on his right.

She takes in the sights the way a canvas drinks paint: the Grand-Place, the Gildehuizen sparkling with gables trimmed in gold, the Hôtel de Ville. When she was a little girl, the family frequently came into Brussels—as she did later with her friends—and the city has always been a part of her. She's home. Her actual home.

Tante and Oncle moved into a new house while Vivienne was in America, but when she sees it for the first time, it's already familiar to her. A generous townhouse in a commune filled with old trees and other stately homes, near where her mother grew up, where her grandparents lived when she was a child. She used to play in the park down the street.

Vivienne falls into a large damask chair in the parlor, exhausted by her trip and her emotions. She's as awash in feelings as she was devoid of them in prison. Relief. Nostalgia. Fear. She's come so far, regained so much, and yet the things that have driven her for the past eight years are still very much in question.

Tante's maid draws her a warm bath, and she climbs into the tub, soaking there until the water turns tepid. By then her luggage arrives, and she pulls a nightgown over her head, crawls into the four-poster bed in a pretty gabled room, settles under a thick feather comforter.

But sleep won't come. Thoughts of Papa and Maman and Franck and Léon. Of Henri. Of how terrified she is to face them.

44

VIVIENNE, 1929

Three days after she arrives in Brussels, Vivienne tells Tante that she thinks she's ready to see her father. Tante sends a telegram to Stuttgart before Vivienne can change her mind, and a response arrives a few hours later. Papa and Franck will be at the house by noon the next day. Vivienne paces the floors all evening and sleeps even worse than she did the previous nights. Papa, her baby brother. Despite Tante's assurances and the obvious fact that they are coming to see her, she can't shake the fear that they'll turn away from her.

When the bell rings a little after eleven, Vivienne races down the stairs and yanks the door open. She freezes there, stares at them in wonder. Franck has grown at least another six inches since she saw him in Paris, and he towers over their father, who's rounder, grayer, his hairline receding a bit. But he's her dear papa, and he's smiling up at her. She throws herself at him.

Franck wraps his long arms around them both. She closes her eyes, breathes in the familiar smell of them, and begins to cry. They both hold her even tighter.

"My girl, my little Paulie," Papa says into her hair. "I despaired that this day would never come."

"So . . . so did I," she sobs into his chest. "It . . . it almost didn't."

"Come in off the street," Tante scolds. "Do you want the whole city to know of your affairs?"

Vivienne doesn't care and clearly neither does Papa or Franck, but they all go into the house just the same. As Tante leads them to the parlor, Vivienne holds on to her father and brother, presses into them, kisses them each on both cheeks. When they enter the room, she chooses the settee, placing each of her men on either side of her, holding their hands, grinning so hard that her cheeks ache.

"Papa, I'm so sorry," she begins, but he shakes his head vigorously.

"I am the one who is sorry," he says, his voice wavering. "You made a child's mistake, and we should never have sent you away. We were wrong, very wrong. You were just a girl. I was the one who decided to invest with Everard, and the fault for what happened is mine alone. It was entirely—"

"Papa, it's—"

"No. Let me say what I must say. A few weeks after you left, I was beginning to return to my senses and was ready to come for you. But then we heard that you were seen with him in Paris, hugging him, I think I went mad. It—"

"I wasn't hugging him," Vivienne cries. "Or . . . or I was, but that was because I thought he'd come to explain, to make it right. As soon as I realized . . . when I realized, I slapped him and sent him away. I promise you, I knew nothing. Had no idea what he was up to. I hate him. Will always hate him."

"I believe you," her father says, his voice gruff. "And even if I did not, I would not blame you. If I, a grown man running an international business, was taken in by him, then why not a young girl in the throes of first love? I was supposed to protect you, and instead I abandoned you."

Vivienne puts her finger to his lips. "I accept your apology, and if you accept mine we'll never have to talk about it again."

Franck turns to Tante Natalie. "I think this calls for champagne!"

"It is still morning," Tante begins to protest, then stops. "You are right. This is a momentous event, one we have all been looking forward to for a very long time." She hurries off to find the maid.

Papa takes Vivienne's hands in his. "You have turned into a beautiful woman. I am amazed and overjoyed that you have returned to us." Then he frowns. "But I do not like your dark hair. And it is too short."

"Don't be such an old fuddy-duddy," she tells him, laughing delightedly. "This is much more fashionable."

"I do not care about fashion," Papa grumbles. "My little girl's hair is blond."

She hugs him and cautiously asks, "Maman?"

Papa and Franck share a glance. "She has missed you," Papa says slowly. "But she's still angry with me."

"You know how Maman is," Franck interjects. "It isn't easy for her to let go of grievances. Léon, too."

Vivienne presses the spot between her eyes to hold the tears back. That's what she is to her mother, a grievance.

"It was the loss of standing that bothered her the most, I think," Franck continues. "More than the loss of the estate or even the money. You know how she's always cared about appearances, the proprieties, being a Mertens."

Papa takes her hand. "She will come around. Léon, too. Soon, I believe."

Vivienne aches for what she did to her mother, to her annoying but dear older brother. "I'm so sorry."

"No more 'sorrys,'" Papa reminds her.

She has Papa, Franck, and Tante Natalie with her, more than she could ever have imagined just two months ago. Maman and Léon's rejection hurts, as does her part in causing it, but she can't allow this to mar her homecoming. This—these people, this place—is what she's yearned for. She pulls them both closer. This.

The maid enters the room holding a bottle of champagne and a silver tray with four crystal flutes. Tante is right behind her. "Let's celebrate!" she cries. And so they do, quickly polishing off the bottle and then opening another, which they drink with lunch.

They're happy and silly and have a wonderful time. Then they all take naps and meet back in the parlor for tea, where Oncle joins them. Once again she tells her story, and Papa and Franck tell theirs. But she doesn't tell them everything. There's no reason for any of them to hear the more gruesome details.

The next morning, Vivienne goes with her father to the Royal Museums of Fine Arts, a Beaux-Arts building that reminds her of the Bradley. They wander through the Rubens Room, then into galleries of Flemish painters, taking in Van Dyck and Robert Campin and Brueghel's *Landscape with the Fall of Icarus*, the inspiration for W. H. Auden's poem. She tells him about her mapping of post-Impressionism, and he's delighted, although they still disagree about whether the Cubists are inside or outside the frame. It's as if no time has passed since they last visited the museum.

They talk about art the way they did years ago, but now she's instructing as well as being instructed. When she tells him she's co-written a book about Matisse, he has to sit down on a bench. After they leave the museum, they go directly to a bookstore where he orders ten copies of *The Art of Henri Matisse* to be sent to Stuttgart.

"It is by Edwin Bradley and Vivienne Gregsby," Papa tells the proprietor. "And it just so happens that is the nom de plume of this beautiful young woman standing next to me, my daughter."

The proprietor takes off his reading glasses and peers at her. "You wrote that book?"

"Co-wrote," she corrects him, blinking back tears. How long has she waited for Papa to hold her book, afraid it would never happen? Fearing that if it did, he wouldn't know she was the author? Now he will hold her book, and he will know she wrote it.

The proprietor offers his hand. "It is a great pleasure to meet you, Miss Gregsby. I have heard many good things about your work. I am proud to have you in my store."

Her father beams, and they walk back to Tante's house.

"I've had an idea about the colonnade paintings," Vivienne tells him as they stroll. "I'm going to contact a lawyer in Philadelphia to try to get them back for you. It might be possible to swap them for the money I'm supposed to receive from the state in the settlement. To pay me in kind rather than in cash. They were stolen from you—"

"There was no thievery involved. I sold them to your Edwin Bradley." He shakes his head, clearly amazed, once again, by the many threads she's woven. "I took his money."

"Because you were swindled and needed to pay off the debts," Vivienne argues. "You never should have been in that position. George stole them from you the same way he stole everything else."

"Oh, Everard stole from me, that is true, but not the paintings."

"They should be with you," she insists.

"This is not necessary," Papa declares. "Nor is it what is best. The pictures should stay in the Bradley Museum, where they can be seen." He brushes a piece of hair from her forehead and kisses her. "It is time to leave the past where it belongs. I have my girl back, and that is all that matters to me."

HENRI ARRIVES FOUR days later. Vivienne goes to the station to meet his train so they can have some privacy—if seeing each other for the first time in almost two years in front of hundreds of people can be considered privacy. She's wearing a deep red dress with a slightly promiscuous neckline that she and Tante bought just the day before. She knows it flatters her and that Henri loves her in red. If he still loves her.

Henri doesn't know she's coming to meet him, and she watches as he steps onto the platform, searching for the exit and heading toward it. His stride is purposeful and his expression determined. Other than a slim case not much larger than a sketchbook under his arm, he has no luggage. Her heart squeezes.

Vivienne takes a deep breath, sidles up to him, and says in a low voice, "Is that you, Monsieur Matisse?"

He turns with a frown on his face, clearly expecting an admirer who's going to impede his progress. When he sees who it is, he stops, then reaches out his finger and touches her cheek. "You have returned to yourself."

She nods, unable to speak.

"You were barely alive. A ghost. Perhaps not even that."

"I . . . I wasn't me," she says. "And everything I told you that day was a lie."

"I believed I would never see you again."

"And here I am," she whispers.

"And here you are." But instead of kissing her, he grasps her shoulders and holds her at arms length, taking her in slowly, almost sadly.

"What?" she asks, suddenly afraid. "What is it?"

"I heard what happened to the Bradley. I am sorry the collection did not become yours and that you are not able to return your father's paintings."

Vivienne closes her eyes against his kindness.

"I have brought something," Henri says. "Let us sit down."

She numbly follows him to a bench and watches him undo the laces holding together the case in his lap. He carefully removes half a dozen sketches. "These are for you. Or for your father." He offers them to her along with the case. "That is your choice."

Vivienne looks down, her vision blurred by tears. Preliminary sketches for *The Music Lesson*. A lovely, thoughtful gift. A generous gift, but a parting gift, she's sure. "He, Papa, he will treasure them," she manages to say around the boulder in her throat. "I will, too. Thank you."

"Vivienne."

She shakes her head, unable to meet his eye. "There's someone else."

"I am sorry. More sorry than you can know. I thought you were gone. Forever gone. And now she is here and I cannot . . . I just cannot."

Vivienne puts the sketches back in their case, ties it, and stands. "I'm happy for you, Henri," she says, her voice steadier than she would have expected. "I truly am and wish you only the best. I'm sad for myself, but so many good things have happened that I know I won't be sad forever." She squares her shoulders. "I will not be sad forever."

He takes her gently in his arms, and Vivienne presses her forehead into his shoulder. They stand that way for a long time, then she pulls away. "Go," she tells him.

He does.

45

GEORGE/TEX, 1930

His home in Monaco isn't a house, it's an estate. Much more majestic than Ker-Feal. High on a rocky cliff facing the Mediterranean, the multilevel structure lined with wide terraces juts out over the sea. It's made almost entirely of marble, and it's surrounded on three sides by a narrow strip of olive groves. A twenty-foot iron fence runs along the edge of the groves, barring the curious.

He loves his new house and, at the beginning, loved his new gig as Tex Carver, an American from Oklahoma who transcended his humble roots to make a fortune in oil. He wrapped up his art-forgery con last year, making a cool $2 million just before the American economy and everyone else's turned sour. "Dang," Tex would say. "A mighty nice haul." And now he's taking a well-deserved rest.

The forty-two Bradley paintings as well as the original works he purchased as Ashton King are hanging throughout the mansion. It's his greatest pleasure to wander from room to room, appreciating his masterpieces, touching them because he can. As most of the pictures are stolen property, he hires only servants who he assumes won't recognize a Matisse or a Picasso and overpays them to cement their loyalty and silence.

He drives his Mercedes-Benz SSK "Count Trossi" into Monte Carlo for food and fun and women and gambling. Tex is welcome at any table at the casino, where he routinely cleans everyone out, as they consistently underestimate the man with the overly large mustache and booming voice. They forgive him when he uses his winnings to spring for a round of drinks. But it's too easy, and after less than six months, he's getting bored.

Often he finds himself sitting at the dining room table, staring at Paulien's adored *Music Lesson*, reliving their days in London. How exciting it was to be with her, how much he enjoyed her company, how he'd been so focused on his con that he didn't notice any of this. It had been the same those last months in Philadelphia. He's glad it was he who freed her from prison. It's good to know she's safe.

He thought he saw her at the casino the other night, and it was as if he'd been punched in the stomach. He leaped from his seat and ran toward her, calling her name. When the woman turned and it wasn't Paulien, he was crushed. As he ponders these unfamiliar emotions, he realizes that ever since she was arrested, he's been uncharacteristically concerned about her. He keeps telling himself that she's nothing to him, but it doesn't ring true.

He misses her, wants to be with her just because he wants to be with her. No ulterior motive. He wants to make her happy just because he wants her to be happy. Insane. He loses himself for a moment in *Music Lesson*, remembering Paulien's stories about curling up in front of this very same painting when she was a little girl. She must have been a pistol. He wishes he'd known her then.

He abruptly stands and leaves the dining room. He's always prided himself on his ability to remain detached, to withhold emotion and empathy, and definitely not to fall in love. Such weaknesses throw you off your game.

IT DOESN'T TAKE long to find her. She's living in Paris, around the corner from Gertrude Stein. Just moved there, in fact. Even though he's shaved his beard, grown a handlebar mustache, dyed his badly cut hair blond, and he now walks slightly bowlegged like a cowboy who just got off his horse, he was in Paris as Ashton King not that long ago, so he skates in and out of the shadows to follow her.

She's as beautiful as she was in Philadelphia, and much looser. She and Gertrude go to galleries and parties and dinners. They wander through the city, chatting and laughing. His stomach twists at the sight of her.

He's relieved to discover that she and Matisse are no longer an item and pleased that she's going to start her own collection with the $5 million she received for the seizure of the Bradley. But he's got no interest in her windfall, startlingly so. She should do whatever she wants with that money. She deserves it. He wants her, but not just in a sexual way. He wants her to be with him. He wants to be with her.

One day he spies her alone, sipping tea and reading a book at a small café. He slides into the chair across from her but finds he's speechless. He's never speechless.

Paulien raises her eyes from her book, appears less surprised than he expected. She puts a napkin between the pages to hold her spot and lays the book on the table. "I wondered when you'd show up."

"So, ah, so did I." Being this close to her, feeling the heat coming off her body, smelling her familiar scent of lavender and something intrinsically Paulien, is intoxicating. Debilitating.

She looks at him sharply, raises an eyebrow.

"And here you are," he says in his southwestern drawl. He needs to get back into his Tex persona. Tex is too much of a hillbilly ever to be flustered. "Looking damn purdy, too." He lifts his Stetson, then puts it back on and pulls the brim down to hide his face.

"Texas?"

"Tex Carver, ma'am. From the great state of Oklahoma. Nice to make your acquaintance." He drops the cowboy accent. "You look great."

"I heard Ashton King wrapped up his game."

"I'm giving it up."

"So why the costume?"

"Protection, as you well know."

She sits back in her chair and crosses her arms, but he can tell she's glad to see him, even if she's trying to hide it. As he's learning, there really is nothing like your first love.

"I'm happy everything worked out," he says. "But I'm sorry about what you had to go through."

She lowers her eyes. "I suppose I need to thank you."

"No, no, you don't. I did what anyone would do."

"Not what George Everard would do."

He reaches over and touches her hand. "I'm not that man anymore, something's changed. Everything's changed."

"Like you're now an American? Let me guess, you made a fortune in oil?"

He has to smile. "I've come to tell you that I love you. For real. That I want to be with you. That I'm sorry for everything that happened, and I'm going to spend the rest of my life making it up to you."

Her laughter is full and loud and turns his stomach to jelly. "Now where have I heard that before?"

PAULIEN GRUDGINGLY CONSENTS to see him once a week. Just as in Philadelphia, they agree to be circumspect and that there will be no physical contact. He's willing to agree to anything if it means he can be near her. Which is different from Philadelphia, when all he wanted was to get his hands on the Bradley collection. Occasionally he experiences an odd twinge, a murky vagueness in his stomach, the desire to bow his head and hide away. Each time, he wonders if this is what shame feels like. But no. The rich French food just disagrees with him.

A couple of months after they start their weekly dates, he takes her to a jazz club. Although it's clear she's crazy in love with him, she maintains her reserve, stepping away from him whenever she comes too close to those feelings. He's making progress, but he doesn't know how to persuade her to let go of the past, to accept him for the new man he is, to accept his devotion as genuine. Despite all that happened to her in the

United States, she often talks wistfully about it, and he hopes she'll get a kick out of the American feel of the club.

As soon as they enter, her face lights up. "A mind reader," she says.

They order drinks, listen to the music, and smoke a few cigarettes, chatting idly. He clears his throat. "I want to tell you something about me that no one else knows."

"Don't I already know lots of things about you that no one else knows?"

"I want to come completely clean."

She stiffens.

"My real name is Clem Knipper," he says quickly. "I grew up in an coal-mining town in Kentucky."

"You've got to be kidding me."

"Not kidding."

"Clem?" She presses a hand over her mouth. "Knipper?" Then she starts to laugh.

"Right," he says, slightly offended. "That's why nobody knows. And that's why I wanted you to."

"So this is the reason you always choose such manly names," she sputters. "That's hilarious."

He frowns. It's not that hilarious. "I'm telling you this so you'll see that there's nothing I won't share with you. That I love you so much that I'm willing to stand naked before you."

She stops laughing and appraises him thoughtfully. "That's so poetic."

"I didn't mean it to be poetic, I meant it to be true."

Later that night, she agrees to close up her apartment for a few months and come to Monaco with him. On a trial basis. Separate residences. No touching.

He puts Paulien up in a suite in the best hotel in Monte Carlo, and he takes another down the hall. He can't bring her to the house, where the Bradley paintings are, until she's finally committed to him, and he doesn't want to be that far away from her. It's five kilometers to the house. She adores the sun and the warmth and the sand under her toes, the perfection of the blue-green sea, and he woos her for all he's worth.

He sees that his ardor and sincerity move her, knows she wants to let go of her concerns. She's so close to believing him, to believing in him, to believing in them. But she can't seem to take that final leap. He needs to make her feel the same way she did when she cared for him so much that everything he did was perfect. He has a replica made of the engagement ring he gave her on the train to Brussels, ten years ago Christmas, and suggests a walk on the beach.

It's a perfect day, the sky that deep Mediterranean blue, the sea azure and clear, lazy clouds billow overhead. Paulien throws her arms up in the air, wiggles her fingers and does a little dance. "I love it here!"

He grabs her around the waist and twirls her in circles, although he's still not supposed to touch her like this. "So stay here. Forever. Marry me." He places her down on the sand and pulls the ring box from his pocket. It's nothing like the last time he offered her a tiny jewelry box. Then he was gloating over how he had tricked her into begging him for exactly what he wanted. Now he's terrified of rejection.

She opens the box, stares at the ring, stares back up at him, at the box again, her expression inscrutable.

He doesn't move. "Happy or sad?" he finally asks.

She throws herself at him, clings to him, covers his face with kisses.

"I take it that means you're happy?"

"Yes," she cries. "Let's stay here forever."

"You love me?" He needs to hear her say it.

"Oh, you stupid fool. Of course I love you. I've always loved you."

An eruption of joy like nothing he's ever felt before, far better than executing a successful con. He can't believe he actually thinks this, but he doesn't care. She loves him. She always has. Just as he's always loved her. She wants to stay here, with him.

A remnant of his usual restraint cautions him not to take her to the house. He assumes she knows he has the Bradley paintings, yet their presence is proof positive that he stole them. Which she could use against him. But that was his old way of thinking, before he understood what it was like to be in love. She's agreed to marry him, to be with him forever, and he wants her in his house, their house. They kiss, deeply, passionately, and he takes her home.

As he hoped, Paulien is enthralled. She adores the open rooms, the terraces, the views, and the privacy. Best of all, she's ecstatic to be reunited with her colonnade seven, thrilled that he managed to wrest so many others from Quinton's clutches. They roam the house, hand in hand, taking in the artworks, her old friends and Ashton King's new ones. She wants to stay the longest in the dining room with *Music Lesson*. She sits at the table, starts to cry.

"It's yours again," he says, wrapping his arms around her. "This one and every other one in the house. Give anything you want to your father. We've got all the money you'll need to create the collection you always dreamed of."

She kisses him deeply, warmly, lovingly. Then they go into the bedroom and make love the way they did a decade ago.

46

VIVIENNE, 1930

Vivienne gives it a month or two. She writes to her family and Gertrude explaining that she needs time alone with the sea and the sun. Time to meld Vivienne and Paulien. Then she does just that. She allows herself to fall into life with George, allows herself to enjoy it.

Monaco might be the most exquisite place on earth, the weather a balm, loosening her muscles, soothing her apprehensions, buoying her hopes. No matter where she stands, where she looks, there's grandeur of every sort, including inside George's house. The colonnade seven are finally free, each hanging on its own wall, liberated from its ensemble, no hinges or scissors. She wishes she could invite her father here, but he'd never approve of his paintings being a part of a private collection. Not to mention that they were stolen. But it warms her to see them unencumbered, present in her daily life, just as they were when she was a girl.

And then there's George, who appears to be in love with her, actually and truly in love with her. She knows he's a master con artist, a great actor, a liar par excellence, but there's a new softness to him, to the way he views the world. He's different from the George of London and Philadelphia, his restless edginess gone, the crafty spark in his eyes diminished, even his dimple subdued.

He spends his days responding to her every possible desire—the ones she has and the ones he conjures for her—from walks on the beach to excursions into town to extravagant gifts of post-Impressionist art. He talks constantly of the Mertens Museum. And then there's the sex, which is always about her, hardly ever about him. It seems he cares only about her pleasure, with no endgame beyond, and although it's her third time around this particular waltz, she's becoming convinced of his sincerity.

Of course, what matters is that he becomes convinced of hers.

THE HIGH MEDITERRANEAN light whitewashes the marble terraces surrounding the house, and salty air wafts through the rooms. The waves froth beneath her, and Vivienne is already nostalgic as she awaits the arrival of the Monte Carlo police. They will be escorting a team of American FBI agents, who will determine whether, as she claims, the artworks hanging on the walls are the ones that disappeared from Philadelphia a year ago. George is in Nice buying her an engagement present. She suspects a painting, most likely a Matisse.

After she lets the men in, the uniformed Monacans remain in the main living area while she escorts the dark-suited agents on a tour of the mansion. She points out the forty-two stolen paintings. As she speaks, one of the agents, an authority on art theft and clearly the highest ranking of the group, consults a file containing black-and-white reproductions of the missing pieces. A second agent takes photographs; the other two take notes.

The agents inspect the works carefully but ask few questions, which is good. The more quickly this transaction is completed, the better. When they finally rejoin the policemen, the eight of them wait silently for George to return.

"Hey, doll!" George calls as he walks in the door. "You're never going to believe what I have for you."

Vivienne stands, as do the men.

George places a bulky package wrapped in brown paper against the wall. Then he straightens, his smile generous and welcoming. "Well, howdy, sirs!" he booms, slipping easily into his cowboy persona.

The lead agent produces his badge for inspection. "I'm Agent Nathan. United States Federal Bureau of Investigation. These are my colleagues from America, and I'm sure you recognize the Monte Carlo police."

George looks at the badge and then shakes the agent's hand heartily. "Tex Carver from the great state of Oklahoma," he says. "Good to see some friendly faces from home. Please, please sit, all of you. Make yourselves comfortable. How can I be of service?"

No one sits, and Agent Nathan picks up his file of reproductions from the coffee table. "We were wondering if you knew anything about these paintings, Mr. Carver."

George nonchalantly flips through the pages. "Why, they look like copies of some of the paintings in my own collection. Where did you fellows get them?"

"I was about to ask you that same question," Agent Nathan replies. The other three agents position themselves around George. The policemen step behind them.

George surveys the room, clearly assessing his options and seeing none. "Vivienne had nothing to do with it," he tells the lawmen. "She's completely innocent. I took the paintings from the Bradley by myself. She wasn't even in Merion at the time."

"We're aware of that," Agent Nathan says.

"You are?" George turns to Vivienne.

She meets his gaze. The fact that his first impulse was to protect her is touching, but not enough to cause regret.

George's expression shifts from confusion to comprehension, and she can't help being impressed by his self-possession. A peculiar smile flits across his face. "A true protégé," he says to her. "Well done."

ALL THE TIME Vivienne was incarcerated at Riverside, she never knew what it looked liked on the outside. Now, standing on the sidewalk leading up to the entrance, she sees it's a boxy brick structure, topped with turrets and barbed wire, its facade as stern as its innards. She shivers in the cold rain, raises her umbrella.

She watches as he's led into the prison, one guard hovering close at his right and another at his left. He's handcuffed and shackled, pale and haggard, a crushed man. Not George Everard anymore. Nor Ashton King or István Bokor or Tex Carver. No, it's Clem Knipper who stares at the sidewalk as he shuffles along. Just as she saw in her imaginings. But this didn't come about because she imagined it. It came about because she learned well at the feet of the master. Planning and patience and playing a role.

He's been convicted of multiple counts of grand larceny in the Bradley heist, while charges are still pending for tax evasion and money laundering in both the Pennsylvania and the United States federal courts. He's awaiting trial on similar charges and a raft of additional financial crimes in six states and at least seven countries. He'll spend the rest of his life in this grim building—or one like it—his cash and property distributed among his victims, the forty-two paintings returned to the Bradley Museum.

A veneer of sadness coats her triumph. A twinge of regret followed by a surge of satisfaction as the prison door closes behind him. As always, she is of two minds about George.

AUTHOR'S NOTE

The Collector's Apprentice is a work of fiction loosely inspired by the lives of the art collector Albert Barnes and his assistant, Violette de Mazia, as well as the history of the Barnes Foundation, which he founded and they both nurtured. *Loosely* is the operative word here, as events that took place over a span of ninety years have been collapsed into ten, legal issues simplified, details rearranged, and names changed. The dialogue is invented, as is almost every storyline, including the confidence games, the romances, and the murder trial. Although certain aspects of the situations, locations, and persons may be recognizable, all incidents, characters, and their actions are the product of my imagination.

There are a number of historical figures who interact with the fictional characters in the novel, including Gertrude Stein, Leo Stein, Alice Toklas, Scott Fitzgerald, Zelda Fitzgerald, Pablo Picasso, and Henri Matisse. I did extensive research on each, which forms the basis of their personalities and actions, but obviously none of them knew anyone named Edwin Bradley or Vivienne Gregsby, although they did know Albert Barnes and Violette de Mazia. On the other hand, George Everard is a complete fabrication, as are many others who inhabit the novel. This mix of history and invention continues throughout the book.

All civil and criminal lawsuits and trials are fictional, but I did try to imbue them with as much verisimilitude as possible. In a few instances this wasn't feasible. The Commonwealth of Pennsylvania would not have had the power to appropriate personal property in the manner described, although the Barnes Foundation was moved, through various legal maneuvers and against Barnes's written directive, from Merion to Philadelphia. An irrevocable trust—which is what Albert Barnes had— would not be dissolvable without approval of the court and the Office of the Attorney General. The reading of a will would not have been post-poned twice owing to a lawyer's attempt to contest it, nor would there be only two weeks' notice of a trial to seize property.

While the Bradley art collection bears a strong resemblance to the Barnes collection, the two are not the same. In the novel, many of the Bradley artworks were created, acquired, shipped, and hung at different times and in different places than those in the Barnes, and they were purchased from different sources. These include works by Matisse—for example, *The Joy of Life* and *Dance II*—Renoir, Gauguin, and Van Gogh. *The Art in Painting* was published in 1925 rather than three years earlier as stated in the book. *The Art of Henri Matisse* was published in 1933, not in 1926. Likewise, the Arboretum School, which is shown as operational in the 1920s, did not open until 1940.

I also played with some of the events in Henri Matisse's life. The apartment in Paris described in the book is actually his apartment in Nice. He did paint his odalisque series in the mid-1920s, but the order and timing of these works has been changed. Matisse created a mural for Albert Barnes called *Dance II*, which had to be redone because of a measurement mistake, but it wasn't installed until 1933. Matisse was nominated to sit on the jury for the Carnegie International Exhibition in Pittsburgh, but it was in 1930 rather than 1925. He did not divorce until 1939.

In the novel, the post-Impressionist movement is accurately portrayed in terms of its evolution, principles, artists, and works of art. But perhaps the greatest deviation from the historical record is my representation of the amount of time it took for the movement to become an accepted part of the artistic canon. The school was given its name in the show *Manet and the Post-Impressionists* in 1910 and is generally considered to have taken place between the 1880s and 1920s, yet it remained unappreciated and even mocked by many well into the mid-twentieth century, particu-larly in the United States. There was no *Painters of Paris and Nice* show in 1918 or at any other time.

In Pennsylvania in 1928, maximum-security female inmates were housed at the Industrial Home for Women in Muncy, and maximum-security males were housed at the Eastern State Penitentiary in Philadelphia. I took literary license and placed both men and women at Riverside Prison, which didn't open until years later.

The undergraduate Columbia College did not accept women in 1922, although many of the graduate schools at Columbia University did, and Barnard doesn't award doctorate degrees.

Neither Mondrian nor Klee was included in the academy show in Philadelphia in 1923. The economy in France was not stagnating in 1926. And the Federal Bureau of Investigation was not referred to as the FBI until 1935; in 1930 it was called the Bureau of Investigation, the BOI.

ACKNOWLEDGMENTS

As is always the case, this book could not have been written without the help of many friends and colleagues, but special thanks are in order to the Ragdale Foundation and the Strnad Fellowship that supported my work there. I began this novel at Ragdale in 2014 and finished it in 2017 at the same little desk tucked under a window overlooking the prairie. It's an enchanted place, and I have no doubt that its magic had a powerful effect on these pages.

Many thanks to my readers, whose patience and honesty is a priceless gift: Jan Brogan, Scott Fleishman, Gary Goshgarian, Jessica Keener, Vicki Konover, Maryanne O'Hara, and especially Dan Fleishman, who not only read and reread every chapter, but also brainstormed with me over too many dinners to count. Thanks also to my experts: Adam Gusdorff, Michael Segal, Richard Segal, and Ben Zimmern. And then extra, extra thanks to the two women who always have my back, Ann Colette and Amy Gash, without whom none of this would be possible.

DATE DUE

10/5?	SEP ? 2019
NOV 1 2 2018	
DEC - 5 2018	OCT 1 0 2019
JAN - 2 2019	
JAN 2 5 2019	DEC 2 0 2019
FEB 1 5 2019	JAN 1 6 2020
MAR - 7 2019	MAR - 5 2020
MAY - 3 2019	MAR 2 2 2020
MAY 2 1 2019	AUG 2 5 2020
JUL 1 1 2019	
AUG - 1 2019	

PRINTED IN U.S.A.